THE DARK ROOM

Sam Blake is a pseudonym for Vanessa Fox O'Loughlin, the founder of The Inkwell Group publishing consultancy and the award-winning national writing resources website Writing.ie. She is Ireland's leading literary scout and has assisted many award-winning and bestselling authors to publication. Vanessa has been writing fiction since her husband set sail across the Atlantic for eight weeks and she had an idea for a book.

Also by Sam Blake

Little Bones
In Deep Water
No Turning Back
Keep Your Eyes on Me

THE DARK ROOM

SAM BLAKE

CORVUS

First published in Great Britain in 2021 by Corvus,
an imprint of Atlantic Books Ltd.

10 9 8 7 6 5 4 3 2 1

A CIP catalogue record for this book is available from the British Library.

Trade paperback ISBN: 978 1 78649 860 1
E-book ISBN: 978 1 78649 862 5

Corvus
An imprint of Atlantic Books Ltd
Ormond House
26–27 Boswell Street
London
WC1N 3JZ

www.corvus-books.co.uk

Printed and bound by CPI Group (UK) Ltd, Croydon, CR0 4YY

For Niamh and Andrea, for their wonderful advice and friendship, and because no writer creates alone.

The dead may be invisible but they are not absent.

– St Augustine

Prologue

ALFIE'S HAND SHOOK as he slipped the letter into the mouth of the postbox, his bitten nails black against the cream of the envelope. He hesitated, holding it on the cold cast-iron lip, glancing behind him, checking the road again. The traffic was almost stationary, lights dazzling. He looked in the opposite direction, to the column of blazing red tail-lights.

Safe.

For now.

Above him, the ornate clock on the station tower clicked on another minute.

The letter was thick, his spidery handwriting spread over many more sheets than he'd expected. Once he'd made up his mind and he'd begun, the whole story had come out with detail he'd thought he'd forgotten. The smell of the car, the heat of the sun as they'd driven down from Dublin. The laughter. The roads had been so bad, winding and narrow, the tarmac potholed and loose. And no signposts; he didn't know how tourists found their way around the country at all.

It was important to get the story right. Exactly right. This could be his only chance. Things would spiral as soon as it was received. And everything would change.

He'd ended up writing the last page in cramped letters, the ink beginning to fade as he squeezed his initials into the corner.

A. B.

Alfie Bows.

It wasn't his name, but that's what they called him on the streets, and it had become part of him. Like the violin he was named after, held firmly now under his arm.

Still holding the letter poised to drop, he lifted his other hand, the carrier bag handle looped securely around his wrist, and shook back the tattered sleeve of his tweed overcoat. He looked at the illuminated dial of his watch, at the minutes flicking past. He didn't know when the letter would arrive – Frank in the hostel had only had a second-class stamp and he'd missed the post today – but it would get there eventually.

And when it did, they'd know the whole story.

They'd know what had happened.

Would they believe him? He wasn't sure. He was invisible now, his voice silent, like a whisper in the night. Not like before, when he was younger. He'd been someone then, had been loud and popular and laughing with the others; he'd partied hard but aced his degree, had had a glittering career ahead of him. That's what they'd been celebrating. A weekend away after the results, their last summer of freedom before the real work started and life began.

And then …

In that one moment, everything had changed.

It was trying to get it all out of his head that had always been the problem, to switch off his imagination. Getting away, becoming someone else, had been the only way he could cope. But it was still there, every day. Like the dull incessant ticking of a clock in the background of his life. He didn't think he'd ever be free.

It had all come roaring back that night, all the alarms ringing together, like white water, filling his ears, choking, drowning him in the memories, suffocating him.

It had only been a week ago, but it felt like a lifetime. Longer than a lifetime. Before, he'd looked forward to what life offered; afterwards he'd lived day by day. Now it was hour by hour.

He'd had always thought of it as 'his' car park; he was the oldest one who camped there, had been there the longest. He didn't know why he kept going back. There were better places, but Alfie knew he liked the isolation, liked the fact that there were no security cameras, that he was usually alone. He was like a rat, he had familiar runs. Even if they weren't ideal, he knew them – what did they say, 'better the devil you know'?

He wasn't sure about that one.

Alfie had been shocked when he'd seen him swinging out of the cab of the lorry, his face illuminated by the interior lights. The devil himself. He'd had a heavy torch in his hand, and perhaps sensing movement in the darkness beside the bins, had swung the beam around on Alfie just as he'd started to pull his head back into his tent.

His muttered 'What the fuck …?' had told Alfie he'd been recognised too.

Perhaps he hadn't changed that much.

His hand still on the edge of the postbox, Alfie smiled sadly to himself; normally the long hair and the dirt, the odd assortment of clothes, was a disguise. But not now. Maybe the recent graduate with his rugby jersey, the stiff white collar turned up, hadn't really changed that much, despite what life had thrown at him.

The torch had clicked off as another truck pulled into the yard, Nemo Freight emblazoned on its side. Alfie had a good idea what was going on, why they were here, but he didn't want to know any details. Crawling back inside his tent, he'd pulled his violin to him, buried himself into the furthest corner so he could feel the wall against his back. Shrinking down into all his layers – the sleeping bags with the broken zips, the torn tweed coat he wore now – he had rocked silently, sick with fear.

He'd been seen.

He'd got so used to not being seen – even when he was playing outside a Tube station people heard him, but they didn't *see* him. Now he'd been seen – and worse, recognised. And not by just anybody. By the one person who had every reason to want him to stay quiet, to silence him. He'd been quiet; he'd slipped into obscurity, getting by, not talking to anyone, keeping his story to himself. Until he'd met Hunter, and then it had started to change. He hadn't planned to tell anyone anything – ever – but Hunter was interested. He wanted to know what life was like on the streets, whether Alfie had people out there somewhere. He'd looked out for him, bought him the watch.

But why. Always why.

That was the question he wouldn't answer. Why.

And then Hunter's TV crew had arrived with their cameras and mics and questions in the car park. Alfie cringed again at the timing of it all. Why had it had to happen like that? As they were unloading their equipment, another Nemo Freight truck had pulled into the car park, this time turning and pulling out again just as quickly.

And Alfie had known he was in danger.

The driver had cleared out so fast he knew a message would

go back. It wasn't how it looked, but would he have time to explain?

Maybe he'd got paranoid living on the streets but this time he didn't think he was being alarmist.

He'd been found, and he'd been seen speaking to the documentary crew. Something was going to happen. He could see it in the shadows, feel it in the air. And whatever happened next, Hunter had been good to him, he owed him the truth.

The rain was getting heavier now, falling like a gossamer curtain illuminated by the street lights. Alfie took another look at the envelope and caught his breath as he dropped it into the box.

His violin under his arm, he pulled the carrier bag to himself protectively. He shivered. He'd got a new woolly hat when he'd called in to see if they had a stamp at the hostel, and a pair of fingerless gloves. They helped a bit, but Alfie knew he wouldn't feel warm again until it all came out. He'd been cold with fear from the moment that torch beam had fallen on him, like a spotlight centre stage.

But he wanted his voice heard – whatever happened, he wanted them to know the truth. It wasn't pretty. It was dark and dirty and had changed the entire course of his life – Christ, the number of times he'd wished he'd gone home that weekend instead of chasing a high. But there had been the promise of booze, of lines, of a country house by the sea and a long hot weekend. They'd had everything.

And then they'd had nothing.

In the road beside him, the traffic began to roll forward again. Alfie looked over his shoulder. He was sure he'd been followed before, but he'd been careful this time.

It had taken him all day to write the letter. But it was done now. All of it. And whatever happened they'd know; they'd have to hear him now.

Chapter 1

Thursday 9 January

THE TWO POLICE officers shifted uncomfortably in the steel and glass reception area of Red Fox Films as Rachel approached them. She'd only just got back to her office, had been collecting her backpack when she'd heard her desk phone ring and seen Stacy in reception's light flashing. *At least they'd been quick.*

She looked at the officers anxiously; the second one had his back to her, looking at the stills plastered over the walls. They seemed to have brought the January chill in with them; cold air hung in the normally warm atrium like a cloud.

'Rachel Lambert? I'm PC Miller from Kennington Police Station. This is PC Anand.'

'Thanks for coming so fast, the lady I spoke to said you might not be down till later.'

'I'm sorry?'

PC Miller frowned, confused. He looked about twenty-five, acne still peppering his jawline. He was probably only a few years younger than her, but he made her feel old.

'The break-in, I reported it about an hour ago?'

'Oh.' He seemed to falter for a moment. 'We're not here about that, I'm afraid.'

Not ...? What on earth could they be here for?

Rachel's mind raced over the wrap on their last location.

It had been a big one; as well as the core cast, they'd had fifty extras in a wedding scene. Catering trailers, costume and make-up. A farmer getting in a sweat about his cows being disturbed. It was her job to ensure that when the cast and crew left, everything was exactly as it had been when they'd arrived. Sometimes it wasn't and then the shit could hit the fan – but it didn't normally involve the police.

Rachel frowned, slotting her hands in the back pockets of her jeans.

'So what's the problem?'

Why had he said 'afraid'?

'Can we go somewhere more private?'

This had to be really bad.

As if getting the barge broken into wasn't enough trouble for one day. And Hunter still hadn't called her, despite her endless messages. He'd said he was going to a meeting but it seemed to be going on all day.

Christ, what could it be?

PC Miller was still frowning, as if whatever it was, was *very* serious. Had something happened after they left the location? Had someone had an accident falling over a prop she'd missed, or tripped in a hole? Her job was all about building relationships: first finding the right location, often one that a director had in their head and was little more than a squiggle on a piece of paper, a vague description; then making sure *everyone* was happy – the locals, the cast, the crew, the director. But they all knew that anyone in this business was only as good as the last job.

Looking at the police officer, Rachel could feel her mouth going dry.

'My office is this way.'

Nervously tucking her unruly strawberry blonde hair

behind her ear, she indicated with her head and turned back down the corridor. The police officers followed her, and she could feel the occupants of the offices they passed swinging around to look at them.

Pushing open her own door, Rachel indicated they should go inside. Jasper stirred in his bed, making a grumbling German shepherd noise at the interruption to his snooze. The officers looked surprised to see a dog in the corner. Or perhaps it was just that Jasper was a very large dog.

'Come in, it's okay, he was a police dog, he's very safe. How can I help?'

Jasper lifted his head and cocked his huge ears forward as the officer cleared his throat.

'We're afraid there's been an accident, Ms Lambert.'

'It's Rachel.' She kept her voice level.

Here it came. She braced herself. People saw 'film company' and automatically assumed that meant millions of dollars in payouts – and her job was all about that *not* happening.

'Rachel. We believe you are listed as the next of kin for a Hunter MacKenzie?'

Rachel felt her knees go weak. 'Hunter's my partner – what's happened?'

She could feel the panic rising inside her, reached out to grab the back of one of the chairs pushed away under the table. Immediately picking up on her mood, Jasper stood up, sleep forgotten, eyes bright. She glanced at him as the police officer continued.

'There was an accident earlier today near Lambeth Bridge – on Millbank Roundabout.'

'Jesus. He goes that way to work. What happened, is he okay?'

'He was involved in a traffic accident. He was knocked off

his bike. We're looking at the CCTV in the area to find out exactly what happened. It's a very busy roundabout.'

'My God.' Rachel's hand shot to her mouth, the diamanté eyes in the heavy silver skull ring on her middle finger catching the light. 'But … Is he …?'

'He's in the Royal Hope – A & E. We can take you to the hospital.' PC Miller paused. 'He's in good hands.'

'Holy Christ. That's why he didn't call.'

Rachel crossed her arms and stared at the blue carpet tiles for a moment, seeing Hunter's smiling brown eyes and broad grin as she'd headed in to work this morning. The way he pushed his glasses up his nose and rubbed his hand over his shaved head when he was thinking. She'd forgotten to get milk; they'd both had their coffee black, Jasper stretched on the sofa looking at them critically, whining occasionally. He'd wanted to be let out, to run the length of the marina snapping at the heels of the ginger cat that lived on the *Marie Claire*, a houseboat two down from them. PC Miller's voice interrupted her thoughts.

'Does he have any family we can contact – anyone we can call for you?'

Rachel shook her head, her bobbed curls falling into her face. She realised Jasper had moved to her side, pushing his head into her thigh. Uncrossing her arms, she tucked her hair behind her ear again and gave him a rub. He sat down, looking at the officers steadily. Feeling his weight against her leg, she took a moment to answer PC Miller's question.

'His mum and dad are at home in Jamaica. He's a sister in America, in Los Angeles. There's only me here.'

'You think he was going to work?'

'Yes, he's a documentary director. He had a meeting. Can I see him?'

'Of course. But we need to ask you some questions—'

'Later? I can answer all your questions. I need to talk to the doctors, find out what's happening.' Rachel's voice was brisk, the one she used to organise the guys on a shoot. She needed to get things moving.

Rachel glanced at her watch, Hunter's watch, a chunky silver Aviator. It was already after four. *When had this happened?*

'I need to get someone to look after Jasper. We've a houseboat down at Limehouse – there was a break-in this morning so I can't take him back. That's what I thought you were here about.' She put her hand to her head; there really was too much happening today. 'They said the scenes of crime man would be down about five.' Rachel looked around the office, not even sure what she was looking for – her skiing jacket? Her backpack? She picked them both up. 'I'll ask Nathan. He's one of the animators. Jasper loves him.' *Why was she telling them that? Was it even relevant?* 'Can we go now?'

Chapter 2

CAROLINE KELLY WASN'T sure that she could ever remember seeing a day that had changed so suddenly into night as it had this afternoon. It was only 4.30, but the darkness surrounded the taxi like a physical thing, as if they were underwater and it was seeping into every crevice, absorbing light as if it was feeding on it.

When she'd come to West Cork as a child it had always been during the three-month Irish schools' summer vacation, or at Easter when the evenings were lengthening and the promise of spring was fresh in the air. Log fires and laughter, beachcombing despite the weather, and in the summer, days on the beach, long walks in sun-kissed meadows alive with insects and scurrying animals.

Steadying herself as the car hit another pothole, she took a ragged breath. Had coming here in January really been such a good idea? Had she even had time for thinking an idea through? West Cork had been her automatic default and realistically there was nowhere else on earth she wanted to go to lick her wounds, to reconcile the events of the past two days – which, let's be honest, she really couldn't have made up if she'd tried.

Greta's voice still rang in her ears: '*We'll have to suspend you while the case is pending ...*' For once in her life Caroline had been utterly speechless, had turned and headed back to her desk, picked up her bag, pulled on her coat and left the building.

So much for your editor backing you up.

The snow had started falling again then, hitting her face like needles. She'd pulled her fur-lined hood up and looked for a cab, navigating the grey New York slush to the kerb, so stunned she'd hardly registered when they'd drawn up outside her apartment block, only realising where she was as she'd stepped out of the elevator on her floor.

None of this had been on her agenda as she'd headed into the week. She'd had a meeting planned with a key source in the prison service, had research to do on the Texas State Penitentiary. It had taken her months to get the meeting, and days to come up with a covert plan to make it look accidental.

And then, after all the work, it all had to be shelved.

Greta's request for an audience had been on her voicemail the moment she'd arrived at her desk at eight o'clock that morning, and whatever was happening in her diary, denying her impossibly elegant, narcissistic, absolute weapon of a boss a meeting wasn't an option. Greta wielded her authority like an avenging goddess.

Which was, as Caroline had to remind herself every day, why she was so successful.

She'd presided over the *New York Messenger* for every year of the past three that Caroline had been its lead crime reporter. Anyone who thought *The Devil Wears Prada* didn't have its equivalent in news only had to stick their head out of the elevator on the fifth floor to see how close to the truth it really was.

Teeth gritted but holding her head high, Caroline had felt like she'd been hit by a forty-tonne container truck as she'd left the office. Her hopes and dreams, everything she'd built, decimated in one glancing blow. How could Greta question her integrity for *one second*?

What the hell was happening to this world? Caroline didn't deal in fake news; she never had. The real problem here was that she'd exposed too much of Rich Slater's actual life in her articles, the areas he thought he'd kept neatly tucked away and compartmentalised. She had exposed all his sleaze and exactly how he'd manipulated his female employees as he'd built his cyber-empire. People talked to her; they always had. And she had a knack for understanding what they didn't say, for reading between the lines and ferreting after the truth.

And now he was accusing her of tapping his phone and defaming him by implying his treatment of his female employees was questionable. As if he hadn't done a good enough job of making a spectacle of himself all on his own.

Caroline glanced out of the window of the cab into the encroaching night and pulled her dark hair out of her face, adjusting her glasses as she mulled over the last few days. You'd think you couldn't be hit by a truck twice in a lifetime – it was a bit like being hit by lightning – but as she'd headed across the news floor, her mouth dry and her stomach about to reject the skinny latte she'd grabbed on the way in, it had happened again. From her desk beside the window, Nancy – young, blonde, all-American Barbie doll – had sprung up, her brows furrowed, her worried expression hiding what Caroline was a million per cent sure was a satisfied smirk.

She knew what was going on and she was going to do everything she could to step into Caroline's shoes while they were still warm.

And from the wide-eyed way Nancy looked at her as she caught her eye, Caroline was also sure she had something to do with what was happening here.

What had actually made the whole thing worse was Tim jumping up the minute he'd heard Greta's door close – Caroline was sure he'd been sitting on Nancy's desk. She had taken one glance at the pair of them, and stalked straight through to the landing and hit the call button on the elevator. Behind her, she could hear him calling her, his voice heavy with concern and bewilderment. She'd pushed her new tortoiseshell glasses firmly up her nose and hadn't turned around; she couldn't trust herself to look at him. *Maybe he could ask Nancy what was going on.*

He'd only got back from his skiing trip late the previous night, was looking deliciously tanned. Had he known, even had a hint? Maybe he'd had the voicemail summons too and had been heading into Greta's office to get a full briefing. The lawsuit against the paper, naming her, must have been filed while he'd been away. *Well, he was due some serious catch-up.*

But what had he been doing chatting so cosily to her so-called colleague? Caroline didn't even want to think about that. She had been out to dinner with him a few times but they weren't dating – she had no input into whom he did, or didn't, speak to.

Sitting in the back of the car, even this far away across the Atlantic, Caroline could feel her temper rising again. She'd been utterly blindsided by Greta, had literally walked out of the building, not even stopping to clear her desk or collect Harvey, her cactus plant, from beside her monitor.

Hurt and anger and confusion had bubbled into rage – rage that, as soon as she got through the front door of her apartment, had rapidly turned itself into a need to escape and the search for somewhere to stay and a plane flight home.

There was no way she was going to sit around feeling miserable, waiting for the axe to fall.

She was going to take two weeks' vacation and send out the message that she wasn't in the slightest bit worried about the impending case. About the fact she could be about to lose her job and how nearly fecking impossible it would be to get another staff job with healthcare in the current market. Optics were everything in this business.

The taxi hit another rough bit of road and Caroline was jerked back from her tiny apartment in snowy New York to icy West Cork. Looking out of the window, the darkness was complete, only the narrow beams of the headlights dancing on the road ahead, on the high-sided hedges, gave her any clue as to where they were. Perhaps she'd got too used to New York, to a city where it was never truly dark.

The driver hit his indicator and turned off the winding lane they seemed to have been following for miles. Caroline closed her eyes for a moment, taking a deep breath, trying to steady her nerves.

So much had happened in the last forty-eight hours that her head was exploding. She wasn't sure if she was running away or running to, but one thing was for sure – she hadn't had a vacation in four years and she needed some headspace.

She'd worked so hard to get into news, had pulled off coup after coup making her column one of the most read ever, spawning a host of talk show items. Everyone was interested in crime, it seemed – death in particular, the more gruesome the better.

Only a few weeks ago, on the afternoon of the office pre-Christmas party – the one she hadn't been able to go to because she was sitting in a freezing town car at a stake-out, following a so-called lead – Greta's husband – who was the real boss, the owner of WordCorp – had taken her to one side and told her how pleased he was with her progress, what a difference she made to the office and the positive energy she brought. The whole situation was insane.

The cab driver interrupted her thoughts.

'Almost there, lass, I'd say you'd be glad of a cup of tea when you get in. They're only lovely at Hare's Landing.'

She could feel him looking at her in the rear-view mirror as he spoke. He'd been chatting since he'd picked her up at the airport, asking question after question. He knew exactly who she was; it was almost as if he'd googled her. She'd hardly had the energy to answer.

Yes, she'd written the piece about the Iced Tea Killer. No, she was on vacation; yes, it was snowing in New York. She covered all sorts of crime, and yes, there was plenty in New York. She was originally from Dublin; no, she wasn't moving back.

Unless she got the sack, of course.

Would she mention she was currently jobless because she was being sued by a serial molester for defamation?

Even as she thought about it, it all sounded ridiculous. But she had two weeks' enforced leave while, as Greta put it, 'they got their shit together' and worked out her defence. Defence? Why did she even need to explain? It was just all farcical. She'd met a lot of crazy people over the years but Rich Slater and his gaming empire really took the crown.

'Thanks for coming to get me, I wasn't expecting that.'

'Least we can do for our transatlantic guests. You should have got an email but the internet at the house is only woeful.'

It had taken her a moment to understand his sing-song Cork accent when he'd met her at the gate in the airport, and as she'd been lulled by the movement of the car, she felt as if it had become thicker.

17

She'd evidently been in New York too long if she couldn't understand her own countrymen.

Trying to think of something banal but friendly to reply, Caroline realised she was still gripping her phone in her hand. She looked at the time; she was starting to feel delirious from lack of sleep. She closed her eyes for a second, realising that the upward intonation at the end of his sentence didn't actually make it a question. He was just trying to be conversational.

'How much further is it?'

'About another ten minutes. The hotel's right on the edge of the estate, has some mighty views of the estuary, right out to sea. Lovely and quiet. Some say it's haunted, but that's only talk.'

Chapter 3

RACHEL HAD BEEN in the back of a police car on more than one occasion, but it had always been on a shoot and the guy driving was usually an actor. Not always – they used all sorts of professionals to get scenes right, dog handlers and forensics – but today was different. Normally there was banter, a laugh about the weather or complaints about the catering.

This time the journey was silent.

Tweedledum and Tweedledee were very short on conversation – not that Rachel wanted to talk to them – but something to break the tension on the thirty-minute journey to the Royal Hope would have kept her mind still. Images of Hunter lying in the road merged with stills from a horror shoot she'd done last year, the make-up so realistic it had turned her stomach.

How badly injured was he? Had he seen her message on his phone about the break-in and lost his concentration? Anxiety gripped Rachel's stomach, making her feel physically sick. She twisted her ring, but the normally comforting smoothness of the heavy silver didn't make her feel any better.

She pulled the polo neck of her black sweater up over her face as she tried to think of the positive, trying not to be sucked into a nightmare place that burned her eyes like hell. There were ghost bikes all over London, bikes painted white and left as memorials to cyclists who had been killed – there were just so many accidents. *Hunter couldn't be one of them.* She chewed the edge of her nail as the squad car negotiated the traffic.

She was always nagging Hunter to take his ancient beaten-up Land Rover to work instead of cycling. He was right about the impact of diesel on the environment, and the fact that it could take him longer to get the five miles there than it did on his bike – plus he loved the freedom, and he reckoned it kept him fit – but the traffic in London was vicious on a good day. He kept saying his camera equipment weighed a ton and apparently going to the gym three times a week and walking miles with Jasper wasn't enough as he headed for thirty-three; he needed cycling too. She'd opened her mouth to protest at that when he'd said it last time, and now she felt his finger on her lips as he'd hushed her. Tears pricked at her eyes. She couldn't lose him; it wasn't even an option, he was her soulmate. He might be from a different island on the other side of the world, but when she was with him, she felt whole.

She closed her eyes tightly. She'd bet he hadn't been wearing a helmet either, would have had his felt Boston Jack hat on. He'd traded in his fedora for it in New York, and hadn't taken it off since. It was chocolate brown, only a shade darker than his skin, the same colour as his eyes, and Rachel had loved him in it from the moment he'd tried it on.

He'd been wearing it this morning when she'd left for the ten-minute walk to work. A mug of coffee in his hand, he'd been waiting on a conference call with the production team to discuss the broadcast schedule for the documentary series he was working on before he went in for his meeting.

He had to be okay.

Rachel didn't know if she could cope if anything happened to him. In the three years she'd known him, two living on the boat with him, he'd never been sick. He claimed it was all the fresh fruit his mother had fed him as a child, the sea and sunshine and clean Caribbean air. He was probably right – she caught every cold that was passing, but that's what rain did for you. Her own home in County Wicklow, the garden of Ireland, had been half an hour from Dublin city. She loved how you could see the weather gathering on the mountains, but there wasn't a whole lot of sunshine.

Rachel shifted in the back seat. The heating was on in the car, but despite pulling on her padded skiing jacket as she'd left the office, she still felt cold.

Would Nathan be okay with Jasper?

She closed her eyes. This was too much in one day. She felt sick, really ill, anxiety spiralling in her stomach like a black hole. Her mind rolled back to the morning – it had all been so *normal*. Absolutely no precognition of anything dreadful to come. An ordinary day.

They'd been chatting about Hunter's documentary, about the rushes and editing slots … If she could only capture that moment, like scent in a bottle, put a cork in it and keep it for ever. He'd been frowning, wondering why the homeless guy he'd befriended when he'd started on this documentary project hadn't turned up to meet him the day before.

'I hope he's okay, it's so unlike him. He's never let me down before. I always get him something to eat when we meet but he never showed up.'

Hunter had picked up the glass coffee pot and leaned over to top up her mug. As he sat back down again, the houseboat had rocked gently, buffeted by a gust of wind that had found its way into the marina from the Thames.

It was snug inside, the heating efficient and the insulation all new, one of the first things to be replaced when Hunter had first bought the Victorian barge, but Rachel had put her hands around the earthenware mug, looking for something to warm her. Poor Alfie; she'd only met him once, and had been a bit daunted by the intensity of his stare, but she'd been mesmerised as he'd started to play his violin – Mozart's 'Concerto No. 5', his favourite piece. Neither of them really had any idea how old he was – he looked almost seventy, his skin lined and weather-beaten, his grey hair long. Hunter had been worried about him since he'd first met him, busking outside Tottenham Court Road Tube station. Alfie was always saying that there were factions on the street they couldn't understand, that people could take against you for little or no real reason. Although neither of them had been able to see how a man with a violin could be in any way threatening.

'But you left a message for him with Frank at the hostel, and with the other lads you were talking to? I'm sure he'll get in touch when he's ready.' Rachel had rinsed her mug, getting ready to go.

Hunter hadn't looked convinced as he stared thoughtfully out of the window across the boats moored between them and the marina office.

'I hope so. There's so much I don't understand about him. I mean, he's educated, you'd know from his accent and vocabulary that he's really intelligent, but he's been on the streets for years, like forever from what I can gather.'

'Has he told you what happened yet, how he ended up homeless? That's the whole point of the series, isn't it?'

Hunter shrugged. 'Some. The others have been quite open, but he gets upset whenever I bring it up. Nothing he's said so far has made a whole lot of sense. He said you couldn't trust anyone in life.' Hunter had paused. 'But you know how stuff happens – one of the dudes I was talking to got thrown out by his wife, another one lost his job and couldn't pay his mortgage, ended up sleeping in his car. From what he's been saying the past few months, I think Alfie had a nervous breakdown, something happened and he just fell apart. I wondered if he has schizophrenia? He's seriously paranoid about people coming after him, coming to find him.'

'Perhaps he's a victim of care in the community and he just ended up dropping out and nobody noticed. The health system is so overstretched.'

The whole point of the documentary was to show how easy it is for everything to go wrong for normal people. Whatever 'normal' was. Hunter wanted to show that people on the streets were just as human as the viewers, that they had lives and families, and how maybe just one or two things went wrong and their lives spiralled out of control. Alfie Bows, as the street people called him, was the perfect example. Hunter had met him the first or second day he'd been out talking to people, looking for stories. One of the shelter workers had suggested they have a chat and Hunter had gone off to find him. Alfie had had his violin with him even then, tucked in under his tattered coat to protect it from the biblical rain. Later Hunter had told her that he loved it like a child. It was how he'd got his nickname. Hunter wasn't even sure his real name was Alfie, but that's what he went by, and Bows suited him.

She'd had to leave then, had kissed him quickly and gone out into the frosty January chill to walk briskly to work, Jasper at her heels, her mind moving quickly from Alfie to whether the hotel in Matlock she'd found would be big enough to take all the crew. Rachel looked out of the window of the squad car and wiped away a tear.

How could your life turn so completely upside down in a split second?

Chapter 4

*H*ARE'S LANDING WAS *haunted?*

That was all she needed. Perhaps *that* was why it was so cheap, and it was nothing to do with it being out of season or recently opened? Caroline sighed as the taxi hit another pothole and her glasses almost jumped off her nose. She pushed them back on. She didn't really believe in ghosts; ever since school when they'd set up a paranormal club and had spent their lunchtimes discussing stories like the disappearance of the girls at Ayers Rock, she'd felt sightings were all about pockets of energy, that time ran somehow in parallel lines and sometimes when the energy was right, you caught a glimpse into another time frame. One day she needed to talk to a physicist about her theories, but today wasn't it, that was for sure.

She was really too tired for conversation. Any conversation.

Perhaps if she asked the questions, the driver would just chat and she could zone out.

After the flight and all the delays, zoning out was about all she wanted to do. Zone out, have a shower and a very tall, very chilled glass of white wine.

And she was going to arrive in darkness, so she wasn't about to indulge in whatever gossip the driver wanted to share about things that went bump in the night. She needed to keep the conversation practical. One where she didn't have to actually answer.

'It said something about the hotel having new management when I booked. Has it been open long?'

'I don't reckon it's quite open yet. Local girl she is running it, went off to see the world, married a chef and ran a hotel in Italy. But now she's back. Hasn't forgotten her roots, like. The restaurant is open all right, that was very popular coming up to Christmas, bit pricey, mind, but not too foreign. They must be getting the rooms ready now though, if they've booked you in.'

'I'm not in the main hotel – I've taken a place called the Boathouse for a couple of weeks.'

'The Boathouse, is it? That'll be lovely, I'd say. On your own, are you?'

He sounded surprised. Caroline didn't have the energy to explain, and it wasn't any of his business anyway.

'I need some space.'

'Well, one thing we've got lots of in West Cork is space. You don't get much of that in New York.'

That was for sure.

Adjusting her seat belt and sitting back, Caroline closed her eyes again. Taking a break from New York and coming home was the right thing to do, even if this wasn't really home. When her mum had died, just before she'd got her American visa, they'd sold the family house. To really go home, she'd have had to stay with one of her inquisitive sisters or friends in Dublin. And she needed time to be on her own, to recalibrate. And to work out what she was going to do next. West Cork was a much better idea. She'd always loved it here. *Perhaps she could capture some of that childhood magic again.*

When she'd calmed down enough to answer his texts, Tim had been all professional corporate lawyer, firing questions at her as if she was on the witness stand. She could almost see him shaking his head at the reason for her suspension, which, she had to be honest, sounded like a fairy story.

Tim had said she needed to stay and fight, to show she thought it was all nonsense, but she'd just *had* to get away from New York, to find the space to work out a plan B if she needed it. And let's face it, she was exhausted. Americans didn't take holidays – vacations, as she'd come to call them – and to keep at the top she worked eighteen-hour days.

It was time to stop.

When the Boathouse had popped up on the hotel booking site, with its granite walls and Gothic windows, she'd felt Hare's Landing was calling to her. Even more so when she saw that they had a special rate for January – *supposedly* because they weren't fully open. Overlooking the Atlantic Ocean, everything about the cottage was perfect – totally private, separated from the hotel by a wood and gardens but serviced, the fridge filled so she didn't have to worry about making small talk with other irritating, nosey guests in the dining room over breakfast.

The peace and isolation were exactly what she was craving, and the note on the booking form that the internet and phone signals were currently intermittent made it absolutely ideal. It meant she didn't have to answer the phone or her email, could blame the lack of connectivity for her silence. She'd take the ghosts if it meant some peace and quiet.

It was time she took stock of her life and worked out where she was going. She was almost thirty, and had been suspended from one of the most influential reporting jobs in New York. And it would be virtually impossible to keep the news private in a business where gossip was currency. Even if she *did* manage to keep it quiet and, instead of waiting for Rich Slater's nonsense defamation case to get to court, resigned to protest at the paper's lack of support, that was as good as admitting it was all true.

But Caroline wasn't made like that – ever since she'd been able to walk and talk, she'd been stubborn to the core. Perhaps it came from having three sisters and having to fight for everything, but she was damned if some creepy misogynist bastard, millionaire or not, was going to get the better of her. She'd take her two weeks' vacation, refuel, recalibrate and come back fighting.

How could she have damaged Slater's professional reputation, really? He'd posted photographs of his secretary's cleavage on social media. *How could Greta doubt her?*

Speculation would be rife across the whole industry as soon as anyone spotted the case listed.

And would Nancy keep quiet about Greta's stance? Really?

If this wasn't handled right, she could find herself unemployable.

And that didn't even bear thinking about.

She adored her job, adored news, loved the adrenaline rush of covering the courts but also of getting to an active scene fast. She had so many contacts within the NYPD at this stage – half the force was of Irish descent – that she often knew about incidents even before the ambulance crews. But if they thought she'd hacked phones to get information, like Rich Slater was suggesting, she could lose that trust, which would be catastrophic if she wanted to have any sort of future on the crime beat.

Her thoughts were interrupted as the taxi rattled over a cattle grid between two high granite pillars, the entrance presumably, although she couldn't see any actual gates in the dark. To her right, in the distance through the woods, she caught sight of a flickering light, yellow like a cat's eyes – a gate lodge perhaps? Ahead the road was narrow, the headlights picking out trees crowding on either side, their arthritic fingers reaching out to scratch the sides of the car. The drive seemed to go on for ages, twisting downwards.

Anxiously leaning forward in her seat, Caroline kept her eyes on the road, the full beam headlights of the car again catching the flash of eyes watching them steadily through the darkness – foxes maybe? Caroline hoped so. There were no wolves in Ireland any more, hunted to extinction, like there were no bears. And there had never been snakes. She shivered.

They swung around a final bend and the house rose in front of them, set into thick foliage on either side. She almost heaved a sigh of relief. It rose over three floors, mullioned windows lit from inside. And the gabled porch looked warm and welcoming, light spilling onto the sweep of gravelled drive. Waist-high statues of two seated hares flanked the entrance. As they pulled up, a woman came to the door, her arms folded. Silhouetted by the porch lights, Caroline couldn't see her properly, only that she was tiny, almost bird-like, her hair steel grey, her cheekbones sharp.

'Here we are, lass. This is Hare's Landing.'

Chapter 5

RACHEL HURRIED ALONG the hospital corridor, glancing up for the signs to St Patrick's Ward. Her police minders had got a call they'd had to take and, in all honesty, she was glad they'd gone; she wanted to do the next bit alone.

She still couldn't believe this was happening after everything this morning. *Was Mercury in retrograde or something?* Hunter always laughed at her, but perhaps if she'd read her horoscope there would have been some hint that would have prepared her for this.

She'd thought she'd reached peak shock today when she'd arrived at the barge. Standing there, frozen, Jasper poised at her side, his low growl like something from the underworld, she'd felt physically sick. *But if she'd felt sick then, it was nothing to how she was feeling now.*

Turning another corner, her mind flashed back to their gorgeous cosy living area. Through the windows she'd been able to see the cushions and brightly striped throws tossed all over the polished boards, every drawer turned out, every cupboard door open.

Rachel stood back to let two orderlies pushing a bed pass her, the elderly man in it hooked up to a drip. She anxiously tucked a wave of hair behind her ear. She'd only gone back to the boat this morning because she'd forgotten the memory stick with the shots of Matlock and the Peak District on it. She'd clipped on Jasper's lead and nipped back to the marina, running all the way, Jasper's claws clattering on the pavement as he lolloped along beside her, happy to be out of the office. She almost always brought him to work; the boat was too small to leave him locked up all day.

She'd known something was wrong before she'd even reached the stout cobalt-blue barge, and Jasper's reaction as they'd slowed and walked down the pontoon had reinforced that feeling. Then she'd spotted the splintered wood on the companionway door and she'd taken her phone out to call Hunter, giving up when he didn't answer and calling the police instead.

And now this. She glanced around her and saw another sign for St Patrick's Ward. That would make Hunter smile – he found her accent constantly amusing, was always teasing her about home.

Around the next corner Rachel saw a reception area and nurses' station.

'I think my partner's been brought in. He was in a cycling accident – Hunter MacKenzie. Downstairs they said he was on this ward.'

The nurse behind the desk held up her finger for a moment as if trying to remember and then, moving back to her chair, sat down, her flingers flying over the keys of her computer.

'Brought in by ambulance this morning. West Indian male, thirty-three years of age?'

Rachel nodded, 'Sounds like him. He was probably wearing a hat.'

The nurse grinned as if the description matched something she had on her screen.

'You Irish as well, pet?' She had a midlands accent, Tipperary perhaps. A tiny part of Rachel felt relieved. It connected them.

'Yes, Dublin. Rachel Lambert, I'm his partner.'

The nurse smiled and nodded as she read her screen.

Why was she taking so long? Rachel's mouth went dry. *Did she have bad news?*

'Can I see him? I really need to see him.'

'Of course, pet, he's on the left, by the window. He's had a bad time. He's got a nasty femoral fracture and a traumatic pneumothorax – a punctured lung. More than a few ribs have gone the same way as the leg, but he's a lucky one.'

'I … Can I talk to him? Is he asleep?'

'I'm not sure. Just keep your voice right down, visiting hours are over, but you're grand to go in for a few minutes. He might have difficulty talking, so not long now.'

At the heavy swing door, Rachel hesitated for a second. She could see that it was a male ward; some of the beds had blue curtains pulled around them. One man was sitting up in bed reading the newspaper.

Hunter was in the end bed. He was wired up to all sorts of machines, and even before she reached him properly she could see he was ashen against the bright white pillow, his dark skin several shades paler than normal. As Rachel reached him, a nurse slipped out of the curtains around the bed opposite. Her eyes lit up as she pushed a pen into the pocket of her tunic.

'He'll be delighted to see you love, he's just conscious now. Only be a few minutes, though, he needs to conserve his energy.'

Rachel mouthed her thanks as the nurse indicated she should sit in a chair beside the bed, and pulled the curtain closed around her. At the sound of the curtain hooks on the rails, Hunter moved his head marginally. Trying to hold back tears, Rachel picked up his hand. He turned towards her and opened his eyes.

'Rach? What …?'

She stood up from the chair and perched on the side of the bed, rubbing the back of his hand and kissing it.

'What am I doing here? Where else would I be?' She rubbed his arm. 'You're here. Do you think I'd be able to keep away?'

He smiled weakly. 'I'm fine, got knocked off my bike. Some bastard in a BMW 4 × 4.' He paused, catching his breath. 'Did they find my hat?'

Rachel hid her grin, shaking her head. 'Your hat?'

Hunter rolled his eyes and then closed them as if the expression had worn him out.

'I love that hat.'

'I'll find out. I think you need to rest, my love.'

His voice was barely a whisper. 'I'll be fine, babes. I'm not going anywhere – for a couple of weeks anyway.' He took a couple of jagged breaths. 'Bastard almost flattened me, came out of nowhere. I had that hi-vis vest on too. I'm not exactly invisible.'

'That roundabout's lethal.'

He nodded, his eyes closed. 'I was early for once too.' He opened his eyes. 'They've confirmed the slots. Spring schedule.'

'That's great news.'

She rubbed the back of his hand, about to tell him he needed to focus his energy on getting better when he interrupted her thoughts.

'Babes, can you see if you can find out what's happened to Alfie? There's more we need to ask him. No one's seen him for a few days and his story is the missing piece. If I can't find out why he's on the streets we can't use any of his footage and it'll balls up the production timeline.'

'Alfie?' She shook her head, trying to hide her impatience:

what was he like? 'You need to *stop* thinking about work and focus on getting better—'

Hunter interrupted her. 'But he's disappeared. Zack's been to all his usual hangouts and can't find him. There's no one in his car park, even the bins have been tidied up … And nobody's seen him at the soup kitchen. It's January, it's freezing …'

'But that's not unusual, is it? He's a free agent, perhaps he's found somewhere better to sleep and he went to a different place for his dinner?'

Hunter shook his head weakly. 'I don't know. I told you I was supposed to meet him and he never showed. He's never done that before, he's as reliable as my watch. As his watch. I gave him one so he'd know when to meet me. He has my number – he would have called—'

'I'll do my best. You need to rest.'

'Please, babes, I'm really worried about him.'

He looked so fragile there against the bright white of the pillow; she ran her hand around his face and kissed him.

'Don't you worry, I'll find him. I want you to focus on getting better.'

The news about the boat would have to wait.

Chapter 6

As THE DRIVER opened the rear door of the taxi, Caroline was immediately hit by a blast of icy air and the distant sound of waves pounding the coast. She knew that this close to the sea the temperature couldn't be as low as New York with its drifting snow, but here it was a different type of cold, a damp creeping chill, the wind keen. The driver had the boot open and was carrying her case into reception before she fully realised she needed to get out herself.

'Careful there, it's fierce cold. Mrs Travers will look after you, she knows all there is to know about Hare's Landing.'

'Thank you.'

Pushing the car door closed behind her, Caroline glanced at the diminutive figure of Mrs Travers waiting in the doorway, and for a moment felt an even deeper chill. Pushing her bag up onto her shoulder again thankful for her padded, fur-lined parka and thick-soled leather boots, as she reached the door, Mrs Travers pushed it open wider to allow her in.

'Good evening. You're later than we were expecting.' Mrs Travers held out her hand, the bones prominent against paper-thin skin.

Good start.

Caroline returned her handshake. The old woman's hands were icy. Caroline retracted her own hand as quickly as she decently could. In the light from the hall she could see Mrs Travers was wearing a black cardigan over a white blouse and straight black skirt. Her tights, like her shoes, were thick and sensible. She reminded Caroline for a moment of the nuns in school, except that her grey hair was neatly cut in a short straight bob, every strand in place as if she'd just stepped out of the hairdresser's.

'I'm sorry to keep you waiting. My plane was delayed. Can I check in and get settled? I'm exhausted.'

'Of course, come inside and I'll get someone to take your case to the Boathouse. We've had the fire lit since four so it should be lovely and warm.'

She held the glazed door open for Caroline. The porch, and the main hall beyond it, were floored with huge grey flagstones. The tick of a clock echoed in the lofty space; a grand staircase carpeted in a rich blue ran up to what appeared to be a mezzanine level. The hall was panelled in oak, polished, like the newel post and banisters, to a deep shine. As she looked around she caught the gentle tones of classical music playing softly in the background: violins, beautiful, haunting.

The unmanned reception desk was tucked in to the right of the door, a pen laid across the visitors' book waiting for her on the dark wood counter. Her booking information was on a separate sheet beside it, a pile of stamped, hand-addressed letters neatly stacked beside an old-fashioned brass bell. Picking up the pen, Caroline quickly signed the paperwork and glanced around her. A fire was burning merrily in a huge fireplace, the mantelpiece alight with stout cream candles. The hall smelled wonderful, of a delicate floral fragrance with a hint of spice.

To her left there was a glass door leading from the hall into what looked like a huge sitting room, firelight flickering on cream walls. A wide corridor opened off the hall to what had to be the back of the hotel. Caroline had looked at the photographs on the booking site thoroughly; she was sure the passage led to the restaurant and bar, and on to a ballroom. Curious, but too tired for a guided tour – not that Mrs Travers looked like she was going to offer one – Caroline turned and feigned a smile. The whole building was wonderfully cosy but felt surprisingly empty for a Wednesday evening.

'It's very quiet.'

Mrs Travers's expression hardened. 'The restaurant's open, but it's early in the year, people don't have the money to be wasting on eating out.' She looked disdainfully at Caroline's Samsonite hard-shell suitcase and distinctive Louis Vuitton shopper. 'You're the first proper guest. That was on the website when you booked, we're not running at full capacity – that's why the price is good. It was very clear.'

'I saw that.'

Caroline suddenly felt more like a guinea pig than a guest, a guinea pig who was clearly under scrutiny for her lifestyle choices and shopping habits. She didn't think it would help to explain that half her wardrobe came as a perk of living next door to Trixie in fashion, working the same crazy hours she worked, six days a week, so they often shared a cab home, and that the bag was a gift to Caroline for feeding her cat when Trixie travelled to Paris and London Fashion Week.

She cleared her throat. 'It's lovely, I'm sure it will be very popular.'

Mrs Travers regarded her stoically. 'There's one or two rooms ready for letting, and the Boathouse of course, but January is always quiet. Always has been. Not many places are open at all.'

'Have you worked here long?'

Mrs Travers's eyes looked black in the weak light from the brass chandelier above their heads.

'Came here first when Mrs Smyth got married, she wanted a housekeeper and someone to run the place when she was in London. She needed help with young Sheridan too.' Mrs Travers put her hand on the counter proprietorially. 'He was a delicate lad, very bright.' Her voice softened for a moment, before she continued briskly. 'Then when it was sold as a hotel first, they needed someone who understood the house. Banks took it in the end.' She sniffed. 'Bronagh bought it about a year ago, they've been working non-stop restoring the place. She's from the village. He's Italian, his family are in hotels, but he spends all day in the kitchen. He's away in Italy at the moment.'

Caroline felt she really had too much information after this long speech, information laced with judgement and vitriol. She didn't have the energy to analyse it, much less the interest. Obviously none of the owners had got into the realms of customer service training with Mrs Travers. Before she could think of a suitable reply, a young man with a mop of sun-bleached sandy hair tied up in a man-bun arrived. He looked like he'd be more comfortable in board shorts than the black trousers and white shirt he was wearing. Good-looking, his face angular and lean, he had a screwdriver sticking out of one pocket and a pencil behind his ear.

'Ah, here you are, Conor. Ms Kelly has just arrived. Can you take her down to the Boathouse?'

As Conor grabbed her suitcase, Caroline heard the sound of chiming. Turning around, she realised there was a huge antique clock on the wall behind the reception desk, obviously the source of the ticking too. Its dial painted with Roman numerals, it had the words 'Waiting Room' in the centre. It had probably come originally from a station but somehow it couldn't have been more appropriate for its current location.

'It's this way.' Interrupting her thoughts, the surfer headed out of the main door at a brisk walk.

Caroline glanced at Mrs Travers, smiling her thanks, and followed him, relieved to be leaving her frosty stare behind. She'd come here to get away from women like that; Mrs Travers reminded her distinctly of Greta – they shared an air of judgement that no matter what you did, it would always be lacking in some way. Caroline had always put it down to Greta's own insecurities but it had become wearing over the years she'd worked for her, and as Caroline had secured her position with scoop after scoop, it had become more intense.

At the front door, Caroline felt her cheeks freeze as she was hit again by the intensity of the cold air outside. She could see Conor was already crossing the gravel ahead of her, completely oblivious to the chill. Pulling up the fur-lined hood of her coat, she trotted to catch up with him, her breath steaming in the night air, her glasses fogging.

Weaving between thick evergreen bushes down a narrow gravel path lit by softly glowing lights at the edges, he kept up a brisk pace. Caroline was surprised when they suddenly emerged from the woods beside a Victorian lamppost, somewhat incongruously throwing a pool of soft yellow light onto a semicircular paved area in front of a granite building shaped not unlike the hull of a boat, the prow pointing skywards. An arched door was flanked by small circular windows.

Caroline grinned to herself; it was just as awesome as it had appeared on the website. She'd looked at all the photos, knew the original boathouse doors on the seaward side had been replaced with huge windows that mirrored the shape of the building and looked out over the estuary. The light was very special here at any time of the year, clear and intense, and it had been one of the things that she'd always loved as a child. In the same way artists flocked to the South of France and Cornwall, they came to West Cork too. She breathed in; the air was as clear and sharp as a diamond.

Conor pushed open the door, painted a dull marine blue.

'Here we are. It's nice and warm inside. There's a bottle of wine and the fridge is full.'

Chapter 7

THE POLICE WERE still at the barge when Rachel finally got there after leaving Hunter at the hospital. He'd named it *Carpe Diem* soon after she'd moved on board, cracking open several bottles of Prosecco and inviting all their neighbours to celebrate. It had just had a number until then. They'd felt it approved of its new coat of paint and striking blue livery.

As Rachel swung open the steel gate that guarded the pedestrian entrance to the marina, she could see a crowd had gathered around the barge, the distinct shapes of their neighbours punctuated by dark blue uniforms.

Nathan from the office had texted to say he'd taken Jasper home to his mum's, and Tony, the marina manager, had texted to say the police had arrived and he had everything under control. *She was so lucky to have so many good friends around her.*

She bit her lip, her emotions swirling. She felt terrible not telling Hunter, but there was really no point worrying him until she had all the information. She needed to find out what the situation was here before she broke the news; he had enough to contend with right now. *Perhaps nothing had been taken at all, perhaps it was just kids messing.*

Rachel just prayed that the boat hadn't been completely trashed. She'd only glanced in earlier, unable to do anything until the police arrived, had gone back to the office to collect her backpack and tell her colleagues that she'd be out for the rest of the day. And then Tweedledum and Tweedledee had arrived to tell her about Hunter. They hadn't known anything about the break-in, but as she'd told them about it on the way to the hospital, she'd seen them exchange glances. She wasn't sure if that was to do with the delay in Limehouse station sending out someone to take all the details, or what – everyone knew the Met were grossly undermanned these days – but she hadn't been up for mind-reading just then, she had had too much to think about.

Today was one long nightmare.

The barge had been their home for the past two years and they both adored it. It cost a fortune to heat and the bilge pump kept breaking but it was theirs and it was home.

Rachel knew how devastated Hunter would be at the thought of anyone damaging the *Carpe Diem*. He'd rebuilt her from a shell, had spent hours sanding and painting, hauling the engine out and fixing the bilge. Looking across the marina now, she knew she just had to face it and find out from the police what had happened. Get the worst over with so that she could call him and tell him it would all be okay.

And she needed to call his mum to tell her what had happened. She'd want to come over straight away, but where would she stay? She'd be fussing and worrying and issuing orders in an accent as soothing as the midday sun on golden sand. She was wonderful and warm and she had an infectious laugh that literally made others smile, but she'd been a staff nurse when she'd worked in London and everything had to meet her standards.

Rachel hurried towards the group hovering at the side of the marina. Darkness had arrived while she was at the hospital, the marina lights now throwing glowing pools across the broad pontoon that connected the office with the berths.

The police officers on the edge of the group turned as she started to jog towards them, arriving slightly breathless.

'Can I get on board now?'

'Ms Lambert?' One of the officers turned to her, his notebook open in his hand.

'Yes.'

'We've got one of our techs in there taking fingerprints. As soon as they're finished, you'll be able to check to see what's missing. Was there much of value on board?'

Despite her resolve to be positive, Rachel suddenly felt another wave of anxiety. She stuck her hands in the back pockets of her jeans and looked at her feet, taking a moment to calm. Her heart was racing. Panicking wouldn't help anyone, and it wasn't her usual mode, but right now she was in emotional overload.

'Hunter's cameras. He's a documentary director. His laptop's been playing up so that's in for repair, but he's got TV cameras, sound equipment.'

'Is it insured?'

She wasn't completely sure which of them had asked, but she nodded.

'Yes, but that doesn't get the film back. Most of it's backed up, but you always miss something.' She took a breath, aware that they didn't need to know any of this and she probably wasn't making a whole lot of sense anyway. 'He's working on a documentary at the moment. None of it's been edited yet, the crew are still reviewing the rushes.'

From the deck of the boat, she heard a woman's voice.

'All clear. I've got everything I need.'

A figure in a hooded white overall appeared at the companionway door and headed towards them across the deck, handing a huge steel toolbox to one of the police officers and deftly climbing off onto the pontoon.

'Whoever it was had to have been waiting for everyone to leave. I can't imagine anyone would fancy their chances against that dog in a confined space.'

Answering her, Rachel said, 'He's a bit of a softie actually.'

The woman pushed back her hood revealing glossy black hair. She was of Asian origin, Chinese, or perhaps Korean, with a local accent.

'He's gorgeous, we met up at the office when I arrived. I can't imagine he'd let someone break in.'

Rachel smiled. 'You're right, he's an ex-police dog. He's retired now, and more focused on chasing cats than criminals.'

The crime scene officer chuckled. 'I hope I'm that well looked after in my retirement.' She glanced back at the galley door. 'I'm sorry they made so much mess, I've tried to keep mine to a minimum.'

Rachel met her brown eyes with a grateful smile. It was hardly her fault.

'Thank you. Did you find any fingerprints?'

'It looks like they wore gloves.'

'How can you tell?'

Rachel imagined the whole boat had to be covered in fingerprints; how could she tell one from another at this stage?

'Smudges. Gloves leave their own prints, albeit blank. It's a very professional job.'

Taking her equipment case back, the scenes of crime officer jumped off the deck onto the pontoon.

'I'll process all of this as fast as possible. You and your partner are fine to go back on board now.'

Rachel nodded slowly. 'He's in hospital, he got knocked off his bike this morning at Millbank.'

'My God, you are having a bad day.'

Chapter 8

THE BOATHOUSE WAS even more lovely than Caroline could have imagined.

Open-plan, the kitchen area formed a small L shape to her left, a counter with stools dividing it from the living room. To the right, a log-burning stove had been lit, a comfortable sofa in a soft oatmeal shade in front of it, the window she'd seen in the photographs at the far end. Beside the stove, there was a dark green leather high-backed armchair with the day's papers resting on the seat.

Her hosts seemed to have thought of everything.

Conor walked into the flagstoned room and popped her case down with a rattle.

'Thank you for bringing my bag down. You'd better nip back before you freeze to death.'

Conor grinned. 'Don't worry, I don't feel the cold.' He pointed towards the living area. 'There's a file with instructions for everything on the coffee table and the heating's a smart system. It knows when you're in and keeps the ambient temperature at nineteen degrees.'

'Wow, thank you. That sounds pretty sophisticated.'

'If you need anything just call. When Leo's away I do pretty much everything. They're making the most of me … before I catch the next wave.' His tone was ironic.

Caroline laughed. 'Do you enter competitions?'

'Surfing? When I can. I'm a marine biologist, I'm just waiting on confirmation of a job in New Zealand.'

'Wow.' Caroline really hadn't expected that, wasn't quite sure what to say next except, 'That's awesome.'

He was obviously used to people being surprised.

'I trained as a chef though, so until then, I'm double jobbing here part-time and in a restaurant called Graylings in Sommerville.'

Caroline did a double take. 'Is there anything you don't do?'

His eyes twinkled. 'History – that's my sister Imogen's thing. You'll meet her tomorrow. Boring as hell, but don't tell her I said that, she's totally fascinated by the past. And random I know, but I'm not good with arachnids and I've been known to faint at the sight of blood.'

Caroline laughed as ducked out of the door, pulling it firmly behind him. She followed him to check it was locked and, turning, leaned back on the smooth wood to look at the open-plan living space. Side lights had been switched on, illuminating the cream walls and several stunning paintings of the sea. To her right was a spiral staircase up to the bedroom and bathroom.

It was just perfect.

Unlike the rest of her life. Caroline sighed; she'd been like Conor once, excited and ambitious, the whole world in front of her. She'd worked so damned hard, had used everything she had to land ground-breaking stories for the *New York Messenger*, and now this …

If truth be told, Caroline had known that she'd needed a break for a while. Her thirtieth birthday was looming and, caught up in the relentless deadlines of a daily newspaper, she was starting to feel that life was passing her by. She had no time to go on dates with anyone, even Tim, whom she hardly saw – his schedule was just as heavy as her own. His firm were retained by WordCorp to look after the whole group, not just the *Messenger*, and that kept them very busy. He was building his name as one of New York's most successful corporate lawyers, but the type of cases he handled involved thousands of pieces of paper and marathon prep sessions.

She had no idea what he'd been talking to Nancy about, but the movement she'd caught in the corner of her eye as he'd shifted off her desk had had *guilty* written all over it.

And Nancy was gorgeous – if you liked the all-American white teeth and straight hair to the waist look. She'd thought he was deeper than that, but he was a very good-looking man, had been gifted all the very best Italian genes without the paunch: melting brown eyes, thick wavy hair that was always a little out of control. The courtroom version of Doctor McDreamy. And he was one of the youngest, most successful lawyers Jarvis, Fielding and Jarvis had ever had on their team.

One thing was for sure: Caroline wasn't about to ask him if he was sleeping with her arch-rival – she really wasn't ready for an answer to that. There was only so much she could cope with at once, and right now she was definitely on overload.

But whatever his relationship status, Tim *was* on her side, and she was angry. Greta had everything: the good-looking husband who had put her into one of the top jobs in New York; the Central Park penthouse; the perfect figure and the perfect skin – both expensive to achieve so naturally.

What she didn't have was Caroline's burning ambition, the ambition that had taken her from convent school to her masters in journalism while she, the last one of the family unmarried and at home, cared for her invalid mum.

There was no way Caroline was going anywhere without a fight.

She slipped off her coat, hanging it on the back of one of the counter stools, and, heading to the fridge, pulled out the bottle of white wine from the door. It was deliciously cold. She ran an eye over the label: *impressive*. As well as cooking, Conor, the marine biologist, obviously knew his wine. She reached up to the cupboards above the counter. The first one contained plates and cooking dishes, the next, glasses.

She pulled one out and unscrewed the lid from the bottle. She was well overdue a little self-care.

Chapter 9

As THE SCENES of crime officer headed up the pontoon to her car, Rachel's neighbours began to drift back to their own boats, patting her arm and giving her a hug as they left. She turned to the uniformed officer, who still had his notebook out, shaking her head.

'There are so few burglaries here, between the gates and the office, and there's always someone about on the marina ...'

His eyes widened as if it was a familiar situation. 'Hopefully someone saw something. What were you saying about your partner?'

'Hunter? He got knocked off his bike this morning.' She sighed and ran her fingers into the roots of her hair. 'I mean, what are the chances?'

The officer screwed up his nose thoughtfully. 'That's what I was thinking. Is he normally here during the day?'

Her eyes on the open companionway door and the mess she could see through it, Rachel shook her head.

'Not often. He works from here sometimes but the internet's better in his office.'

'And what time did he leave this morning?'

Rachel frowned. 'I'll have to ask him. It was after me. It had some stuff to do first, so maybe around twelve?'

The officer flipped open his notebook. 'Do you want to go on board and see what's missing?'

Rachel bit her lip. This was the bit she'd been dreading. 'Of course.'

A few minutes later she'd climbed through the hatch and stood at the bottom of the companionway steps, twisting her ring around her finger as she surveyed the main living space. Whoever had been here had made a right mess: sofa cushions were tossed on the floor, the storage spaces under the benches pulled apart. She took a step down into the saloon. Hunter kept his equipment in a padlocked cupboard under the counter that divided the kitchen and living areas. The padlock had been wrenched off and the cupboard was empty. Rachel felt a chill run up her spine.

This must have happened just after Hunter had left.

Whoever had broken in had obviously known what they were after, and had waited until they were all out of the way before trying anything.

The police officer waiting for her on the deck leaned down the steps.

'Can you make a list for us, love? Serial numbers, make and models of the stuff stolen.'

'Hunter has all the serial numbers – every item. I'll need to print off the list at the office, but it looks like everything is gone. There was a lot of gear.'

Rachel glanced back at the officer, frowning, trying to work it out. As she spoke she heard someone coming on deck. The officer turned as Tony, the marina manager, came into view. He moved to allow Tony space to stick his head in through the companionway hatch. He was a big man, had been a boxer, and he filled the space.

'Jesus, that's some sort of mess. I looked in earlier but it's worse close to. I'm gutted, Rach, I don't know how they got in. We're checking all the entries up at the gate. I'm wondering if someone had a tradesman organised and they slipped in after him.'

Rachel looked up at him. 'It's really not your fault, Tony, they must have been very determined to get down here. Did any other boats get broken into?'

Tony shook his head. 'Only yours. They must have been after Hunter's equipment.'

Rachel looked puzzled. 'How, though? How did they know it was here? It's all locked away. They must have known to pick us.' She could feel anxiety bubbling up in her stomach. 'Are you sure no one else was broken into?'

'I checked everything. As soon as you told me, I sent the boys out to look at every boat. It's definitely only you.'

'Well, I suppose that's good.' She put her hands on her hips, still not quite accepting what he was saying. 'Do you think they were disturbed and left before they could try the other boats?'

Tony shrugged. 'No idea. They must have looked kosher, though, because no one noticed anything strange.'

'And the CCTV. It covers the whole marina? They must have been caught on that somewhere?'

Tony put his hand on the roof of the barge and leaned down.

'That's what the plods asked. But some bastard cut the wires to the cameras positioned on this side of the marina.'

Rachel's eyes met his and she shook her head slowly. 'Jesus Christ, that's very organised, isn't it? The forensics lady said it looked like professionals.'

The policeman, who had been listening to their conversation, cut in.

'The type of equipment that was taken is valuable. It's very specialist, it could have been stolen to order, so they knew exactly where to go. We'll have a look at the street cam footage too, hopefully they will have been caught on film somewhere.'

Rachel ran her hand over her face and sighed. 'My God, I hope so. I don't like the idea that they might have been watching, that they knew what Hunter had here.'

Tony cleared his throat. 'Have you got somewhere to stay tonight?'

Rachel sighed. 'I'm grand, thanks. The lad that's looking after Jasper said his mum has a spare room. She's very generous to have us both so we'll be fine tonight. Hopefully I can get all this fixed tomorrow so we can come back tomorrow night.'

Tony held up his hand. 'You leave that with me. I've already got a carpenter and locksmith coming down in the morning. We'll get everything double-checked and the cameras fixed up first thing.'

'Thank you.' Rachel smiled at him weakly, suddenly overwhelmed.

The officer standing beside him looked thoughtful. 'You don't think this could be connected to your partner's accident? Perhaps someone was looking for him but he left earlier than expected?' It took a moment for Rachel to register what he was saying. She turned to look at him, horrified, as he continued. 'Is he working on anything sensitive at the moment?'

Pulling her hair out of her face, Rachel shook her head. 'He's working on a documentary about the homeless.' Thoughts collided in her head. 'Do you think they could be connected? This and his accident? My God, that's awful.'

Chapter 10

HALF PROPPED UP on the generous pillows, Caroline stretched in bed. Out of the window at the end of the bright room, she could see thick woods on the other side of the estuary, the azure blue of the water rippling in the winter sunshine. She hadn't bothered to close the curtains last night and was glad now. The view from here was heavenly.

Reaching for her phone, she checked the time. It was almost one – she'd slept for nearly fourteen hours. She wriggled back into the pillow and closed her eyes again.

For the first time since her conversation with Greta – although she wasn't sure if 'conversation' was the right word; that sort of implied a two-way exchange, not a single barely controlled voice – but anyway, for the first time since she'd left the office, she felt a little of the grimness of the situation had lifted. Being here was definitely helping her put everything into perspective.

As if she was haunting her, Nancy's face loomed into her mind and Caroline felt a surge of irritation and disappointment. When she'd caught her eye, Nancy had, for the briefest second, looked like a rabbit facing a fox, which had told Caroline all she needed to know.

The little bitch.

It was as if she was aware of exactly what was going on – had she found out before Caroline and not warned her?

Caroline pulled the pillow up behind her and, pursing her lips, stared blindly out of the window at the end of the bed, not seeing that the sky had turned grey, that a squall seemed to be heading up the river. All she could see was Nancy's fake worried eyes and her guilty-as-sin face.

Caroline had realised a long time ago that when she got really upset about something, she felt wretched for a while, but then, rather than slipping into some deep dark depression, she got angry. Really angry. And rage was an awesome emotion if you learned to channel it. She'd used it to great effect over the years. She had her best ideas when she was mad, and was at her most insightful and creative. Nothing could stop her.

Men who got their kicks hurting women made her angry. And injustice. And situations where people unable to defend themselves were attacked by anything – the law, lawbreakers, society. That's why she was so good at what she did, and why she'd uncovered scandal and dirt from Fifth Avenue to City Hall.

And she didn't let something go when it made her mad; she pursued it until she had all the info and then she took the perpetrators to task. The stubbornness that had made her, aged three, stamp her foot in the kitchen at home when she thought something was unfair was precisely the quality that delivered her the best stories.

Stubbornness and rage were her superpowers.

And rage was what she was going to need to get her through this.

Almost as if someone had heard her thoughts, her phone chimed with a WhatsApp notification.

Tim's name and avatar popped onto her screen. Caroline looked at her phone. There must have been a glimmer of reception for a moment, but now the little triangle indicating signal strength was back to blank.

It didn't matter. She wasn't in the mood to speak to him yet. Was he having a fling with Nancy? Or maybe he hadn't got that far, was only thinking about it. He was Italian, after all – affairs were the norm in Italy apparently. She'd read that in a magazine in the hairdresser's on the morning he'd asked her to lunch, had laughed it off at the time.

Part of her was sure Nancy was involved in this somehow, but, Holy God, if they were having a fling was *that* why he was in the office the morning straight after he'd come back from his vacation? Jealousy clouded her mind, irrational perhaps, but she felt her heart grow heavy, the betrayal cutting deep. It was just another thing on top of this whole mess. As if Slatergate wasn't enough, there was Nancygate to deal with too.

Caroline threw back the duvet. She was cross now, wasn't in the mood for staying in bed at all. She needed to get up and do something constructive with the day. She'd never been very good at switching off – even at the weekend and in the evenings she'd research stories, keeping an eye on the news all over the world and how it might affect the country. As he'd got to know her better, Tim had started giving out about her hours – not that he wasn't just as bad – but she ran on full steam and damping that, even for a vacation, was incredibly hard.

Putting the phone back on the bedside locker, Caroline reached for the soft white robe she'd found on the back of the bathroom door and pulled it on.

She hadn't been able to see much of the room last night, had stumbled into bed utterly exhausted, vaguely aware of the sloping ceilings, the view out across the river. She smiled –

she couldn't not – and looked out across the estuary. The sky had gone dark now, but the view was magnificent: a passing fishing boat coming back in from the sea; a crowd of seagulls around it, screaming in a frantic cloud of excitement.

Whoever had decorated the Boathouse had literally brought the outside, inside. Cream walls were punctuated with beautiful paintings of the sea, all of them stormy – waves whipped by the wind, the water as many colours of blue and grey and green as she could imagine. Even the en suite bathroom was tiled, as she'd discovered last night, in white and a rich cobalt blue.

Beside her, to one side of the window, was an antique walnut dressing table, gleaming brass handles on the drawers on either side of the knee nook. On the other side of the window stood a matching art-deco-style wardrobe. Caroline went to open the door, looking for a mirror. As she'd expected, there was one inside, polished to a shine. She opened the other door. On one side there was hanging space, silk-covered padded hangers with lavender bags slung around their necks sitting in a neat row. On the mirrored side, the door opened to reveal shelves and drawers, each one with an ivory label, the lettering picked out in bold black letters: hats, gloves, brushes. The wardrobe was beautiful, petite and incredibly elegant. As she closed the door she looked up and noticed what looked like the letter *H* entwined in marquetry across the top. *H* for Hare's Landing? Perhaps the wardrobe was original to the estate.

How many stories could this piece of furniture tell?

What had the driver said about this place being haunted? Caroline's theory about ghosts and energy focused on extremes of emotion – she'd always felt that love or hate or anger could lodge in a place like a stain. It was part of her personal explanation as to why some places felt cold and bad, others like they were smiling. The Boathouse felt warm and welcoming to her. Caroline ran her hand over the polished wood of the wardrobe.

What could it tell her about the women of the house who had used it before her? What secrets did it hold?

Chapter 11

'ARE YOU SURE – nobody's heard from him at all?'
Hunter frowned and turned his head away from
Rachel, closing his bloodshot eyes. The nurses had told her
that he was asleep when she'd called this morning, and he was
obviously still exhausted.

She'd spent the morning with the locksmith on the marina
and then, after checking in with the police, she'd headed
straight to the hospital, all geared up to tell Hunter about the
break-in. But the minute she'd arrived, he'd asked about Alfie.

Hunter turned back to her. 'It's just so strange, his vanishing
right now. We're nearly there with the filming. He knew that.'

Rachel let out a sharp breath, biting back the need to tell
him that he had to forget about work, and rest. She knew him
too well – his world was spinning; he couldn't control the
pain or how fast he healed, but he *could* keep a grip on the
documentary and all the work they'd done. And if he focused
on that, it would distract him from everything else.

'I checked with all of your crew. Zack's been checking too.
And I dialled into your voicemail but he hasn't left a message
on your phone.'

'My phone's toast. And he doesn't have one.' Hunter
sounded uncharacteristically terse.

'He could have used a landline. And I've brought your old

phone. I charged it last night. If you call Vodafone and explain, they might be able to forward your calls or something.'

He gave her a withering look. 'I doubt it.'

Ignoring him, she continued. 'At least I'll have the number. And I'll give it to Zack. Between us, we can send you a lot of the key contacts you'll be missing. It's better than nothing.' She glanced at her watch. 'Look, it's almost two o'clock. When I leave, I'll call over to the hostel. I'll ask Frank, he'd know if anything was wrong. You said he was really on the ball.'

'But you need to get back to work.'

'I've taken the day off.'

He looked annoyed. 'But why? I'm not going anywhere, there's no point using your holiday. I thought we were going to try to get home at Easter. I need to feel the sun on my bones.'

Rachel searched for the right words. 'There was a problem with the boat yesterday.' She drew in a shaky breath, then just decided to go for it. 'Someone broke in. It's a bit of a mess.'

'What?' His response was explosive. 'Why are you only telling me now? What happened?'

She was about to say it was fine, it was all fine – the line she always used would be etched into her gravestone – but actually it wasn't fine at all. She'd planned to go back to the boat tonight, but the thought that Hunter's accident could be connected to the break-in was freaking her out.

'It's not that bad …' She stopped herself. 'Well, it's not great—'

He interrupted her. 'What did they take? Was it kids?'

Staring blindly at the edge of the bed, she played with her ring, rotating it on her finger.

'The police don't think it was kids. They seem to think it was someone professional who had their eye on your camera equipment.' She hesitated. 'They were wondering if it could be connected to your accident.'

As if he hadn't heard the last part, he closed his eyes.

'It's gone, hasn't it? All my gear – everything?'

'Well, your laptop is still in the shop, but ...' She stopped speaking for a moment, trying to think of a way of putting it gently and failing. 'Basically, yes, they broke in the door and turned the whole place over.'

The groan that escaped from him sounded like a train releasing steam.

'Christ. Christ.' He closed his eyes, his mind clearly moving fast. 'My kit, the bastards. It's taken me years to build that kit. And we're going into editing next week.' He stopped, sucking the air in between his teeth as he frowned in thought. 'Zack's got most of the footage about the hostel and the guys. And Jake's got most of Alfie's bits – we just need the last tiny part of his story.' He clenched his fist against the sheet.

And then it was as if her words finally registered. His expression changed as he said slowly, 'The cops think it's got something to do with this wanker knocking me off my bike?' He let it sink in. 'That's fucked up. Why the hell would anyone be after me?' He frowned. 'Unless we've upset some gang with something we've filmed.' He shook his head. 'Maybe we caught a deal going down or something. Do the police want to see our footage?'

'I've only spoken to the team looking after the break-in so far – I'll ask.'

He hesitated before replying. She could see him fighting the pain, trying to think.

'I don't want you going back to the boat, not on your own. Not until we know what this is about.'

Rachel had a feeling he was going to say that. Not that she didn't agree with him; the more she thought about it, the more frightening it got. Hunter had had run-ins with Yardies in the past when he was filming in Toxteth and Brixton, he understood how bad it could get. And so did she. She sighed, putting her face in her hands.

'Where should I go? I can't move into a hotel until you get out of here, it could be weeks.'

His voice was decisive. 'Your mum's. Can you take a week off work? That'll give me time to fix something up. The insurance should cover alternative accommodation for a few days if we haven't come up with a solution by the time you get back. I'll sort it out, I promise. We need to find out what the fuck's going on.'

'You're in hospital, sweetheart. You need to concentrate on getting better so you can get out of here. Let me work something out. I'm sure the boat will be secure by now. Tony's looking at all the security and—'

He interrupted her. 'Rach, we don't know what this is. If someone's trying to bump off a journalist that's pretty heavy. Go to your mum's, please – she'd love to see you and you'll be safe in Dublin.' He shook his head, sighing, then closed his eyes tightly as a wave of pain seemed to wash over him. 'Christ, I wish we knew where Alfie was. I've got a bad feeling with all this going on.' He hesitated for a moment, to let the pain pass. 'The last time I saw him he kept muttering about somewhere called Hare's Landing. Wouldn't say where it was, but something happened there, I'm sure, something that changed the path of his life. I reckon he ended up on the streets shortly afterwards. He almost told me – almost.' He shook his head again. 'It never fucking rains, does it, it just pours? Alfie's disappeared, someone's nicked my cameras, maybe they tried to kill me too, and I can't do anything about it because I'm in here.'

Rachel felt a kick in her heart. She loved him so much and she couldn't bear to see him so unhappy. They were solutions people, both of them, and not being able to see a way through a problem was the worst thing that could happen to him mentally. He needed to be free of any worries so he could focus on getting well and getting out of hospital.

She leaned forward and linked her finger through his. 'You're right about my mum's, but it's going to kill me to leave you on your own—'

He cut in. 'Darlene will be here soon, I'd put money on it.'

He rolled his eyes and Rachel stifled a grin. His mother, Darlene, was wonderful but a force in her own right.

'Okay.' She cleared her throat. 'I'll call my mum. I can fly back if you need me, it's less than an hour by air. And I'll find Alfie, or ask Frank anyway. The police are all over the break-in, they said they'd keep an eye on eBay to see if any of your gear turns up there. And Zack and the crew will too. Tony's being brilliant. He organised a guy to fix the door on the hatch and a locksmith – I've asked them to put a steel bar on the inside of the hatch, just to be sure.'

Hunter listened, his face serious. 'I couldn't bear it if anything happened to you, you know that. Once I know you're safe I don't have to worry about anything else.' He paused. 'Speaking of which, where's Jasper?'

'Currently, in the Land Rover. I can't leave him for long or he'll eat the seats. He ate two hand towels and a slipper at Nathan's mum's last night.'

Hunter fought a smile. 'He's bored and missing me.'

'He's not the only one.' Rachel stood up. 'Right, I'll be back at dinner-time to bring you something nice, and hopefully some news.'

'Thanks, babes. But where are you going to stay tonight?'

'Well, it won't be Nathan's mum's.' She bit her lip. 'I'll be fine. I'll look for an Airbnb, see if there's something close.' She leaned forward to kiss him. 'I'll be back later.'

Chapter 12

FINALLY SHOWERED AND dressed in her jeans and a dark grey cashmere sweater, Caroline grabbed her coat. Her glasses fogged the moment she stepped outside. Pulling the door behind her, Caroline wrapped her scarf around her face, covering her mouth and ears. She'd put her glossy dark hair up into a ponytail, which had seemed like a good idea until she'd got outside; now her ears were frozen. The air was damp with unshed rain, and through the trees, the patches of blue she'd seen when she'd woken up this morning had been thoroughly obliterated by thick grey cloud. Behind her she could hear the haunting cries of gulls.

The winter nipping at her fingers and cheeks, Caroline hurried back up the path she'd come down last night, her footsteps silent, the fallen pine needles and leaf mulch soft underfoot. A moment later she emerged from the woods to see the hotel rising between the trees.

Inside, Caroline was hit again by the scent of perfumed candles, warmth and the delicate sound of classical music. The place looked empty, and again there was no one in reception.

Caroline pushed the door open into the lounge area she'd seen last night, expecting to see someone in the bar in the adjacent room. She had a sense that someone had been there, but had popped out for a moment. A pile of tea and coffee cups had been left on a side table beside a slab of Madeira cake.

The lounge felt warm and welcoming, as if it hadn't really shrugged off being a house. Caroline looked around the walls at more paintings of the sea, breaking waves iridescent in the light from the side lamps and chandelier. Two sofas were positioned in front of the fire, facing each other over a long low coffee table.

Over the fireplace, a stunning portrait of a woman wearing scarlet lipstick dominated the room. Her wavy shoulder-length blonde hair was clipped back on one side. Her eyes were a deep blue, the colour picked up by the cornflower-blue silk evening dress she wore. Her expression was haunting, hard to read, but Caroline felt as if the woman was looking straight at her. She felt a shiver head up her spine.

Pouring herself a coffee and cutting the thinnest sliver of cake, Caroline carried them to a small octagonal room, like the base of a turret, that opened off one corner of the lounge area. She glanced back at the painting. It was almost as if the woman's eyes were following her. *Creepy.*

An ornate central lantern hung from the high ceiling in the turret room, casting a warm glow that supplemented the weak light coming in from the tall ivy-clad windows on each side. In the centre was a coffee table constructed from old books. Caroline put her coffee down on its glass top. Taking a look underneath it, she realised the books were all old editions of *Burke's Peerage*, leather-bound with titles picked out in gilt, held together in a tight circle by a very practical-looking leather strap. Someone had evidently been *very* keen to find out who was who.

Caroline slipped off her coat, the khaki colour almost the same as the soft green of the window seat cushions, and sat down so she could keep an eye on the portrait. For reasons she really couldn't explain, she didn't want to sit with her back to it. The painting – like its subject – was quite beautiful, the woman perhaps in her mid-forties. It was so real it was almost photographic, as if the artist had literally captured a moment in time. What looked like evening light highlighted her angular cheekbones, the fine lines around her eyes. There was something complex in her stare, a sadness somehow. Caroline wasn't sure; it was almost as if she was trying to look happy.

Below the portrait, leaning on the mantelpiece, was a glazed plaque: cream, decorated with a hare painted the same shade as the dress in the painting. Intricate lettering circled the image. Caroline couldn't quite read it from this distance, but intrigued, she stood up to look more closely. Pushing her glasses up her nose to look at it properly, she picked it up. It was beautifully made, the background crazed with a powder blue.

'*She believed she could, so she did.*' Caroline read the legend etched onto the clay out loud. *It was as if it had been made for her.*

Setting it back on the mantelpiece, she turned to get her coffee and caught sight of the same blue hare printed on a leaflet on the oak coffee table, a local newspaper lying beside it. Picking up the leaflet, she reached for the paper, glancing over the headline: '*Where Are They Now?*' Below it there was a pair of photographs, one of a young girl, her hair blonde and thick, styled in a 1980s curly perm. Beside her, a dark-haired youth looked like he was being smart with the photographer in a forced school year photo, his skin pockmarked, one ear pierced. They looked to be around the same age – seventeen or eighteen. Caroline scanned the article but, suddenly uncomfortable, she looked back up at the portrait. It was as if the woman was judging her, looking down and wondering why she was there, what she was doing. *Super creepy.* What had the driver said about this place being haunted?

Shaking off the feeling, and with the leaflet and the paper in her hand, Caroline headed back into the turret nook to look at them. Before she quite got there, a voice behind her made her jump.

'That all happened so long ago. Her sister says she's long gone to the bright lights. Glencurragh was always too small for her. I don't know why they want to drag it all up again, it's no mystery. That lad, though, he was never any good.'

Quite sure Mrs Travers had crept up on her deliberately, Caroline took a deep breath, turning slowly as if not at all startled. *What on earth was she talking about?* The housekeeper looked exactly the same as she had the previous night, dressed in black, her mouth carved in a hard line.

'Oh, hello, Mrs Travers.' Caroline sat down, her tone cool. Glancing back at the paper she had hardly had time to read, she realised Mrs Travers must be referring to the headline. 'Glencurragh is near here, isn't it?'

'Next village. She was up in Dublin, though, when she went missing.' Mrs Travers said it as though the city was to blame.

Caroline looked back at the paper; they had both vanished in 1990, the year she was born.

'It says it's thirty years this summer since they disappeared. There's a quote from his mother, she's planning a big campaign.' Caroline read on a little further. 'She's got breast cancer. She wants answers, the poor woman.'

It had definitely been a different world then. Nobody had mobile phones and the internet hadn't even been invented. Caroline scanned the page. The girl, Meg Cassidy, had been seventeen, the boy nineteen. The article was really about Johnny O'Connor, quoting his mother extensively, saying how hard Christmas and New Year were, and how his birthday was in January. Perhaps that's why they were running the story now.

'It says they both just vanished. Nobody knew what happened?'

Mrs Travers made a humphing noise. 'There were rumours she went to England first, with some lad, they say. She had her sights set on the stage, from what I heard.'

'And the boy?' Caroline checked for his name again. 'Johnny O'Connor. Did she go with him? His mother says he'd been away, but he called her when he landed in Cork. After that, she heard nothing.'

'That's assuming he *was* calling from Cork. No one's any idea what happened to him. He was in with a rough lot though, and his family weren't much better. Never in school, always hanging around the harbour in Ross Haven. Reckon he came to a bad end somewhere.'

'That's terrible. Not knowing what happened. Did they know each other?'

Mrs Travers pursed her lips as if it was none of her business and bent down to stoke the fire as Caroline read the rest of the page. Families never got over their loved ones going missing. Caroline had seen it at first hand, in the interviews she'd done with grieving parents over the years. Robbed of an opportunity to find solace in any sort of finality, the not-knowing literally ate them up. A psychologist she'd spoken to once had explained that the human brain couldn't let go unless there was evidence of transformation from life to death – without that, there was always hope they'd return, making it incredibly difficult for those left to move on mentally, to move house or even change job. Caroline had spoken to parents who were convinced they'd caught glimpses of lost relatives in the aisles of supermarkets, in crowd scenes on the news, hope flaring every time.

'Some people don't want to be found.' Mrs Travers stood up decisively.

Caroline looked up. 'It says her sister's had postcards from Meg, that she's living somewhere in America. But nobody knows why she left or where she is.'

She scanned the rest of the page. Johnny O'Connor had been to Spain, celebrating his nineteenth birthday. She glanced up at Mrs Travers, but she was tidying the leaflets and magazines on the coffee table.

The parallels between the two cases seemed to be pretty tenuous – the journalist was trying to make a splash out of something that was only half a story. She had to give him marks for trying, though. It was a good interview with the boy's mother and there was a link with his birthday – January had to be a pretty slow news month in an area where the population tripled in the summer.

Mrs Travers sniffed. 'It's a long time ago.'

Caroline put the paper onto the bench beside her as if she was completely unaware of the poisonous vibes she was picking up.

She had no idea what Mrs Travers's problem was – after her frosty greeting last night and now this, Caroline was starting to think it was with her, or maybe she just didn't like visitors. Caroline had spent too many years dealing with Greta to be daunted by a dour housekeeper, but before she could come back with a suitably smart answer, Mrs Travers continued.

'I trust the Boathouse meets with your approval?' She was clearly finished with the subject of the local news.

'It's lovely, thank you, and the furniture is awesome. Is it original to the house?'

'Most of it is. It was all stored in the stables between the last lot and Bronagh buying the place. She used as much of the old furniture as she could when she did the place up. Saving money.'

'It's lovely to keep that connection with the past. It must be nice for you to see it being used.' Caroline paused, amused at Mrs Travers's pursed lips and hard expression. She didn't seem to approve of spending money on designer suitcases, or saving money by using antique furniture. And Caroline thought Greta was hard to please. 'You said you worked for the original owners? Were they a local family?'

Mrs Travers shook her head. 'Mrs Smyth was from New York. Hare's Landing was her grandmother's house. *He* was English.' She said it as if it left a bad taste in her mouth. 'Spent most of his time in London, but she preferred to be here.'

'Why did they sell if she loved it so much? Did her son not want it?'

Caroline raised her eyebrows in question, remembering Mrs Travers had mentioned helping with the owner's child the previous night; it had sounded like she had been his nanny.

As if she'd pried too much, Mrs Travers didn't answer; instead she began plumping up the cushions on the sofa.

'Will I get Imogen to get you more coffee? That'll be cold.'

Caroline let out a sigh. Why were people such hard work? Mrs Travers could have been Greta's maiden aunt; they were cut from the same – she was now sure after their brief exchange – block of marble. Folding the newspaper beside her, she picked up the leaflet with the hare on it. The address of a pottery was printed along the bottom: *Cassidy Ceramics, Glencurragh, West Cork: studio, shop & workshops*. That was exactly what she needed to take her mind off work. Now she was finally away from New York, she wanted to use her time well: to read, to walk, to do something creative, to absorb the energy of the place she'd loved so much as a child.

She said brightly, 'Coffee would be lovely. I've been living in New York for years – I think the city runs on coffee.' Mrs Travers didn't answer but Caroline continued breezily. 'I love that hare plaque on the mantelpiece. I might visit this pottery and do a workshop – do you know if it's far from here?' She pointed to the leaflet she'd picked up.

'That pottery course is run in the village, Ava is a friend of Bronagh's – but she only does workshops in the summer as far as I know, you'll be lucky to get her out of season.'

'How far is the village?'

'About twenty minutes by car, longer walking.'

'Logically enough. I think I'll give them a ring and see if I can book in. They might be glad of the business at this time of year.'

Mrs Travers's mouth was set in a hard line. 'I'll get that coffee organised.'

'I'd love a skinny latte, thank you,' Caroline replied sweetly.

Mrs Travers didn't quite roll her eyes, but she wasn't far from it.

'I'll get the girl to organise that.'

Chapter 13

A LIGHT RAIN WAS falling and it was beginning to get
dark by the time Rachel got to the hostel in Holborn
that Alfie had told Hunter he occasionally stayed at. Parking
in a neighbouring street, the moment they got out of the Land
Rover, Jasper tugged at his lead, eager to see where they were
going, his chain collar rattling as he trotted along beside her.

Rachel was hit by a wave of heat as she pushed open
the glazed door of the hostel. She unwound her scarf and
unzipped her skiing jacket, the neon lime bright against her
navy polo neck and short denim skirt. At least the intruders
hadn't done much damage to their bedroom, tucked away in
the prow of the boat – perhaps they hadn't had time. She'd
been able to collect several changes of clothes, stuffing them
into a kitbag, hoping she wouldn't be homeless for too long.

The girl on reception looked up as she approached.

'Rachel Lambert to see Frank.'

'Of course, he's expecting you, go through.'

Frank's office was tiny and piled high with plastic bags of
what appeared to be clothes. It had a faintly musty smell. His
desk was just as busy, scattered with paperwork and invoices.
He stood up as she came in, his hand outstretched.

'Frank McGahern.' He grinned broadly at Jasper. 'And
who's this?'

Rachel accepted Frank's warm handshake. 'This is Jasper. Is it okay to have him inside?'

'Of course, we don't turn anyone away here. How can I help?'

'I'm Hunter MacKenzie's partner.'

'The documentary maker? How's he getting on? We were delighted to help him out. It's a constant battle to keep the homeless in the news.'

Rachel took a deep breath. 'He's in hospital actually, we've had a bit of a run of bad luck.' Frank raised his eyebrows as she continued. 'He was knocked off his bike at the Millbank roundabout.'

'Good God. Is he okay?'

She pulled a face. 'Broken leg, punctured lung, lots of bruises and grazes. He's very cross but he's alive.'

'Well, that's good to hear – not the injuries bit – the alive bit. Several of my staff cycle and I don't know how they do it. The number of accidents is horrifying.'

Rachel ran her hand through her hair, pulling it out of her face.

'Hunter's almost finished filming the documentary. But he's worried about Alfie – Alfie Bows. He's got quite close to him while they've been filming and he really wants to ask him a few more questions. He hasn't heard from him – they were due to meet but Alfie didn't turn up.'

Frank hesitated before he spoke. 'Sit down, won't you, please. Did you know Alfie?'

Rachel pulled out the chair in front of the desk. Seeing her sit, Jasper collapsed to the floor with a sigh.

'I only met him once, but Hunter told me all about him.'

Frank picked up a pen from the muddle on his desk and played it through his fingers for a moment before he spoke.

'I'm afraid I've bad news for you. Alfie's passed away.'

Rachel's hand shot to her mouth. 'Oh my God, what happened?'

'His tent caught fire.' Frank cleared his throat. 'We won't know the full details until after the post-mortem.' He shook his head sadly. 'The last time I saw him, he dropped in to see our barber. We had a chat about the melancholy and joy of Sarasate's *Gypsy Airs*.' He cleared his throat again, his eyes damp. 'It's been so cold. I gave him a new hat and gloves, but a lot of the street people light braziers and fires at this time of year to keep warm. We're always warning them but …' He shook his head. 'What can you do?'

Rachel shivered despite the warmth of the office. 'That's horrible. How awful.'

As if understanding, Jasper sat up and put his head on her knee, the grey hairs peppering his muzzle bright in the fluorescent light. She rubbed the top of his silky head.

'I'm hoping that perhaps he'd been drinking and wasn't aware of what was happening. It's all we can hope for really.'

Rachel could see from Frank's face how upset he was.

'And they're sure it's Alfie?'

'Well, as sure as they can be. A bag of belongings was found nearby – his tent was in a car park tucked in beside some wheelie bins. The bag they found didn't contain much but it did have a jar of rosin in it – it's used for softening violin strings. When the police brought it to us, we couldn't think of anyone else who might have owned it.'

'And no one has seen him for days …'

'Exactly. It's not concrete proof but it means they can check his dental records. We have a dentist here who sees the men every so often.'

For a moment Rachel was lost for words. There was just too much bad news this week and she felt as if it was rising up to overwhelm her.

'Does he have relatives? How …?'

Frank sighed. 'We may never know.' He cleared his throat, 'Once his identity is confirmed we'll see if the national papers might run something. It's a long shot but he didn't teach himself to play like that, so there's a chance someone might recognise him.'

'What about a funeral? What happens there?'

'The council will take care of it – it'll be something small. Just the staff here, I'd imagine, and anyone we can find who he was friendly with.'

'It's so tragic that he's gone and his family don't know.'

'It's often the case. There can be lots of reasons people drop out of society – losing a job, a relationship break-up, mental health issues …'

'That is the whole point of Hunter's documentary. He wants to show how close we all are, how they are exactly like you and me.' She sighed. 'He'll want to be at the funeral, if he can get out of hospital.'

'That would be great. It won't be for a while, I'd imagine. The official identification process takes time.'

Rachel nodded silently. Surely there had to be someone out there who had known Alfie, who would want to or need to mourn his loss. Or perhaps they'd lost him long ago.

How could they find out?

Chapter 14

IMOGEN, 'THE GIRL' who brought the coffee, turned out to be not much older than seventeen herself – the same age that the girl in the paper had been when she disappeared.

Caroline had tried to read more of the newspaper article about the missing teenagers while she'd been waiting. She needed something to distract her from the drama in New York, but it wasn't this. Greta kept popping into her head, opening a black hole of anxiety in her stomach.

Arriving in Caroline's turret nook with a tray and a smile, Imogen bent down to put a tall glass of coffee on the glazed top of the book table, pushing a stray stand of highlighted blonde hair out of her face as she did so. Her hair was pulled back into a bun, and she was wearing a white shirt and black trousers, a white cloth tucked into the waistband.

'Thanks so much. Mrs Travers seems a little …' As Caroline searched for the word she caught a knowing look crossing Imogen's face – obviously her manner wasn't all in Caroline's head. '… Sharp?' Caroline kept her voice low.

Imogen tried to hide a smile as she replied. 'She's grand when you get used to her. She's always a bit off with new guests.'

'But she's supposed to be running the hotel, isn't she? Guests are kind of important in that equation.'

She could see from Imogen's face that she knew exactly what Caroline meant.

'I think Bronagh only keeps her on because she's got nobody else now. She's lived in the gate lodge for ever. I don't think she's ever left the estate to go further than the village. She thinks she runs the place but Bronagh actually does everything, she just makes Mrs T. feel like she's in charge.'

Caroline shook her head, her voice low. 'I think if I was Bronagh, I'd keep her away from front of house.'

The girl shrugged. 'She's sort of a feature, but you get used to her. Her bark's worse than her bite. I think she's just lonely. This is her whole world.'

'Doesn't she have any family?'

The girl shook her head. 'A nephew, away in London, but nobody else.'

'I get the distinct feeling she doesn't like me one little bit.'

'It could be your accent. Mrs Travers was very close to the original owner, Mrs Smyth – when she died, she left Mrs T. the gate lodge in her will. Mrs Smyth was from New York. She must have sounded a bit like you.'

'But I'm from Dublin.'

Caroline knew she'd been living in New York a long time, but according to the natives she hadn't picked up much of the accent. Perhaps she sounded more American to an Irish ear than she thought.

Imogen checked over her shoulder to see if Mrs Travers was nearby.

'Mrs Smyth went to boarding school in Ireland. Hare's Landing was her family's holiday house, but she was brought up in New York.' She shook her head. 'It was such a tragedy.'

Caroline looked at her, confused for a moment.

'What was a tragedy?'

Imogen glanced up at the portrait over the fireplace before she replied, as if it might hear her and be offended if she spoke too loudly.

'Mrs Smyth. She died. That's her portrait.' She lowered her voice even more. 'She committed suicide.' She glanced back at the painting again. 'I'm not sure how true it is, but rumour has it that she was having an affair with one of the staff, and he found her first, and then drove his car off the cliff. Mrs T. found her later, over in the castle. She'd hanged herself from one of the beams.'

Caroline took a slow sip of her latte. She'd been here less than twenty-four hours and already the place was tangled in mystery. She glanced up at the painting, which still seemed to be watching her, and tried to focus hard on her coffee, fighting her need to ask Imogen another hundred questions. She really had enough problems.

But the part of her mind that loved getting to the heart of a story – and, if she was honest with herself, needed to be kept occupied or it would dwell dangerously on this stupid court case – was already alight with curiosity. There was something about this place that intrigued her, and her imagination was hungrily looking for more fuel. That painting was calling to her.

As if she could read her thoughts, Imogen glanced at it again.

'I'm studying history in Cork, second year. That's why I love working here, it's like time's standing still sometimes. In the summer you can almost hear the garden parties the Smyths must have had with their guests from London. I feel like she's still here sometimes – Honoria Smyth, I mean.'

Following Imogen's gaze, Caroline spoke without thinking. 'Perhaps she wants someone to find out her story.' She trailed off, then a moment later snapped back to the room. 'I'm Caroline, by the way.'

'Imogen. Nice to meet you.'

She held out her hand. Smiling, Caroline shook it. She liked Imogen a lot; she was clearly passionate about her subject.

Imogen looked back at the portrait. 'She's beautiful, isn't she?'

'She sure was. I keep thinking she's watching me.'

Imogen drew in a sharp breath, her face clouded. 'A lot of people say that. And sometimes it gets really cold in here.' She opened her eyes wide. 'I think you're right about her story. I sometimes feel like she's trapped here, that until someone finds out what really happened, she won't be able to move on.'

Caroline felt the hairs standing up on the back of her neck as a gust of wind blew down the chimney and the fire flared.

'Woha, I felt that. And the guy who picked me up told me the place was haunted. I didn't believe him at the time, now I'm starting to wonder. How long ago did Honoria die?'

'About thirty years ago now.' Imogen pulled out the cloth at her waist and bent down to wipe an invisible mark off the glass coffee table. 'I feel her here a lot. The house was empty for years before Bronagh bought it. I think Mr Smyth couldn't face it after his wife died, never mind the gossip, so he sold up the whole place.'

'Mrs Travers said all the furniture was put in the stables.'

'A lot of it's still there. Bronagh can't afford to get it restored yet, so the best pieces are in the house, but there's loads more.'

Caroline felt a chill again. 'I'd love to see it. There's a beautiful wardrobe in my room ...'

'That was one of the original pieces. Did you see it has Honoria's initial on it? Well, it actually belonged to her grandmother originally, but they had the same name. There are H's all over the place …' Imogen pointed at one of the windows behind Caroline. As she turned the clouds outside seemed to part, illuminating an ornate letter *H* etched into the glass. 'They're everywhere.'

'I thought it was *H* for Hare's Landing.'

As she said it, Caroline caught a waft of perfume. Imogen's? For a moment she wasn't sure.

*

Caroline looked at Imogen in amazement as she opened the stable door and reached in to switch on the electric light, the overhead tubes buzzing into life with a brightness that was dazzling in the dusky yard. Caroline leaned in to get a better view; inside the air was freezing, as if it had never got warm, dust motes dancing, disturbed by the movement of the door.

'This lot must be worth a fortune.'

'I know, it's mad, isn't it? It's like an antiques warehouse. When the house was first sold, everything was put in here by the new owner apparently. Bronagh's been working her way through but there's just so much stuff. I don't know if she'll ever get time to look at it all.' Stepping back, leaning on the bottom half of the open stable door, Imogen grinned. 'I reckon there's treasure in there somewhere, some of Honoria's jewellery maybe, that got put away and forgotten.'

Caroline looked back at her, her eyes wide. 'I don't know how you stay out of here – I couldn't leave until I'd been through every single drawer.'

Imogen laughed. 'I wish there was time. I've got it on my to-do list for the summer though, when we can pull some of the bits out and make more space to see what's there. Bronagh's got a plan to make the stables into a spa, and to put a pool in the yard here eventually, so it'll all have to be moved some time.'

The stable was literally packed to the rafters, Victorian mahogany chairs stacked seat to seat, wardrobes and armoires, chests of drawers pushed up against the rough whitewashed walls. The overhead lights cast deep shadows, but Caroline could see Chinese and Afghan rugs had been laid over some of the pieces, perhaps to protect them. Vases and bunches of silk flowers lay on others. Caroline almost expected to open a cupboard and find it full of suits hanging to attention.

'Can I go inside? The curiosity is killing me.'

'Just be careful. We're probably not insured to have guests in here, Bronagh could kill me.'

'I take total responsibility for my own actions. I'll be really careful. It's wonderful, isn't it? Like an Aladdin's cave.'

Imogen laughed again. 'The historian in me goes a little bit nuts every time I open this door. Wait till you see what's in some of the drawers. Bronagh hasn't even got started.' She indicated the house with her head. 'The writing desk that's in the lounge now was buried under a carpet, and it was like nobody had emptied a drawer for about a hundred and fifty years. There were old pairs of glasses and pens, odd keys, receipts, parish newsletters, theatre programmes. All the type of stuff you have in those drawers at home with batteries in them … you know, the odds and ends.'

'Wow, I love all that ephemera …'

Caroline could hardly contain her excitement. One of the things she missed in New York was a sense of heritage. There were beautiful art deco buildings but she often thought of her grandparents' house with their dark polished boards and darker furniture, passed down through generations of Kellys.

Imogen tapped the top of the stable door with her hand.

'Will you be okay on your own? I'll call Conor from the landline to tell him you're here so he doesn't accidentally lock you in. Bronagh's gone into Ross Haven to the accountant, she won't be back for ages. Just knock when you're finished and I'll come and lock up.' She inclined her head towards the kitchen.

Smiling her thanks, Caroline stepped inside. Immediately to her right was a huge bow-fronted chest of drawers, the veneer badly water damaged where there must have been a leak. On top of it were piles of china plates, teacups and saucers, all thick with dust and grime. Caroline wiped one of the plates with her finger, revealing a pink willow-pattern-style design, its edge delicately fluted.

Had this been Honoria Smyth's china? The teacups she used out on the terrace in the summer? Caroline felt herself shiver, the image of summer tea parties suddenly strong.

Taking a step forward, she squeezed between a circular walnut table, its edges carved like they were bound with rope, and the firmly closed doors of a huge wardrobe. The dust covering the table was thick, grey, punctuated with bits of straw and bird droppings. A thick felt cloth had been draped over half of it – it looked like it would easily seat twelve. Caroline bent down. The underside was in shadow but she could just see it had a staunch central pillar that splayed into ball and claw feet on the ridged concrete floor. She was sure it would be magnificent if it was polished, would look stunning in the entrance hall with a huge arrangement of flowers in the middle.

Slipping past the table, Caroline ventured in further, the smell of straw and damp mingling with a memory of beeswax, like a whisper, barely there. To her right two wardrobes stood staunchly face to face; beside them, what looked like the headboard of a bed, the wood dark, the edges bevelled. Taking another step, Caroline saw another chest of drawers, tall and narrow, like a linen cupboard, and on its top a small mahogany chest with six drawers set into it. Perhaps it was a writing box?

Leaning forward to get closer to it, a movement in her peripheral vision made her cry out. Turning, she realised it was her own reflection, caught in a dressing table mirror. Caroline put her hand to her chest, her heart pounding. *She'd been sure someone was there watching her.* Taking a deep breath, she yanked a strand of hair that had come loose from her ponytail decisively back, tucking it into her hairband. *She was never going to get anywhere if she let her imagination run riot.*

Then, over the smell of dust and damp, she caught a waft of the perfume she'd smelled earlier in the lounge.

What the …?

Pausing, Caroline breathed in deeply to see if she could catch it again; it reminded her of Chanel No. 5. But she couldn't be sure if she could really smell something, or if it was all in her head. She felt the hairs rising on the back of her neck again and shivered, the movement bringing her back to the stables. *Perhaps she should have come here earlier in the day.* She shook herself. She was being silly. Imogen was just across the yard; Caroline could hear the radio on in the kitchen, classical music carried into the stables on the breeze.

She turned her attention back to the little chest.

A row of metal handles fell like teardrops down the centre of it – they must have been brass once, but now were as black as the dark wood surrounding them. It was delightful, the type of thing that featured in period country house dramas.

Edging closer, she put one hand on top of it to steady it as she slid the bottom drawer open and peeped in. Mildewed

81

envelopes were packed inside it. She opened the next drawer. Blank postcards and paper in this one. The middle drawer was stuck tight. She wiggled it but she didn't want to damage the chest. She was sure the wood could have absorbed moisture and swollen; it would probably need to be in more hospitable surroundings to open for her. Opening the second drawer from the top, she found a fountain pen and several biros, the illusion that this had been some nineteenth-century poet's correspondence box immediately shattered.

Caroline almost laughed out loud at herself. Her imagination was flying in here, wondering about where the pieces of furniture had been in the house, what conversations they had heard. But if there were biros in the chest, it had to have been in use relatively recently – could perhaps have been something Honoria Smyth herself had used. Caroline pulled the drawer out further, and a roll of camera film and a fountain pen rolled towards her. Picking up the film, she peered at the numbers on the side. It was Kodak, but in the dim light she couldn't see if there was a date on it. She slipped it into her coat pocket to show to Bronagh later – she was looking forward to finally meeting her. The pictures were probably spoiled by now, but there might be salvageable photos of the house and its previous occupants.

Sliding the drawer closed, Caroline took another step into the stable. Even with their chunky soles, her boots were loud on the gritty concrete floor. She eased open the door to a wardrobe. It was similar to the one in her room, although so dirty she couldn't see if there was an *H* in the scrolled carving of what looked like acanthus leaves across the top. Inside, old wooden hangers hung linked together with spiders' webs so thick with grey dust that it looked almost as if you could knit with them.

Caroline closed the door quickly, the movement sending dust up her nose. She sneezed loudly.

'What on earth are you doing?'

Her back still to the door of the stable, Caroline felt herself start at the sound of Mrs Travers's voice ringing out like an alarm bell, the sound bouncing off the rough stone walls.

How long had she been there?

Caroline looked over her shoulder, keeping her face open and smiling.

'Imogen was telling me about the old furniture and I persuaded her to let me have a look. All this stuff is amazing. I always feel furniture can tell so many stories, don't you?'

Mrs Travers glared at her, her grey wool coat buttoned to the neck, the harsh light casting shadows on her angular face.

'There's nothing of interest in there. And we can't have guests poking around the stables, I'm afraid. Insurance.'

Mrs Travers held the stable door open pointedly.

Caroline looked back at her, surprised. Even from what she'd seen of Mrs Travers so far, she was distinctly acerbic. *What was her problem this time?*

'I'm here entirely under my own steam, and nothing's fallen on me yet. I'm sure I'll be fine.'

Mrs Travers glared at her again.

'I think you need to come out. Nasty things can happen quite unexpectedly.'

Chapter 15

RACHEL SAT DOWN beside Hunter's bed and unwound her fuchsia-pink scarf, folding it neatly on her knee. His eyes were still closed but she could see that he was gradually surfacing from sleep, the sounds of visiting time, the chatter and the clatter of the tea trolley percolating through his drug-induced haze.

Turning, he slowly opened his eyes.

'You're a good sight to wake up to.'

He wrestled his hand out from under the sheet and reached for hers, rubbing his thumb over her ring.

He'd bought it for her in New Orleans, a reminder – if they needed one today – that life was short and you had to make the most of every day.

'How are you feeling?'

'Like I got hit by an idiot in a Beemer. Bastard. The police better bloody well find him, or I'll be after him.'

'Have they identified the vehicle yet?'

He inclined his head slightly, as if it hurt to move. 'They have it on video but the plates were covered in mud, so unless they can track it to where it was parked after it hit me, we may never find out if the driver even noticed.' He closed his eyes again; it was clearly an effort to speak. 'You know the percentage of traffic accidents involving cyclists that are actually prosecuted in London is woefully small. Even in fatalities. It's fucking depressing.'

She could hear a *but* coming in his voice, raised her eyebrows in question. He grinned at her reading of him.

'*But* it would make for a very interesting ob. doc. Cameras on the helmets, dashcam footage, I want to show the public exactly what it's like out there. It's the bloody jungle.'

'Could you focus on getting better first? It only happened twenty-four hours ago – you've got a lot of time.'

He scowled good-naturedly. 'You're not my mum, you know.'

She threw him a withering look. He always said that when she worried about something, like if he'd got a sensible coat on. His mind was usually two steps ahead, and sometimes he missed the practical things.

He looked serious for a moment. 'To do this right we need a crew following me through from now to recovery. I've got a request in to the head of programming. He's a cyclist too. If the police don't get the BMW, I will. One thing I've got while I'm stuck in here is a lot of time to plot my revenge.'

She wasn't even going to ask how he'd managed to message the head of programming while he'd been here, sedated, supposedly resting. He never stopped.

He grinned, a hint of the old Hunter shining through the pain like a chink of light through a curtain.

'So how was your day? Did you track down Alfie?'

Rachel looked away, could feel a tear forming, hot in the corner of her eye. But she couldn't cry now. The last thing Hunter needed was her falling apart.

'Sort of. I went to Holborn to talk to Frank.'

'Has he seen him? I was starting to wonder if the cameras had spooked him. I was really pushing to find out what had got him on the streets, Maybe I was too intense. He kept clamming up on me. He really didn't want to go there.'

'I don't think it was that.'

Rachel's voice was quieter than she'd intended. He looked at her sharply. He could read her as well as she could read him.

'What's happened?'

Rachel fiddled with the fringe on her scarf with her free hand. There wasn't an easy way to tell him.

'There was a fire. Last week I think, or maybe the week before, I forgot to ask the exact date.'

Hunter's eyebrows creased in a frown. 'A fire? Is he okay?'

Rachel shook her head, unable to meet his eye. Then, biting her lip, she took a deep breath.

'He died, honey – he was camping beside those bins in that car park and his tent caught fire. The police are investigating.'

'He's dead? Alfie?' Hunter fell back on his pillows and looked up at the ceiling. 'Christ. Christ, that's awful.' He was silent for a moment. 'I told him not to light that barbecue thing close to the tent. *I told him.*' He closed his eyes and shook his head. 'I don't believe it. We talked about it, about how fast those nylon tents can catch fire. Bloody hell.' He let out a sharp breath. 'First the boat, and now this. What a fucking week.' His eyes were damp with tears. 'I think I was his only friend – he didn't trust anyone.'

Rachel sat forward in the chair beside his bed, fighting back her own tears. She gripped his hand.

'Did he mention any family or where he was from? Frank says they will try to find relatives, but he didn't seem very hopeful.'

'Some people just want to disappear. I think Alfie was one of those. You'd know from his accent. He tried to hide it, but it would creep out every now and again. And he learned to play the violin somewhere.'

'He must have family. They'd want to know, surely?'

Hunter was only half listening. 'Something happened, something big that landed him on the streets.'

'Did he give you any idea of where he was from?'

'I always felt he was from London, though I'm not sure why, and he mentioned going to Ireland one time when I told him about you.'

Rachel looked at him, surprised – more at the fact that she'd been discussed than the Irish connection.

'What did he say?'

'He said he'd had friends there, I think. I can't remember.' Hunter closed his eyes.

'You're exhausted. We need you to get better and then you can think about Alfie.'

'I just wanted to get to the bottom of his story, to find out why … To see if I could help. He was almost ready to tell me – I know he was. I just really wanted to help him. He was such a gentle, lovely bloke.'

'You need to sleep. We'll talk in the morning. Oh, I collected your Mac, it's all working. There was dog hair in the fans apparently.'

Hunter half smiled. 'Well, that's not my fault, you're the one who lets him on the sofa.'

'And you're the one who works in the living room instead of the office.' She leaned over to kiss him. 'Rest, please. Your mum called to confirm her flights, she's coming over to make you proper food.'

He rolled his eyes. 'Christ, I've only just lost the weight from her last visit.' And then, as if it had suddenly occurred to him, 'Have you booked the ferry? I don't want you on the barge alone. Whoever broke in had to have been watching us. They could come back if they think they missed something.'

Rachel sighed. 'I'm going to book it tonight.'

She stood up before he could ask her again where she was going to stay. She'd been so busy she'd only had a few minutes to try and find somewhere that took dogs, and so far she'd drawn a total blank. It was rapidly looking like the barge was her only option, for tonight, anyway. The locksmith had been, so it was secure and she had Jasper. Tomorrow she could sort out the ferry and be on her way to Dublin.

Chapter 16

CAROLINE AWOKE WITH a start, her eyes rapidly adjusting to the dark room. She'd left the curtains open when she'd gone to bed, and through the window opposite she could see heavy cloud blocking the starlight, its edges glowing eerily silver in front of the winter moon, not strong enough to penetrate the window and the high-ceilinged bedroom. She strained her ears. What had woken her? A sound outside, or something inside the house?

Groggy from waking suddenly, Caroline felt disorientated, had no idea what time it was. She'd been so exhausted she'd come to bed early, had crashed into a deep sleep. But now her heart was pounding in her ears as she shifted slightly in the bed, scanning the room, peering into the dark corners. Beyond the distant ghostly glow of the moon, the night was black. Outside she could hear the trees in the woods whispering, the stiff wind that was sending the cloud across the sky agitating them. She'd been completely at home here in the daylight, but as she leaned forward to look out of the side window cut into the sloping ceiling, she could almost feel the trees watching her, the sound of their movement echoed by the roll of the waves crashing on the shore below the Boathouse and the beating of her heart.

Perhaps she'd been having a bad dream. She couldn't

remember, just felt the panic and cold sweat, the shock of a sudden awakening.

Another sound. A movement, soft and measured. Stiffening, she turned over as slowly and quietly as she could and peered towards the top of the spiral staircase. She was sure she'd left a lamp on downstairs but there was no sign of its soft light now. Perhaps she'd turned it off? She wasn't sure. Jet lag played havoc with her memory.

Listening hard, she focused on the sounds of the building: the creak of the wooden frame as the wind picked up, teasing the eaves, moaning gently. Suddenly fully awake, she lay back, rigid, starting at another sound – soft, like a magazine being moved. She pulled the duvet to her chin. Was there someone or something downstairs? What on earth could it be?

Nobody had mentioned the Boathouse being haunted, but after talking to Imogen, she'd started to believe the rumours about the main house.

She'd locked the front door when she came up, she was sure of it – hadn't she? In this part of the world people still left their front doors open – they always had when she holidayed here as a child. But she was conditioned now to lock up. She'd spent too long in New York.

Wouldn't she have heard if someone had broken in? A window smashing or something?

How else *could* someone have got in? She was sure they had duplicate keys in reception but why would anyone from the hotel want to come in, in the middle of the night? She reached for her phone; it was only ten o'clock. Not late but definitely not a time for the cleaning staff to be dropping by.

Sliding her phone back on her bedside table, Caroline shifted again, trying to listen for movement downstairs. There were days when she wished she had a regular office job, that she hadn't reported on almost three hundred cases of burglary with and without menace.

Another sound, like something being moved.

It couldn't be a ghost. She pulled the duvet up closer to her chin. It really couldn't. Maybe this house was on some sort of energy line or something and the time zones kept slipping. Was that even possible? *Perhaps her teenage theory was about to be proven.* Caroline tried to listen harder, but all she could hear was her own heartbeat.

Perhaps a cat had got in. Or maybe it was mice. Should she get up and go and see? The external phone was in the kitchen and her mobile had no reception – calling for help was only an option if she could get downstairs. And who would she call anyway? Ghostbusters?

Before she could finish thinking she heard a gentle click and felt a blast of icy wind whistle up the stairs. A loud clatter almost lifted her out of the bed. The front door was banging. Throwing back the duvet, Caroline grabbed the robe from the end of the bed and dragged it around her, then ran down the spiral stairs, the wooden treads cold on her bare feet. Spinning around the last turn, she almost cried out. The front door was wide open.

Caroline crossed the tiled floor as fast as she could, her robe swirling around her as she slammed the door closed, her heart hammering in her chest. Turning, she fell back against the door. *Holy God.* She scanned the living room, looking for signs of a disturbance.

Had the door just blown open and the wind caused the noises she'd heard?

She finally caught her breath and tried to think rationally. She was in the middle of nowhere; this wasn't the Upper East Side – this was a vacation let, it was hardly going to be filled with her best jewellery or tech equipment … Her eye darted to the kitchen counter where she'd left her laptop charging. It was still there, sitting in plain view.

It must have been the wind. With all the stress of the past few days, she hadn't been sleeping – she must have been so tired when she went up to bed that she'd not shut the door properly. Leaning on the counter, Caroline tried to calm her breathing, fighting for a rational explanation.

Chapter 17

RACHEL PUSHED OPEN her office door, relieved to see all her Post-it Notes and photographs on the giant map of the Peak District were still in place. It was ridiculously late to be coming to the office, but after leaving Hunter, she'd gone back to the barge to clear up. A fine film of black fingerprint dust had coated all of the surfaces, smearing as she'd wiped it up. She'd picked up the cushions and straightened the throws and then, exhausted, had sat down in the middle of the mess and had a good cry.

Jasper had tried to climb into her lap and lick away her tears, but it hadn't altered the feeling of invasion, that somehow this wasn't her home any more. Eventually pulling herself together, sniffing, she'd piled all the detritus from the upturned drawers back into them, and had pushed them under the saloon table. She could go through them all in daylight when she was feeling a bit more on top of things – they probably needed a good sort out anyway. As she knelt on the floor picking up stray dice that had escaped from somewhere, she'd started thinking about Alfie again. And then she'd remembered she needed to test Hunter's MacBook and make sure all the footage he'd filmed so far was backed up.

It hadn't been a hard decision to make. She knew she was reaching for excuses not to hang around the barge until the last possible moment, but the internet connection at the office *was* super-fast, and she really did want to see what Hunter had of Alfie. He'd mentioned this hare's place a couple of times and Rachel wanted to see if she could find the reference herself.

She just wanted whatever it was that was going on here, all to be over. She had no idea what could be the cause of the break-in, and Hunter being knocked off his bike. Perhaps they *had* caught something going down on camera, something in the background of a shot. And the only way they'd be able to know that, to find something that might help the police, was if she went through the footage.

It had been well after ten o'clock by the time she left the marina, but the Red Fox Film building operated close to twenty-four hours a day, was a lot warmer than the barge and would be empty on a Friday evening. She'd stopped to pick up Chinese on the way. Her second good decision of the night.

Her stomach was already rumbling from the aromatic smells rising from the brown paper bag, as Rachel swung it onto her desk along with Hunter's battered MacBook, the lid covered in stickers. Jasper happily flopped into his bed in the corner with a satisfied sigh. He was a heat lover too.

Sitting down, she flipped open the lid of the computer and pulled her dinner towards her, fishing in the paper bag for a fork. Her stomach rumbled again. She'd had so much on her mind that she'd forgotten to have lunch earlier and now she really needed to eat. A sweet chilli chicken noodle box and prawn crackers had never smelled so good. It was comfort food, and right now she needed some comfort.

Powering up Hunter's MacBook, Rachel could see the shop had done a very neat job of replacing the cracked screen, as well as fixing the fans that had finally given up. Despite her nagging, it was only because it had started overheating that Hunter had had the screen fixed at all.

Scrolling through his files, she found the folder containing all the uncut footage for the show. If Hunter was right and they'd caught some sort of criminal activity in the back of a shot, it would be a marathon job to go through it, one she didn't really have the energy for now. Rachel sighed. *What on earth could have brought this down on them?* She looked at the number of folders in the file. She didn't often feel overwhelmed, but where should she start? Scanning down the list, she could see Hunter had set up a folder for Alfie. *The poor man, what a way to go.* Curious to see what he'd said to Hunter, she clicked through to the first video and hit play.

Shot at the end of the summer, Alfie was sitting on a park bench beside Hunter, sunshine dappling the ground around them, playing through the dense foliage of the leaf canopy that almost created an outdoor room. She felt a pang of sadness.

Zack, the cameraman, had sized up the shot, focusing on Hunter's smiling face as he laughed at something Alfie had said. Part of her heart broke all over again. He'd been such good friends with Alfie, had felt he was getting somewhere with him, that he could perhaps help to get him back on his feet and integrated with society.

But now Alfie was dead and Hunter was lying in a hospital bed. Life really could change in an instant.

As she watched the screen, the camera panned to Alfie. He was nodding, smiling at first as if they were sharing a joke, but then his face changed, like the weather closing in over the mountains at home, sunshine obliterated by clouds.

Her fork poised over the cardboard box in front of her, Rachel slid the cursor back through the frames, turning up the sound so she could hear it more clearly. They were talking about her – she caught Hunter saying her name. Alfie was staring into the distance, his hands resting on his knees, his famous violin lying on the bench beside him. He sounded sad as he spoke:

'I had a friend from Ireland. I was only there once. Visiting his place. It's a beautiful country. Green. Very green. Terrible roads.'

'Where did you go, Dublin? Or over to the west?' Hunter said it like he belonged.

'A long drive. To the sea. Down to the sea.'

Alfie shuddered, his face tense. In the video Hunter was nodding in response as if he knew what Alfie was talking about.

Rachel rolled the counter back and watched the few minutes play again. She knew Hunter had been burning up, wanting to find out about Alfie's background; this gentle questioning wasn't just idle chatter.

Rachel played it back again. Listening to Alfie carefully, she was sure Hunter was right – Alfie was English and had been to a British public school. She turned up the volume again and scrolled on a few more seconds. Hunter was frowning, his elbows on his knees, his eyes on the ground. Beside him Alfie was staring into the middle distance, his face tense as if he was remembering something.

'Hare's Landing.' He shook his head, as if he was only verbalising half of what was going through his head. On camera, Hunter turned and looked at him as Alfie's voice dropped. '"Hare before, trouble behind. Change ye, cross, and free me." Have you heard that before?' His face twitched ironically and he shook his head.

Perplexed, Rachel watched as Alfie stopped speaking, a sad smile on his face. Hunter had said he'd mentioned a place called Hare's Landing – was that somewhere in Ireland or was he just rambling, his memories jumbled?

Hunter had clearly heard him but as Rachel watched, he glanced at Alfie sideways and changed tack a little. Rachel could see the concern in Hunter's face; he thought Alfie's mind was starting to wander, wanted to pull him back.

'Did you like Ireland? Was Hare's Landing a place?'

It was as if the light had suddenly gone off, and the room had gone dark. Alfie's face closed; he rubbed the tops of his arms and stared into the distance. He obviously thought he'd said enough.

Hare's Landing didn't sound in the slightest bit Irish. Was he getting mixed up?

The Irish for 'hare' was *an giorria* – 'the short deer'. In the myths and legends they'd all learned at school, Rachel was sure that they were thought to be messengers from the Otherworld – and seeing one was believed to be a blessing. But was there a village associated with a specific tale that might account for the name? Rachel couldn't think of one. The only hares that came immediately to mind were the ones at Dublin airport – the car parks were full of them, as big as dogs, lolloping around the acres of parked cars.

She replayed the recording, looking at Alfie's face. Hunter had asked him another question about where home was, where he remembered as a child, but he'd clammed up, shaking his head as if he didn't want to say more.

So the only lead they had on his background was somewhere called Hare's Landing, that seemed to be connected to Ireland. And trouble, going by the phrase he'd quoted, although she'd never heard that before either. That wasn't a whole lot to go on. But it was a start. And Google was her friend.

Rachel chewed her noodles thoughtfully, spearing a piece of chicken as she pulled her keyboard towards her, waking up her own monitor. Clicking through, she entered *Hare's Landing* into the search bar and hit Enter. Immediately a booking.com ad popped up for a hotel. It looked vaguely as if it had been built in the 1920s, its half red-brick exterior giving way to mock-Tudor beams and mullioned windows.

Hare's Landing welcomes you to West Cork.

The image switched to shots of the sea.

There it was. Hare's Landing. Had Alfie stayed in the hotel? *Had something happened here?*

Jasper grumbled in the corner as she swung around in her chair, scrolling through shots of the interior. It looked lovely, warm and welcoming, as if it had once been a family home.

Rachel's phone pinged with a text. Looking at the screen, she almost laughed. Hunter.

Gotta get out of here, food is crap.
Bring supplies.

She texted back, Breakfast roll?

A row of hearts pinged straight back. He must be on the mend if he was hungry. She took a screenshot of the hotel and sent it over to him.

Found Hare's Landing. Hotel in West
Cork. They're dog-friendly.

Chapter 18

THE TAXI DRIVER pulled into Glencurragh village, slowing for a black cat that was elegantly making its way across the main street. He had the heater in the car on high but Caroline shivered, chilly from lack of sleep. She yawned. She'd lain awake in bed for ages last night, trying to find a rational explanation for the noises she'd heard – surely it must have been a draught, shuffling things about?

'Here we are, lass, did you say you wanted Mahony's shop?'

'Yes, thanks, this is great.'

There had been just as many questions in the twenty-minute drive to the village as there had on the way back from the airport. Questions disguised as conversation: how was she liking Hare's Landing; had she met anyone interesting; did she go to pottery workshops in New York?

At least he hadn't mentioned ghosts.

Caroline had answered the first few questions as briefly as possible and then pulled out her phone, pretending to check her social media. About halfway along the main road they'd caught a wave of receptivity and all her message platforms had updated together, creating a cacophony of sounds. She'd busied herself checking through everything, pretended she was concentrating.

Indicating, the driver pulled up.

'Will I give you a lift back, lass? You're going to the pottery after?'

Swinging the door open and climbing out of the car, Caroline bit back a sarcastic response.

'That would be great.' *Like hell it would, but she could hardly fly back.* 'I might want to go for a walk afterwards. Could you pick me up here about seven?'

'That'll be a long walk. It'll be pitch dark by then.'

Holy fecking God, was it any of his goddamn business?

'I might have a drink in the pub, I guess it'll be open?' She did little to hide the hint of sarcasm in her voice.

'It will so. See you then, back here at seven.'

'That would be great.'

She said it through gritted teeth, trying her best not to be irritated. If you took negative energy on board, it just dragged you down. And she had enough negative energy around her at the moment to sink a battleship.

Caroline slammed the rear door of the car closed and looked around. Glencurragh wasn't much more than a single road steeply sloping to the sea. Above her on the hill was a pub, its walls painted a rather surprising purple, and below her she could see a cheerful cafe. Across the main street a church rose, its clock tower facing the village, marking time.

It had been years since she'd been here, but she was sure there had been more stores when she was a child. Hadn't there been a fish and chip shop? She could remember a post office that sold fishing nets and brightly coloured buckets, a stand of postcards on the pavement outside. But that had been almost fifteen years ago. They hadn't had a family vacation since she was seventeen, and her mum had shown the first signs of the aggressive multiple sclerosis that had taken her just a few months before Caroline received the results of her degree.

Her mum knew Caroline would get a first, but not having her there when the envelope had arrived had almost broken her.

Caroline shook the memories from her head. She had enough going on without dwelling on the past. The first thing she needed to do was to call Tim and see what was happening at home. She looked at her phone and almost cheered. She had full reception. She checked the time. It was just past 9.30 a.m. in New York; with luck she'd catch him in his office before his meetings started.

She found his cell number and hit call. It was picked up immediately, his New York accent making her smile.

'Caroline? Why haven't you answered my emails? It's like you've fallen off the planet.'

'Sorry, the phone and internet are non-existent at the hotel I'm staying at, it's miles from anywhere. I'm in the village now, standing in the street.' She glanced up at the sky. It wasn't actually raining but the sky was thinking about it. 'What's happening there?'

'Rich Slater is pushing through with this case.'

'And Greta's taking him seriously.'

'I know – it's ridiculous. It's the bit about you invading his privacy and breaching data security by getting hold of his phone records and bank statements that she's getting hung up on apparently.'

'That's total nonsense.'

'I know. But how did you get the information about his spending habits and his salary?'

'I stalked him on social media. I've got all the notes, Tim. He used to take pictures of every damned thing he did. I could see what sort of car he drove, how often he changed it. He posted from the auto dealer where he bought the new one, so I went and talked to them about the cost of that exact model.

It's not rocket science really, it's just good detective work.' She was sure Tim could hear the exasperation in her voice. 'He was always posting from restaurants, and he has this thing about fancy cooking, and wine.'

'Interesting. He'll be a lot more careful in future if this comes to court.'

Caroline let the glimmer of a smile escape as she continued. 'Everything is out there – I just cross-referenced a load of things and joined the dots. I'm observant, Tim, that's all.'

'And you've got everything recorded?'

'Every screenshot, every link. Due diligence. I tried to tell Greta all of this.'

'Well, she's got a real bee in her bonnet about you. I'm starting to think it's personal.' He left it hanging there.

'Why the hell ...?'

He made a humphing noise. He sounded uncomfortable when he answered.

'I reckon it's got something to do with Clive and the Christmas party. Remember he had that big chat with you in Greta's office, that afternoon?'

'You what ...? Yes, we had a meeting earlier in the day, but I didn't go to the Christmas party – I was sitting outside a 7–Eleven all night freezing my butt off.'

What the hell could Greta's husband have to do with any of this?

Caroline turned around and began to pace up and down the pavement, lining the toes of her leather boots up with the cracks as she took each step. At moments like this she was very grateful that she'd invested in good clothes. Her cashmere sweater and scarf, and her thick padded parka, were the very least she needed right now. *Not that she had anything else to spend her money on – like a social life, for instance.*

It took a moment for Tim to answer; it sounded like one of his assistants had brought him coffee.

'And why was that again? Why didn't you go?'

'I told you that night, I was following a lead. Nancy picked up a message from the front desk for me. It was to do with that story I'm working on, on illegal workers.'

'I remember. You told me you were going but not what happened?'

'Where?'

'At the 7–Eleven?'

'Nothing. Nothing happened at all. There was a lovely Hispanic girl behind the till, she wants to be an actress. I couldn't see any illegal activity at all, it was a bum steer.' Caroline took a breath, her anger rising again. By the time she'd realised the red-hot lead was mortuary cold it had been too late to go home and get changed for the party. She'd been seriously pissed off. She cleared her throat. 'What's this really about, Tim? Why isn't Greta backing me? This is going to be thrown out the minute a judge sees my records.'

Caroline paused to let him answer; even with her snug layers on top, the cold was starting to seep through the soles of her boots.

'That, I have yet to discover, but trust me, I'm working on it.'

He sounded sincere but she couldn't resist her next question, her tone deliberately innocent.

'Thanks – Slater's some piece of work but Greta's not far behind him. How's Nancy doing in my absence? Picking up all my leads?'

'She's been out of the office a good bit, I think – that story she was working on before Christmas is coming to a head apparently.'

'That would be the one she can't tell anyone about, the top secret one?'

He grunted. 'Look, I'm going to have to go. I'll make sure Greta knows you've got all the paperwork.'

'I'll try and check my email every few days. If you need me urgently ring the hotel. It's called Hare's Landing, it's in West Cork.'

'Cool. I've got the details in your last email. I'll have a talk to Greta and see if I can find out what the real issue is here.'

'We need to stop it before it comes to court. It's such total nonsense, the whole industry is going to be wondering why my editor isn't backing me. No smoke without fire.'

Caroline could hear the weariness in her own voice. They were going around in circles here.

'I'm on it.' His voice softened. 'Really, try not to worry. I've got your back. We'll have dinner and laugh about this when you get back.'

The call dropped.

Don't worry? That was easy for him to say. But she liked the sound of dinner, and he was looking out for her. She couldn't ask for more than that.

Maybe she had got the Nancy thing wrong after all; she was definitely up to something but perhaps it wasn't trying to sleep with Tim.

Caroline put her phone back in her pocket and looked down the street, rerunning their conversation through her mind.

Really, what on earth had the Christmas party got to do with anything?

Caroline shook her head. If her career wasn't on the line here, she wouldn't even be taking this seriously. The whole thing was mad. But there was definitely something niggling her about Nancy. What had taken up so much of her time, coming up to Christmas? They all had cases they couldn't discuss, sources they had to protect, but she'd been very cagey, since, now Caroline thought about it, about a month after she'd started in the newsroom. *Curious and curiouser.*

Caroline walked the few paces to Mahony's store. Pushing her glasses on firmly, she opened the door. She could see a post office sign at the back. Perhaps this was the store she'd remembered from her childhood holidays after all.

It was tiny and dark inside, the shelves crowded with all manner of things from copybooks and twine to milking pails. There didn't seem to be much logic in the display. As the door closed behind her, a bell jangled, and an elderly man wearing a brown leather apron shuffled out from the back room. He looked at her over the glasses perched on the end of his nose.

'Hello there, how are you finding our little village after the bright lights?'

Stunned, Caroline didn't know what to say.

'I'm sorry?'

What was this, the bush telegraph?

'Imogen mentioned you might have a film for me to develop?'

'She said you have a dark room.' Flustered, wondering when Imogen had had a chance to discuss her business with the shopkeeper, Caroline unhooked her bag from her shoulder and searched for the roll of film she'd found. 'I was wondering if there were any pictures on here of Hare's Landing. Could you take a look and see if there's one you could enlarge. I'd love to surprise Bronagh.'

His face crinkled. 'Of course, I'll take a look.'

'I hope they *are* pictures of the house – they could be all of someone's cat.'

He chortled. 'Is there anything else I can get you?'

He indicated a stool in front of the counter. He was obviously very well set up for a gossip whenever a customer came in.

'Thank you, I'd love to stop but I'm on my way to a pottery workshop, it starts pretty soon.'

His face clouded for a moment. 'Are you now? Ava's doing a grand job down there. Mind, she's had a tough time.'

Caroline wasn't sure how to reply to that.

'I'd better get moving. I can collect the photos when they're ready?'

'Probably be tomorrow. It's quiet today so I'll get started now.'

Chapter 19

RACHEL FLICKED ON the indicator and turned off the main road that wound its way towards Fishguard and the ferry terminal, the Land Rover rattling over the uneven Welsh road. At least it had been well signposted all the way here. Behind her, Jasper grumbled in the back seat.

Rachel still couldn't believe she was on her way to West Cork, or that she'd spent the last five and a half hours on the road. She was starting to feel as if she'd slipped into some sort of parallel universe. They'd been talking about going to see a show in the West End at the weekend, maybe having a meal first. Now that seemed like a different life. One where her points of reference didn't shift hourly and where there wasn't a constant undercurrent of fear.

After she'd texted him with the details of the hotel, Hare's Landing, Hunter had remembered more and more fragments of Alfie's conversation, and kept texting her as it came back to him. It didn't take long before he was totally convinced this was the house Alfie had talked about. He'd been so sure that he'd called her at 2.00 a.m., his voice low as he'd whispered into the phone, trying not to disturb the other patients in the ward.

Rachel pushed a curl of hair out of her face, slowing as she came around a bend to find a caravan in front of her.

She hadn't realised quite how far Fishguard was – as they'd crossed rural Wales, passing a sign to Haverfordwest, she'd been sure they were almost there. Rachel shifted in the seat, her bum numbed from sitting down for so long. She hadn't had time to stop on the way here, and once they docked in Rosslare she wanted to get across country as quickly as she could. She just hoped there was a shop of some sort in Fishguard where she could get a coffee and a sandwich before they left. She glanced at the time on the dashboard, double-checking it against the watch on her wrist. She should arrive about ten minutes ahead of schedule, assuming the caravan ahead didn't meet a tractor on the way.

There was no question that the barge wasn't a safe place for her to stay on her own until they knew what was going on, and there was no arguing with Hunter when he got an idea in his head. He was right that she had a holiday due from work and Jasper would love a break in the country. He'd be in hospital for at least another three weeks, *and* his mum was on the way over from Jamaica so he'd have someone to fuss over him.

This could be the only lead on Alfie's past they had. She had to go, if only for the weekend.

She'd been wide awake herself when Hunter had called, the duvet pulled to her chin, Jasper lying full length next to her, snoring just loudly enough to disturb her. Or perhaps it had been the sounds of the marina, her ears sensitive to every noise, that were preventing her from sleeping. She'd answered the second the phone had rung.

'You've booked it already?'

She'd fought to keep the smile out of her voice. She'd been one click away from booking a room at Hare's Landing herself when Jasper had decided he needed to go outside last night. Realising it was almost midnight, she'd decided it was time to get back to the barge.

'You know they probably won't remember him? Alfie, I mean? Really, what are the chances?' She'd lain back and rubbed her eyes. 'You're mad, but it will be lovely. It'll just kill me that you're not with us.'

'I know, babes, but I'm absolutely sure that's the place Alfie meant.' He continued, keeping his voice low. 'And there's a ferry tomorrow at lunchtime from Fishguard.'

'Tomorrow? Good God, Hunter …'

'I know, but you've already taken the time off work and we need to get to the bottom of his story, to find out what happened to him. He must have people, Rach, could you imagine not knowing …?'

'But even if I go there, how on earth are we going to find out what happened? I mean, we've no idea *when* he was there for starters.'

'Go and ask around. You're always saying how small Ireland is, how everyone knows everyone else. Someone has to remember a posh lad from England visiting.'

'You know, if it wasn't that I needed somewhere to stay this would be totally mad. But I haven't had a chance to call Mum yet, and it's so much cheaper than anywhere in London …'

'Exactly. And you work too hard, you need a break. You might not find anything, but at least you'll be safe there and I'll get out of here faster if I'm not worrying about you. We only need a tiny bit of info to help us on to the next step, and if anyone can dig up the information, it's you. I'll go through all the out-takes and see if there are any more clues … Please will you go – for me? I'd kill to come with you but …'

'You're broken. I know.' Rubbing the sleep out of her eyes, she'd turned over and put her arm around Jasper. 'Okay, I'll see what I can do.'

'I booked the ferry for you. The hotel is dog-friendly and Jasper's passport's up to date. You can have a couple of days in luxury while I get Zack to check the boat and make sure it's totally secure.'

Now Rachel shook her head, remembering their conversation. It was a totally mad expedition, but if someone had a problem with Hunter that had caused them to knock him off his bike and break into the barge, she'd be much safer in Ireland.

Pulling up at a small roundabout, Rachel could see the sea ahead of her, and down to her left a parade of shops. The ferry was already in, sunshine reflecting off its white paintwork, a stream of vehicles disembarking.

'Almost there, Jasp. You can have a run before we board.'

Chapter 20

WALKING BRISKLY DOWN the hill towards the turning for the harbour and the pottery, Caroline pulled out the leaflet featuring the image of the hare that she'd found in the lounge at the hotel. Perhaps there was a local story or tradition around them. If Ava the potter didn't know, she was sure Imogen would. Caroline had meant to ask her about the name of the house but she had got distracted by looking at the furniture, and it had slipped her mind.

Following Glencurragh's main street downhill, Caroline passed a brightly lit cafe and swung down right towards the water. Even at this distance she could hear the waves breaking on the shore, the sound so regular it was like time ticking.

Suddenly the lane came to an abrupt end, opening out into the little stone harbour. Caroline looked around, thinking she must have missed the pottery, but turning, she saw a beautiful sign on one of the buildings to her right: Cassidy Ceramics. Trailing ivy entwined around the lettering, which was a deep cobalt blue against a white crackle-glazed background.

The house and pottery looked as if they had grown out of the harbour itself, the front windows looking directly out over the little slip and the brightly coloured hulls of upturned boats. Built of substantial blocks of grey stone, it was much more impressive than she'd expected, Georgian, austere and imposing, but warmth radiated from the sash windows.

Caroline glanced into the window closest to her as she walked up to the front door to knock. Before she had time to take in any detail, the door was opened by a woman in her early fifties, her crinkly straw-coloured hair peppered with grey. She was wearing a denim apron over a bright green sweater and jeans, her hair tied up in a messy bun that she had stuck a pencil through, as if she was worried that she might lose it. She held the door wide.

'Hi, I'm Ava, you must be Caroline? I really don't normally do workshops in the winter, but come in.'

'Thanks so much for taking me. I know it's late notice too.'

Surprised, Caroline tried to sound warm in response to Ava's frosty welcome, always her default with difficult people – it usually disarmed them. After their chat on the phone, Caroline hadn't expected her to be quite this hostile, despite Mrs Travers saying the same thing. Ava *had* said she was about to do a firing though, so perhaps this workshop really was a nuisance, but she was one of those people who couldn't say 'no'. Or perhaps she'd changed her mind since their call. Caroline felt a twinge of guilt; she knew what it was like when she was writing and someone called, it broke her flow completely.

Caroline followed Ava into what was obviously her workroom, the concrete floor, like her apron, splashed in silver grey slip. In the middle of the room a huge pine workbench was crowded with a series of damp, dove coloured clay tiles – she clearly *was* right in the middle of working. On the far wall a big square steel box stood with the door open – the kiln. Its shelves were already half full of pieces.

As Caroline slipped off her parka, she could feel Ava taking her in. She seemed a little edgy, which made Caroline feel even more like she was interrupting. *Perhaps she just wasn't a people person.*

'Have you done any ceramic work before?'

As she answered, Caroline looked for somewhere to hang her coat, careful to keep it off the floor. There was a fine layer of dust covering everything – she could feel it in her mouth.

'I haven't done pottery since school, but I did art for my leaving cert and my piece was a pot based on a poppy head. It wasn't thrown, more sculpted. It was my favourite part of the course.'

Ava took her coat to hang on an empty hook on the back of the door beside another one laden with bright red aprons, pointing to a window seat where Caroline could put her bag. She passed her an apron.

'I think potters have a unique connection to their work. Being able to hold it, to create three-dimensional objects that are functional, that people can use every day, it's a different form of art. On one of the courses I run in the summer, each participant creates a bowl and in the last session I make soup and we use them for lunch. I think ceramics are about community as much as art.'

'That's so true. It's the functionality that I love, it's so practical.'

Ava pulled out a stool from under the bench.

'Sit down. We don't have time for a bowl today, but we'll make something lovely. And you can tell me all about why you've come to West Cork in January.' Ava's smile was cold. Caroline looked at her in surprise, but she continued smoothly, as if her comment wasn't laden with innuendo. 'I use an encaustic technique to make the tiles you've seen – it was developed in the thirteenth century.'

She moved along the bench and turned around an oval-shaped piece of damp clay with a design cut into it, so Caroline could see it better. It took a moment for Caroline to tune back into what she was saying. Had she misheard Ava? Or was it just that everyone in this village was incredibly nosey and so incredibly bored in the winter that a new face got them all excited? Caroline wasn't sure, but the way Ava had implied she had some ulterior motive for being here was definitely strange.

As if she was completely unaware of the impact of her words, Ava continued.

'I hollow out the design and add tinted slip, creating a layer of colour. It's very tough once it's fired. There are tiles on the floors of cathedrals in Europe that have been made using this technique and the colour never fades. They are just as bright as if they were made yesterday.'

Keeping the interested expression on her face, Caroline nodded as if she was totally caught up in what Ava was saying.

'Are the plaques with the hares on that I saw up at Hare's Landing, and in your brochure, made the same way?'

'That's right. I apply a crackle glaze and more coloured slip to finish the tile off. Each piece goes through around ten different processes before it's finished.'

Ava seemed to relax a little as she warmed to her subject. Perhaps Caroline was imagining things? *The taxi driver's incessant questioning and the storekeeper knowing her business before she walked in the door was making her paranoid.* She tried to focus on the tiles.

'They are really beautiful – and I love the quotes on them.'

Caroline ran her finger over the surface of the finished tile closest to her, feeling how smooth it was.

'You can make one like that. I have some here you can look at to give you some ideas. You don't have to draw a hare – I just love them because they are magical somehow, such free spirits. There's so much mythology around them.'

Ava pulled out several large plastic containers from a shelving unit behind the door, each one filled with tiles. They looked incredibly heavy but she did it with ease. Taking one from each box, she handed them to Caroline.

'Each one is unique, the glaze dries slightly differently each time.'

'They are really wonderful.'

Caroline laid them out on the workbench in front of her as Ava selected scraping tools and brushes from pots on a huge pine dresser at the back of the room, and laid them out ready for her to use.

Caroline felt Ava glance at her.

'So, how are you finding Hare's Landing?'

Was that an innocent question? Caroline wasn't sure. She answered with a genuine smile.

'Gorgeous. I'm staying in a separate house, the Boathouse, but it and the hotel are stunning. Bronagh's done an amazing job restoring it.'

'She works really hard. We were in school together. She and Leo ran a hotel in Verona for years but she'd always wanted to come home. It's great she's back, areas like this need employment.'

'I guess she'll be busier in the summer, it's very quiet now.'

'Not much happens here in the winter. It's no harm, it gives her husband a chance to get home.' Ava continued, 'Conor is brilliant in the kitchen, he's one of those people who takes everything in his stride. I'm sure the restaurant will pick up once they get into the season properly – he's got quite a following over at Graylings but they only open for lunch. Imogen will be back at college by then but I'm sure she'll stay on – she doesn't have many college hours.'

Surprised Ava seemed to know them so well, and was prepared to share so much, Caroline nodded. *She really must be getting paranoid.*

'I was chatting to Imogen. She mentioned she was doing history.'

'Much to her father's chagrin. He's the local GP, and his father before him. He's got six kids and they are all brilliant, but only one of them is doing medicine.'

'Conor said something about fainting at the sight of blood.'

Ava chuckled half to herself. 'So I've heard. I don't know how that works in the kitchen though. I reckon he just told his father that so he could study fish instead of people.'

'Their parents must be very proud. Imogen said she was loving her course – she was telling me about it.'

'She's fascinated by local history and there's plenty around here.' Ava reached for one of the scraping tools in the middle of the table. 'She has a lovely Instagram account with pictures of the house and village on it, it's really beautiful.'

Caroline couldn't keep the look of surprise from her face.

'How does she make Instagram work here? I'm not used to being so cut off.'

'The internet's a bit patchy in this area. But that's the beauty of it for some people.'

'Very true, it was one of the reasons I chose Hare's Landing, I have to admit.'

'Really?'

Ava's smile was fixed but didn't reach her eyes. Caroline felt her tense. There definitely *was* an issue here, but what on earth could it be? Wary, Caroline continued.

'The house is fascinating. Imogen told me a little about it, about Honoria Smyth and her story. It sounds so sad.'

116

Ava sighed. 'I don't think we'll ever know what really happened. She was a writer, not so well known here, but big in America, and quite prolific. She wrote romance mainly – but from what I've read, she could be quite dark. And she was a talented artist.'

Perhaps this was it: Ava had an issue with her in connection to the story of Honoria Smyth's death. Caroline still wasn't sure.

'Are those her paintings in the house? There are lots in the Boathouse too, they're fabulous.' Ava nodded as Caroline continued. 'They are all of storms, she really captures the power of the sea.'

'I think her life was more turbulent than we know. It looked perfect from the outside, she had everything – the big house, a career, and her paintings were exhibited all over the place. But I think she must have been lonely with her son away at school. They were very close by all accounts, but her husband sent him off to England when he was eight or nine.' Ava cleared her throat. 'Outward appearances can be deceptive.'

Caroline looked up at her sharply. But suddenly she didn't feel as if Ava was talking about Honoria. Before she could ask, Ava continued.

'Now, let's get some clay and get started. What sort of decoration would you like?'

'I'd love a hare on it. There's something a bit mysterious about them, isn't there.' She hesitated. 'Do you know why the house is called Hare's Landing?'

Ava carried the remainder of the sausage of clay back to the box she'd taken it from.

'The first customs officer who lived there was a Captain O'Hare. Along the way the "O" got lost. His house was originally closer to the sea. The castle's all that's left, it was the original gaol, but I'm sure you read that on the website.'

'Are you originally from Glencurragh?'

Ava arched her eyebrows, her eyes cold, as if the question was too personal.

'I went to art college in London. But let's get on with making this tile and you can tell me about what you do in New York.'

Chapter 21

THE LAND ROVER bounced into another pothole and Rachel felt her bones jar. She just hoped to God that this was the right lane and she wasn't going to end up in a field with a bull at the end of it – or worse, on the edge of a cliff. After the trip from London, three hours on the ferry – which thankfully had docked early – and another three and a half hours on the road crossing the south of Ireland, she'd left in the dark and was arriving in the dark – at least she hoped she was. She'd lost 4G and Google Maps about half an hour ago and was following her nose and what she could remember of the map now.

One thing was for sure, she was going to sleep well when she eventually found this place.

She'd caught glimpses of the sea as the road twisted downhill, her headlights playing onto dense hedges on either side of the lane. She smiled to herself. Here they were called ditches. Before the thought could develop, a white shape dipped across the road in front of the windscreen, making her jump. She slammed on the brakes, making Jasper yelp in the back.

'I'm so sorry, Jasp, are you okay, boy?' Rachel turned to find his head thrust between the two front seats. 'I think that was a barn owl, we're in the country now. You'll love it when we get there.' He whimpered in response. 'Won't be long, I promise.'

Thrusting the Land Rover into first gear, Rachel set off

again, her headlights finally picking up a sign.

'There we are.'

She almost said *thank God*, but she was pretty sure Jasper understood everything she said, and she was supposed to be the adult here.

Following the sign, Rachel turned off the main road down a winding lane. Another sign took her rattling between two huge gate posts and over a cattle grid down a narrow, heavily wooded track. When Rachel reached the end, she didn't think she'd ever been happier to see a building. It was a magnificent house, elegant and well proportioned, a round turret on the far left of the porch.

The lights were on across the ground floor, a welcoming glow after the tar-like black of the night.

Thank God.

Pulling up on the gravel, Rachel swung open the door and eased her stiff legs out. Behind her, Jasper was pushing through the front seats, desperate to get out and explore. She caught his collar as he jumped down beside her, his paws crunching on gravel. As she turned to grab her bag and his lead from the footwell, slamming the door closed with her hip, she heard another car approaching. A moment later it swung into the drive behind them. Jasper pulled at his collar for a moment, but Rachel clicked her tongue and he settled down immediately. Watching the new arrival intently, he sat quietly beside her, his ears cocked forward, senses on alert.

Rachel bent to clip on his lead as the car pulled up and the back door swung open. Illuminated by the light from the house, a young dark-haired woman got out, pulling a Louis Vuitton shopper onto her shoulder. She was wearing a thick parka over skinny jeans and black leather boots.

She pushed her glasses up her nose as she bent to speak to the driver.

'Thanks so much, can you charge it?'

Rachel didn't catch the driver's response, but she saw him wave an acknowledgment as he pulled away.

The woman's face lit up as she came up to them.

'What a beautiful dog. Have you just arrived?'

Her accent was mid-Atlantic; educated Dublin, Rachel guessed, with an American edge. Illuminated by the lights of the hotel, her high cheekbones drew Rachel's eye to striking violet eyes behind her tortoiseshell glasses.

'Literally this minute. He needs a run – he's been cooped up all day.'

The woman walked up to the front door of the hotel, guarded on either side by two huge stone hares, and held it open.

'It's this way, I'll show you. Once you've checked in, he'll have an awesome walk – there are loads of paths through the woods and along the headland. He'll love it. I'm Caroline, by the way.'

'Lovely to meet you – Rachel. And this is Jasper.'

Before Caroline could reply, they heard another voice greeting them both from the hallway of the hotel.

'Good evening, ladies! Come inside and get warm.'

Following Caroline, Rachel was astonished at the elegance of the hallway, the sweeping staircase, candles burning on the mantelpiece. The whole hotel smelled divine.

Behind the reception desk a woman stood up, her hand outstretched. She was tiny, about five feet tall Rachel reckoned, her hair flame-red and cropped, setting off the red and blue print on the shirt she was wearing under a smart boxy navy blazer. It suited her; she gave off an air of efficiency.

'I'm Bronagh, welcome to Hare's Landing.' Shaking Rachel's hand, she turned to Caroline. 'I'm sorry I wasn't here when you arrived, we had a slate blow off. I got tied up trying to sort it out. How are you finding the Boathouse?'

'Gorgeous, thanks.' Caroline hesitated and Rachel thought she saw a shadow pass over her face, but perhaps she was imagining it. Caroline continued cheerfully. 'And the full fridge is a big bonus. I hadn't expected that.'

Bronagh smiled broadly. 'Least we can do, when you're staying a while. Just let us know if you're missing anything.'

Rachel liked Bronagh immediately. She had the right personality for hospitality, was warm and clearly enjoyed meeting people.

'I'll see you later maybe?' Caroline touched her arm, her face warm. 'I'll be in the lounge making the most of that fire.'

Rachel nodded, smiling. She had no idea what she'd be doing later – collapsing on her bed probably – but Caroline seemed nice and looked interesting. It would be great to have some company for the few days she was here. Bronagh interrupted her thoughts.

'Now let me give you your key …'

'Rachel – Rachel Lambert. But I think my partner made the booking.'

'He did indeed.' Bronagh picked up a booking form from her side of the counter. 'I just need you to sign in and Mrs Travers can show you to your room.'

A movement on the staircase made Rachel look up. An elderly woman had materialised at the turn of the stairs, one hand on the banister. She was dressed in black, and reminded Rachel instantly of her Mother Superior in school. She had that same serene but disapproving expression. Beside Rachel, Jasper leaned into her leg, his eyes fixed on the stairs. Unaware of any ripple in the atmosphere, Bronagh continued.

'Mrs Travers is our housekeeper, she knows everything there is to know about Hare's Landing.'

Chapter 22

THE RECEPTION AREA was empty when Rachel got back downstairs, Jasper at her heels. She'd been very tempted to order room service, but Jasper really was desperate for a walk and curious as to his new surroundings. He'd wolfed his dinner as soon as she'd put it down in the en suite bathroom, anxious he didn't make a mess on the bedroom carpet. The hotel was dog-friendly but that didn't mean they wanted to have to deep clean after every stay.

Jasper's claws tapped the flagstones as he followed her across the hall, his ears pricked. Looking through the glazed doors into the bar, she couldn't see Caroline, but the whole hall was welcoming, the chandelier casting a warm glow, a fire burning merrily in the huge fireplace opposite the front door.

Rachel's room was gorgeous too. And when she looked out of the sash windows, she had an uninterrupted view of the gardens, some sort of tower or small castle a dark shape to her left. Buried in the trees to the right, she could just see the roof of a building beside the water's edge. Across the estuary the steep hillside was thickly wooded, not a light in sight. There was definitely no danger of anyone looking in.

Rachel had been on a lot of period film sets over the years, but here at Hare's Landing, she felt as if she'd really stepped back in time.

Wrapping her scarf around her neck, Rachel zipped up her skiing jacket. It had been a present from Hunter – super warm and such a zingy lime green that there was definitely no danger of getting lost in the snow when she was wearing it. She pushed the front door open and Jasper shot outside, cantering into the darkness and circling back to see if she was following. He spotted a large dog bowl full of water beside the porch wall and drank noisily, then, checking back with her, looped between the two magnificent statues of hares outside the door and ran backwards and forwards, almost leaping in the air as he changed direction, his tail wagging hard.

'Go on, Jasp, go explore, boy. See what's there.'

He didn't need to be told twice. She knew he'd rush around investigating, but would keep her in sight even if she couldn't see him. He loved woodland with all its scents and hidden places. Sometimes she felt bad that he lived on a houseboat, but he was a city dog and made up for it when they took him for walks at the weekends in the London parks or further afield. He made them both get out and keep active, which wasn't a bad thing. Being fit would help Hunter get better faster. Rachel felt a pang of emotion. She knew she was tired after the drive and the trauma of the past few days, but Hunter's accident felt like a weight on her chest. She rubbed away a tear.

It could have been so much worse.

Looking around at the gravelled area which gave way to the tree-bordered drive, Rachel knew Hunter would love it here; they'd have to come back when he was better.

She felt another pang. What was Alfie's connection to this place? What could have happened here that had had such a dramatic effect on his life? It was so peaceful, so far away from anywhere – she could almost hear Hunter voicing one of his favourite expressions: 'the arse end of nowhere'. He was usually talking about the locations she found for filming, but Hare's Landing really did feel as if it was on the edge of civilisation.

In the distance she could hear Jasper barking. She followed the direction he'd taken, around the front of the hotel, past some outbuildings into what appeared to be a stable yard that opened off the side of the property. He was running around in circles barking, stopping on each circuit to stretch in the middle of the yard, putting his front legs out like he was in the circus, his back legs straight. She laughed – after being cooped up in the car all day, she needed to stretch her back too. He barked sharply and she called him to her, worried he'd disturb other guests with all his noise.

He came to heel immediately, looking at her questioningly.

'Come on, boy, let's see if we can find the sea.'

She looked around as she walked back to the front of the house. Through the lit windows of the turret-like room, she could see it opened on to the very cosy-looking period lounge.

Had Alfie stayed here for a holiday or a break? He'd said something about an Irish friend. But how could she find out who he'd been here with if she didn't know the dates, or even what his real name was? In all honesty, it seemed utterly hopeless. And Rachel was already missing Hunter. She pulled out her phone, her thumb on dial when she saw that there was no reception. She looked up anxiously, the need to talk to Hunter overwhelming. But she couldn't go back to the hotel yet. Jasper had disappeared ahead of her into the darkness and really did need a proper walk. He'd been incredibly patient all day. Above her, the night sky was clear, the moon bright. It was going to be a cold one, and she didn't want to hang about.

She looked around again, glancing back at the hotel. *Had Alfie been here?* All she could hope for was 'the luck of the Irish' that Hunter was always reminding her she had, and that someone might remember something. She had to admit Ireland was like that; it was an incredibly small country and everyone seemed to be connected somehow. She sighed. She'd just have to ask around.

The glow from an antique lampstand lit a path into the woods to her left, heading down towards the sea. She could hear the waves breaking on the shore and turned to walk that way. If Jasper wasn't already on the beach he soon would be, and tonight she needed to keep him out of the water. Once she'd asked if the hotel had a hose, she could let him roam – they might be dog-friendly but a very large, muddy, wet dog was a different thing.

Following him down the path, a few moments later she came across a two-storey cottage built like the prow of a ship. A light glowed inside but it looked empty.

'Jasp, where are you, boy?'

A moment later he appeared, running at high speed from the woods, streaked around her and off again down a path that ran beside the house. The sound of the sea was louder here, waves pulling at shingle. She was always amazed at how sound travelled differently at night, and even more so across water. A moment later she could hear paws on the shingle, and set off at a jog to catch up with Jasper.

Chapter 23

RACHEL COULD FEEL her face glowing as she headed back to the hotel. Jasper had run the entire length of the beach, up and down, stopping to nose at the piles of seaweed and driftwood, dark shapes in the night. Occasional clouds obscured the moon, but her eyes quickly adjusted to what little light there was and she could see patterns of phosphorescence in the water as the waves rippled into shore.

From the beach she'd seen a squat stone building higher up on the hill. Watchful and solid in the darkness, Rachel had no idea what it was, but it commanded a fine view of the estuary. Intrigued by it, she kept glancing up, imagining it as the perfect location for a medieval battle. It was definitely somewhere she needed to come back to explore in the daylight.

Closer to the soft lights of the hotel, the shadows deepened, and ahead of her, Jasper was a dark shape loping through the trees. He ran back around the building to the stable yard again, barking sharply.

Reaching the porch, Rachel called him and waited for him to reappear. He drank deeply from the bowl, and as she opened the door, he pushed past her into the tiled hallway, shoving her sideways, then stopping abruptly, his head on one side. Someone must have just left. She could see him catching their scent.

'Come on, boy, let's find some food and get warmed up.'

She headed into the bar that linked the dining room and lounge. The lounge area looked cosy, decorated to match the period of the house, a huge fire burning hungrily in the hearth, old books lining the mantelpiece, above it a striking portrait. Rachel headed towards it. Before she'd gone a pace, she heard a friendly voice.

'Did you get settled in?'

It was the dark-haired American she'd met earlier. For a moment Rachel struggled to remember her name, then it came to her: Caroline. She was sitting on a window seat that ran around the tiny turret-like room Rachel had seen from the drive. The tall windows were uncurtained, and outside the darkness was complete, the windows a canvas reflecting the room. Rachel took off her scarf and unzipped her jacket, dropping them over the back of one of the sofas. She perched next to them as Caroline smiled warmly at her.

'Yes, thanks, the room's absolutely lovely. And we had a gorgeous walk. I came down to get some food.' She turned and looked back at the bar. 'But there doesn't seem to be anyone about.'

Caroline pushed her glasses up her nose.

'We can ring. It's very quiet at this time of year apparently, they've got a skeleton staff on.'

'Looks more like they've bypassed the skeleton stage and turned straight into ghosts.'

'Oh God, don't say that. There are rumours this place is haunted. There seem to be all sorts of stories and mysteries about the previous owner.' Caroline indicated the portrait over the fire. 'She committed suicide apparently.'

Rachel turned and looked up at the painting. It was beautiful, as clear as a photograph, and even though she was smiling, the woman's eyes looked sad. She shivered despite the warmth of the room.

'Would you like to join me for supper? The menu is quite limited just now because they aren't fully operational, but the food is amazing.'

Caroline leaned forward to pick up a menu off a circular table in front of her. The table had a glass top but appeared to be made entirely of books. Rachel made a mental note to take a photo of it in the morning for her files.

'Do they stretch to a Caesar salad? I'm a creature of habit, I could happily live on that and poached eggs and avocados on toast.'

'You might need to order that in advance, but the chef is excellent. He's actually a marine biologist.'

'Seriously?' Rachel laughed as Jasper came back from his exploration of the bar and headed straight for the fire, flopping down in front of it with a loud sigh before rolling onto his side. 'I don't think he's going anywhere for a while.'

'He'll love it here. There's loads of space to run around. And that fire.'

As she spoke, Rachel could hear stronger traces of an Irish upbringing in Caroline's accent.

'That's for sure. Where are you from, originally?'

'The Dublin mountains, but more recently New York, as you can tell. I'm a journalist, crime mainly … for the *New York Messenger*.'

Rachel picked up on her hesitation, her curiosity immediately piqued.

'Tough job?'

Caroline ran her hand into the roots of her shiny dark hair. 'It has its moments. I'm well overdue a vacation and New

York's under two feet of snow, which looks great on postcards but is a total nightmare.'

Rachel moved from leaning on the sofa to join her in the little octagonal room, sitting down opposite her on the window seat.

'That I can relate to. I work in film. I'm a location scout, and there's nothing good about snow unless it comes out of a machine and you can hoover it up afterwards.'

Caroline raised her eyebrows. 'That sounds like a very cool job.'

'Crime journalist is definitely way cooler.'

'Touché.' Caroline laughed. 'So what brings you to Hare's Landing – work or pleasure?'

Rachel grabbed a cushion and pushed it in behind her.

'Honestly, a bit of a wild goose chase. It's a long story ...'

'Let's order and you can tell me about it.'

*

Once Caroline had rung the bell on the bar, a young waitress seemed to appear magically. As did their dinner shortly afterwards. Sitting in front of the fire, their plates on the solid oak table between them and a bottle of white wine open, they chatted easily. It didn't take as long as Rachel had expected to explain the background to Alfie's story and how she'd ended up here; Caroline was very quick picking it up.

'That's scary. You're right to get away. How long's your partner going to be in hospital for?'

Rachel shrugged. 'At least a couple of weeks. His mother's coming today though. She'll stay for at least a week, so I would be fairly redundant even if I was there. She doesn't think anyone can look after him like she can – she'll be delivering all his meals to the hospital.'

Caroline picked up her wine, taking a sip. 'And you don't know anything about this Alfie character at all?'

Rachel ran her hand into her wiry curls. 'Very few actual facts. His name might not even be Alfie. Frank, the guy from the hostel, thinks his first name is Alfred, but who's called Alfred these days?'

'Perhaps he was known as Freddie?'

Rachel picked up her glass and stared into the flames.

'Maybe. I've really no idea where to start. I mean, what could have happened in a place like this that was so life-changing?'

'Plenty apparently.' Caroline leaned forward, adjusting her glasses. 'Imogen, the waitress, was telling me the house used to be owned by a family called Smyth.' She looked up and indicated the portrait above them as she spoke. 'That's Honoria Smyth. She came from a very wealthy Irish-American family and married an English barrister. She hated London so she spent a lot of time here. Apparently she took up with the gardener.'

'Very Lady Chatterley.'

As Rachel spoke a door banged somewhere near reception, making them both jump. The movement caused a draught that made the fire splutter. They looked at each other, alarmed. Eyes bright, ears cocked forward, Jasper looked up, but a moment later the fire settled and he put his head down again. Rachel leaned forward to rub his back.

'I'm sure that was the wind, there are storms forecast. It was on the radio on the way down.'

'I hope so.' Caroline took a sip of her wine and glanced up at the picture. 'I keep thinking she must have been terribly lonely, living here by herself. It's gorgeous for a vacation, but Glencurragh is a twenty-minute drive and there's literally a pub, a cafe, the pottery and one store that sells everything, and that's all. It's tiny.' Caroline frowned. 'Something must have gone wrong because the gardener disappeared and she committed suicide, or perhaps it was the other way around … Nobody seems to know.'

Rachel shivered. 'That's awful. The poor woman. Perhaps it was his leaving that did it.'

'I'm not sure. I mean, we've all had break-ups and they don't usually end like that. There must have been more to it.'

'When did all this happen?'

'About thirty years ago, Imogen said. I figure there must be something in the local paper about her passing, so I'm going to go down to the village tomorrow to see if the pub has Wi-Fi.'

Rachel grinned. 'I thought you were on holiday?'

Caroline's eyes gleamed as she glanced up at the painting again.

'I'm fascinated by her. I can almost feel her presence. Her initials are all over the house – on pieces of furniture and etched into the glass on some of the windows, even on the tiles. I've got a beautiful wardrobe in my bedroom with an *H* worked into the marquetry.' Caroline picked up the bottle to top up Rachel's wine. 'It would be mad if your Alfie turned out to be the gardener.'

Rachel looked at her, her eyes wide. 'That's for sure. I don't think he ever mentioned gardening to Hunter, his passion was definitely the violin. I heard him play once, he was quite brilliant.'

'Perhaps he came here to give a concert?'

'He was good enough.'

It had never occurred to Rachel that Alfie could have been a professional violinist, but it made sense. She'd worked with

132

all sort of musicians and could tell when they had a real gift – they could take an ordinary piece of music and make it exceptional. Which was exactly what Alfie had done when she'd heard him play. It was if the music lifted him from the dark room of his mind and lit everything up.

Her brow creased in thought, Caroline tapped a manicured finger on her lips.

'Perhaps he came and stayed here at the hotel while he was doing a concert in Ross Haven or Sommerville?'

Rachel instinctively reached behind her for her phone.

'There might be something online about a concert. Maybe if we google his first name, assuming it was Alfred, and possible venues? It's the longest of long shots I know but …' She tailed off, her mind drawn back to the painting over the fireplace. She frowned, thinking. 'Would the local paper have carried a report of Honoria's death? I mean, I assume there would have been a funeral notice, but suicide was illegal until the early nineties. Rural Ireland is still cagey about it even today.'

'That's very true. Hopefully there might be an obituary of some sort that might tell us a bit more about her. This was the "big house", I guess, its owners would have been well respected and her passing would have been marked somehow.' Caroline pointed at Rachel's phone. 'But you'll be lucky if that works here.'

'Damn, I forgot about the signal.'

'Bronagh said it's okay to use the phone at reception if you need to make a call.'

Rachel looked at her gratefully. 'That's a relief. I need to tell Hunter I've arrived in one piece.'

'There's phone reception in the village, it's just here we seem to be in a black spot. I'm going down in the morning if you'd like to join me for a coffee. I did a workshop at the pottery there this afternoon – I want to see if the tile I made fired properly.' Caroline pointed towards the mantelpiece. 'I made one like that.'

Rachel looked across at the blue and white plaque wistfully; she'd noticed a similar one in the hall, had stopped to look at the glazing technique.

'It's gorgeous. I haven't done ceramics since I was in college. I did an art degree – I started in the film business in set design.'

'I'd love to make another one – would you come and join me? The potter doesn't normally do workshops in the winter, but we might be able to persuade her if there are two of us. The history of the method she uses is fascinating.' Caroline hesitated. 'She's a bit odd, I'm not sure she warmed to me, but it's so relaxing doing something totally different.' She sat back on the sofa. 'When we're down in the village we can check our email.' She laughed ironically. 'I never thought trying to keep in touch with the outside world would be such a challenge.'

Chapter 24

A s CAROLINE CLOSED the door of the Boathouse, she made a point of checking she'd locked it from the inside, rattling it to be sure. There was no bolt, which was worrying if someone from the hotel did have access. Looking at the door she suddenly realised that anyone who had stayed here previously could have had a duplicate key cut.

But she was being dramatic.

Who would do that, and why?

And they'd probably have to go all the way to Ross Haven to get one made, unless Mahony's sell-everything store could do it. She hadn't noticed when she'd called in earlier with the roll of film. Entering the shop, part of her had felt as if she'd stepped back in time, not to her childhood but to some distant point in the past where it was normal to stock everything from wellington boots to bread.

The intensity of interest in strangers, the hunger for gossip, also gave it a quaint, old-fashioned feel. Like the taxi driver, the elderly shopkeeper – John Francis Mahony – had been blatantly curious as to who she was and what she was doing in Glencurragh in January. And Ava the potter had been very interested in what she was doing there as well, but had been quite cagey about her own background. Perhaps word had travelled that she was a journalist.

Perhaps they all thought she wanted to write about them.

Dumping her bag and coat on the sofa, Caroline headed up the spiral stairs to her bedroom to take her make-up off, mentally shaking her head. As if she was going to find a story in Glencurragh, with its fifty-nine residents and one bus a day. But perhaps at this time of year, anyone new was a diversion. When news got out that Rachel was here, no doubt the story would travel that she was secretly scouting for a Hollywood blockbuster.

They'd had a lovely evening, chatting. They were both emigrants, outsiders in the world they'd settled in, had experienced similar problems moving country. And coming home. That was the bit that you didn't realise when you left: fitting back in at home was hard too – you were still an outsider. Things changed and adapting back was strange.

Flicking on the electric blanket that Bronagh had thoughtfully put on her bed, Caroline bit her lip, thinking about Alfie's story. It sounded tragic – he'd clearly been an outsider too. Where had he called home? Rachel had met him and was sure he wasn't Irish, as so many homeless were – those who'd left in sheer desperation over the years but for whatever reason had failed to find their place.

Would she be able to discover his story? That type of digging was what Caroline did for a living, but Rachel had so little information to go on, it was hard to know where to start. As they'd dithered over whether crème brûlée was really a good idea for dessert, Rachel had explained that finding locations was her job and she loved the detective work involved, but this was a whole new challenge.

Switching on the light in the en suite bathroom, Caroline took off her glasses and found the hairband she used to hold her hair back when she took off her make-up. Looking closely at her face in the mirror, she could see dark circles were beginning to form under her violet eyes. Not a good look. The fresh air and her walks were doing her good while she was here, but she still needed to catch up on her sleep. Getting woken up by strange noises and lying awake half the night wasn't sitting well with her jet lag.

Finishing up, Caroline rinsed her face and pulled off her sweater as she headed for the wardrobe, kicking off her boots under the bed on the way. Folding the sweater onto one of the shelves, she undid her belt and slipped off her jeans, pulling open the drawer labelled *Lingerie* to find her nightshirt.

She could imagine Honoria pulling out a silk nightdress from this drawer, something simple and elegant. If Caroline had a wardrobe like this at home, it would definitely be a strong case for upgrading her nightwear. Hers might be DKNY but it was black jersey, and not the silver silk she could picture folded here. Pulling her nightshirt over her head, Caroline was suddenly paralysed by the scent of perfume, something sweet but old.

The same scent she thought she'd picked up in the lounge and the stables.

Frozen, she breathed in slowly. There was definitely something there, and it definitely wasn't hers.

Where had it come from?

A cold sweat broke out down her back. There had to be a rational explanation. Perhaps there was a scented sachet in the drawer.

Leaning forward, she slowly pulled it open wider. The only thing she could see was a drawer liner, the floral paper faded, sprigged with little posies of flowers. It didn't look as if it had been touched in years. Caroline sniffed the drawer but all she could smell was the wood. Had the liner been sprayed with Honoria's perfume? Fascinated, she drew the nightshirt to her nose again. The smell was dissipating but it reminded her of Chanel No. 5.

Reaching into the drawer, Caroline eased the paper away from the sides. It had been perfectly cut to size and fitted snugly, but it wasn't stuck down and once she'd peeled back one corner, it came up easily. Lifting it out, Caroline caught the scent, much stronger now; she was sure it was Chanel.

Suddenly she felt much closer to Honoria, as if she was somehow in the room. But this time it was a warm presence, not dark and chill like the feelings she'd had in the main house. Caroline shivered involuntarily and went to replace the liner, but there was something else in the drawer: another piece of paper that had been put in underneath the floral paper. Plain cream, it looked like a piece of writing paper folded in two. Caroline reached in for it gingerly, realising as she picked it up that it was a letter, the handwriting beautifully flowing in faded blue-black ink.

Her heart thumping, Caroline slipped the lining paper back into the drawer and took the letter to her bedside table, closer to the light. Excitement fluttered inside her as she sat on the edge of the bed, angling it closer to the bedside lamp. Despite the clear hand, it was hard to read, the ink smeared and faded by drops or splashes that had splayed out across several lines. Had it been left out in the rain?

She could make out an *H*, signed with a flourish in the bottom corner. Had it been written by Honoria?

Caroline felt her heart heave, suddenly sure that the splashes weren't raindrops, but tears. Had she cried so much over this draft that she'd had to write it again? Perhaps she'd kept this copy so she had a record, and could remember what she'd said.

Caroline's exploration of the stables earlier had proven exactly what Imogen had said about the furniture being full of the previous occupants' bits and bobs, apparently abandoned by Mr Smyth when he'd sold the house. Imogen had mentioned that the new owners who bought Hare's Landing in the early 1990s had had all the art deco furniture put in storage, furnishing the interior with stencilling, faux finishes, and sponge painting. It had taken Bronagh a full year to return the house to its period glory. Doing so much of the work herself, she hadn't had time to look in every drawer and cupboard.

But it seemed those drawers and cupboards still held secrets.

Caroline looked at the notepaper again. She was so tired she could hardly see the letters. She could pick out odd words, *heartbreak* being one that jumped out at her. She was desperate to read it, but she needed coffee first. She needed to be able to give it her full attention, and to hell with the possibility that caffeine might mess up her sleep cycle even more.

Carefully she folded the letter, feeling a wave of exhaustion and emotion threatening to overwhelm her. She'd had so little sleep in the past week it was all catching up on her now. But she couldn't leave the letter until the morning. She had to read it properly now and see if she could decipher the blurred-out words. Coffee was definitely the answer, and the light was better downstairs. Reaching for her robe, Caroline slipped it on and padded down the spiral staircase. Her legs felt leaden but another hour awake wasn't going to kill her.

Would this letter tell her what had happened to Honoria Smyth, or at least give her a clue? She knew exhaustion played tricks on your mind, but she was starting to feel as if she'd found Hare's Landing for a reason. She was a journalist, after all, and it felt as if Honoria Smyth had a story that needed uncovering. She'd felt bizarrely connected to her ever since she'd seen the portrait; it was almost as if Honoria was speaking to her, guiding her. And now this.

Caroline's theory about extremes of emotion staining a place – creating an energy that revealed itself across dimensions – suddenly seemed even more real. Honoria must have been deeply unhappy to have cried so much while she was writing this.

Putting the letter on the end of the L-shaped counter, Caroline went to fill the kettle.

And stopped.

Beside the kettle was a white feather. About an inch long and delicately curled at the end, it was resting on the counter beside the sink.

What did they say about white feathers? That they signified a visit from the other side? Frozen for a moment, confusion and surprise blending to root her to the spot, Caroline looked at it. It couldn't be a sign, could it?

Was Honoria trying to tell her something?

Caroline took a tentative step towards it and realised there was something in the sink. She'd left it empty when she went out – she'd only used it to fill the kettle and rinse a mug. Puzzled, Caroline looked more closely.

In the bottom of the sink was an old plate, the edges fluted, the pattern a soft rose pink like a willow pattern, but the design showed a country house set in a rural landscape. Or it would have done, if it hadn't been broken right across the middle.

And lying across the two broken halves of the plate was a carving knife, its cutting edge covered in something red.

Caroline froze, sweat breaking out down her back as every hair on her body stood up.

What the hell?

Chapter 25

RACHEL HAD ALREADY had breakfast in bed and taken Jasper for a long walk by the time Caroline appeared the next morning. The fire had been lit while they were out and Jasper was making the most of the heat as Rachel looked through the Sunday papers, spread over the coffee table. Hearing footsteps, she looked up.

'My goodness, you look exhausted, didn't you sleep?'

Rachel tried to keep the surprise out of her voice, but the dark circles under Caroline's eyes and the strain on her face were undeniable. Caroline peeled off her jacket and collapsed on the sofa opposite Rachel.

'Eventually. I …' Caroline stopped. 'I found something last night when I got back to the Boathouse and it spooked me a bit.'

'What?'

She screwed up her face for a second before replying.

'You remember I told you all the furniture from the original house is in storage, and Imogen said they keep finding things in drawers? Well, I have this gorgeous wardrobe in my bedroom.'

'The one with the *H* on it?'

'Exactly. It's got these adorable ivory labels on the drawers and shelves so you know where to put your gloves and hats.'

'Really? I had to get one of those built for a set. I'd love to see it.'

'Come down and look … But …' Caroline paused. 'There's more …'

She reached for her shopper, pulling out a leather-bound diary and flipping open the pages. Inside Rachel could see a folded letter, the notepaper a thick cream vellum.

'What is it?'

'I think it's a letter from Honoria Smyth. Look – it's signed "H". It was under the lining paper of the lingerie drawer, as if it had been hidden.'

'Let's see.'

Rachel stood up and, pulling up the sleeves of her black roll neck sweater, moved around the coffee table to sit next to Caroline as she continued.

'It's really hard to read. Her writing was beautiful but I think she must have been crying when she wrote it.' Caroline smoothed the letter out on the table. 'See, these splodges look like tears to me.'

Rachel leaned over to read it. It was addressed to 'My Darling D—'. Rachel glanced at Caroline and pulled an OMG face that made Caroline smile. 'Who could "D" be? Diarmuid? Daniel?' Before Caroline could answer, she continued reading out loud. '"I love you so much and I know this is going to come as a terrible shock. It doesn't change anything; I need you in my life. I don't know how to tell you but the doctor in London …"' The next few lines were impossible to read, obliterated by tears. Rachel looked up from the page. 'Do you think she was pregnant?'

'That's exactly what I thought.' Caroline paused. 'But that's not all …' Rachel lifted her eyebrows at the seriousness of Caroline's tone as she continued. 'I wanted to read it in a good light and I was wrecked, so I came down to make coffee. And … This sounds so mad in the cold light of day, but there was a white feather on the counter.'

Rachel nodded slowly; she knew all about the significance of white feathers being interpreted by many as a sign from beyond the grave.

'And …'

'Go on.'

'When I was in the stables the other day I found a lovely set of china, and this picture jumped into my head of Honoria Smyth sitting on the terrace in the middle of the summer, having tea. It was so strong. The whole set was filthy, but it had a design like a willow pattern, just in pink.' Caroline took a breath. 'I saw the feather, and then I realised one of the plates from the set was in the sink. It was broken right through the middle, through the country house scene in the centre. It looked a lot like Hare's Landing. And there was a carving knife lying across it.'

Rachel pulled a face, perplexed. 'What on earth would someone leave that in the sink for?'

Caroline opened her eyes wide. 'I've no idea. The knife must have been used to cut a Swiss roll or something, there was jam smeared along the cutting edge.' She put her hand to her chest unconsciously. 'I almost died right there. I thought it was blood on the knife. That's what it looked like – it was only when I got closer I realised it was jam.'

Rachel sat back in her seat and looked at Caroline, mystified.

'I know, it doesn't make sense. But it felt like some sort of warning. And with the feather, maybe a warning from Honoria. Does that sound totally bonkers?'

'It would sound utterly mad if I hadn't been sitting with you here last night when that door banged. I didn't say it, but it was like someone was listening to us talk about her and wanted to make their presence felt.'

Caroline shook her head. 'She's done that all right. I think this letter is the key to her story. If she was pregnant she couldn't have gone to a doctor around here in case news leaked out. Even someone seeing her go to the surgery could have put two and two together, and if it was her lover's and she didn't want to keep it ...'

'When do you think it was written?'

Caroline shrugged. 'There's no date but presumably she wouldn't have left it there for any length of time in case someone found it, so I'm guessing right before she took her life.'

Rachel scanned the next few lines, reading aloud:

'"These years have been the happiest of my life. I love you so deeply that sometimes I can hardly breathe. You have shown me so much about myself, brought me to places I had never been before ..."'

Rachel raised her eyebrows again and glanced at Caroline as she continued.

'"We need to talk about it all, I know, but I didn't know how to tell you. I love you so much, my darling, I never want to be apart from you." Jeepers, I can't read the next bit, it's all splotched.'

'I know. She was pouring out her soul.'

'Why do you think she kept it?'

'So she could read it again and remember what she'd said? She knew what the missing words were, but it might have been hard to remember as she was so emotional. I presume she gave whoever it was meant for a legible version. These days we do everything on a computer and write and rewrite to get the tone right. Perhaps it was something she needed to get right – she was an author, she would have been used to drafting and redrafting. But it's clearly so personal it's not the sort of thing you'd type.'

'Something must have been really wrong, though, for her to take her own life. Perhaps she was pregnant and she wanted to leave her husband and have the baby, but its father, whoever D was, didn't want it – or her?'

Caroline pulled a face. 'Maybe we can find out more about her online. Imogen said that Mrs Travers was her housekeeper, that she came to work here when Honoria got married, but she's so spiky I don't really want to ask her anything yet.'

'If she knew anything, she'd probably keep it to herself anyway. She wouldn't want anything said about an employer who left her a house – that would suggest they had a very strong bond.'

'Will we head down to the village now? We can get coffee in the pub, and we can use their Wi-Fi. After last night I could do with getting out of here for a few hours.'

Chapter 26

'SORRY IT'S NOT a bit more comfortable.' Rachel flipped her seat forward for Jasper to get into the back of the Land Rover and jumped in herself. 'I walk to the office and Hunter uses it for all his equipment – it's a bit of a workhorse. Functionality is more important than glamour.'

'It's grand. That taxi driver the hotel use asks so many goddamn questions. The only thing I haven't told him is my bra size.'

'People around here do seem to have a natural curiosity. Imogen was trying to find out all about me this morning. I told her I was tracing my family tree and looking for a cousin.'

'Alfie?'

'Exactly. I didn't want to get into the detail of Hunter's documentary or everything else that has been happening. And people go a bit odd when they know you work in film or TV.'

Heading into Glencurragh, Rachel pulled up outside the brightly painted pub and looked down the hill. Deserted except for parked cars, it was the narrowest main street she'd ever seen, and seemed to be almost entirely residential, brightly coloured cottages fronting directly onto the road. Outside the front door of the Spaniard pub, a pair of dog bowls indicated that Jasper would be welcome. They didn't need to look further.

Inside the bar was busier than they'd expected, the low ceiling beams covered in sporting badges and ancient memorabilia. Neither of them had any idea what they were, but the pub had Wi-Fi and the coffee, it turned out, was surprisingly good. They could feel the locals assessing them as they found a corner table. Jasper fell onto the tiled floor with a sigh, obviously not impressed with this interruption to what he'd thought would be another walk.

Rachel opened her email to see several messages from Hunter. She scrolled back through them, smiling. His mother had arrived and things were not to her liking. She'd worked at the London Hospital for years, retiring back to Jamaica to look after her own mother. Rachel could imagine she'd be running the ward before she left. She sent him back an email explaining the lack of connectivity and that she hadn't got anywhere with Alfie yet, but that she'd met Caroline and was going to see if she could find out if he'd visited the area for a concert. Perhaps he *had* been a professional musician.

As she was typing, over the top of her laptop, Rachel could see Caroline chewing the end of a pen.

'Found anything?'

'Not as much as you'd expect. The archive for the local paper has been digitised and there's an article from June 1990, but I can only see half of it. Something about mourners filling the church. The grab on Google has her name and the name of the church in it, so it has to be her funeral.'

'The church on the hill that we could see when we came in?'

Caroline put the pen down. 'I think so. There's a photo of a hearse filled with flowers. That must be it.'

'She was lucky they let her be buried in Church ground in 1990.' Rachel did a quick search, keeping her voice down. 'Suicide was only decriminalised in 1993.'

Caroline scanned her screen. 'It's a Protestant church, that probably helped.'

Rachel grimaced. 'Imogen might be able to confirm the date. You said she was writing a history of the house? We could go up to the church and see if we can find her gravestone. I'm not sure that will tell us anything more about the actual circumstances, though. Whatever happened, it's such a tragic ending.'

Caroline eyed her. 'I'm not sure I'm up for visiting the graveyard after last night, but you're right. We need to talk to people. There's only so much Google can tell you. Let's look for Alfie next, although I think we'll have the same problem.' She tapped her keyboard and wrinkled up her nose as the results appeared on her screen. 'I'm getting lots of venues and concerts, but no hits on an Alfred who plays the violin.' Caroline spun the screen around for Rachel to look at.

'We need one more piece of information – anything, his age, a date.' Rachel shook her head. 'I did have a feeling I'd hit a wall. When Hunter remembered he'd talked about Hare's Landing, he was convinced we'd be able to find out more about Alfie's background.' She drank the rest of her coffee. 'Let's take Jasper for his walk and we can call into the pottery on the way. Didn't you say it's down on the quay?'

Outside it was already getting dusky. Rachel wrapped her bright pink scarf around her neck again, thankful she'd brought her skiing jacket. There was a distinct chill, the air heavy with the scent of rain.

'It's this way.'

Her hands in the pockets of her parka and a charcoal beanie hat pulled down over her ears, Caroline started walking down the hill, Jasper keeping pace between them. A few minutes later they reached Mahony's shop. Rachel stopped at the window to look at the display, a muddle of the practical and the decorative – an alarm clock beside a dustpan and brush, behind them framed prints of Glencurragh's main street.

'Look at these photos, they go back years.'

Caroline pulled her hat down against a cold blast of air that had found its way up from the sea.

'Imogen said the owner, John Francis, has been documenting the locality forever. He's got a dark room out the back. This is where I brought that film I found. I don't know where you'd get it developed nowadays, everything's digital. Hopefully he's had a chance to look at it. I wonder if he knows anything about Honoria Smyth – will we ask?' She looked at Jasper. 'Is he okay outside? Do you need to tie him to something?'

'No, he'll be fine, won't you, Jasp? We'll only be a minute.' Rachel frowned. 'Let's ask Mr Mahony about Alfie too – nothing ventured.'

A voice greeted them as they pushed open the shop door.

'Good afternoon, ladies, what can I do you for? Oh, 'tis you, young lady. I've got those pictures developed. There was a lovely one of the house. I blew it up like you asked. It's all ready to go if you want to take it back with yous.' He turned away from the counter to go into a back room. 'And I've got the rest here for you too – Bronagh might want another one to display. I'll hang on to the negatives and she can ring me if she wants more copies or any more of them enlarged. They'll look good around the place. Will you tell her I did this one in black and white because the colour had deteriorated over the years. It's nice and crisp now, sure it is.'

'Brilliant, thanks so much. Can we get it on the way back up? We're just going for a walk.'

'You'd want to be quick, there's a storm brewing – it'll be here before it gets full dark. I've got it all ready for you. I close at five on a Sunday, mind.'

Rachel and Caroline exchanged glances, getting the message very clearly that he didn't want to have to wait for them. Caroline reached into her shopper for her wallet.

'Don't worry, we'll take it with us. If you can wrap it up?'

'Look, I have it all ready to go, I've brown paper to wrap it in, the lot. And here's the other pictures.'

Caroline looked for her credit card as he put the framed print on the counter. It was almost too dark to see it properly in the store, but it was a shot of two people standing outside the porch with the two hares standing proud in front. Exactly what she had been hoping for. The shopkeeper put a bulky envelope on the counter and tore off a length of brown paper from somewhere under it to wrap the framed print in. As he reached for the Sellotape, Caroline glanced at Rachel.

'We were wondering if you could help with something else. My friend here is over from London, she's looking to trace some family. There was a violinist she thinks played around here. He was English. He became known as Alfie Bows but she thinks his name was Alfred.'

The shopkeeper looked at them blankly. 'Don't know him, I'm afraid. There's a lot of English who come here to live, and the place is full in the summer. I don't rightly remember a violinist though – when would it have been?'

Feeling sheepish, Rachel took a step forward, twisting her ring as she spoke.

'About thirty years ago, maybe longer?'

''Tis a straw in a haystack you'd be looking for now. Do you know anything else about him?'

Rachel wrinkled her nose and shook her head.

'Well, good luck to you is all I can say. But keep asking, you never know who might remember.'

As Rachel followed Caroline out of the shop, she was shaking her head. They both knew he was right. Caroline looked back at her as she picked up Jasper's lead.

'I think you nailed it with "long shot". Come on, if we get down to the pottery quickly, Jasper can have his run back at the hotel before it rains.'

Caroline bent down to give Jasper a tickle. Rachel sighed. She was right.

'Let's put that picture in the Landie and drive down. Those clouds are moving fast, they look really angry.'

*

Pulling up outside the pottery, Rachel looked out of the windscreen, glad she'd been out with Jasper earlier in the day. John Francis Mahony might not have known anything about Alfie, but he was right about the weather closing in.

'Do you want to run in and I'll wait with Jasp?' Rachel picked up her phone from the slot beside the gearstick, checking the signal strength. 'I should try to call Hunter and see how he is while I can.'

'Grand, I won't be long. I'll ask about us doing another workshop together and ask her about Alfie too. You never know.'

As Caroline slammed the door, Rachel looked back at her phone. She had a tiny signal. Glancing back at Jasper, she rang Hunter's number. He answered immediately.

'Hello, stranger, I was starting to think you'd found a handsome Irishman and left me.'

Rachel laughed, relieved to hear him joking; it was a sure sign he was on the mend.

'How's it going?'

'Tough. Everything bloody hurts, there's a guy here who talks in his sleep all the fucking time – and my mother's arrived.'

'At least the food will improve with her in situ. Where's she staying?'

'She didn't like any of the hotels you suggested so she's staying with my cousin for a few days.'

'But they fought like cats the last time she was there. Wasn't that why I spent ages looking for a hotel for her?'

'Yes. It was. But you know Darlene MacKenzie, she's nothing if not unpredictable. How are you doing? Anything on Alfie? I've been looking at the Hare's Landing website. I think I'm going to need a holiday to recuperate, it looks pretty stunning.'

'It's gorgeous. Jasper loves it, he's getting in huge walks. There's no one else staying apart from a journalist called Caroline Kelly. She's from New York. She's lovely. It seems Alfie's adventures aren't the only mystery around here. She found this incredible love letter hidden in her wardrobe and we think the house is haunted.'

'Haunted? Good God.' He started to laugh but it sounded more like a cough as he tried to catch his breath. 'Talking of letters, Tony called. He's got all our post at the marina office. I'm going to get Mum to pick it up in case there's anything from the insurance company. I'd presume they'd email but all we need is for them to send out an assessor when neither of us are there.'

'Very true. I don't think I'll be here too much longer—'

He interrupted her. 'Stay for a few more days. Zack's getting some extra security put on the barge, you're better off there until the police can tell us something about all this. Does the hotel have booking records or visitors' books or something you can check for Alfie?'

Rachel glanced at the door of the pottery to see if Caroline was coming.

'It's under new ownership. Caroline told me it was a hotel before, but not for long, that it was a private house before then.'

There was a pause at the end as if he was thinking.

'So, where do we look? Maybe he knew the original owners. We need to talk to them – can you get details? It'll be on the land registry.'

Rachel rolled her eyes to herself; he made it sound so easy.

'There's a woman here who's been the housekeeper for years. I'll ask her – if anyone will remember him, it's someone like her.'

'Perfect. Oh Christ, I can hear Mum arriving. I love you, babes. Find what you can out about Alfie and try not to enjoy it too much without me.'

Rachel laughed as he blew noisy kisses down the phone.

She ended the call just as Caroline came out of the potter's studio door. Behind her, a woman wearing an apron lingered in the doorway, leaning on the door jamb, her arms folded. Holding something wrapped in newspaper, Caroline pulled the door open and climbed in. She wasn't smiling as she glanced back at the woman in the doorway nervously.

'Did it fire okay?'

'Yes … Yes it did.'

Something was wrong. Rachel wasn't sure what, but she put the Land Rover in reverse and pulled back to do a three-point turn out of the yard. She flicked the headlights on full and headed slowly up the narrow lane that joined the quay area with the main street. It was barely wide enough for one car, the road here bordered by stone walls made from dark grey flat stones. *Famine walls*. Rachel wasn't sure if they were, but they reminded her of the ones around an estate near home where the landowner, like some of the few good landlords during the Irish famine, had kept his tenants fed and their dignity intact by employing them to build walls around his land.

'What's up? Did something go wrong with the design?'

'No, not that, not that at all. Ava just asked me straight out why I was here. I explained there was a court case in New York and I needed a vacation. I didn't want to go into too much detail. She was behaving really strangely. I didn't get a chance to ask about Alfie or us doing a workshop – sorry.'

Rachel glanced across at her. Caroline was biting her lip, her face creased in a frown.

'Tell me more.'

'When I was down here the other day, she wouldn't tell me anything about herself, she was really cagey and nervous. I thought that was a bit weird at the time, but I was concentrating on making my tiles. Plus she's an artist, she works on her own – I thought perhaps she wasn't great at meeting new people or something.' Caroline sighed. 'But it turns out, she thought I was there to do some sort of tabloid story on her sister's disappearance.'

Rachel glanced across at her, her face creased in a frown. 'What happened to her sister?'

'That's it – nobody really knows. She literally disappeared thirty years ago. Ava thinks she's somewhere in America, she's had a couple of postcards from her. Why she went and where to is a mystery. But it happened in June 1990.'

Chapter 27

'ARE YOU SERIOUS?' Frowning, Rachel did a double take. 'Her sister went missing around the same date you found that reference to Honoria Smyth's funeral?'

Caroline put her hand to her forehead. 'Honoria was July. But it's *so* weird – I was reading about these teenagers disappearing in the paper when I first arrived. A boy disappeared at the same time. Apparently his birthday is in January and his family is launching an anniversary appeal to get some publicity. Ava is furious, she says Meg just ran away, she doesn't want the whole thing dragged up again, that it looks bad for the family.'

'But the press is linking their disappearances?'

'They're trying to. But Ava says she had postcards from Meg – one a few months after she vanished that was sent from London, and one six months later from New York. She says there's no mystery. Meg just hasn't told Ava where she is or been in touch properly, but she's reached out. Ava's father brought them up on his own and he was an alcoholic apparently, so she really didn't have much to stay for.'

'They weren't close as sisters then?'

Caroline's forehead puckered. 'Obviously not. You'd think they would have been in those circumstances, but families are strange things. Ava reckons Meg was always headstrong and must have got an offer she couldn't resist. She reckons Meg went to London, and by the time she got there it was too late to explain where she was – half the country was looking for her – so she just kept going.'

'Maybe she was running from something or someone, too.'

'That's what I thought. But that's why Ava was so edgy yesterday – she thought I'd booked in to try to get information out of her. Apparently there was a bit of a local smear campaign when Meg vanished because of some gossip about her seeing an older man. Ava thought I was looking to rake all of that up.'

Rachel switched down a gear. 'Did you tell her you worked for the paper though, when you booked the course?'

'Nope. She must have found out from someone else and put two and two together to make five. I suppose I'd only just arrived when I rang to book the workshop. Perhaps that fed into her suspicions.'

'Sounds to me like you're the major topic of conversation in the village. Obviously not much happens around here.'

Caroline smirked. 'We probably both are. Did you use your work email to book in?'

Rachel shook her head. 'Nope, Hunter made the booking. He would have used his Gmail. He doesn't use his work email for anything for precisely this reason. How old was Ava's sister when she disappeared?'

'Seventeen.'

Rachel shivered. 'That must have been horrible, until they heard from her.'

She bit her lip, thinking about Hunter and Alfie.

Had someone put out a missing person's report for him when he became homeless? How could she check that when she wasn't even sure of his full name?

156

'I know.' Caroline adjusted her glasses as she continued. 'I think I was so surprised when she told me, that she believed I didn't know anything about the case. She opened up a bit then. She said that even though she knows Meg's okay somewhere, she doesn't know anything about her life. It's like a bereavement but the person's still alive.'

'Christ, and this place looks so idyllic. You don't have to go far below the surface and it's *all* bloody dark.'

'That's life though, isn't it? Look at your Alfie friend. From what he said to Hunter, it sounds like something happened to him that pushed him right over the edge. It has to have been a pretty big thing to make him totally drop out of society.'

'I know. I was wondering if it could have been something to do with Honoria's death. Nuts, I know, when I've really no idea when he was here – it could have been ten years later. I don't even know how old he was.' Rachel changed gear to crawl around a tight corner. 'But whatever about the chances of Alfie being here when Honoria Smyth lived at Hare's Landing, it is a bit odd that this girl goes missing and Honoria kills herself around the same time. What was the girl's name again?'

'Meg – Meg Cassidy. I didn't connect Ava's surname with the newspaper article or I might have twigged sooner.'

'You're on holiday. It's okay to switch off occasionally, you know.'

Caroline glanced at her. 'That's very kind but I'm a crime journalist, the investigative kind.' She shook her head. 'On vacation or not, I'm supposed to see connections like that.' As Caroline was speaking it began to spit. 'That store guy was right about the storm – this must be the start of it.'

Rachel put on the wipers and glanced over to Caroline.

'So what are you going to do? Can you do anything to help separate the two cases? Do a profile on Meg maybe, or something focusing on the lad?'

'I don't know who I'd do it *for*. If Meg *is* in America, there could be a bit of a story, but nobody's going to be interested in the boy in New York – people go missing all the time there. His family are from Ross Haven, she said. They've got RTÉ coming to film for *Crime Call* – they think a reconstruction might jog someone's memory. The papers here will pick it up from there, which is good for his family and the story, but that's the thing Ava's worried about. And she thought I was going to try and sensationalise the whole thing and scoop RTÉ.'

'Why would the *New York Messenger* want to scoop RTÉ? Isn't there enough crime in New York to keep you busy?' Rachel couldn't keep the disbelief out of her voice.

'I know. I don't get it either but like you say, once people get something arseways everything you say feeds into whatever nonsense they've come up with.'

'True.' Rachel pulled out onto the main road, flicking the wipers up a notch. 'It would be good to know a bit more about them, though – Honoria and Meg, I mean. And this lad – do you think they could be connected, that they knew each other?'

'Maybe, but Meg disappeared in Dublin – Ava said she'd gone up to Bewley's for an interview in the restaurant.' She glanced out of the window, saying half to herself, 'It's amazing more people didn't disappear before mobile phones were invented.' Snapping back to the conversation, she continued. 'Apparently she called home to say she'd arrived in Dublin. She was planning to stay with a relative. And she got to the interview all right, and then went to some of the shops on Grafton Street, but that's the last time she was seen. Everyone thought something dreadful had happened but a few months later Ava got a postcard from London from her. She has it there in the studio – both of Meg's cards, in fact, pinned to a noticeboard.'

'So that mystery's not a mystery?' Rachel raised an eyebrow. 'That's probably a good thing. So all we've got to worry about now is finding out what happened to Alfie and why you're being haunted.'

Caroline looked across at her, half smiling, shaking her head.

'I am *not* being haunted. It's to do with energy lines or something. There's always an explanation for these things.'

Keeping her eyes on the road, Rachel opened them wide in disbelief.

'You think?'

*

It didn't take Rachel long to get back to Hare's Landing – she was definitely getting the hang of the roads here. After the first time, when she'd almost missed the turn to the main hotel and followed the winding lane that ended in the stable yard instead, she hadn't made that mistake again. Now, although it was dark, driving down the lane into the estate was no longer quite so terrifying.

As they got out of the Land Rover, the wind was starting to pick up, driving the now heavy freezing rain down their necks. Even Jasper seemed happy to be inside in the warm, his walk forgotten. He shot into the hall as soon as Caroline pushed open the door.

'I wonder if I can leave the Landie there tonight. I don't fancy walking back from the stables in this weather.' She shook the raindrops from the shoulders of her jacket. 'I was planning to take Jasp to investigate that castle thing too, but I think we'll have to wait.' Rachel unwound her scarf. 'Do you want to get a drink before dinner or go back to the Boathouse for a bit?'

'It's not so much want a drink, as need it – and seriously, I'm not going back outside until the last possible minute.' As if to underline Caroline's words, a gust of wind sent rain against the windows like spit shot. 'Jeez, it's getting worse.' She glanced out of the porch door into the darkness. 'Let's give Bronagh her picture and these photos and see if she knows anything about Honoria Smyth. I'm still nervous about asking Mrs Travers in case she gets upset, but if Bronagh doesn't know anything, we might have to.'

Rachel unzipped her jacket, slipping it off.

'You know Mrs Travers probably thinks you're here investigating Honoria's death, that's why she's so spiky. Perhaps she thinks you want to befriend her to extract some juicy gossip.'

'That would actually explain a lot. Perhaps she was the one who told Ava I worked for the paper. Someone here must have done, because no one else has seen my email address.'

Rachel leaned back thoughtfully on the reception desk, watching Jasper snuffle around the fireplace, while Caroline reached for the bell on the reception counter. According to the waiting room clock behind the desk, it was almost six o'clock.

A few minutes later she heard heels on the wooden floor in the corridor leading to the back of the hotel. Bronagh appeared around the corner, a clipboard in her hand.

'Oh, I'm sorry, were you waiting long? It's Imogen's day off and I'm making an inventory of the cellar, it's taking forever.'

Caroline lifted the framed photo from where she'd rested it on the reception desk.

'Surprise for you. I found some film in a drawer in the stables the other day. Imogen told me I could get it developed at the store and Mr Mahony framed it. I collected it this afternoon. I asked him to see if there was a picture of the house.'

Bronagh put the clipboard down on the counter.

'Wow, that's amazing, thank you. There's just so much in the stables, I don't think I'll ever get through it all.' Taking the picture and peeling back the brown paper, she held the frame out at arm's length. Rachel and Caroline peered over her shoulder, seeing the image clearly for the first time. 'This will be fantastic over the fireplace here in the hallway. It looks almost vintage in black and white.'

It was a photograph of the house itself, Hare's Landing, in what looked to be a warm and sunny summer. A pair of teenage boys stood casually in front of the open front door, leaning on the statues of the hares positioned exactly as they were now, on the edge of the drive. The boys were smiling, two good-looking lads in T-shirts and shorts. One of them was wearing glasses.

'I wasn't sure there'd be anything retrievable on the film when I found it. When do you think it was taken?'

Bronagh wrinkled her nose. 'Hard to tell, they look a bit generic teenager, but their haircuts are definitely 80s or 90s, don't you think? That doesn't exactly narrow it down though.'

Rachel looked hard at the photo. 'That holly bush next to the door doesn't look very big, it's huge now. Maybe if we find out how long that takes to grow it will give us a better clue?'

Caroline leaned in to take a look. 'Holly's slow growing, isn't it?'

Rachel shrugged. 'I don't know anything about plants, I've only ever had a window box.'

'I wonder who they are?' Bronagh held the picture up, experimenting to see how it would look over the fireplace. 'With a bit of luck, Mrs Travers will know. We'll see what she thinks in the morning. Let's see what's in these other photos and if there are any more people in them. I'm fascinated by the history of this place. I've loved it since I was a child – sometimes when I'm here on my own I feel like the house is talking to me.'

Rachel exchanged a glance with Caroline, her eyes wide. Rachel knew they were both thinking the same thing:

Perhaps it wasn't the house trying to talk to her.

Chapter 28

THE FIRE WAS blazing in the lounge when they walked in; the room was filled with the delicate sound of classical music. Caroline put her head on one side, listening to it. Was it Mozart? She wasn't sure. She must remember to ask what the CD was, it was so beautiful.

While they'd been talking in the hall, Jasper had got bored and stationed himself almost on the hearthstone, stretched out his full length. Arriving ahead of Bronagh and Rachel, Caroline laughed when she saw him, pointing to him as she sat down on the end of the sofa closest to the fire.

'He's going to hate leaving here.'

'Do you have a fire at home?' Bronagh turned to Rachel as she leaned the picture frame against the coffee table.

'We've a stove but we live on a houseboat. It's really well insulated but it doesn't exactly have the space you have here.'

'A houseboat? Goodness.' Bronagh put the envelope of photographs down on the table. 'Is it moored in the same place all the time, or do you move it about?'

Caroline plumped the cushion behind her. 'That's like a barge, right?'

Sitting down opposite her on the other sofa, Rachel nodded.

'It *is* a barge, actually. It used to move coal through the canals, but Hunter bought it and converted it. It's bigger than you'd think, about sixty feet long and sixteen wide.'

'Sounds bigger than my apartment.'

Rachel reached down to tickle Jasper. 'But that's New York – we're in Limehouse Basin near Rotherhithe. We keep it moored in the marina. We could move it about but it's a bit of a faff, to be honest.'

'Can I get you a drink, ladies?' While they'd been speaking Bronagh had gone behind the bar. 'How about a hot whiskey for the night that's in it? On the house – I know we're thin on the ground in terms of staff at the moment.'

'Sounds lovely, and don't worry, Conor is a genius in the kitchen and the fire's always lit, so we have everything we need.'

'Thank you.' Bronagh said it as if she meant it. 'Conor and Imogen are fantastic. My husband's using the quiet period to go and see his mother. It's preferable to her coming here.'

Rachel laughed at the expression on her face.

'I know that feeling.'

Bronagh chuckled. 'Right, kettle's boiled, Jameson or Powers?'

*

Sitting down, warming their hands on their glasses, Bronagh opened the envelope of photographs, spreading them out over the coffee table so they could all see them. Caroline felt a frisson of excitement, wondering when they had been taken, and whether they would tell them anything more about Honoria Smyth.

The photographs were colour, although it looked like the deterioration that had led to the framed photo being printed in black and white had affected these too. There were lots of shots of the gardens – individual flowers and bits of stonework, the colours faded, with a magenta tinge.

'Look, you can see a car in this one – and part of the licence plate. It's not in the format that's used now, is it? When did they change?' Caroline looked over to Bronagh, her eyebrows raised.

'Years ago – late nineties? I can't remember to be honest. The house was first sold in 1992, according to the deeds – I've a feeling these must be from before then. Honoria Smyth loved the garden, according to Mrs Travers. She organised all the planting, so perhaps she took these?'

Picking up the framed picture, Caroline adjusted her glasses and leaned forward, angling it into the light from the chandelier to look at the two boys again.

'Maybe one of these guys is Honoria's son. I think Mrs Travers said his name was Sheridan. It stuck in my head because it's so American.'

As she spoke, the fire spluttered and flared and Jasper looked up sharply, making a whimpery noise in the back of his throat as if someone was disturbing him. Caroline passed Rachel the picture quickly, her eyes wide.

Taking it from her, Rachel looked at the figures in the image.

'That's a tour T-shirt – the Who's twenty-fifth anniversary tour. The Union Jack in the middle is so distinctive, and the band were on the British posters and shirts but not on the American ones.' Rachel put her finger on the glass, pointing to the boy wearing glasses. 'That tour was in 1989, my boss is mad about them, he's got a wall full of their album covers and tour posters in his office. Their last gig in the UK was the Royal Albert Hall, in October I think. Red Fox did an ad campaign for a vintage store in Camden using the images.' She wrinkled her nose, thinking. 'So perhaps this *is* the summer of 1990? The print looks quite crisp, not faded by washing and years old.'

Bronagh reached for the envelope of photographs.

'Mrs Travers will know for sure if that's Sheridan Smyth.' She leafed through them. 'Here are some people – and this must be Honoria. Oh, there are two pictures.' Bronagh held out a photograph of a pretty blonde woman sitting at a table on the terrace, a cup of tea in her hand. She glanced up at the portrait above them to check. 'She looks just like her painting.'

'Oh, can I see?'

Caroline couldn't keep the excitement out of her voice. She could feel an energy in the room; perhaps it was her own anticipation, but it was making her skin tingle.

Bronagh handed her the photos. Caroline felt her stomach hollow as she looked at the first photograph. Honoria was laughing, a book open on the table beside her, a pretty teacup in her hand. It was hard to see the colour but it looked distinctly like one of the cups from the pink set she'd seen in the stables. A plate from which had wound up in her sink.

Caroline passed the photograph to Rachel wordlessly and looked at the next one. It showed the same blonde woman, sunglasses holding her hair back, leaning on one of the hares outside the front door of the house, obviously laughing at whoever was taking the photo. She was wearing a green sundress with some sort of flower pattern – it was hard to see. The deterioration of the film gave it a surreal orange glow but she looked like she was wearing red lipstick. *Perhaps that was her signature colour.* In her hand she held a book, her finger marking her page. She was beautiful, high cheekbones setting off a warm smile, and she radiated happiness.

Caroline passed the second photo across to Rachel, meeting her eye. Rachel cleared her throat.

'Imogen told us what happened. She doesn't look like someone on the edge of taking their own life, here.'

Bronagh looked thoughtful as she leafed through more pictures.

'Perhaps this was taken a long time before it happened. You know how film used to stay in a camera for ages if it wasn't used up – we've no way of telling.'

'At least she was happy here. That's good to know.' Caroline drew a shaky breath. 'After I found the film, I found a letter that I think might be from her, under the lining paper in my wardrobe. I brought it up to show you earlier, but then we went into the village.'

She reached for her bag, pulling out her diary and passing Bronagh the letter. Bronagh's eyebrows rose at the splotches.

'This place never stops throwing up surprises.' She frowned as she read. 'It sounds like she was pregnant.'

Rachel took a sip of her whiskey. 'That's what we thought. We wondered if this rumour of her affair with the gardener was true, but that maybe he left her when she told him. She could have had a termination in London, but perhaps she wanted to keep it.'

Bronagh took a deep breath. 'That's so sad. There are so many rumours about her. I don't know if any of them are true. Some people say he left her and that's why she killed herself, and others say he found her and then killed himself. I think it's more likely he left the property than jumped off the cliff, but who knows? If she was pregnant it maybe explains it a bit. Mrs Travers won't say a word about it, but perhaps this is why.'

Caroline looked thoughtful. 'But there would have been a body found, if he killed himself too, surely?'

'It depends. The estuary has a really strong tide – sometimes a body can be washed straight out to sea.'

'And the Atlantic's pretty big.'

'Exactly. It's all about timing and water temperature apparently – but people don't tend to be thinking about that when they go in.' Bronagh picked up another photograph. 'Nobody seems to know what happened, to be honest, it's all speculation. Some people say he was the handyman or gardener, and some the chauffeur, and there are other rumours he was dealing drugs. There's a lot of illegal activity along the coast here. It's so rugged and isolated it's extremely difficult to police.' She shook her head. 'Leo reckons the rumours about the place being haunted are to do with people seeing lights at night when drugs were being landed. And no doubt those sorts of rumours help keep people away too. Apart from the odd draught and doors slamming, I've never felt that there was anything *really* supernatural here.'

The way she said it made Caroline doubt she was being completely candid with them. After all, they were paying guests, and they were both here on their own. Finding out there was anything majorly spooky going on could send them home.

'What about her son, Sheridan – what happened to him?'

'Mrs Travers said something about him being a judge in London. His father was a barrister as far as I know, he must have followed him into the law. She's still in touch with him though.'

Rachel gave Jasper a tickle, her voice thoughtful. 'If we can find a photo of him, we might be able to tell if he's one of the boys in the picture.'

'Mrs Travers will know, we can see what she thinks tomorrow.' Bronagh continued to leaf through the photos. 'Look – there are some more of the boys. They're very blurry, looks like they were messing about with the camera.'

'I wonder if there's more film kicking about the place.' Caroline looked over at the writing desk in the corner of the room.

'There could be in the stables, I really don't know what's in there. That desk was full of old fountain pens and glasses. I've got a big box of stuff in my office that one day when everything is up and running, I'll have a look through. No more letters I'm afraid, though. This is a real find.'

Rachel sighed. 'It's utterly tragic, isn't it? She's so beautiful and she seemed to have everything.'

Chapter 29

CAROLINE HAD TO battle the wind back to the Boathouse that night. It was coming straight off the sea, the rain cutting into her face like glass. Falling into the shelter of the wall, she rooted for the key, hauling it out of her pocket and scrambling through the front door. Slamming it closed behind her, she heaved a sigh; the atmospheric heating – or whatever Conor had called it – was working beautifully and inside it was wonderfully snug. It was past nine now, according to the digital readout on the oven, and she was tired but her mind was racing with everything they'd talked about earlier.

A gust of wind hit the huge glass windows at the end of the open-plan room – windows that would once have been the boathouse doors. Caroline had a feeling she'd have trouble sleeping tonight. The weather was brutal now and this was only the start; another storm was due tomorrow. *But you didn't come to West Cork in January for the weather.* Shaking the raindrops from her hair, she slipped off her coat and looked apprehensively at the sink. *No surprises tonight, thank God.*

About to reach over to put the kettle on, she thought better of it and opened the fridge instead. She pulled out a fresh bottle of wine that had been left while she was out. Conor was really looking after her. The hot whiskey had been very welcome this evening, and now she fancied sitting in front of the fire with a chilled glass of white and going over Honoria's letter again. Seeing her photograph had made it all the more personal.

The fire had been laid by whoever had filled the fridge – Conor or Imogen, Caroline was sure – and she only had to pop in a firelighter and it was burning away merrily. Switching off the lights so only the firelight lit the room, she stood looking out of the door-shaped window at the end of the living room, nursing her wine. It was really wild, the estuary whipped into a frenzy of white horses, the waves splashing up against the jetty and reaching the window.

Her mind wandered to the situation at work. She hadn't told Rachel that Tim had emailed, checking to see how she was. Part of her wondered why it was the company lawyer mailing – he wasn't even a direct employee of WordCorp – and not Greta, her boss, but that was a pointless query. She knew why. For some reason none of them could work out, Greta hated her.

Tim had said he'd spoken quietly to her colleagues at the other papers. The feeling was that Rich Slater was attacking one of their own and looking for media attention, and they were very happy not to feed that particular fire.

The whole case was nonsense; she was sure the judge would throw it out, but it was going to cost them all a lot of time and money until then. And more importantly, his assertion that she had broken the law by hacking his charge card and cell phone suggested she'd been less than professional in the pursuit of a story, and it was things like that that could really damage your career. She shook her head half to herself. He was so damn clever. He knew she couldn't reveal her sources – to do that would be guaranteed professional suicide. She'd just have to fight her case based on the records she'd kept.

Still, at least she had Tim rooting for her. He'd said something about Nancy fielding any enquiries that came in. Anything that sounded interesting and could wait, she was apparently slotting into a holding pattern and would keep the informant happy until Caroline got back. Caroline would believe that when she saw it. More likely, Nancy was picking off the best stories and cementing her position. The good news was that everyone who wasn't in the immediate defamation case loop seemed satisfied that she'd gone on vacation.

She'd wondered about telling Tim about the plate in the sink, but it had sounded a bit ridiculous when she'd repeated it to Rachel. Perhaps it was just lack of sleep that was making her jump to conclusions. Fear bred fear at night. Working her job with the *Messenger*, covering crime, she'd seen some pretty terrible things and some serious people had tried to frighten her. This didn't even compare, but something about Honoria's story had got right under her skin. Had Honoria been afraid? Was that what this was all about? Afraid of her husband, or afraid of being alone? Of being found out? Had she left ends untied when she took her own life, ends that needed tying before she could rest?

Caroline's unsettled mind wandered again, landing back on Rachel. She wondered if this guy she was trying to get information on, Alfie, had been frightened at the end. The police were apparently still investigating but what if it hadn't been an accident? With everything else going on – the break-in on her boat and Hunter being knocked off his bike – what if someone had deliberately set Alfie's tent on fire?

Caroline shivered. She'd come here to get away and seemed to have landed in the middle of a tangle of mysteries. She bit her lip. The one thing that drove her as a journalist was the victims' stories. Everyone talked about the killer when something happened, but after the initial shock and speculation, after the trial – if there was one – people forgot the victims, when they were the ones who had lost the most.

It felt to Caroline that Honoria had been a victim – perhaps a victim of her own obsession, but a victim nonetheless. And Meg Cassidy ... Had she been afraid of something that had driven her away from home, so frightened that she had simply vanished? And then Alfie. What had happened there?

Caroline sighed, surfacing from her thoughts and tuning back into the room. The fire was blazing now. She closed the vent to keep it under control and looked for her notebook. She was sure she'd left it on the sofa this morning before she'd gone out. But it wasn't there now. Perhaps whoever had topped up the fridge had moved it. But she couldn't imagine Conor or Imogen doing that. She looked around. Her magazine was still on the coffee table, but at a different angle from how she'd left it.

Maybe whoever had tidied had put the notebook in the kitchen. She'd made notes in it on Hare's Landing before she came – the bits of history on the house she'd found on the internet. The journalist in her didn't let her go anywhere without getting the fullest picture possible.

She wanted to look back over it and add the information she'd learned tonight about Honoria Smyth before she forgot any of it. Tim was always laughing at her obsessive note-taking, but that was why she was good at her job: she didn't trust her memory. When you physically wrote things down longhand your brain stored the facts differently, and somehow relationships between different pieces of information suddenly became apparent that perhaps you wouldn't have seen before. She had a whole shelf of notebooks in her apartment. Caroline took a sip of her wine. She also, thankfully, had extensive notebooks on Rich Slater, including records of her interviews with his employees and a folder in Dropbox with screenshots of every piece of social media she'd used to build a picture of his habits.

Picking up the wine bottle from the counter and topping up her glass, she glanced around the kitchen, checking the drawers to see if her Hare's Landing notebook had been put away. She couldn't see it. But at least there were no broken plates in the sink this time. *That was just so weird.* And she'd had such a strong image of Honoria using that exact china, the picture in her head so similar to the photograph on the film she'd found, that even now it made the hairs stand up on the back of her neck.

Shaking away the thoughts, Caroline wondered if she'd left her notebook upstairs. She was sure she hadn't, but her disturbed sleep was making her weary – perhaps it was affecting her memory. She put her glass down and skipped up the spiral staircase, flicking on the main bedroom light as she did so.

And stopped dead.

Lying in the middle of the pure white cotton duvet cover was her notebook.

A feeling of dread spiralling in her stomach, Caroline took a step towards the bed so she could see it better.

It was open in a double-page spread.

And the word LEAVE had been written in capital letters across both pages in something smudgy and red.

Her mouth dry, the beat of her heart drowning the sounds of the wind howling around the building, Caroline leaned closer, trying to see the lettering more clearly.

It looked as if it had been written with lipstick.

Closing her eyes and taking a deep breath, Caroline tried to catch her racing mind. It was flying in all directions like a hare being chased by hounds. Hounds that were closing in.

She could hear their baying, feel their breath on the back of her neck.

What the hell was going on? Who had been here? This was her bedroom, for Christ's sake – *the ultimate violation of her personal space.*

She couldn't imagine that Imogen would have done this, or Conor. Mrs Travers? Well, that seemed a whole lot more likely. *But why?*

Caroline felt paralysed, suddenly cold as if she'd literally been turned into ice and frozen to the spot. Forcing herself to move, she walked slowly around the end of the bed, pulling her sleeve down over her hand so she could open the bathroom door. With the sleeve pulled over the other hand, she switched on the light. Her red Chanel lipstick was open on the back of the sink, the lid lying beside it, the end squished. As if it had been used to write something. Raising her eyes, she realised whoever had graffitied her notebook had also been busy in here. LEAVE was written across the mirror as well.

She narrowed her eyes. *Bastards.* Whoever had done this wanted to frighten her. And had used a $100 lipstick to do it.

They were wasting their time there.

That colour might have suited Honoria Smyth but it had never suited her.

Caroline felt the fear suddenly replaced by a seething rage. How dare someone come into her home, albeit a vacation home – into her *bedroom* – and try and scare the shit out of her?

Never mind white feathers and plates and now her red lipstick; there was no way this was some sort of apparition. Ghosts didn't daub mirrors.

She'd been frightened yesterday, so they'd succeeded there, but she was blind mad now, so angry she could feel her temper surge like a huge wave.

Was someone trying to warn her away from following Honoria's story, or finding out more about the missing teenagers? Did that someone think she was engrossed in some sort of covert investigative operation? Was this something to do with Honoria and the letter?

Who had she told? Only Rachel. But where had she been, and who had been listening? Questions raced around her head like tracer fire.

Caroline skirted the bed and headed down the stairs again. As she'd come through the airport she'd picked up some spare plastic bags for her liquids and toiletries, and had stashed them in her bag.

A few minutes later she was back in the bedroom, her fingers encased in one bag as she reached for her notebook and dropped it neatly into a second one. She was sure it had been wiped clean of fingerprints but there was no point in contaminating what could be evidence.

Looking at it closely, through the clear plastic of the bag, she could see the same lipstick that had been used on the notebook was the one used on the bathroom mirror.

Caroline headed back downstairs and laid the bagged notebook on the counter, then picked up her wine, thinking before she took a sip.

If she was being sensible, she should go back to the hotel tonight and see if they had a room she could take. She could hear Tim's voice loud in her ear, telling her to leave right now. But she wasn't going to do that. She was far too single-minded. Someone wanted her to leave Hare's Landing, which gave her every possible reason to stay. And stay right here.

There was no way she was running scared, like some sort of prey. She turned to glance at the front door, wondering again if its opening the other night had been her fault at all?

Perhaps someone – a real someone – *had* been wandering around down here?

She felt a flutter of anxiety in her stomach, but it was quickly diluted by another surge of rage. Glancing around the room, she looked for something she could block the front door with. It was the only way in and the ancient-looking latch wasn't going to keep anyone out.

Particularly if they had a key.

She should have thought of buying a bolt for the door when she was in the village.

The armchair would do the trick for the moment. There was every chance whoever had done this thought she'd see the bed and head straight back to the hotel, up the dark and tree-shrouded path that connected the two buildings. She would be massively vulnerable to attack if she did that, especially in this weather where you couldn't hear yourself think, never mind someone creeping up on you.

Marching over to the leather armchair positioned beside the stove, Caroline pulled on the back, testing its weight. She reckoned if she edged it along she could just about move it into the kitchen. Her anger gave her extra strength. Hauling it across the polished floorboards, she was relieved to see the legs didn't scratch the floor; they seemed to have some sort of felt pads on the bottom. They made it slide relatively easily and she quickly had it wedged up against the front door. It wasn't a perfect barricade but it would sure slow someone down.

There was no way she was getting attacked outside – or inside. It wasn't going to happen. She wasn't going to play into anyone's hands. She wasn't going to get jumped in the dark because she wasn't leaving.

Whoever it was could just fuck off.

Chapter 30

'WHAT?'
Rachel's shock was written all over her face as Caroline explained what had happened the previous night. They'd arranged to meet in the dining room for breakfast after Jasper's walk. They were sharing a table beside the window that would have looked out onto the walled garden if the rain hadn't been lashing against the windows, obliterating any sort of view. Rachel held her spoon poised in the air over her half-forgotten muesli, the overhead lights picking up the diamanté eyes in her chunky ring.

'Who on earth would do that?'

'That's what I wondered. After what Ava said, I reckon it *has* to be someone who thinks I'm poking around after a story.' Caroline pushed her glasses more firmly onto her nose. 'But I'm sure it's not connected to her. We only spoke yesterday and I think she believed me when I said I wasn't looking into her sister's disappearance – I mean, there is no story there anyway.' She picked up a glass of orange juice. 'Whoever spoke to Ava about me was trying to make trouble, but I think it's something closer to Hare's Landing that they want me to keep away from.' She took a sip of her juice. 'My notebook had all the notes I'd made about the house in it.'

'Do you think it's something to do with Honoria's death? Perhaps it wasn't suicide at all?'

Caroline pursed her lips meaningfully. 'Funny you should say that. That's exactly what occurred to me. Either that or her pregnancy was the secret, and someone doesn't want us raking up the story. My finding that roll of film, and getting it developed, must have really upset someone.'

'But who could it have been? Who knew about the photographs or about Honoria's letter? And who would care about it after all this time?' Rachel took a spoonful of her muesli and chewed thoughtfully. 'It has to be someone who thinks you're on to something that will threaten them *now* – that you're about to expose something that maybe happened in the past, but will have an impact on their reputation or liberty today.'

Caroline picked up her coffee. 'If it *is* to do with Honoria, it has to be someone who was connected to the house at the time. Someone who has something to hide, or wants to keep part of the story hidden.'

'It's like something out of Agatha Christie, one of those country house mysteries.'

'Indeed.' Caroline rolled her eyes. 'Or *Rebecca*. Mrs Travers could be related to Mrs Danvers. She was literally as mad as a march hare in that movie.'

'So, who was here when Honoria died?'

Caroline counted off on her fingers. 'Honoria was, obviously. Mrs Travers, whom we know was devoted to her. Her son Sheridan, if that's him in those pictures, and I think it could be. He looks a bit like her, and it would make sense that he might come home from university for the summer.' Caroline paused. 'If you're right about that T-shirt, it means the picture definitely can't have been taken before The Who went on tour in the UK in October 1989. Bronagh's right that the film could have stayed in the camera until it got used up, but there were so many random pictures of the boys messing that I reckon it would have been finished pretty quickly. And all the pictures were obviously taken in the summer.' Caroline pulled a stray strand of hair behind her ear. 'Honoria died in July 1990, so that narrows the time frame a lot, doesn't it? To be super sure, we could check to see if 1990 was a hot summer. Google should be able to tell us that.'

Rachel glanced at her phone, beside her on the table, double-checking the reception bars.

'We'll have to go back to the village for that. Bronagh said last night she has an internet connection in the office, but it's painfully slow and very intermittent. And with the best will in the world, we don't want anyone walking in on our conversation or checking our search history.'

Caroline frowned, looking over her shoulder at the increasingly ferocious weather.

'Exactly. We'll see if it calms down a bit first. So, Honoria, Mrs Travers, Sheridan Smyth, presumably her lover – the handyman cum gardener, maybe chauffeur – would all have been here.' She stopped and looked intently at Rachel. 'And perhaps her husband. He was a barrister and their son was studying law and later became a judge. If Honoria was murdered, they'd both be very familiar with the law and police investigations.'

'And if either of them was even implicated in something to do with Honoria's death, surely they'd have to resign? If there was any suspicion of foul play, their careers would be over.'

'I think you're right that someone has a lot to lose from me being here now. But they've picked the wrong person to try and frighten off. I just keep thinking that my notebook being deliberately put in my bedroom is some sort of message that someone's watching me when I sleep.'

'That is seriously creepy.' Rachel picked up the teapot to top up her tea. 'But why write on the mirror? Is that supposed to be some sort of message about reflections or looking into something?'

'Maybe, or maybe they've been watching too many movies? Perhaps it was just supposed to scare me. I was thinking the plate thing and the white feather could have been supernatural, but ghosts don't write on mirrors.'

Rachel's eyes widened. 'That's true, but would you not move up to the hotel just to be on the safe side? The phone reception's so bad, if something happened, how would you call for help?'

Caroline shook her head. 'I'll be fine. I'm very cosy where I am.' She took a sip of her coffee. 'When this rain stops, we'll head for the village, will we? And do some proper googling. It's Monday, so the cafe might be open, we won't have to go to that pub. I felt like there was way too much interest in what we were talking about in there.'

'That would be better. It was like we were some sort of sideshow last time.' Rachel hesitated. 'But whoever broke in didn't touch your laptop?'

'I had it with me all day.'

Caroline rooted in her bag under the table for her laptop, double-checking it was there. The movement caused Jasper's head to shoot up. He had been lying beside them, pretending to be asleep, his ears twitching every time another gust of wind hit the window. He looked at Caroline quizzically for a moment and then put his head back down on the wooden boards.

Rachel reached for her tea. 'Just as well you didn't leave it behind, they could have taken it.'

Caroline sighed. 'But that would be actual theft, of something valuable – it's different somehow from your basic intimidation.' She ran her hand over her forehead. This was all getting very complicated. 'I'm starting to think we need to have a proper chat with Mrs Travers.'

'I think she's over in reception now. The buffet table was all set up for breakfast when I came down.'

'Could it have been her? She's the only current link between this place and Honoria …' Caroline stopped herself. 'But that's silly, she's about a hundred and ten, she's hardly going to be sneaking about doing mad stuff with lipstick.'

Rachel took the last mouthful of her muesli and put her spoon down.'So what are you going to do? Report it to the police? You have to tell Bronagh at least.'

'Nope, I'm not going to do anything. Whoever it is thinks they are frightening me, that I'll make a fuss and maybe leave. They don't know this sort of thing has precisely the opposite effect on me. God, I was so mad last night. Part of me wished they'd tried to come in again.' She scowled, making Rachel smile. 'The thing is,' Caroline continued, 'I was thinking about the whole vacation let thing. I mean, anyone could have a key – someone who had stayed in the Boathouse before and had maybe lost one and got a new one cut, or the cleaning staff, friends of the cleaning staff … I mean, the spare key is in reception, which is pretty much always empty. The bloody mailman could nip in and borrow it and I don't think anyone would notice. I'm sure you can get keys cut easily in Ross Haven if you don't want to go to the inquisitive Mr John Francis Mahony in Glencurragh.'

Rachel opened her eyes wide in shock. 'My God, you're so right, I've never thought about that before. There's all this publicity about Airbnb hosts setting up secret cameras and filming their guests, but it would be so simple just to walk in and go through all their things.'

'They probably do that too. I'd never book with Airbnb, they're like Uber for me – utterly unreliable, you have no idea what you're really getting.'

'That's because you've got a journalist's suspicious mind.'

'True.' Caroline smiled, then after a moment her face creased in a frown. 'Which is why, and please hear me out, it strikes me as a rather worrying coincidence that your Hunter got knocked off his bike so soon after this Alfie guy died. He's making a documentary about Alfie Bows and all of a sudden, two of the key individuals involved in that have accidents – Hunter could have been killed.'

Rachel's mouth dropped open. 'But Alfie's death was an accident. Hunter told me they'd spoken about how he needed to be careful with fire around his tent.'

'So you've been told, but what if it wasn't?' Rachel looked at her, suddenly pale. 'Sorry, forget I said it. You're right – I've got a journalist's creepy mind. It's just that – and I know this sounds awful – but who cares about some homeless guy dying in what looks like a perfectly explainable accident? The homeless are like invisible people. It's just such a massive coincidence. And if you were going to try and bump someone off randomly in London, and they ride a bike, you've got means and opportunity right there on a plate. And very few accidents involving cyclists are ever prosecuted. Very few.'

'Oh, Jesus – that's what Hunter keeps saying.'

Caroline took off her glasses to clean them on the hem of her sweater.

'It was just a thought. I'm sorry, I should learn to keep them to myself. I'm sure the police are going to catch whoever it was, there's CCTV everywhere in London.'

Rachel twisted her ring as she looked back at Caroline, frowning.

'Except the guy's number plate was covered in mud.'

Caroline put her glasses back on and her mouth formed an O shape.

'Not too much of *that* in central London. Mud, I mean.'

Before Rachel could reply her phone began to ring.

'Good God, the wind must be blowing in the right direction.'

'You better take it before it changes. I'll go and see if the papers have arrived, they might have a weather forecast. Be great if this rain stopped for five minutes.'

Chapter 31

IN THE DINING room, Rachel stood up and walked towards the tall window overlooking the terrace, trying to find a clearer signal.

She had so much to tell Hunter but she was conscious of being overheard. The details of Caroline's ordeal last night would have to wait until she was alone in the Landie with full reception. And their suspicions about what might have happened to Honoria Smyth would definitely have to wait.

Could Caroline really be right about Alfie being killed deliberately? Why hadn't she thought of that? The police were already linking the break-in and Hunter's accident with the documentary, and Hunter had thought that the timing was bizarre, but everyone assumed Alfie's death had been accidental. She felt a sick feeling in the pit of her stomach just thinking about it.

She really needed to have a chat to the police officer looking after Alfie's case. Rachel shivered but tried to sound as upbeat as she could.

'How are you feeling, lovely?'

'Grumpy. I can't bloody sleep here. And my leg hurts a lot.' His voice sounded raspy.

'Are they giving you enough pain relief? Tell them and I'm sure they can make you more comfortable.' She continued, not giving him a chance to tell her off for interfering. 'Have you heard anything from the insurance people?'

'No, I was going to ask you the same thing.'

'This is the first time I've had phone reception in the house since I got here. I'll check my email when we're done, it could have come in. Wasn't there anything in the post?'

'Mum keeps forgetting to pick it up. I'm starting to think I should send someone else.'

'Do you want me to ask Nathan? He could pop it in to you there?'

'Not for the moment. If she thinks we're checking up on her she'll go nuts. We'll keep him in reserve. I want to get this insurance business sorted out, though. I'll give them a ring and be more insistent.'

'How's everything else?' She hesitated. 'Have the police been back? Any news on the BMW?'

'I gave them as much info as I could. Last I heard they were trying to track it across London. They haven't got the reg plate so they can't trace the owner, but they have been trying to follow it on CCTV, to see where it went.'

'Can you remember anything about the accident? I mean, what actually happened?'

'He clipped my back wheel. I came off. Pretty straightforward. I was lucky I didn't go under his wheels. What's with all the questions?'

'Just interested. I'll give the police a call and see how they're getting on.'

'Okay, if you want to – I'm sure they'll tell us when they have anything. Listen, how are you doing on Alfie?'

'Not great. I don't even know when he was here, if he was here. Have you spoken to Frank? Do we know anything else at all?'

'Frank came over yesterday, he brought Alfie's bag.' She could hear the tiredness in his voice. 'There wasn't much in it. The rosin for his strings and a page from someone's bank statement that he'd written my number on the back of. It must have been a piece of scrap paper he'd found by the bins. There was some sheet music. Such a random collection. He had a broken watch in the bottom, wrapped up in a sandwich bag. My God, it just hit me so hard, it's just so fucking sad. He always had that bag with him, that and his violin …'

Rachel could hear his voice catching. He was low enough after the accident, now he had to deal with Alfie's loss … She needed to give him some good news. But first she had to find the good news to give him. There had to be something in that bag that was important, that would give her a clue.

'What's the name on the bank statement?'

It took Hunter a moment to answer. She could hear rustling, as if he was rooting in the bag.

'The nurses are going to have a fit if they see this in here. It's probably a walking germ fest.' He stopped speaking for a moment. 'It's J. A. Stafford. It's from Barclays in Regent Street. Dated …' He hesitated again, as if he was looking for the information. 'Dated last month.'

'Hunter, listen to me. Could that be Alfie? John, or James maybe, Alfred Stafford?' Rachel couldn't keep the excitement out of her voice. Maybe this was the break they needed. 'Can you ask the bank if it's him?'

'The bank aren't going to tell us anything about a customer now, are they? Think about it, Rachel. The police will have to ask.'

'Could Zack take a still from the rushes and go in and see if they recognise him at least? He's very distinctive looking, let's face it.'

'Well, I suppose he could. But when do any of us ever go into a bank these days? It's all electronic banking and cash cards.'

Hunter sounded exhausted; she didn't think he was really grasping what she was saying. She tried again.

'Well, maybe the police can get the CCTV from the cash dispenser and then they can confirm his ID.' She said it slowly, trying to keep her patience. 'You have to tell them. It was in his bag, pet – it has to be important.'

Hunter didn't sound convinced. 'I think it's much more likely to be a piece of litter he picked up. There's only one page, and he's written my number on the back. The guy whose account it is seems to have had loads of money. There's over a hundred grand in there and no withdrawals – it looks dormant. Why would you live on the street if you had that sort of money?'

Rachel felt her frustration rising. Hunter obviously wasn't feeling himself at all, he was never this negative.

'Take a picture of it and send it over to me, will you? I'll have a look. I'm not getting anywhere here at the moment, it might help.'

'It's just so fucking grim, isn't it? Can you imagine only leaving that behind? I mean, a whole lifetime in a carrier bag.'

Rachel was silent for a moment, and suddenly felt bad that she hadn't been more sympathetic. Looking in Alfie's bag must have been heart-wrenching for him. She knew he was trying to hide it, but he'd got so attached to Alfie in the time they'd known each other. Hunter was just like her; he had a natural instinct to want to find solutions for everything. His positive thinking was one of the things she loved about him. His reaction just showed how sick he was feeling.

'I'll keep digging here. Will you ask the police to check that name? Assuming someone did actually report him missing, they could have all sorts of information about him. I feel like I'm wandering in the dark at the moment. And I want to get back to London, there's all sorts of other mad stuff

188

going on here. I can't talk now – I'll have to tell you later.'

She wasn't sure if he'd heard her properly as he cut in.

'Oh God, here's Mum, I'd better hide this bag. Try and find out something about Alfie for me, but you need to stay there a bit longer, until the police find out who knocked me down at least. I want you here, babes, you know that. Darlene is driving me insane, but I need you to be safe.'

Rachel felt a kick in her heart.

'I just want to see you. And Jasper's missing you. Well, he's pretending he is. He loves the woods here – we've been having the longest walks. But I think the weather's getting bad again. There's a red weather warning, Storm Brendan or something coming through, so I need to wait before I can book the ferry anyway. I don't fancy getting seasick all the way home.'

Rachel heard a low growl begin behind her. Turning, she could see Jasper was still lying on the floor stretched out. He was playing dead. She could tell from the angle of his ears that he was fully alert. That, and the growl.

'I better go, love you hon, say hi to your mum from me.'

Clicking off the phone, she went to give Jasper a rub.

'What's up, boy?'

Jasper thumped his tail once on the floor. The growl lowered an octave. What had upset him? Was it hearing Hunter's voice on the phone, or had he felt some sort of spooky presence? She shook her head to herself – the poor baby must be missing Hunter too.

Frowning, Rachel slipped her phone into the back pocket of her jeans and picked up her room key. Sensing that she was moving, Jasper stood up, his eyes trained on her.

'Come on, boy, let's go and find Caroline and tell her about this bag of Alfie's will we, she what she makes of it. And we'll see what's happening with this weather.'

Chapter 32

IN THE HALL Caroline could see the Monday morning papers had been left on the reception desk. She picked up the *Irish Times*, scanning the headline. She was so absorbed in reading the front-page article, she didn't hear Rachel come up behind her.

'Anything interesting?'

She turned, her face serious. 'There's some company called Nemo Freight in deep trouble. Remember that Northern Irish company involved in all those poor Vietnamese dying in that container? This lot seem to be doing something similar.' She scowled. 'That was so utterly horrific.' She glanced at the paper again. 'Apparently the directors of Nemo Freight are denying everything and one of them has absconded.'

'I know them. I've never used them, they've always been way too expensive, but I've seen their trucks around the place.' Rachel shook her head. 'They're Irish I think. An absolute disgrace. I reckon these people start with drugs and get away with that, then start looking for more lucrative cargo.'

'You wouldn't think there could be anything much more lucrative than drugs, given the relative size, but clearly people are.'

Caroline turned the paper towards Rachel so she could see the front page. Rachel scanned it, her face taut.

'The only good thing is that they've been stopped. I bet they're into all sorts of other criminal activity too.'

She let out a ragged sigh. Caroline glanced at her. Talking to Hunter seemed to have shaken her up.

The more Caroline thought about it, the more worried she was that Hunter's accident was directly linked to Alfie's death, and that neither incident had been an accident at all. But she could see Rachel needed to process it before she dug deeper. There had to be a reason they'd met at Hare's Landing, that fate had brought them together right now, and one thing Caroline was very good at was finding connections, uncovering stories in apparently innocent situations. Last night, as she'd lain awake thinking about Hare's Landing, looking at the whole picture from every angle, she'd gone on to thinking about Alfie's death. Hunter must have got close to something that some serious people wanted to keep hidden.

Something that involved Alfie Bows.

Caroline couldn't see how the house – Hare's Landing itself – could possibly be tied in, and nobody was telling Rachel to leave, so what Alfie's connection was to the place, goodness only knew. She had so many questions for Rachel, but now wasn't the time. She felt sure last night's attempt at intimidating her had to have been about Honoria Smyth and her death. She was the one who'd found the letter, after all.

Another gust of wind and rain hit the windows behind the reception desk like a slap in the face.

'Good God, this *weather*. I've never seen anything like it. Let's see what the forecast is.'

Caroline was in the process of flicking through the paper to find the weather report when a voice cut in.

'Red weather warning. High winds and inches of rain coming in. They're predicting flooding right across the county.'

Caroline looked up sharply at the sound of Mrs Travers's voice, at the same time feeling a movement at her feet as Jasper pushed his way between their legs, sitting firmly on her foot. She glanced down, smiling. She'd thought she was a cat person until she'd met Jasper, but he had such a strong personality and intelligent eyes – she was starting to think of him as the third musketeer in their little gang.

'Good morning, Mrs Travers, lovely to see you again.'

Caroline smiled sweetly, conscious that her eyes were giving out a very different message. From the other side of the reception desk, her arms full of the tabloid newspapers that she had clearly been going through from their not-quite-folded appearance, Mrs Travers looked herself and Rachel up and down.

'Good morning. I hope your room's comfortable and there's enough space for that big dog.'

'Plenty, thank you, and it's beautiful. I love all the period touches. I work in film, I spend a lot of time looking at properties like this for location work. Usually something fundamental has been changed, but this house has been restored beautifully.'

There was a warm laugh behind them. 'We'd be *very* happy for it to be used as a film location. Anything you need, you just say. I've got some peacocks arriving in the spring, we're going to set the gold standard for a period retreat.'

Rachel turned to see Bronagh had arrived from the back of the hotel, a hammer in her hand.

'Don't worry, I'm taking lots of pictures, and Jasper loves it so much here, we'd love to come back. If I can get someone else to pay, all the better.'

Caroline smiled. 'You really have thought of everything, right down to the classical music – it's so beautiful and completely in keeping with the house.'

Bronagh looked at her, puzzled. 'What classical music?'

'The violins. They are so subtle sometimes you don't catch them, but it's a brilliant sound system. Sometimes it sounds like there's someone playing in the corner of the room, like last night when we were looking at the photographs.'

Bronagh squinted at her, half smiling. 'We haven't got a sound system.' She cleared her throat. 'But perhaps Imogen had the radio on in the kitchen or something. Sound seems to carry quite remarkably in this house.'

'Perhaps that was it.'

Caroline faked an amused smile.

Surely everyone else had heard the music too? She'd have to ask Rachel later.

Bronagh laughed, but it sounded a little forced. 'We can bring in a full orchestra if you need it, Rachel, a film would definitely put us on the map.' She diverted her attention to Mrs Travers, as if she needed to change the subject. 'Mrs T., can you pass me over that picture tucked under the desk? I'm going to put it up over the mantelpiece. I'd love you to tell us who's in the photo if you can.'

Mrs Travers put the papers down on the desk and leaned down to look for the picture. As she pulled it out, Bronagh called down the corridor.

'Conor, where are you with that ladder?'

A moment later Conor appeared, a fold-up aluminium ladder casually swinging from one hand. Jasper trotted over to give him a sniff, his tail wagging hard. Conor gave his ears a rub with his free hand.

'Sorry, where do you want this?'

'In front of the mantelpiece. I've been waiting for the perfect picture to put over the fireplace, and now we've got it.'

They all turned to look at Mrs Travers, who was holding the picture in both hands, her face frozen, drained of colour.

'Are you okay there, Mrs T.?'

Her voice was barely a whisper. 'Sheridan – that's young Sheridan and his friend.'

Caroline and Rachel glanced at each other. Pretending she hadn't noticed Mrs Travers's reaction, Caroline said casually, 'Isn't it a lovely picture? It looks like the summer. Have you any idea when it was taken?'

Mrs Travers slid the photograph up onto the counter. She shook her head and, turning, went back into the office behind the reception area, closing the door behind her. Caroline turned to Bronagh in surprise.

'It's upset her. Damn, I thought she'd be happy to see an old photo. She was very close to Sheridan, still is, he sends her a huge hamper every Christmas.' Bronagh shook her head. 'She's such an odd old stick. I never seem to get it quite right. I don't think she approves of the house being a hotel.'

Caroline frowned. 'She's not very guest-friendly but surely she'd rather see the place used than turned into a ruin, or owned by people who won't let her near the place?'

Bronagh shrugged. 'Let's get this picture up anyway.' Behind her, Conor was halfway up the ladder. She handed him the hammer. 'Careful up there, we don't want any accidents.'

'Bro, it's a stepladder. If I can ride a wave, I think I'll have enough balance to be okay, don't you?' He grinned down at her, teasingly. 'Now how high do you want it, before I fall off and sue you for ending my world championship hopes?'

Before she could answer, there was a crash from inside the office.

Bronagh's eyes widened. 'Good God, what was that?'

Chapter 33

BRONAGH RAN ACROSS the hall and opened a door cunningly concealed in the oak panelling that led into the office beside the reception desk. They weren't far behind her, arriving in the doorway to see Mrs Travers lying on the utilitarian grey carpet tiles, her face a shade of the same colour. Bronagh was kneeling beside her, holding her wrist, her face knotted in concentration. She moved her fingers to the older woman's neck.

Bronagh glanced up at them. 'I think she's had a stroke or something. I can't feel a pulse. Mrs Travers? Mrs Travers, can you hear me, are you okay?'

'I'll call an ambulance.'

Caroline stepped back out of the room and headed for the phone in reception as Rachel bobbed down beside Bronagh. Conor appeared in the doorway.

'Start CPR – you know how?'

Bronagh looked up at him and gave him a sharp nod, her hands already in place. Rachel felt helpless beside her.

'What can I do?'

'Hold her hand?' Bronagh began pumping Mrs Travers's chest. 'Is this right, Conor? It's years since I did it.'

Bronagh had placed one of her hands over the other in

the middle of Mrs Travers's breastbone, leaning over her, her fingers linked together.

'That's great, do it really hard, use the heel of your hand. I'll take over when you need me to.'

Caroline reappeared at the office door, the telephone receiver stretched on its curly wire in one hand.

'Ambulance is on the way. They said they'd get someone here as soon as they can.'

Conor looked back at her. 'Stay on the line in case anything changes.'

Rachel rubbed the back of Mrs Travers's hand; she could feel her temperature dropping.

'She's getting colder.'

Bronagh's concentration was fully on the housekeeper. 'Can you get a blanket?'

Rachel stood up. 'Two minutes, there are spare blankets in my wardrobe.'

Running upstairs, Jasper beside her, Rachel unlocked her door and flung open the central section of the huge wardrobe. Under the TV there was a row of drawers where she'd thrown in her clothes. The bottom drawer was packed with spare blankets. She pulled one out and ran back downstairs with it.

Bronagh was in the hallway, leaning on the reception desk when Rachel got to the bottom of the stairs. Their eyes meeting briefly, she rounded the corner into the office. Conor had taken over the compressions, making them look easy, as if he could do them all day. He looked up at her and grinned reassuringly.

'Fold it over her and tuck it in.'

Kneeling down, Rachel let out a low whistle and Jasper came through the doorway.

'Lie down here, boy.'

Rachel patted the floor on the far side of Mrs Travers's prone figure and Jasper squeezed in between her and the desk, lying down beside her. He looked back at Rachel enquiringly.

'Good boy, stay now.' Rachel tucked the blanket in over Jasper and Mrs Travers. 'He'll keep her warm.'

'Good stuff. Can you take over for a few minutes? We need to keep up the rhythm. Come in here beside me, so we can time the switch over between compressions.'

Rachel moved in next to him, her hands crossed over.

'Do you know "Staying Alive" by the Bee Gees?' Rachel looked at him blankly, not understanding how this could possibly be relevant. 'We need to keep to that time, one hundred beats a minute. Hum it if it helps. Ready?'

Rachel nodded.

Conor moved out of the way, but kept counting out loud. Rachel picked up the count, pushing into Mrs Travers's chest. There was a sickening crunch.

'Don't stop, keep going. That was a rib. She has to be over seventy, her bones are going to be a bit brittle.'

Rachel could feel herself pale but kept pumping.

Bronagh leaned into the doorway of the office, watching them.

'I can't believe this has happened. I thought that photo would create a lovely sense of nostalgia when people arrived.' Bronagh bit her lip. 'I knew it would be a surprise for her, but I never expected this.'

Still on the phone, the wire stretched over the desk, Caroline hovered in the doorway.

'Are you okay, Rach?'

Staring blindly ahead, concentrating on the compressions, Rachel indicated that she was and kept going. She knew she was probably fitter than Bronagh – she was a regular at the gym – but this was hard going. She was using every muscle in her upper body and her thighs were starting to burn.

But she knew she couldn't stop.

In the reception area the waiting room clock chimed.

'Let me have another go now.' Conor was back beside her. 'We just have to keep going till the ambulance gets here. This keeps the blood moving to her brain.'

Rachel fell back on her heels, her arms and back aching, catching her breath.

'Jesus, I hope they get here soon.'

Conor kept up the compressions, counting half to himself, the sound rhythmic. Rachel could feel her own heart beating, thumping in her ears, and found herself counting silently in time to his counts. From behind her, Rachel sensed movement.

'My turn. Bronagh's keeping the phone line open.'

Caroline climbed past her and kneeled down beside Conor, who nodded wordlessly; despite his level of fitness, it was hard going. Rachel shimmied over, giving Caroline space to get into position.

'One, two, three.'

They swapped hands seamlessly and Caroline took over the count.

'They're here!'

They all heard Bronagh's voice from the hall. Conor stood up.

'Keep counting, don't stop.'

They heard the outer door slam and a paramedic appeared. Conor met him at the door to the office.

'Seventy-plus-year-old woman. She collapsed. We couldn't find a pulse. We've been giving CPR.'

'That's great, we'll take over now. Can we clear the room?'

Before he'd even finished speaking, Rachel stood up to

give the paramedic space. He deftly took over the chest compressions from Caroline.

'Good job.'

'My God, that's exhausting.' Caroline shook out her arms.

Outside they heard wheels rattling and the paramedic's colleague appeared at the doorway, manoeuvring a gurney across the hall. Coming into the room, she knelt down and pulled back the blanket, uncovering Jasper's head. He looked up as she laughed in surprise.

'That's a new take on insulation.'

Rachel clicked her fingers. Jasper slid out from under the blanket and nimbly skipped around Mrs Travers and the paramedic to stand beside her.

'Come on, boy, let's give them some space.'

He trotted after her into the hall and pushed his head into her leg, whimpering. She bent down to give him a rub.

As if nothing had happened, Conor picked up the photograph and the hammer from the reception desk and hopped up the ladder. He leaned the frame on the mantelpiece and banged in two nails, slipping the picture wire over them.

'I'll get this ladder put away, will I? We don't need any more accidents.'

Chapter 34

'COFFEE?'

Rachel pulled over on Glencurragh's steeply sloping main street, and hauled on the handbrake of the Land Rover. Caroline looked across at her as she spoke.

'Actually, I'd really like something stronger after this morning, but you're driving, so yes, that sounds perfect.'

The rain had slowed and they'd taken advantage of it. Bronagh had jumped into the back of the ambulance with Mrs Travers, heading to St Michael's Hospital in Ross Haven. Seeing her off, they'd headed into the lounge, exhausted.

But neither had been able to settle.

Without saying it, they both knew they needed to get away from Hare's Landing for a few hours. Not that Glencurragh was exactly cosmopolitan, but it was a change of scene and it had internet.

Rachel leaned into the back and clicked on Jasper's lead.

'Not that we have boundless choice, but Imogen said the cafe down from Mahony's was lovely. Let's leave the Landie here and walk down. If the rain holds off long enough, we'll be halfway to the harbour and that little beach. We can take Jasper for a run.'

'Do you think they'll have cheesecake? I really feel I need cheesecake.'

Rachel laughed. 'You're so American.'

Caroline looked at her with mock affront. 'I'm not at all. But bloody hell, talk about the morning after the night before.' She shook her head. 'Cheesecake has been known to solve all sorts of problems.'

'Right. I believe you. Let's make a run for it, it's only spitting now.'

Pausing at the door of the cafe to check that Jasper was welcome, they went straight to an empty table in the corner beside the Victorian-style paned window, as far away from the serving area as they could get.

The furniture was a mismatched mixture of upcycled tables and chairs, with pretty antique plates and saucers dotting the walls, bringing a feeling of warmth and sunshine to the cheerily lit interior. It had obviously been busy earlier; brightly coloured cups and chintz style china teapots littered a small group of tables like a patchwork blanket.

The only other customer was a mum nursing her coffee as she gossiped to the girl behind a glazed counter heavy with home-made cakes and biscuits. Beside her, her toddler was colouring and drinking hot chocolate from a red polka dot mug, trying to catch the bobbing marshmallows floating on the surface with his tongue whenever his mum turned to check on his baby sister, who was chuntering happily beside her in a pushchair.

Jasper settled himself under the table with a sigh. Rachel gave his ears a tickle. The toddler was so busy with his marshmallows that he hadn't noticed him arrive.

The girl behind the counter diverted her attention to them. 'What can I get you, ladies?'

Caroline looked at Rachel enquiringly, as she called back, 'Two lattes, please.'

'Perfect for me.' Pulling off her skiing jacket, Rachel slung it around the back of the chair, unwinding her scarf as she sat down. 'Do you think Mrs Travers will be okay?'

Caroline glanced over to the counter, relieved to see that the girl behind the till was distracted enough by her own conversation and making their coffees not to be listening to theirs. Pulling out a farmhouse-style chair opposite Rachel, she kept her voice low as she replied.

'Really, I've no idea. How long were we doing CPR for – almost ten minutes? But she's better off than she would have been if it had happened anywhere else. She gives me the creeps so I'm having trouble with full-on sympathy. I can't stand negative energy – there are enough problems in the world without adding to them, and she just radiates fury.'

'Perhaps being cross with everything was what brought it on. It was just so sudden. She looked a bit flushed when she came out with the papers, and then she picks up that picture of the house, and the next thing, keels over.'

Caroline wrinkled her nose. 'I was thinking about that. She said the guys in the picture were Sheridan and his friend. I wondered if the shock of seeing him again was what did it.'

'But Bronagh says they're still in touch, that he sends gifts at Christmas.'

Rachel picked up a vintage-style menu card from the middle of the table, and put it back down without reading it.

'That's what makes me think there must be something else about that photo, or when it was taken, that gave her a fright.'

'Something to do with Honoria, maybe? I wish we could ask her – Mrs Travers, I mean.'

Rachel stopped speaking abruptly as the waitress brought them their coffees, smiling her thanks.

As the waitress left, Caroline sighed. She felt as if there

was so much more just under the surface at Hare's Landing – so many secrets – and her curiosity levels were absolutely peaking. She felt Honoria Smyth's presence in every room, as if she'd walked out just before Caroline had walked in, sometimes leaving a trail of scent behind her. Caroline could almost hear her voice, soft and ephemeral, her laughter distant, lost in the ticking of the waiting room clock.

Whoever was trying to scare her off was having precisely the opposite effect – they obviously hadn't done their homework very well. Now she *really* needed to know what was going on – and why. The part of her that drove her when she was on to a story was in top gear, and she knew she wouldn't be able to leave until she'd found out precisely what the story was.

'I'm not sure Mrs Travers would tell us. Let's see how good the internet is here and we'll do some more digging. I just know there's more out there we didn't find last time when we were looking for info on Honoria and Alfie.' Caroline took a sip of her latte. 'You know, I really didn't realise how much I'd miss the internet when I booked to come over. I mean, I never thought I had an internet addiction or anything, but being so cut off really is a bit of a problem, isn't it?'

Rachel sipped her own coffee. 'A twenty-first-century problem. Twenty years ago, people just read the paper and listened to the radio, you know.'

'They had TV. But it was like the dark ages in terms of technology.'

A smile flickered across Rachel's face. 'That's exactly what Hunter calls the world pre-internet.' She took another sip and leaned down to pull her laptop out of her backpack. 'I was thinking about what you said, about what happened to Alfie, and I'm starting to think you're right. I don't know why I didn't see it before, it seems so obvious.' Caroline looked at her across the top of her coffee froth as Rachel continued, her face grim. 'You just don't expect people you know to get murdered, do you?'

Caroline wrinkled her nose and put her coffee down.

'Nope, that is for sure. I hate to say it, but it really feels like Alfie's at the heart of the problem. Someone didn't want him talking to Hunter and his crew, and it sounds like they think he'd already said too much.'

Rachel grimaced. 'The question is, what? What on earth could it be that it could get him killed ... and Hunter almost killed?'

'I was wondering if he'd seen something – a drug deal, or maybe something worse, and whoever is involved thinks he might have told Hunter. He's obsessed with finding out why Alfie ended up on the streets at the moment, so he can use the footage they've got in the final edit.' Rachel took another sip of her coffee. 'One of the crew needs to go back through all the rushes to see what Alfie said, or see if there's anything going on in the background that got caught in a frame.'

Caroline glanced up at the Wi-Fi code on the counter and typed it into her laptop. 'Let's do this properly. Tell me everything you know about Alfie. Let's work through all the details.' She pulled out a pen from her bag, then dug around for a few more seconds. 'In the absence of my notebook, we will use ... a shopping list.' She pulled out a sheet of A4 paper that had been folded several times. 'Shoot. Everything you know.'

It only took Rachel a few moments to summarise what she knew of Alfie Bows. She swirled her coffee with her spoon as she spoke.

'Frank – he's the guy who runs the hostel Alfie dropped into – called in to see Hunter at the hospital yesterday and gave him Alfie's carrier bag.'

Caroline chewed the end of her pen thoughtfully, looking

over the list Rachel had given her. It wasn't much, and the biggest problem was how much was actually accurate. But they had to start somewhere.

'Strange he didn't have it with him – in the tent, I mean.'

Rachel tucked her hair behind her ear. 'Who knows what really happened that night? Maybe he was trying to get away from the fire and fell and it went under the bins. The thing is, Hunter says there's a bank statement in the bag – well, one page of one, anyway. It was in the name of a J. A. Stafford. Hunter thinks it's probably just a piece of scrap paper he picked up. It was an old one – he'd used it to write Hunter's mobile number on the back. But I wondered if perhaps it's Alfie's real name.'

Caroline looked sceptical. 'Why would he only have one page if it was his account?'

Rachel's eyebrows rose as she shrugged. 'He was homeless, he didn't have anywhere to store anything. If it was his, maybe he collected it from the bank and he threw the rest away.'

'Was there any money in the account?'

'Yes, that's the thing that made Hunter think it was a bit of rubbish he'd found.' Rachel keyed in the Wi-Fi code. 'Oh God, this being offline nonsense is a nightmare. About a hundred emails just arrived.' She scrolled down through her inbox. 'Here we go, I asked Hunter to send an image of it.' She opened it up. 'Look.' She spun her screen around to show Caroline. 'There's over a hundred k. I mean, if you were the type of person who had that sort of money, you'd be a bit careful about where you left your statements, wouldn't you?'

Caroline peered at the image. 'You'd think so. But you'd hardly be living on the street either, would you?'

Rachel took another sip of her coffee. 'Maybe he wanted to. It's possible. From the rushes I saw, I don't think his mind was completely intact.'

'You know, that looks like an annual statement. And there are no actual transactions, just an ongoing balance. Can you ask the police, get them to check? They'll be investigating his death, won't they?'

'They found the bag. They must have gone through it.'

Caroline pursed her lips. She didn't want to say it, but Alfie was just another homeless guy, apparently with no family to complain about anything the police did or didn't do, and she was sure the Metropolitan Police were as overstretched as their counterparts were in other parts of the world. Things got missed.

'I think I'd check. Just to be sure.'

'Do you think I think I should call Alfie's case officer?'

'I think I'd call them both – whoever is investigating Hunter's accident, and the team looking into Alfie's death – just to make sure they both know there may be a bigger picture. The British police aren't like the guards, it's not a national force. The different teams could have no idea about each other's cases. It's more than likely they *don't*, actually. Unless the team investigating Alfie's death are planning to interview Hunter for background, then there's no reason for him to be referenced in connection with Alfie at all.'

Rachel looked shocked for a moment. 'My God, that's true. And the same person could be behind all three incidents.'

Caroline clicked her tongue on the roof of her mouth. 'Exactly. There's no time like the present. Do it now while you've got reception on your phone.' She looked out of the window. 'The rain's stopped.'

Rachel grabbed her jacket from the back of the chair.

'You're right. I've got the number of the officer investigating the break-in on the boat, and the officer who took me to see Hunter was from Kennington Station, he gave me his card. I'll call there too. And Frank will know who's investigating Alfie's death.'

Chapter 35

RACHEL CALLED FRANK first, to get the details of the team investigating Alfie's case. She caught him just as he was heading out to a meeting, but it only took him a moment to find the number of the station and text it to her.

Rachel could feel the cold cutting into her cheeks as she waited for the inspector in charge of Alfie's case to pick up. She'd got through to one of his assistants very quickly, and had been insistent that she speak to him directly. Now she was on hold listening to Tchaikovsky's *1812 Overture*. She heard the phone click.

'Hello, Detective Inspector Driver, how can I help you?'

Rachel hesitated. She hadn't expected a woman's voice, but it immediately made her feel more secure. She filled the inspector in on what she knew so far.

'So that's it, really. Hunter has Alfie's bag with the page from the bank statement in it. We were wondering if a J. A. Stafford had been registered as missing. But all these things happening – the camera equipment being stolen, Hunter being knocked off his bike – they could be connected.'

There was a pause at the other end. 'It's certainly something we need to look at. I'll get my officers to speak to their colleagues leading the other two investigations. It sounds like they all need to sit down together and compare notes. Has there been any further threat to your partner?'

'Not that I know of. He's in a public ward in the Royal Hope so I can't imagine too much could happen there?'

'I'll check with the nursing staff, see if anyone's been trying to get in touch with him or if he's had any unexpected visitors. Leave it with me.'

'Thank you. I'm going to call him now – I'll let him know to be careful.' Rachel felt anxiety flutter in her stomach. 'Do you think he needs some sort of protection?'

'Let's hope whoever broke into your boat thinks they've got all the film he made. But I think he and his colleagues need to be extremely careful about who they talk to until we've got more information and assessed whether there is an active threat.'

The words 'active threat' were ringing in her ears as she hit 'call' on Hunter's number. Jasper gave the back of her knee a nudge. He'd been wandering up and down the street while she was on the phone, but he was getting bored and needed his walk.

'I won't be long, Jasp, we'll get moving in a minute, I promise.'

He sat down in the middle of the pavement and looked at her, his head on one side. A moment later Hunter answered. He sounded tired.

'Hi, babes, what's up?'

Rachel took a deep breath, not sure where she should start.

'I need you to listen and just hear me out. We've realised something about Alfie and the break-in on the boat.'

'Who's "we"?'

'Me and Caroline, the crime reporter I told you about.'

'Tell me more.'

208

'Okay, I was just on to the inspector who's looking after Alfie's case—'

Hunter interrupted her. 'What have you found out, babes? Was he there at that Hare's place?'

'Shush a minute and listen. I'm standing in the street and it's freezing.' Rachel looked around again to make sure there was no one within earshot. 'Caroline is sure Alfie's death and your accident and the break-in are all connected. It's so obvious when you think about it. She thinks maybe someone didn't want Alfie talking to a TV crew, that there's something going on that—'

Hunter interrupted her again. 'It's Nemo Freight. Zack was here earlier and we came to the same conclusion. He said a Nemo Freight truck came into the car park while he was setting up his kit. The driver took one look at our van and turned around and literally hightailed it out of there. He only thought about it when he saw all the stuff in the papers about the drivers and management being arrested. Did you hear about it? It's all over the news. Drugs and people trafficking, they reckon.'

'I saw it in the *Irish Times*, it's front page here too. Will you contact your case officer about that? They need to know – you might need protection. If they were using that car park as a base for dealing drugs or whatever, Alfie could have been a witness. When they saw him talking to your guys, they must have panicked.'

'Zack went straight over to Kennington nick as soon as he left here. If we're right, that would explain a lot. If someone was worried about who Alfie was talking to, they could have followed me home any of the times I met him.'

'Those guys sound like proper criminals.'

'I reckon what the papers are reporting is only the tip of the iceberg. I'll call Zack right after I get off the phone to you, babes. Trust me, I'm not doing this shave with death thing again.' As if he'd heard what Hunter was saying, Jasper yelped. 'That my boy? Give him a hug from me. And listen, babes, I want you to stay there until this is sorted out, or at least until we've got a better idea of what's going on. There's no way you can go back to the boat.'

'It'll cost a fortune, can't I—'

'The insurance will pay – it's probably cheaper to stay over there than it is to rent somewhere in London. I'll get Mum to collect that bloody mail and find out what's happening with the assessor. Just stay there where I know you're safe?' He paused. 'My battery's on red, I'll call you on the landline at the hotel as soon as there's news. I'd better go.'

Rachel blew him a kiss down the phone. She felt sick. Caroline had been right that something sinister was going on.

*

'How did you get on?'

Caroline had ordered them both more coffee while she waited. She'd been watching Rachel as she paced up and down outside the window, talking to Hunter.

'You were right, the police hadn't connected Alfie and Hunter.' Rachel summarised her conversation. Caroline's ears pricked up at the words Nemo Freight.

'You mean the same Nemo Freight crowd that are all over the papers?'

'Exactly. That's what made Zack remember. Hunter reckons that they might have used that car park before, that Alfie might have seen something.'

'And they think he was talking to a film crew about it?'

'Exactly.'

'Holy cow. They really aren't nice people, going on what the paper said.'

'I know. And I bet they thought no one would miss some homeless guy, but they had to get Hunter's gear in case Alfie had said something on tape.' Rachel shook her head. 'It's horrible.'

Caroline took a sip of her coffee. 'While you were outside, I checked out Sheridan Smyth. He's not on social media, he doesn't even have a LinkedIn profile, which I *did* sort of expect. I'd guess he would have taken down all his social media when he became a judge. You have to be careful in that type of position.'

'Good point, I'd never have thought of that. Is there anything online about him?'

Right now, Rachel needed something – anything – to get her mind off Hunter, and some heavy from Nemo Freight murdering Alfie and then breaking into the barge.

'Indeed there is – he has a Wikipedia page. Which, while being notoriously unreliable, tells us he went to a private school in the south of England, and then to St Jude's College, Oxford.' She took another sip. 'And if we search for J. A. Stafford in connection to either of those institutions, we discover there was a James Stafford at St Jude's, who led the debating team to triumph in 1988 and 1989. A debating team in which Sheridan Smyth was a member.'

'Good God, how on earth did you find that out?'

'A photo on Facebook, one of those reunion "then and now" things.' She made rabbit ears with her fingers. 'They'd helpfully tagged it with everyone's names and the college. Facebook is very useful in my job, people put way more information on social media than they realise and it's brilliant for photographs. I've found people in the back of pictures that have totally blown open alibis. Obviously I need to do a lot more research on James Stafford to see if he's actually J. A. Stafford. Unfortunately, he doesn't seem to have a Facebook page.'

'Nobody had Facebook in 1989, it was—'

Caroline said it for her. 'The dark ages. I know. But most of the other people in the same photo seem to have them. They're all in their fifties now.'

'Can I see the picture?'

Caroline swung her laptop around for Rachel to look at. The photograph was blurry, a group of students celebrating in a pub all waving their glasses towards the camera. It looked like Christmas, one of them had a piece of tinsel draped around his neck. They looked raucous and a bit out of control, their hair longer than students would wear today.

'Sheridan is far left. I found a photo of him when he was appointed to the bench. He's aged obviously, but I'm sure that's him.' Caroline paused as Rachel looked at the photograph. 'Stafford is third from the left. See anything interesting?'

Rachel frowned for a moment as she scanned the image.

'Good God, he's wearing the same T-shirt, The Who tour shirt, the one that's in the photo of the house.' Rachel glanced up at her. 'Maybe lots of people had those T-shirts at the time, but it's some coincidence. It looks like J. A. Stafford was definitely here.'

'That's what I thought. We'll compare the two pictures when we get back, but he looks remarkably like the guy in the photo we've got.'

'And it proves beyond doubt that Sheridan Smyth knew James Stafford, who knew, or perhaps *was*, Alfie Bows.' Rachel raised her eyebrows. 'So *that's* how Alfie came to be at Hare's Landing.'

'So it appears.' Caroline looked across at her. 'Your wild goose chase might just have caught your wild goose.'

'I'd better call Hunter back and tell him we've found a connection to Sheridan Smyth and Hare's Landing while my phone's working. Are we ready to go now?' Rachel dipped her head to look out of the window at the sky. It was getting darker, but the rain seemed to be holding off for the moment at least. 'I want to get Jasper's walk in before it starts lashing again.'

'How about I stay here a bit longer and you take Jasper? I want to see what I can find out about Honoria Smyth now. I haven't even started on her yet.'

Rachel put her scarf back on, winding it around her neck.

'I'll call Hunter on the way down to the beach. I'll probably be about an hour, is that enough time?'

'Should be, but take as long as you need. I need to go through my email too and find out what's happening at work.'

Chapter 36

HUNTER'S PHONE WENT straight to his voicemail when Rachel tried to call him back. She texted him, the cold biting into her fingers, the tugs from Jasper's lead, looped over her arm, making it even more difficult. Finally, she hit send and pushed her hands into her pockets.

The main street was quiet as she headed down to the harbour and the beach. Jasper ran ahead of her, his extendable lead now tucked firmly into her pocket. Nose down, he was focused on following whatever scents he'd found, but stopped every few hundred yards to look back at her, as if he'd picked up on her mood.

She was glad of the walk, needed to be away from people for a bit to get her thoughts sorted out. She could feel the tension in the back of her neck and shoulders, radiating to her jaw. This whole situation had suddenly got really scary. But she was just so glad she'd met Caroline here. Would she have made any of these connections without her input and experience?

Thank God Hunter is okay. Just thank God.

Almost losing someone made you realise how much you loved them, and how much you needed them. She really didn't think she could live without him in her life. In two short years they'd become soulmates, almost finished each other's sentences. They always had something to talk about but found companionship in silence too. It helped that they both worked in the same business – each understood the demands of the other's job. She was away a lot when she was scouting or setting up a shoot, and sometimes filming took him away for weeks on end, but that was good for them both.

Whatever was going on back in London, at least she was safe here.

Caroline had been half joking when she said that the flip side of not having an internet signal meant no one could track your phone, but if Hunter was right about Nemo Freight being at the heart of all their problems, perhaps that was a very good thing. She didn't doubt that whoever had followed him home knew all about her too.

Reaching the solid, cold grey stone of the harbour, Rachel let Jasper off the lead and let him wander around the upturned boats, their brightly painted hulls cheerful against the slate grey of the sky. A young seagull watched them from its perch on a squat capstan, feathers mottled brown and white, its beady eye calculating.

The sea was choppy, eager wavelets dancing as the tide turned. Her mind full of Alfie and Nemo Freight, Rachel didn't hear footsteps behind her.

'He's a lovely dog. He must need a lot of walking.'

Rachel spun around to find Ava standing a short distance from her. Wrapped up in a thick padded coat, she held a letter in her hand.

'Oh, yes.' Rachel hesitated. 'Sorry, I was miles away. He's loving all the space here.'

'You're from London, aren't you? I'm Ava – the potter.' She gestured behind her at the stone house, its windows lit warmly to the growing dusk. 'You're staying with Caroline at Hare's Landing? She did a pottery workshop with me.'

Rachel tried to hide her surprise at Ava's immediate familiarity.

Caroline had been right about news travelling in this village.

'Yes, that's me.' It took a moment for her to think of something to follow it up with. 'I saw your work up at the hotel. Your glazing technique is beautiful. Caroline told me about it.'

'Thank you. It's very ancient. Are you interested in ceramics?'

Ava took a step closer to her, pulling back a strand of greying hair that blew across her face. Thrusting her hands deeper into her pockets against the sea breeze, Rachel nodded.

'I did Art at uni, I loved that part of the course.'

Ava's face was warm and open. 'Really? Where did you study?'

'London. I'm from Wicklow originally, that's how I ended up over there. Feels like a long time ago now.'

'I know, time seems to pass so quickly. And what brings you to Hare's Landing? John Francis mentioned you were looking for a relative who played the violin?'

Rachel hid her surprise. 'Yes. But I think we've found out when he was here. Seems he was a friend of Sheridan Smyth's, he wasn't playing in a concert at all.'

'Really? Well done. John Francis said you didn't have much information to go on and it had been a while ago.' Ava paused, an expectancy in the framing of her sentence.

'Ages ago, as it turns out. About thirty years.'

Rachel deliberately glanced over to see what Jasper was sniffing at. She wasn't sure why, but she didn't feel comfortable sharing information with Ava. Her interest didn't feel like just polite conversation for some reason.

As if she sensed Rachel's hesitation, Ava pulled her coat around her.

'I'm just off to post this, but if you'd like to drop into the pottery after your walk, I can show you some of the bigger pieces.'

'That would be lovely but I need to get back. Caroline's waiting for me at the cafe.'

Ava smiled. 'If you'd like to do a workshop just let me know, I can show you how I do the glaze. I've got a slot free on Wednesday afternoon if you're free. I've another firing scheduled for Thursday. Caroline might like to come too, I think she enjoyed the last one.'

'She did. Thank you. I'd love to, I'm sure she would too.'

'Would two o'clock suit? That'll give us a run at the afternoon and plenty of time for a chat.'

Rachel hesitated, unsure whether she could speak for Caroline. But Caroline had enjoyed the workshop, and she'd said she wanted to talk to Ava again. Perhaps this was the ideal opportunity. And it would get them out of the house for a few hours. Gorgeous as it was, with the lack of internet and what felt like constant rain, it was starting to feel a little claustrophobic.

'Perfect, we'll see you then.'

Nodding, Ava returned her smile. 'Super, I'll look forward to it. I'd better go, I need to catch the post.'

Turning, Rachel watched as she walked up towards the road.

Rachel whistled for Jasper and turned towards the beach. He ran past her enthusiastically, his tail wagging. She could see the tide was coming in, the strip of shingle getting narrower as the dusk drew in. Out to sea the clouds were darkening, heavy with more rain. They needed to be quick.

Chapter 37

IN THE CAFE, Caroline opened her browser window. Now they'd found what appeared to be a concrete link between Alfie, Sheridan Smyth and the summer of 1990, she wanted to know more about Honoria Smyth and how she fitted into the picture. There was so much about her that intrigued Caroline. She was an American living in Ireland, the reverse of Caroline – Irish, living in America. She had a sense that, like her, Honoria had felt a bit dislocated.

Ireland would always be home for Caroline; she felt that New York was a stopgap. Had Honoria felt like that too – as if she didn't really fit, that she was only a visitor? Being on the outside could be lonely. Caroline knew all about that, which was, she'd also realised, why she spent so much time at work. She was forging a career, and the hours paid off, but if she didn't work, what could she do? Go for a walk around Central Park on her own? Was that how Honoria had felt? Alfie had been an outsider too, dislocated from society in a different way. He must have felt lonely as well.

Caroline put Honoria Smyth's name into the search bar and hit Enter. A list of entries appeared linked to her name.

She sipped her coffee as she scrolled down. Honoria's books first, lots of them. She'd been first published in 1967;

there were lots of reviews and vague author biographies but Caroline couldn't find any interviews. Which was a bit strange, but perhaps she really was reclusive, or maybe they just weren't online.

Clicking on, Caroline recognised the oil paintings of the sea she'd seen in the house. They were all square, the paint thick, layered, each one full of colour, vibrant blues and greens against stark white, conveying the movement and power of the waves. On one of the London gallery auction sites, there was an 'official' biography. It was only a few lines, and listed Honoria Franklin Smyth's birth year as 1943. And she had RA after her name – didn't that mean Royal Academy? Which meant she was a recognised talent. She wondered if Bronagh had realised that the paintings peppering the walls of the hotel and the Boathouse could be worth a lot of money.

Caroline glanced at the time on the screen. Rachel would be back soon and her window of opportunity would close. This whole lack of internet was a real problem.

Caroline looked at her screen, her mind focused on Honoria Smyth. What did she actually want to know? She had her year of birth and a feel for Honoria, and her husband – there were pages and pages on the cases he'd acted in. But the gardener? If he had killed himself too, the whole story felt very melodramatic – the knight falling on his sword for his lost love. Caroline had a feeling the truth was a little more sordid: older woman falls for younger man who spends a couple of years living off her in a big house until she discovers she's pregnant, and then vanishes.

Someone must know his name. *Who was 'D'?* And who could she ask without word spreading like wildfire that she was investigating the house and its owners?

The mother who had been chatting to the girl behind the counter began packing up her children. Caroline glanced at them, smiling as they passed her.

'Can I get you another coffee?'

Her attention finally fully on her job, the girl came over to clear Caroline's table.

'Please, I'd love one.'

'Are you working there? That looks very complicated.'

Caroline cleared her throat. 'Family history. Trying to find someone who was here in the 1980s.'

The girl pulled a face. 'Before I was born. John Francis would know though, I'd guess, he knows everyone who's ever lived here. Everyone calls in to him for the milk and the news.'

Caroline had thought of asking Mr Mahony when she was in his store the other day, but was now very glad she hadn't. She had no idea who wanted her to leave Hare's Landing, and there was no way she was going to alert them to what she was working on. She was sure there was a good chance John Francis Mahony could tell her exactly what she wanted to know, but equally that he'd tell everyone else what she'd asked.

'That's a great idea, I'll pop in next time I'm here.'

Looking at the time, conscious that she wouldn't have internet access for much longer, she closed the windows on her searches and opened her email, typing in Tim's name. Her message was short:

'Can you Dropbox me the photos of the Christmas party?'

The party been niggling her since Tim had mentioned it on the phone. Whatever Greta's problem was, he thought it stemmed from that. Though goodness only knew how that could involve her.

Perhaps if she could see who had been talking to who, in the group shots, she'd get a better idea. Had Nancy said something to Greta about her? The photos might be able to tell her if Nancy had been sitting next to Greta and Clive at the dinner. It wouldn't give her an answer, but it would help paint the picture. When she was researching anything, it was about building a picture, taking the morsels of information she could find and seeing how they interrelated. If she could see the photos, she might have some clue as to what had gone on that night.

She hit Send.

And a message came straight back.

Surprised, she hardly noticed the girl putting her coffee down for her, was distantly aware that she was clearing away the mugs and plates behind her. Tim had sent a Dropbox link with a short message 'in haste'. Caroline looked at the clock in the corner of the screen. Would she have time to download them before Rachel got back? It was worth a try. Caroline was sure she wouldn't mind waiting a few moments. She opened the link and hit Download. There was a tradition of everyone pooling the Christmas party photos and sharing them around the office. Mainly because the young ones who went on clubbing afterwards couldn't remember what they'd said or done by the time they showed up at work the next Monday. She'd never been very interested before – she always stayed for the meal, but once everyone had a few jars on board it could get messy and she usually slipped off home.

The photos finished downloading and she saved the file to her hard drive. Now she could look at them at her leisure.

As she picked up her coffee, Rachel appeared at the door looking like she'd been blown up the street, a gust of cold air coming in with her.

'My God, it's freezing. How did you get on?' Before Caroline could answer, she sat down, rubbing her hands together. 'I met

221

Ava down by the harbour.' Caroline's eyebrows shot up. 'She was lovely. She said she'd like to see you again – maybe she feels bad that she misjudged you. She suggested we go down for another workshop on Wednesday. I said yes if that's okay, our diaries aren't exactly booked out.'

'That sounds great. I'd like to have a proper chat with her now I've got the full picture.' Caroline knocked back the rest of her coffee. 'Let's get moving and see if we can get back before it gets dark.'

Chapter 38

'CRIPES, LOOK AT that rain. I've never seen it this heavy. It's just as well we came back when we did, the drive's awash. There'll be ducks out there next.'

Caroline's breath steamed up the lounge window and she rubbed it with the sleeve of her sweater, watching the rain splashing down for a few more moments before she went back to the sofa. Despite having been down to the village, she felt fidgety.

The moment they'd got back they'd compared the photo of J. A. Stafford on Facebook with the photograph in the hall of the two men standing outside Hare's Landing. As well as the matching T-shirt, facially the two images looked remarkably similar. They were sure it was the same person.

Caroline felt as if she was on the edge of learning something important about whatever had happened that summer, and she wanted to keep digging. As soon as Bronagh got back, she was going to ask her if she could use the internet connection in the office. It might be slow but it was worth a try.

Rachel interrupted her thoughts. 'When do you think we'll hear about Mrs Travers? I'm dying to ask her about Alfie staying here.'

Caroline took her glasses off and gave them a polish on the hem of her sweater. 'When Bronagh gets back, I suppose. At least she got treatment really fast. If she'd been at home, she could still be on the floor.' She leaned back on the sofa. Jasper was lying on the hearthrug in front of the fire, stretched out so his stomach got the full benefit of the heat. She felt like joining him. 'She is a bit of a weapon, but being alone when you breathe your last isn't how I'd like to depart this life.'

Rachel leaned forward on the opposite sofa, her elbows on her knees, chin in her hands.

'That's what I keep thinking about poor Alfie. I really hope he wasn't conscious at the end.' She leaned forward to tickle Jasper. 'There's a sort of kinship between homeless people, but it's very brutal on the streets too. Alfie told Hunter he used to be able to get a ticket for the platform in Victoria for a couple of pence. He'd go and find a train that was in the station – there was one he said that arrived at 12.15 and left at 6 a.m., I can't remember where he said it was going. He used to go and get on it to sleep. There were a lot of people hanging around Victoria, using the loos to clean up and pinching leftover food from the cafes. He said people even slept on the night buses, changing when they reached their destination. It's not a way to live. Even if you know people on the street, it's such a case of having to survive that I don't know if you ever really have friends.'

Caroline tilted her head thoughtfully. She was fascinated by Alfie's story, even more so now they had an idea about his true identity – it had her investigative curiosity on full blast. And she knew Rachel desperately wanted to take Hunter some good news. Alfie had trusted Hunter and Hunter felt that somehow he'd let him down. And that was even before he'd known anything about a possible link with Nemo Freight. Now Hunter had to be feeling a whole lot worse. If seeing Alfie talking to the camera crew had brought about his death, it took responsibility to a whole new level.

Caroline pushed her hair over her shoulder, still damp from running to the Land Rover and then into the house.

'We'll find out what Alfie's story was, don't worry. I'm sure I can find out more about him and Sheridan Smyth, now we know who Alfie really was. I spend my life trying to find links between people and events, trying to track down witnesses.'

Caroline wrinkled up her nose, thinking, but before she could say more, Imogen arrived carrying a tray laden with bowls of salad. They'd decided on a light supper tonight, had both agreed that they were enjoying far too much of Conor's cooking.

'I'm so sorry for the delay, ladies.' Her face was worried as she slid the tray onto the table. 'Did Bronagh say when she'd be back? Her phone seems to be switched off.'

'I think she's going to stay until Mrs Travers comes around, or at least until she's comfortable. She doesn't have any family, does she?'

Rachel leaned forward, interrupting Caroline.

'Is everything okay? You look a bit stressed.'

Imogen pulled a face and smoothed her hands down her trousers, obviously very worried about something. Rachel looked at her encouragingly.

'It's okay, really, tell us – we'll see if we can help. Today is definitely a day for teamwork.'

'I don't know what's wrong exactly. Conor's not back here until later, and I can't get hold of him either.' Imogen took a breath. 'It's the plumbing. Well, maybe it's not the actual plumbing but there's something wrong with the pipes. The toilets in the staff area are all backed up and the water's not draining from the sinks.'

Rachel looked at her thoughtfully for a moment and then glanced at the window, the view completely obscured by the rain.

'Have you checked the toilets in the rest of the house?'

Imogen bit her lip. 'They're flushing all right but the water doesn't go anywhere, it's filling up the toilet bowl. One of them has overflowed.'

Rachel pulled a face. 'Lovely. Are you on mains drainage here?'

Imogen made an open handed gesture. 'I don't know anything about the drains. Could it be all this rain? My mum said the water's washing through the village like a river now. Apparently, they've got sandbags outside the pub.'

Rachel stood up, causing Jasper to grumble.

'I hate to say it, but living on a boat you end up with far too much experience of sewage disposal.' Imogen looked even more worried as she continued. 'If there's no flow, everything gets backed up. If you're on the mains there shouldn't be a problem, but I bet you're on a septic tank and all this rain has filled it up. If the ground's waterlogged around the septic tank run-off, then what's leaving the house hasn't got anywhere to go. It's been raining so heavily – I think it's only because you're on a bit of a slope here that the house hasn't flooded.' Rachel went over to the window and put her hand around her eyes to see out more clearly. 'Look, it's getting worse, there are streams running across the gravel.'

'What do we do? Thank God we aren't fully booked.'

'I think you need a plumber to start with, or a drains man. Someone who knows how the system works here.'

'Bronagh's the only one who would know how it works or who to call.'

Caroline glanced at her watch. 'It's almost six o'clock now. If you've left messages, Bronagh would have got back to you already if she'd got them. Have you got a phone book? We'll need to be quick to catch someone tonight.'

Imogen looked flustered, put her hand to her forehead.

'There must be one somewhere. Don't plumbers charge a fortune though? Bronagh will go mad.'

'She'll be a lot madder if raw sewage starts coming back up through every loo in the place. This won't wait until she gets back, by the sounds of things. Can you check the empty rooms and close all the lids of the toilets?'

Imogen put her hands to her face. 'Oh my God, I can't believe this is happening today. First Mrs Travers, now this …'

Chapter 39

THE NEXT MORNING it was still raining hard.

'How does it look?'

Rachel stood up from her chair at the huge farmhouse kitchen table as the plumber came in through the back door, his thick padded jacket glistening. He hadn't been able to get to them the previous night, but he'd been as good as his word and come out early this morning. It wasn't even light when he'd arrived.

He shook the water off his jacket and wiped his face with his hand.

'I think you're right. The ground all around the septic tank is flooded. It's a good one too, never had a moment's trouble out of it since I came back to Glencurragh. Most of them you have to get emptied every couple of years, but if they're properly built you shouldn't have to at all.'

'So what now?'

'We're going to need to get it emptied – can I use the phone? Mobile's useless here. I'll get the lads to come down with a tractor. It's been raining for so long the ground's saturated, there's nowhere for more water to go. I've never seen anything like it. But once the lads are here it won't take them long to get it pumped out and then you'll be back to normal.'

As he spoke, Caroline came into the kitchen, Jasper at her heels.

'Pumped to where? Not into the sea?'

He shook his head. 'No, no, we'll get rid of it for you. Lots of uses for waste …'

Caroline held up her hands, stopping him. 'Some things I don't need to know at this time in the morning.'

He laughed. 'When's Bronagh back?'

'She was exhausted when she got in from the hospital last night. We had a brandy and I told her about the septic tank. I said Caroline and I would help Conor and Imogen sort it out. She thought she'd be gone most of today. She went out early to collect an overnight bag for Mrs Travers on the way back to Ross Haven.'

'I'd say she needed a brandy all right. Never rains but it pours, as they say. Are you both staying here?'

'I am – Caroline's in the Boathouse.'

Rachel inclined her head in Caroline's direction and stood up, heading for the kettle. Caroline had sprinted through the deepening puddles back to the Boathouse last night, despite Rachel's efforts to try and persuade her to stay in the main house. They'd compromised with her agreeing to take Jasper with her. The fact that the howling wind and constantly pounding rain were so loud that Caroline wouldn't be able to hear anything if anybody did break in had worried Rachel a lot, but she knew Jasper wouldn't have that problem. She'd been relieved to hear the night had been uneventful when they'd both come up to the house early this morning.

'I don't know if there's a landline down here or if you'll need to go back to reception. Where's Imogen?' Rachel turned to Caroline.

'She was in the bar when I came past.' She turned to the plumber. 'Follow me.'

As they left the kitchen, Rachel filled the kettle at the huge white porcelain Belfast sink. It was a huge room. It had been modernised by the various owners, professional stainless-steel counters lining the walls, but a dark green Aga that looked like it had been in situ since the house was built was still pumping out heat at one end. Always the first to find warmth, Jasper had flopped down in front of it, was toasting his back against its cast-iron walls.

A few minutes later she heard Caroline and the plumber coming back down the hall. Coming into the kitchen, Caroline pulled out a chair out from the table and sat down as the plumber hovered in the doorway, his hands stuck in his pockets.

'The lads are on the way with the tractor, they've just a job to finish first and they'll be right here. This weather's mad, I've never seen this much rain in all my life.'

Behind him, Imogen came into the kitchen, a pile of tea towels in her hand.

'I've checked upstairs and nothing's overflowed yet, thank God.'

*

'Do you think it'll take long?' Caroline put her hands to the glass and peered out of the kitchen window. Rachel could hear the tractor backing into the stable yard as she continued. 'I'm starting to get a bit stir-crazy stuck inside.'

It was mid-afternoon. The earlier job had taken longer than planned, but at least they were here now. Rachel went over to the window to watch the activity outside.

'Once everything's working here, we can go up to the village. The Landie won't have any problems with the mud.

You should have come with me and Jasper this morning for our walk. He went for miles along the beach. He wanted to go and look at that old castle but I was too wet at that stage. It's really overgrown, and with the mist swirling around it like something from a horror movie. There was a whole flock of crows roosting in it – they all took off when they heard us.'

Caroline pulled away from the window to reply, 'I think they're called a murder of crows.' She raised an eyebrow. 'But I'd need some serious wet weather gear to join you guys. I'm set up for rain in New York where you hold up an umbrella and go from taxi to air-conditioned lobby.'

'You'd *definitely* need wellies.' Rachel glanced back out of the window. 'I brought my sailing jacket as well as my skiing jacket, just in case.'

Caroline shook her head. 'You must have worn Jasper out this morning. He's not moved from that Aga. We'd better hope Health and Safety don't decide to do a surprise kitchen check.'

'Very true. We'll pretend we're friends of Bronagh's, not guests. The place is basically closed really. Especially now Mrs Travers is in hospital.'

'Did Bronagh have any idea of the prognosis when you saw her last night?'

Rachel turned her back to the window and sat on the radiator under it, twisting her ring. Despite the heat from the Aga, she was feeling chilled.

'No, the doctors really didn't know, I'd guess it's too soon to tell. She was exhausted – I didn't want to push her. She did say they've got Mrs Travers hooked up to all sorts of machines, but she was more worried about the drainage here at that stage.'

'Sewage issues are all she needs right now.' Caroline paused. 'More tea? I'll put the kettle on again.'

As Caroline headed over to the Aga, Rachel turned back to look out of the window. Two men had got out of the tractor and were unhooking a giant corrugated pipe from the tanker. With the end ready, one of them leaned down and pulled a huge iron ring that was sunk into the concrete floor of the stable yard, lifting a rusted steel cover. The tube was pushed down the hole. One of the men strode back to the tanker and, Rachel guessed, switched it on. Even with the wind whipping the rain against the window she could hear the pump engine growling into action.

'Right, they're starting. Let's hope it's a fast pump.' Rachel turned back to Caroline, who raised her hands to the ceiling in mock thanks. 'And yes please. They're going to need a cup of tea when they're finished too.'

'You can't have them in the kitchen after they've been doing that. They could be covered in … well, waste.' Caroline sounded shocked.

Rachel stifled a laugh. 'I can take it out to them, don't worry.' She turned back to the window. 'Uh-oh. There's something up.'

'What?'

'They've stopped, look.'

Caroline rejoined her beside the window and, as they watched, the men pulled the tubing out of the hole and both leaned in to inspect the end. One of them moved around, blocking their view so they couldn't see the end of it, but they could tell from their body language that they were puzzled by something. The one bending over with his back to them glanced behind him, looking at the house. Then he slowly stood up. They were obviously having a conversation; the man standing began nodding and pulled out his mobile phone. Pulling off one glove under his arm, he tried to dial.

Caroline frowned. 'That's not going to work. I wonder what's happening? Should we go out?'

The man outside realised he had no signal on his phone and glanced over his shoulder again, then turned and headed for the back door. Rachel reached it before he did, pulling it open to a gust of wind and rain that blew her strawberry blonde hair out of her face.

'Is there a problem?'

'You could say that. I think you need to call the guards. We've found some bones. Human bones.'

Chapter 40

THE BLUE STROBE lights on the Garda car cut through the darkness, bouncing off the windows of the house and the shroud of trees that encircled the sweep of the drive, as it pulled up outside the front door.

Caroline went straight to open it. She'd been completely absorbed in her thoughts while she'd been waiting. The drainage men had found a human skull. It still hadn't sunk in.

Who could it possibly belong to?

Part of her still couldn't believe it. She'd seen some terrible things out on the streets in New York, but here in the gorgeous landscape of West Cork it was worse somehow, utterly chilling. Rachel had gone positively grey with shock.

Leaning on the reception desk waiting for the guards, Caroline had started doodling on a pad she'd fished out from behind it, trying to make sense of everything. But there just seemed to be so many strands, tangled like knitting. She wrote down names in thought bubbles: *Honoria Smyth, Alfie Bows, Sheridan Smyth. How did they all fit together?* And then there was that boy who had gone missing – what was his name? – Johnny O'Connor. Caroline felt her heart skip. Why hadn't she thought of him before?

Could he have ended up at Hare's Landing?

Pulling the door open to let the guards inside, Caroline could see the rain was getting heavier. Carried by the wind, it was virtually horizontal.

'We got a call?'

The guard pulled off his hat as he spoke, raindrops covering it like precious stones, and put it under the arm of his navy bomber jacket. His colleague followed him, his mouth on the radio clipped to his jacket.

'Hi, it's this way. It's quickest through the kitchens.'

Caroline led the way down the corridor to the back of the house, conscious of their boots squeaking on the wide wooden floorboards in the hallway.

'And you are?'

'Caroline Kelly. I'm a guest. I'm staying in the Boathouse.'

He threw her a puzzled look.

'I know, guests don't usually get involved with the drains.' *Where did she start?* 'It's a long story, there's been a lot happening here. I can fill you in once you've …'

He looked at her quizzically, obviously detecting the weariness in her voice.

'One step at a time – let's see what we've got here first. The report said some bones had been found.'

Nodding, Caroline threw him a weak grin. 'In the septic tank. And they definitely aren't animal bones.'

As Caroline pushed open the door of the kitchen Jasper came shooting out, sniffing at the two guards, his tail waving madly.

'Jasper, heel!'

Rachel's voice was sharp and he responded immediately, trotting back to stand beside her protectively.

The first guard nodded to her, his eyes on Jasper.

'Well-behaved dog.'

'Malachi? Malachi O'Brien?' Rachel half stood up from her chair and looked at him incredulously. 'What the hell are you doing here?'

He looked back at Rachel properly and shook his head.

'Rachel Lambert? I could ask you the same thing, I thought you were in London making a fortune.'

'I was … I am. Well, not the fortune bit. What are you doing here?'

'I'm stationed at Ross Haven, got moved out of Dun Laoghaire when I made sergeant.'

'They couldn't have moved you much further.'

'Could have been Muff.' He paused, smiling. 'So why are you here?'

'Holiday … well, sort of.' She sighed. 'It seems to have taken on a whole new direction in the last twenty minutes.'

Malachi came into the room properly and put his hat on the table.

'So what's been going on here exactly?'

'You need to talk to the drain guys. They're outside, they needed a smoke.'

'I bet. Give me your take on it first.'

'Well, it's all quite simple really. Everywhere's flooded with this bloody rain and the septic tank started to back up. Bronagh – she owns Hare's Landing –' from Malachi's expression Rachel realised that he already knew, so she kept going – 'is in Ross Haven. The housekeeper had a heart attack yesterday and she doesn't have any family, *so* we – myself and Caroline – called the drain guys in. Imogen's brother Conor …' Rachel nodded towards Imogen, who smiled weakly. She'd been sitting at the end of the table, her arms wrapped around herself since they'd called the guards. 'Conor would normally look after this sort of thing, but he's got another job in Sommerville at a restaurant and they're *completely* flooded.' Rachel shook her head. 'I've been wondering why Jasper has been so interested in the stable yard and barks his head off every time he's out there, I should have realised.' She sighed. 'God, this is totally surreal, and then you turn up …'

'Go on.'

'Sorry, so they were all set to pump out the tank but the pipe thing …'

'Gully sucker.'

'That's it. Well, it got blocked. When they pulled it up there was –' she drew a breath, paling – 'there was a skull caught in the end. A human skull.'

Malachi kept his face impassive. 'Where is it now?'

'They left it right where it was and came in to use the phone.'

'Good. Sounds like we need to call in the troops. Let's just have a look outside.'

Rachel indicated the back door with a sweep of her hand as Malachi put his hat back on, his voice grim.

'Can you all stay in here, please?'

'Of course. I'll put the kettle on. I guess you might be here for a while.'

As the back door closed on Malachi and his colleague, Caroline opened her eyes wide.

'Well, Rachel Lambert, you're a dark horse. Have you got any more gorgeous friends up your sleeve? How do you know him?'

Rachel laughed, blushing. 'We went to school together, first boyfriend.'

Caroline's eyes opened in surprise. 'What is this country like? You can't go anywhere, can you?'

Rachel shook her head. 'What time is it?' She glanced at her chunky watch. 'Six o'clock? Imogen, do you want to call home and tell them you'll be a bit late? We don't want them thinking you got lost in the storm. Just say you're sorting out the drains? If this gets out there'll be a load of press descending. Bronagh's got enough on her plate.'

'Did you get through to Bronagh yet?' Caroline's voice was full of concern as she sat down at the table, and Jasper trotted around to put his head on her knee. She tickled his ears affectionately. 'I'm all right, you silly boy. I'm not so sure about our friend outside, though.'

'Who the heck can it be? I mean, it could have been there for *years*.'

Imogen leaned forward in her chair, her face ashen. Answering Caroline's question about Bronagh, Rachel shook her head.

'No, I've left a message. I just said to call. There's no point in her rushing back from the hospital, there's nothing she can do.'

Caroline sighed. 'You're right. Whoever it is has clearly been dead a very long time.'

'Christ, what's going on?' As she spoke, Conor trudged into the kitchen from the direction of the hotel, his car keys in his hand, his jacket soaked through. 'There's a cop car outside. I thought you were calling a plumber, not the police … And there's a dog in my kitchen.'

He looked at Jasper as if his presence was more of an issue than the Garda car.

'Where've you been? I've been calling all day. The drains men found a body in the septic tank. Well, a skull anyway.'

Imogen jumped up from the table and punched her brother on the shoulder.

'Sorry, I got caught up at Graylings. I was just coming to pick you up. Can we get the dog into the lounge, do you think?'

Imogen glared at him. 'Jasper isn't the problem. The drain men found a *skull* in the septic tank. We've no idea how long it's been there, I mean, how long does a body take to rot in a septic tank?'

Conor didn't seem in the slightest bit fazed. He narrowed his eyes.

'Decomposition really depends on the conditions. The whole point of a septic tank is that it's filled with bacteria that digest the waste. Bodies decompose more slowly in water than they do in the air, though, so there are a few factors to take into account.'

He shouldered off his wet coat, looking thoughtful as Rachel clicked her fingers to Jasper. He trotted over to her and lay down under the table. Conor didn't seem to notice, was obviously deep in thought about the septic tank.

'Good place to get rid of a body. Not like the bogs where everything gets mummified.'

'Conor.' Imogen sounded aghast.

'Sorry, it's interesting.'

Imogen scowled at him. 'You should have done medicine like Gramps and Dad, not marine biology. Then you could be doing something useful instead of cooking for a living.'

'I like cooking. And it's only a stopgap. Damned sight more useful than history.' Conor leaned backwards on the Aga, his hands on the stainless steel rail that ran across the front of it, his face thoughtful. 'Have the cops said anything? It could have ended up in there quite recently? Like it might not be hundreds of years.' He looked at them keenly. 'Do they think the whole body's in there or just the head?'

'Conor, that's horrible. Will you shut up?' Imogen had gone even paler. 'I think I'm going to be sick.'

He looked alarmed. 'Christ, make sure you go outside. If the septic tank's out of action we won't be able to flush any of the bogs. Have a glass of water.'

'Here, Imogen, come and sit down. You'll be fine.' Caroline turned to Rachel. 'Conor has a point – the plumbing in this house is going to be out of commission until they can clear the scene. If they're fast and they can get forensics and the pathologist down tomorrow, it might only be a few days, but …'

Rachel rolled her eyes. 'Oh, crap.'

'The Boathouse must be on a separate system – I haven't had any problems. I think it's too far away– and it's downhill, so I can't imagine it's linked to this tank or there would need to be a pump house and God knows what.'

Caroline looked at Conor for confirmation.

'That's right. Totally separate system.'

'So come down and stay with me. I think the sofa turns into a bed. And …' Caroline paused meaningfully. 'Having Jasper around will be very nice.'

Rachel tucked her hair behind her ear. 'But you came here for some peace and quiet.'

'And you came here for a break that involved occasional washing and using the facilities. In the absence of those we need a plan B.'

Rachel stood up and leaned on the table. 'Very practical. I suppose you're right.'

Imogen picked up Conor's coat from the back of the chair he'd slung it around and looped it over the stainless steel rail of the Aga to dry out.

'I can drop some bedlinen down and make up the sofa before we go home. We'll get the fire lit too.'

'Don't be silly, we can do that if you can find the stuff for us to take down.' I'll be able to use some of that lovely food in the fridge for dinner. Conor, can I get a couple of bottles of wine from you?'

'No problem, there's plenty in the cellar.'

'Excellent news.' Caroline glanced at Rachel. 'We'll just wait for the guards to come back and see if it's okay for Imogen to get off home. She's had a very long day.'

Before she could answer, they heard the sound of the back door opening and someone stamping in the porch. A moment later Malachi appeared, followed by his colleague. He was about ten years older than Malachi, heavy around the waist, his ruddy face creased with concern.

Malachi inclined his head in a greeting to Conor, choosing his words carefully.

'We're going to need to secure the scene and get a team in. You're not going to be able to use the septic tank for a few days at least, I'd imagine. You'll have to close the main house.' He looked at Rachel. 'Are you staying here?'

'I was. Caroline's staying in the Boathouse, though. It's self-contained so I'm going to stay with her tonight.'

'Grand. Joe here will need all your details. We won't keep you long. Have you got a number for Bronagh?'

Rachel pulled out her phone to give it to him. There was no signal now but it had been coming and going all day. She didn't have any new missed calls, or messages except a text update from Hunter.

'I've left messages, she must still be at the hospital.'

'We'll get someone to find her there. We're going to need to look back over the records she's got, and she'll need somewhere to stay too.'

'Do you think it was someone who was visiting here

241

when it was a hotel before?' Imogen's hand flew to her mouth.

'We don't know anything at this stage. Anything at all. Please be careful what you say when you get home. I'm sure word will travel pretty fast, but we need to keep this as quiet as possible until we have more information.'

Rachel found the number in her phone and looked up at him.

'I'm not sure Bronagh will be able to help much. She's only been here about a year, I think. The person who knows everything about this place is Mrs Travers.'

Malachi pursed his lips. 'We'll need a chat with her as soon as she's well enough.'

Chapter 41

AN HOUR LATER the stable yard looked like the set of a film. Arc lights had been set up to illuminate the area around the septic tank cover and men in white overalls were clustered in groups discussing … Rachel had no idea what. In truth she didn't really want to know. Fascinated by the activity, Jasper was on his back legs looking out, his nose pressed to the window. Every time the back door opened he shot over to see what was happening.

Unable to do anything constructive, Caroline had gone down to the lounge with her laptop to look at some photos that her colleague in New York had sent over. Neither of them was feeling very useful, but Rachel wanted to wait at the main house for Bronagh.

And she was looking for an opportunity to talk to Malachi.

Keeping the coffee topped up was the best excuse she could think of to hang around the kitchen, although at this stage everyone had been in at least once and she had a sink full of crockery to wash. The hotel dishwasher was far too big to put on for a few mugs and probably emptied into the septic tank anyway. Rachel filled a basin, planning to throw the dirty water out of the front door when she'd finished. She was pulling the sleeves of her sweater up when she heard the back door open.

'They're nearly done. We'll need to preserve the scene for a bit but the detailed work is almost finished.'

She turned to look over her shoulder and Malachi gave her a tired grin as he put his hat on the table and sat down. Jasper was beside him in a moment, his head on one side. Malachi rubbed his ears.

'I'm not sure he should be in the kitchen but he's a gorgeous dog.'

'He's invisible, you can't see him, and if Health and Safety or the food people turn up, we'll hide him.'

'I hear you.' Malachi tickled Jasper again as Rachel continued.

'He's retired now but he was a police dog. I think he recognises the uniform.'

As if on cue, Jasper sat down expectantly beside Malachi, his ears forward, as if he was waiting for instructions. Malachi laughed.

'So how are you finding Ross Haven after the big smoke?' Rachel rinsed out a mug as she spoke.

'Actually, a lot busier than I thought. I was in drugs in Dun Laoghaire, which held me in good stead when I came down here, I can tell you.' He rolled his eyes. 'When Dawson O'Rourke left Dun Laoghaire, the whole team changed, it was time to move on. He's a super now, in Limerick.'

'And didn't you work with that girl – Cat someone, the boxer? She was in the papers.'

'I did, she's in the Emergency Response Unit now, although they are all supposed to be anonymous, so you didn't hear that from me.' He gave Jasper another rub and looked up at her. 'So how on earth did you end up in Hare's Landing?'

Rachel finished scrubbing the mug in her hand and put it on the drainer, picking up a tea towel and drying her hands.

'How long have you got?

'It could be all night at this rate, someone's got to stay and Joe's missus is already giving him grief.'

Rachel threw the tea towel onto the drainer and came and sat down opposite him, twisting her ring as she frowned.

'I'm not sure where to start.'

'The beginning is usually a good place.'

'You're just as smart as ever.'

He flashed her a grin, his blue eyes as piercing as they had been when he'd been sixteen.

'Thank you, I'll take that as a compliment that I haven't aged a day.'

Rachel rolled her eyes. 'There's been quite a lot happening ...'

She explained as best he could, Malachi nodding periodically without interrupting.

'So that's it really. Hunter's in hospital and I came to see if I could find something out about Alfie and his background.'

Malachi leaned forward, frowning, and rubbed his chin with his hand.

'Hunter, your partner, thinks Nemo Freight are mixed up in all of this somehow?'

'He's sure of it. He texted this afternoon to say he's spoken to all the different officers now and they are all trying to co-ordinate.'

'That's good, very good.' Malachi tapped his fingers on the table, obviously thinking for a moment. 'Nemo Freight are registered here. Our lads have had an eye on their trucks for a while. There's a lot of drug-related activity along this coast. I'll pass all that on, if you don't mind, and we can follow up with our colleagues in London.'

'Please do. Does it sound plausible to you – that the three incidents are linked, I mean? Just because I think it—'

'It seems extremely likely. Nemo Freight are a bad bunch. But I'd like to know what your friend Alfie was doing here at Hare's Landing, and what might have happened to make him change direction so radically. Particularly taking into account tonight's events.'

'You don't think he could have been involved?' Rachel's hand flew to her mouth.

He raised his eyebrows. 'We don't know anything yet. The body could have been there five years or fifty. We can't make any assumptions until we see the post-mortem report.'

'I'm sure Alfie couldn't have had anything to do with it. I was wondering if it could be this handyman guy, the one Honoria Smyth was supposed to have been having an affair with? The Smyths lived here thirty years ago. Honoria committed suicide. Caroline's been trying to find out her story.'

Malachi raised an eyebrow. 'Before my time. Tell me more.'

Rachel traced a knot in the table with her fingernail, the eyes in the skull ring on her finger flashing in the light from the fluorescent tubes overhead.

'The rumour is that she was having an affair with a gardener or handyman, one of the staff anyway. Caroline's a crime reporter in New York, she was wondering if there was more to the suicide. She can tell you better herself. But no one seems to know what happened to the gardener guy or who he was.'

'And you think …?' Malachi jerked his head backwards towards the stable yard.

'I've really no idea, it's total speculation. But if her husband came home unexpectedly, who knows …? How soon will you know anything about the body?'

'The pathologist needs to put what he's found back together. But he's got the pelvis which will enable him to determine the sex, and I think an approximation of age, and also the upper part of the jaw, so it's possible we can look for dental records. Age, sex and cause of death are his priorities. After that, it's down to us to try and identify it.'

Rachel shook her head sadly. 'Do you think he'll be able to tell what the cause of death was, with only the skeleton to work from? It's horrific isn't it …? I just …'

Rachel tailed off. She had too many questions and no idea if she'd ever find the answers.

Malachi looked back at her reassuringly. 'The tank's been drained now and they've got lights down there. The lads are meticulous. When they're sure they've got everything, then the pathologist will get started.'

Chapter 42

'PASS THAT BOTTLE over, I need it after today.' Caroline leaned forward as Rachel picked up the white wine from the coffee table and handed it to her. She held it up and inspected the label. 'This is really good. I hope Conor hasn't gone and given us something that's about €200 a bottle.'

'To be honest, I don't think I'd care at this stage. We'll split it either way.' Rachel leaned back on the sofa, her glass in her hand as Caroline topped up her own glass. Caroline had whipped up delicious Spanish omelettes – they'd both been far hungrier than they'd expected. 'Thanks for taking me in. What a day.'

Rachel moved a cushion in behind the small of her back, aching after all the running around.

It was late but neither of them felt like sleeping yet.

Up at the house, the stable yard had been taped off as the forensics team from Ross Haven worked through the night. Bronagh had been speechless when she'd arrived at the front door, the dazzling white light spilling out of the stable yard punctuated by blue strobes.

Caroline yawned. 'That Sergeant O'Brien is pretty dishy, what's the story there?'

Rachel took a sip of her wine. 'He was pretty cute when he was sixteen too.'

'I didn't see a wedding ring.' Caroline opened her eyes wide, feigning innocence.

'Perhaps he doesn't wear one at work – health and safety.' Rachel gave her a mischievous look. 'But I can find out.'

Caroline smiled into her glass, the flames dancing in the stove reflected in its smooth side. She took a sip.

'I still can't believe this has happened – what is it with this place? It's like one thing after another. I mean, as if Mrs Travers having a heart attack isn't bad enough, now this. It's not going to be good for business, and Bronagh's put so much effort into the restoration – I love this place.' She paused. 'Although it'd be a whole lot better without the creepy nocturnal visitors.'

'Perhaps you should tell Malachi about that.' Rachel turned to Caroline, her voice serious. 'I know you wanted to keep it quiet, but it's pretty scary. And there's a body in the septic tank.' She shook her head half to herself, still unable to believe it. 'You've kept that notebook safe, haven't you? There could be fingerprints on it.'

Caroline nodded. 'Yes, I've got it in a plastic bag. And you're right, of course. There's no such thing as a dead hero.'

'Will you talk to him tomorrow? There's no danger of anything happening tonight. Jasper's here, for one thing.'

As if he knew they were talking about him, Jasper's tail thumped onto the floor. He was lying in front of the stove, having had a good run on the way down to the house, circling through the woods and down to the beach as the two women had walked slowly, laden with baskets of bedlinen, towels and wine. He'd gone mad barking at something, the sound distant, as if he was at the other end of the field, or right down on the beach. Neither of them had had the energy to investigate and Rachel had called him back.

'Very true. I think we're safe tonight. Particularly with half the region's Gardaí in the stable yard. I'll talk to him tomorrow, I promise.' She paused. 'Did you get through to Hunter again?'

'Briefly, from reception. We didn't talk for long, it was too late.'

Caroline pulled her glossy hair back from her face. 'What did he say about Alfie?'

'He didn't really have an update at his end, it's too soon. And I couldn't tell him much about today – I mean about the bones. We don't know anything, do we really? Until the pathologist comes back with his findings and they get the forensic reports, it's all pure speculation.'

Caroline tapped the side of her wineglass with a polished fingernail, her face creased in a frown.

'Do you think it could be Honoria's lover, the gardener or whoever he was? In the septic tank, I mean.'

Rachel glanced over at Caroline before answering.

'That had occurred to me – I said it to Malachi earlier. I'm starting to think it's a bit of a coincidence – two deaths in the same location. They could have been years apart, I know, but it just feels very unlucky. Could someone have killed Honoria and someone else at the same time?'

Caroline narrowed her eyes, frowning. 'We need more facts, but I'd have to agree with you about the coincidence. Not having the internet is driving me mad, there are so many things I want to check.'

Rachel played with the stem of her glass thoughtfully as she replied. 'Makes you wonder how Miss Marple managed to get anything done.'

'She listened to people. I do, all the time. It's sort of active listening, I use it when I'm interviewing. Often the way someone says something or the way they don't say something, their body language, can tell you so much more than their actual words.' Caroline paused. 'Like when I was talking to Ava originally. I knew she had something on her mind, I just didn't have a clue what it was. Normally I've got a bit more background.'

'Let's go down to the village again tomorrow and you can do some more research – and we both need to check our emails. I want to see if we can find out anything more about J. A. Stafford and if he really was Alfie.' Rachel leaned forward, feeling suddenly chilled. 'I told Malachi about Nemo Freight and he seemed to know all about them.'

'I bet.' Caroline frowned. 'Aren't we supposed to be going to the pottery tomorrow? Isn't it Wednesday? I'm losing track of the days.'

Rachel opened her eyes wide. 'Jeepers, yes. Ava said two o'clock.'

Caroline was about to reply when Jasper suddenly jumped up and ran into the kitchen, his eyes trained on the front door. His movement made her start, spilling her newly filled glass.

'Holy God, what's that?'

A low growl began in the back of his throat as a gust of wind rattled the building. His ears cocked forward; the growling became a sharp bark. Trotting over to the front door, he sniffed for a moment, then gave another bark, this one loud and threatening.

'There's someone out there.' Rachel slowly put her wine down on the table, glancing around. 'Is the only way you can see into this room through those big windows?'

Caroline shook her head. 'There are little round ones on either side of the front door, but they're quite high up.'

Jasper barked again, this time a volley, each one sharp and very clear. Then he put his head on one side and waited, clearly listening. Rachel watched him, her nerves taut. Caroline looked across at her. She was listening hard too, sitting completely still on her end of the sofa as if the slightest movement might alert someone to their presence. Suddenly Jasper whimpered and sat down.

'They must have heard him, they've gone.'

Rachel leaned forward and let out a sigh of relief.

'How do you know?'

'I know by him.'

They watched as the big dog sniffed the bottom of the front door, then, looking up, trotted past them to the other end of the room, as if he was looking for someone out of the huge window at the end. His ears cocked forward, he gave another sharp yelp.

Caroline shook her head. 'Jesus Christ, as if finding bodies isn't enough for one evening ...'

Chapter 43

MALACHI O'BRIEN PUT down his coffee cup sharply and looked at Caroline, doing a double take.

'Are you serious? Someone broke in and you didn't think to mention it – to *anyone* except Rach?'

Suddenly feeling like a complete and total idiot, Caroline felt her colour rising. She looked out of the windows at the estuary. The rain had blown through last night and this morning was beautiful, bright and clear, the sky so blue it lifted your heart.

And hers needed lifting.

Neither of them had slept well. She'd heard Rachel get up from her bed on the sofa and boil the kettle at 3 a.m.; had woken in a sweat at six, her heart thumping and mouth dry, images from her nightmare still vivid. A foul-smelling dark room, pitch black, that she could feel rather than see, slowly filling with water. She'd been paralysed as the icy cold had crept up her leaden limbs, the sound still in her ears when she'd woken up, rushing like a mountain waterfall, overwhelming, her chest tight with panic.

She took a deep breath and looked back at Malachi, wincing inside. He was way too good-looking to be a guard, which really wasn't helping. Not only did she feel a complete arse, but he probably thought she was one too. Any kudos she thought she might have had as a Crime Reporter (albeit suspended) for the *New York Messenger* had just gone out of the window.

'I really don't think it's serious. I've met some really scary people and been in some difficult situations and this is—'

'Beautiful Ireland, where there's zero crime, a pot of gold at the end of every rainbow and a leprechaun guarding the front door.' He shook his head in disbelief. 'You've been in New York too long.'

She glared at him. 'Look, it's probably some sort of prank – the whole lipstick thing was way over the top. I mean, I'm not even here to work. *There is no story.*'

He looked at her, shaking his head.

He was right, she was deluding herself there.

She cleared her throat. 'Okay, so there are stories, like maybe more than one, but whoever did this clearly thinks I'm on some shit-hot lead and getting close to something ...'

'And are you?'

He leaned forward on the sofa, his elbows resting on his knees. Caroline pushed her glasses up her nose and did an exaggerated shrug, indicating that she had no idea.

'None of it makes much sense. Look.' She put her hands on her knees, emphasising the point. 'There's clearly a whole *load* of stuff going on here, like there are secrets everywhere you turn. I am very suspicious about Honoria Smyth's death – I don't know if it was ever investigated. I mean, was her husband ever questioned? Had she been to her GP with depression—'

He cut in. 'Mental health was a different story then. I don't think people even knew they had depression, never mind the medical profession. But I'll check and see if there's a file.'

'Oh, thanks. That would be great.' Surprised, Caroline took

a moment to think. 'And then we've got Rachel's homeless guy, who it looks like was an Oxford graduate … And I read in the paper about two teenagers going missing thirty years ago, but it turns out one of them isn't missing at all. And then there's the whole Nemo Freight thing going on …'

Malachi sighed. 'If anything happens again, can you call? Really – we've got enough bodies turning up around here.'

'Jeez, thanks for your concern.'

He ignored her sarcastic tone. 'I'll ask the scenes of crime lads back at the station to put this notebook of yours through the system and see if we can lift any prints. It might give us something. And at least you've preserved it.' His tone held a note of grudging respect that made her feel a tiny bit better.

'If they had any sense they'd have been wearing gloves.'

'Obviously, but you never know. It could have been a spur of the moment thing. It's worth checking.'

'Thank goodness I had Honoria's letter in my bag. I almost tucked it inside the notebook but my diary was closer to hand at the time.'

He opened his mouth to comment when they heard a knock on the front door.

'That'll be Rachel back with Jasper.'

She stood up to answer it, flicking on the kettle as she passed.

'My God, it's cold but it's a gorgeous day.' Rachel pulled off her scarf as she came into the house, her hair ruffled by the wind. Jasper almost knocked her over as he bounded over to Malachi. 'He likes you.' She grinned at him. 'How did you two get on?'

She opened her eyes wide at Caroline, her innuendo not lost on her. Caroline leaned against the kitchen counter.

'He thinks I'm an idiot and he's probably right.'

'Well, I did say it.'

'I know.' Caroline held up her hands in mock defence. 'I know. More coffee, Malachi?'

'I should go, I need to see what's happening up at the house.' He started to stand.

'Have another cup? I'm desperate for one.' Rachel peeled off her jacket and hung it on the coat stand under the spiral staircase. 'Then we'll let you go.'

'Thanks a bunch. You know it's an offence to hold a member of the Gardaí hostage.' He grinned. 'I've got work to do, you know. This place is busier than Dublin.'

The kettle boiled and Caroline brought two cups of coffee to the table, heading back to get her own as Rachel sat down. Perching at the end of the sofa, she took a sip.

'Do you know anything about this Johnny O'Connor's disappearance? It happened at the same time as Meg Cassidy's, if the paper is to be believed. Do you think it could be him in the septic tank?'

'That was before my time down here – the O'Connors are well known though. The lads reckon Johnny got caught up in something his uncles were up to – they're fishermen, but they've been busy in other areas over the years.' Malachi reached for his coffee. 'I know the O'Connor family want the case reopened, that's why the publicity now. There was a family rift after he vanished. His mother gave our lads a very frank description of what'd been landed along the coast here, and it wasn't fish.' He took a sip before continuing. 'They've a cold case squad up in Dublin and I'm sure it's on their list. I'd guess they can't say anything about opening it yet, in case there's a break in another case and it gets pushed back. Families get up so much hope when we go back to something. They are very fragile, we have to be careful, whatever their background.'

Caroline's face creased in thought. 'The paper said *Crime Call* were going to do a reconstruction. That might jog some memories. It's alarming how so many people go missing. It happens in the States all the time. I follow a Twitter thread about missing people, and there's one trying to identify people. There are so many bodies found there and nobody has any idea who they are, it's tragic.'

'For the O'Connors, all publicity is good, I suppose. Maybe someone will remember something. Whatever about Dublin, a teenager disappearing down here was pretty rare in the nineties. When Ava told the case team she'd heard from Meg, her case was closed, whatever the papers say.'

'Clearly whoever landed up here has been missing for a good while. I keep wondering, without all this rain, would the body have ever been found?' Rachel cradled her mug in her hands, the light catching the diamanté eyes on her ring. 'I'm absolutely sure it's Honoria Smyth's lover. I think you need to have a chat to her husband.'

Chapter 44

'WHEN SHE FINDS out what's happened, this really will bring it all back for Ava, won't it?' Caroline felt Rachel glance across at her as she switched down a gear, heading down Glencurragh's steep main street. 'I mean, before she heard from Meg, I bet every time a body was found Ava must have thought it was her. You don't forget that.'

Rachel indicated and turned into the narrow lane running down towards the harbour. The rain had cleared for the moment and the single-storey cottages on either side of the road looked picture-postcard pretty in the sunshine, just how Caroline remembered them as a child. A total contrast to the grim scene they'd left in the stable yard.

Seeing where they were heading, Jasper thrust his head through the front seats, pressing his nose on her arm. Caroline reached back to give him a rub as she sighed.

'It'll all be dragged up again as soon as the press discover a body's been found. Everything she was worried about when she thought I was doing a story will happen tenfold. But, you know, Ava still doesn't know where Meg actually is, so she is kind of still missing.'

'You really would wonder what drove a seventeen-year-old girl so far away that she never wanted to come home – to call, even. Postcards are so anonymous somehow, aren't they, sort of flippant.' Rachel paused. 'I hope she's okay for this afternoon. She would have called to cancel if she didn't feel up to it? I half expected her to, to be honest. But maybe she thinks we can tell her what's happening?'

'It's not going to be easy but let's just see if we can navigate around it. We don't know anything really anyway, and we don't want to say anything that could turn into Chinese whispers.' She shook her head. 'Talk about the elephant in the room.'

Caroline glanced down at her phone again to see if she had reception. A fraction of a bar appeared; the signal wasn't strong enough for her social media to update. She opened her sent mail. The email she'd written to Tim last night still hadn't gone yet. She'd need to get Rachel to stop outside the cafe on the way back so she could jump on their Wi-Fi.

While Rachel had been making cups of coffee for the guards in the kitchen last night, she'd gone through the photos from the Christmas party.

And they'd thrown up a few questions.

'Here we are.'

Rachel swung down into the harbour, sending a gaggle of seagulls into the air, and pulled up alongside the elegant building housing Cassidy Ceramics. Even in the sunshine she could see the lights were on inside the house.

'We better leave Jasp here or we could need a second mortgage to pay for the breakages. I'll take him for a super long run afterwards.' Hearing his name, Jasper whimpered. Rachel leaned between the seats and rubbed his head. 'Sorry, boy, we won't be long.' She swung open the door. 'You coming?'

Momentarily lost in her thoughts, Caroline looked up.

'Yes, sorry, ready now.'

She threw her phone into her bag.

Ava opened the door as soon as Rachel rang the bell, stepping aside to let them in. Caroline hitched her bag onto her shoulder, smiling warmly at her.

'Thanks so much for doing this. I …'

Before she could finish, Ava's face creased and she burst into tears.

'Good God, are you okay?' Caroline stepped inside and put her arm around Ava's shoulders, glancing behind her at Rachel as she did so. 'Let's go and sit down.'

Guiding Ava into the pottery studio, Caroline pulled out a stool with one hand.

'It's okay, have a good cry.'

Looking over Ava's head Caroline caught Rachel's eye. She was hovering in the hallway; she mouthed 'she knows'. Caroline rolled her eyes. She was sure Imogen and Conor wouldn't have said anything, but had one of the drain clearance men said something to his wife, maybe? This village could set records for the spread of news. Who even needed the internet? But why hadn't Ava cancelled the workshop?

Perhaps she did want to find out what was going on from them.

Coming into the studio properly, Rachel put her bag down on the workbench.

'Will I make some tea?'

'Through there.' Caroline indicated a door at the back of the room beside the dresser.

While Rachel was boiling the kettle, Caroline sat down beside Ava. How did she find out what the problem was, without mentioning the Garda activity at the hotel? Anything could have happened to upset her. Perhaps her cat had been run over. Caroline had a feeling that was very unlikely, but she knew she couldn't say anything until Ava did.

'Tell me what's wrong. I want to help, really.' Caroline rubbed the top of Ava's arm.

After a few minutes Ava pulled herself together. Pushing a loose strand of hair out of her face, she closed her eyes.

'What's happening up there?'

Caroline hesitated, making a rapid assessment of how much of the truth was actually required. She wanted to be straight with Ava, but sometimes being too straight just made things worse. Thankfully, at that moment Rachel appeared with the tea and a bowl of sugar, slipping it onto the workbench and going back to the kitchen for her own and Caroline's mugs.

'Here, do you take sugar?'

'Please, just one.'

Adding the sugar, Caroline turned the mug around towards her. It was hand-thrown, a gorgeous bowl shape, the white slip not quite reaching the bottom of the dark grey clay. She glanced at Rachel, who opened her eyes wide and pulled out a stool to sit down on the other side of the bench.

Caroline could feel Ava's distress seeping out from her like ink, flowing into every corner of the room and washing over her and Rachel. The photo she'd seen of Meg in the newspaper jumped into her head: a beautiful, smiling girl, slightly frizzy bleached hair blowing across her face.

Ava sniffed loudly and took a sip of her tea. She shook her head, incredulity written all over her face.

'I can't believe it. Everyone's saying—'

'Ava, you know it's not Meg. She went missing, but she got in touch with you, didn't she? And the guards really have no idea who they've found yet. We were there, but we have zero information. They can't say anything until they've done all sorts of tests. They don't know age or sex or anything. It could be a middle-aged man who's been there for a hundred years.'

'How did you find out?' Rachel leaned on the table, her voice soft.

'John Francis told me this morning, when I went up to get the paper. He was bursting with it. He was the one who told me you were booked in to Hare's Landing. Then when you came here, I assumed it was because of Meg.' She took a shaky breath. 'Then Mary O'Connor rang me this morning – Johnny's mother. She was in bits.'

Caroline shifted on the stool. 'Like I said before, I read the story in the local paper but I had no idea you were related to Meg. I didn't even get a chance to finish it.' She sighed.

Ava shook her head and took a sip of her tea. 'It's going to rake it all up again …'

'Tell me about Meg. What sort of girl was she when she lived here?'

Caroline knew it helped relatives to talk, to remember; it helped release the pent-up emotion. She'd been in this situation too many times before.

Ava took another shaky breath. 'Do you want to write this down?' The hint of sarcasm was thinly disguised and Caroline felt it hit her in her stomach.

'No, we're here as friends. We know how painful this is. Talking about her will help, I promise. What was she like?'

Ava sipped her tea, her hand shaking. 'She loved music, she had the radio blaring in her room the whole time, had this Walkman she wouldn't leave the house without. She read all the magazines, *Mizz* and *Just Seventeen* and *Smash Hits* – she left them all over the house, but they were so expensive. She did any job she could to save up for them, worked weekends in Mahony's and evenings in the pub, cleaned the holiday lets in the summer. She was saving up to go to London, she wanted to be a singer. Everyone said she had a gorgeous voice, she sang in the choir for years. I don't know where she got it from, I haven't a note.'

Ava stared into her tea, frowning. 'She always had it easy at school, got good grades without having to work at all – unlike me – but art was her favourite subject. I always thought she might go into fashion design. She used to make her own clothes, long skirts and denim jackets with embroidery and sequins all over them. Whenever she went up to Dublin she'd look in all the vintage shops for buttons and braid and clothes she could customise. That's where she found her watch. It was a bit like yours –' she indicated the Aviator on Rachel's wrist – 'a man's watch, but she made this really colourful strap for it, she never took it off.' Ava sighed deeply, her eyes filling again. 'We used to fight like cat and dog but she was my sister.' She cleared her throat. 'When will they know who the body is?'

Caroline took a deep breath. 'I've no idea. They still have the stable yard blocked off so they may not have even finished looking yet. It could be a while.'

All sorts of thoughts were careering through Caroline's head. What had made Meg leave and not tell anyone where she was? Had she started chatting to someone in one of the vintage shops, someone she thought was a kindred spirit? Had they promised her the sun, moon and stars if she came to London with them, that they could help her follow her dream? Caroline felt the hairs standing up on the back of her neck. From what Ava was saying, Meg was ambitious and focused. Ireland had changed a lot in the nineties, but London was still the place you had to go if you wanted to make it.

'It really is going to drag it all up again, isn't it? It doesn't matter that she's been in touch, the press just wants a good scandal. There was so much muck printed that was just nonsense.' She sounded bitter. 'The landlord at the Spaniard fancied his chances, and then when the media came sniffing around he thought he'd have his fifteen minutes of fame because she'd worked for him. He gave photos of her to *The Sun* and some other rag, and then his ex weighed in, saying Meg was a flirt and the media created the whole story. Chinese whispers. It really didn't help – everyone was talking about her being a slut and not concentrating on what had actually happened to her.'

Caroline bit her lip. 'I can see why you aren't comfortable with the media.'

Ava took a deep breath as she spoke. 'Some reporter came sniffing around, pretending they were on holiday and had got lost. They asked all these questions. I didn't realise until they'd gone what was happening, what they were really after. So then when you came and John Francis said you worked for a newspaper, I thought that's what you were doing too.' She paused. 'I agreed to do the workshop so I could find out and put you straight. Dear God, Mary O'Connor's been in touch every five minutes telling me about this reconstruction, and RTÉ. It's like she's got no one else to talk to.' Ava took a sip of her tea. 'I don't want Meg's name dragged up again.'

Chapter 45

RACHEL'S BOOTS CRUNCHED on the shingle as she walked across the beach, one eye on Jasper and one on Caroline.

'You really should have brought wellies.'

Caroline looked over at her, shaking her head, a smile creeping on to her face.

'I told you, I don't own wellies.'

Rachel tutted. 'Everyone has wellies, how can you be Irish and not have wellies? Just be careful, if the salt water gets onto those leather boots it'll leave a line when they dry out. They'll be ruined.'

'I'm good. I'll just stay up above the tideline, you can get wet.'

'Thanks a million.' Rachel bent down to pick up a piece of driftwood for Jasper, who was dancing up and down the beach, playing with the waves, then glanced back at Caroline. 'Do you think Ava will be okay?'

'Honestly, no – at least not until she gets proper news from Meg. She can't move on until she has some sort of closure on why she went. I can understand that, I'd be the same.'

'That's how Hunter feels about Alfie.' Rachel looked down the estuary. The sky was an incredible blue, washed clean after the rain. She could imagine how wonderful this area was in the summer. 'I could stay here all day, wandering – just listen, there are just so many birds.'

Caroline didn't answer. Rachel glanced back at her. She'd stopped walking, had her hands in her pockets and was staring down the estuary out to sea, deep in thought.

'A penny for them.'

'Oh, sorry.' Caroline suddenly realised she was being spoken to. 'I was thinking.'

'Yes, I could see that.' Rachel rolled her hands. 'About …?'

'My boss actually. Greta. About this whole lawsuit thing and her not backing me. You know, that just doesn't happen in my job – it can't, or the machine stops working. The press has to be able to report the news, the truth, without comment or interference. We're like the thin black line that keeps the bad people at bay. I know there's lots of different shades of reporting – the sensationalist tabloid stuff Ava was talking about doesn't serve any useful purpose, but … Anyway, I'm still trying to work out why Greta took the stance she did.'

'And have you? Worked it out, I mean?'

Caroline bit her lip. 'Maybe. I need some more information. I need to send an email on the way home if you don't mind stopping. I should be able to pick up the Wi-Fi in the cafe from the car, so we don't have to go in if you don't want to.'

'I think I'd like to keep a low profile today. I'm not sure I'm ready for questions – not that we have any answers, but people don't understand that. But sorry, go on.'

'So, here's the thing. Greta is a bitch, she's always been a bitch, but usually she's a fair bitch. I mean, she has a tough job – she's got all the trimmings but she really does put the hours in.' Caroline teased the stones at the tideline with the toe of her boot. 'We've never got on particularly well. Tim, he's the colleague I mentioned – the company lawyer – reckons it's because I'm twenty years younger than she is and she can see herself in me.' She shook her head. 'Nonsense, probably. But he said something changed at the Christmas party.' She looked thoughtful for a minute and then added quickly, 'It wasn't at Christmas, it was right at the start of December, we always do it early.'

'What did you do – spill your wine on her?'

'Well, that's the thing, I wasn't even at it.'

Rachel looked at her, puzzled. 'So what changed?'

'That's what I've been trying to work out. I asked Tim to send me all the photos he could find of the night, so I could see who was talking to who. That's what I was going through last night while you were on coffee duty.'

'Did you see anything? Anyone under the mistletoe who shouldn't have been?'

Caroline frowned. 'It was more who *wasn't* under the mistletoe, actually.' She moved the stones around again with her foot. 'The Christmas party is the big one each year. The date is set in stone and everyone knows about it from about September. We go somewhere really fancy and it's a sort of tradition, it's a bonding experience. Everyone brings their partners, so it's a chance for them to meet the people their spouses get to spend the night with when they're not with them.'

Nodding, Rachel turned to see where Jasper had disappeared to; she couldn't see him.

'Come on, walk and talk so we can keep up with Jasp.'

Rachel walked up towards the tideline, her feet slipping on the shingle and Caroline fell into step beside her as she prompted: 'So, fancy party ...'

'Yes, sorry. So, fancy party – an opportunity to get dressed up, out of the jeans or the suit. Nice night, everyone goes.'

'But you didn't.'

'No. I've been working this story about people trafficking, illegal migrants being forced to work all hours for nothing. It's been trailing on for months. The traffickers are very good, every time I think I'm close, they slip away.'

'Like Nemo Freight – till now.'

'Exactly. So, the night of the Christmas party I get a tip-off that some illegals are being moved to a 7–Eleven downtown. I've been on this story for months. I couldn't pass up the opportunity, so I had to bail on the party. I use this freelance photographer, Joni. We spent most of the night playing cards in her car. About two o'clock I reckoned there was nothing happening so we split. I went home.'

'And this is significant, how?'

'When I went through the photos of the party, I wasn't the only person missing. Clive, Greta's husband, wasn't there, and nor was Nancy – at least not for the whole night.'

'Nancy?'

'My arch-nemesis in news. She's flying up the tree right behind me and I don't trust her, to be honest. She's been promoted really fast and she's good, but she's not that good.'

'So you think something's happening, between Nancy and this Clive?'

Caroline raised her eyebrows. 'She's gorgeous.'

'I'm playing devil's advocate here, but being gorgeous doesn't seem to be quite enough of a reason to suspect she's having an affair with your editor's husband.'

'Well, that's the thing. He's actually her boss – Greta's, I mean. He's her husband, but he also owns the paper. And he has a bit of a history, if gossip can be believed. But it really doesn't matter what I think. It's Greta that's the problem. There's a picture of Nancy talking to her early in the evening, so Greta thinks she

268

was there, but I can't see any pictures of Nancy later on, not even in the background of other people's shots.'

'You're still lacking a bit of evidence there.'

'I know, it's entirely supposition. That's why I need to email Tim. I want him to try to remember if he saw her later in the evening. He's on this health kick and isn't drinking, so he was probably the only person who was sober.' Caroline screwed up her face, deep in thought. 'The thing is, Nancy's been working this big secret case for about three months and keeps disappearing from the office.' Caroline looked over at Rachel. 'I know this sounds mad, but I think I was set up with the story about the 7–Eleven so I didn't go to the party. Nancy gave me the lead – it was handed in at the front desk apparently, a note on a piece of paper. I think she knew Clive wasn't going, and she wanted to make it look like he was having an affair with me, when actually she spent the evening with him.'

'Isn't that very complicated? You've got your photographer as a witness to where you were.'

'Nancy wouldn't have known I'd call Joni in, and Greta's not the cops – there's no reason for me to tell her who I was with, or for her to ask.'

'I suppose so, but it's bit of a strange night to choose.'

'I agree one hundred per cent, but it's very Nancy – she's got such a convoluted mind. And when you think about it, it's the only night where it would have been obvious to Greta that I wasn't there. And if Greta was a bit suspicious, she only needed to hear a few choice words that would implant the suggestion that it was me who was seeing Clive, not Nancy.'

'Nasty. But you can't prove it?'

'Probably not, but I *can* get Tim to drop into the conversation that I spent that night with Joni in a parking lot and see what happens.'

'I'm not seeing how that gets you off the hook with this lawsuit?'

'It doesn't, but that's not so much the problem. I can prove my every move with Rich Slater. I know a court is going to laugh in his face – but Greta not backing me is much bigger. It raises questions about my competence, about whether I can do my job. And I have a feeling the next stop could be her firing me. That couldn't happen here, but it happens in the States all the time, the employment law is totally different. The thing is, it's my professional reputation on the line.'

'Which is the type of revenge you want to get on your husband's mistress.'

'Precisely. She's never going to call him out because he holds the purse strings, but she must have been dropping hints or something, implying she knew he was up to something. I'm guessing he told Nancy she was suspicious, and I was the solution. Two birds, one stone. Nancy gets the guy and my job as head of the department.'

'And your friend Tim can help you sort it out?'

'I hope so. I really hope so.'

Chapter 46

EMERGING FROM THE tree-shrouded lane, Rachel pulled into the drive at Hare's Landing, the wheels crunching on the gravel. A brand-new navy-blue Mercedes E-Class saloon was parked beside the hares guarding the front door, its sides flecked with mud where it had been driven down the lane from the main road. From the angle of the splatter, it looked like it had been going pretty fast.

'Oh God, somebody's arrived – do you think there might be more guests? I need to hose Jasper down – but the hose is in the stable yard.' Rachel hauled on the handbrake and, screwing up her face, slapped her forehead. 'I should have thought of that before I let him go after that seagull on the beach. I'm sure it's still sealed off.'

Caroline looked out at the car speculatively. 'I wouldn't worry. Bronagh can't take in anyone new, not with the plumbing the way it is and the stables cordoned off as a crime scene. And I'm sure there's another hose somewhere. Conor will know if he's here.' She looked at the car curiously. 'It looks like a hire car. Perhaps it's someone who called in on spec? I've never seen a reporter in a new Merc, so I think we can assume it's not press. No journalist gets paid enough to drive a fancy car, not a new one anyway.'

Rachel swung open her door and flipped her seat forward to let Jasper out, grabbing his collar.

'Sorry, old boy, we need to get you a bit cleaner before you can go anywhere near the public.' Caroline got out of the other side as she continued. 'I'd better take him around by the stables and see if the guards will let us in to use the hose. It's on this corner beside the entrance, well downwind of the septic tank so I don't think there'd be any problem with the water running into it.'

'Tell you what, why don't I do that? Malachi might still be here. I can say hi.'

Rachel laughed. 'Do I guess from that tone that you don't want me tagging along? Wouldn't it just be easier if we asked him over for dinner?'

Caroline looked as if she was thinking about the idea.

'I don't really want to put him off with my cooking this soon. He already thinks I'm a total eejit for not reporting the graffiti artist in my bedroom.'

Rachel came around the back of the Land Rover.

'I'm sure he doesn't.' She held out Jasper's lead. 'Here.'

Caroline grabbed the lead from her and clipped it on Jasper's collar. Obviously thinking she was taking him for a walk, he jumped up excitedly, pawing at her parka with wet sandy feet.

'You'd better be quick or that coat will be ruined.'

Caroline dusted herself off. 'It's fine, just a bit of sand.'

Rachel laughed. 'On a $500 coat. Totally fine. Well, don't say I didn't warn you. I'll order you a coffee. You might need it.' She leaned in through the passenger door to haul her backpack out of the rear seat. 'Will I take your bag in? You really don't want to get that wet, it's far too good.'

'That would be great. Wish me luck.'

Waving theatrically, Caroline disappeared around the side of the house to walk down to the stable yard entrance, Jasper trotting beside her.

As Rachel pulled the front door open and stepped into the porch, she could see that there was a man in reception. He looked like he was in his early fifties, heavily built, wearing a navy pinstripe suit with a sky blue shirt and navy tie. Rachel couldn't work out what the design was on his tie from this distance, but it seemed to be a club crest of some sort.

Standing right in the middle of the hall, he was glaring at whoever was behind the reception desk, impatiently jiggling the change in his trouser pocket. He turned to Rachel as she pushed open the inner door, scowling as he looked her up and down, no doubt noting her mucky wellies and the splashes of mud on her jeans. Rachel raised an eyebrow and looked right back at him. She was about to speak when she heard Imogen's voice.

'I'm really sorry, I've checked and we don't have any rooms available right now. I'm so sorry.'

'But it's January – the place must be empty.' He sounded British, with a full-on public-school accent that came with its own sense of superiority and entitlement. The impatience in his voice was thinly disguised.

'I'm afraid we're in the middle of renovations. All our available rooms are taken. Will I try Ross Haven for you? Did you say you were visiting someone there?'

'Yes, at the hospital.'

Rachel's ears pricked up. She put her own and Caroline's bags down beside the reception counter and unwrapped her scarf, dropping it on the top before unzipping her skiing jacket. Trying to defuse the tension, she kept her tone upbeat and practical.

'At least the weather's improved for your visit. It's so lovely to see the sun after all that rain.'

The man obviously didn't think she was talking to him as he continued to glare at Imogen. She'd slipped on a navy jacket over her white shirt and looked very smart and capable behind the desk. From the empty coffee cups Rachel could just see under the lip of the counter, it looked like she'd been there all day. She'd probably been fielding phone calls and curious passers-by since she'd arrived. Rachel was sure half the village had found a reason to drop in once word had spread about the Garda operation on the septic tank.

Rachel could see Imogen wasn't sure what to say next – he hadn't responded to her offer to call another hotel. Rachel caught Imogen's eye as she picked up the phone.

'Let me call the West Haven, they're sure to have rooms. And they have a lovely pool.'

'Do I look like I've got time to use the pool? Go on, try them. I need somewhere to stay and the mobile reception in this area is woeful. I don't know how you expect people to communicate.'

Imogen blushed and, tucking a loose strand of blonde hair back into her bun, busied herself with the phone.

Rachel glanced up at the huge waiting room clock, wondering how long it would take Caroline to hose off Jasper and make headway with Malachi, assuming he was there. She'd probably be ages, and she'd kick herself if she missed an opportunity to meet this guy, deeply unpleasant as he was. He looked heavier and older than he did in his Wikipedia photograph, jowly and very overweight, but Rachel was pretty sure she knew who he was. Perhaps she should try to keep him talking to give Caroline an opportunity to appear. It was worth a try.

'Some people like the lack of connectivity. I certainly do, I think it's a huge bonus.'

The man turned and looked at Rachel. He was only about five feet nine, but he used his bulk to command the space. He reminded her for a moment of Alfred Hitchcock – there was a distinct resemblance. Hitchcock had only been five feet six, but he'd always controlled his environment. And right now, this visitor was reinforcing her theory that men who needed to get the upper hand in a simple situation like this must have serious inadequacies in other areas.

'Perhaps you don't need to be connected in your business while you are away, but I do.'

'Really? What business is that? I work in the film industry, we're pretty teched up.'

Rachel managed to sound offhand, but also as if whatever he did couldn't be as glamorous and high-rolling as her job. Her apparent attempt at one-upmanship worked. He turned around and glared at her.

'The law.'

Obviously not considering either her or Imogen worthy of further consideration, he turned his back on them and, his hands behind his back, scowled at the fireplace. Rachel hid a smirk as Imogen pulled a face behind his back. She mouthed 'sorry' to her, just as she got through to the hotel she was calling.

The man tapped his foot, glancing behind him to scowl at her, and then, turning back, took a step towards the fireplace as if he'd just noticed the picture above the mantelpiece. He seemed to shake for a moment, then, standing stock-still, he leaned forward, peering at the photograph.

'What the hell's this?'

Imogen didn't get a chance to answer. The receptionist at the hotel she was calling was asking her questions at the other end of the phone.

'Yes, that would be wonderful. You can upgrade to a suite? I'm sure that will be much appreciated.' Imogen cleared her throat. 'What name will I say, sir?'

He turned and looked at her, his face a strange colour, pallid but mottled with red blotches.

'Smyth with a *y*, Sheridan. I'll be driving straight over from here.'

Rachel kept her face blank. She'd been right. She had been sure this had to be Sheridan Smyth from the moment she'd walked in. Ignoring Rachel, he pointed at the picture and opened his mouth to speak, but realised Imogen was fully absorbed in the phone conversation. Watching him, Rachel leaned on the counter, trying to make herself look as if she was actually waiting for Imogen rather than hanging about listening in to his conversation.

Imogen hung up and was about to speak when he cut across her.

'This photograph – where did it come from?'

'Erm … I'm not sure, I'm sorry. Bronagh, the owner, put it up the other day.'

'Is she here?'

'No, she's at the hospital with our housekeeper Mrs Travers, she's been really sick.'

'I know how unwell she is, young lady, that is *precisely* why I am here.'

His voice went up a notch, the increase in sound accompanied by an increase in the blotches on his face. He didn't follow it up with 'Don't you know who I am?' but the implication was there. Rachel was quite sure Imogen knew exactly who he was and was just as unimpressed as she was by his bombastic behaviour.

'How do I get hold of the owner? I want you to take that

photograph down immediately. She cannot put my family photographs up in this hotel without my express permission.' Imogen looked at him in surprise, her mouth open as he continued. 'Don't just stand there like a fish, girl. Get me her number, I'll speak to her myself.'

Imogen found a business card on the desk in front of her and held it out across the counter.

'The West Haven are expecting you.'

He didn't comment, instead snatched the card from her hand and turned abruptly. He seemed to have forgotten Rachel was there and almost bumped into her as he headed for the door. He glared at her as he marched outside, letting the porch door bang. She heard a car door slam and the engine start.

'Well!' Behind the reception desk, Imogen put her hands on her hips.

'Nice man. Did I hear him say he was Sheridan Smyth?'

'With a *y*, yes, you did indeed. *The* Sheridan Smyth, who thinks his family still own the place. Do you think he'll sue Bronagh for putting up his family photos?'

Rachel shrugged. 'There are all sorts of copyright issues with photographs but if he's nice about it she might just take them down. I rather doubt he'll be asking politely though. He really didn't seem to like this one being up one little bit, did he?'

Imogen scowled. 'It probably reminded him of when he was younger and thinner.'

Chapter 47

BEFORE RACHEL COULD comment on Sheridan Smyth or the photograph, they heard another car pulling up outside. Imogen's eyebrows shot up.

'My God, do you think he's back already?'

She turned to look out of the reception window as the porch door slammed again and Malachi O'Brien walked in.

'Who the hell was that arsehole in the Merc? He almost ran into me.'

Rachel couldn't resist a grin. 'Sheridan Smyth. He's in "the law", though, so he probably thinks police officers are a lower form of life, like us women.'

'Sheridan Smyth, the judge – from here?'

'The one and only.'

Malachi took off his hat. 'Tosser. If I had more time I'd have pulled him. Is Caroline around? I need to speak to her. I tried her phone.'

'She's out the back with Jasper, hoping to bump into you actually. I'll go call her.'

'Can I get you both coffee?'

Malachi smiled appreciatively to Imogen. 'That would be great. In the lounge?'

'No problem, go through. There's no one around so it's nice and private.'

Looking at Malachi's face, Rachel suddenly got the feeling this wasn't a social call.

'Give me two minutes.'

Leaving Malachi in reception, Rachel walked quickly down the corridor to the kitchen. It was empty; she went straight through and out the back door. Across the stable yard, the guard who was securing the scene around the septic tank, raised his hand. The whole area was still cordoned off with blue and white crime scene tape, but it looked as if everything was winding down. They'd worked quickly. She waved to him.

'Have you seen a woman with a large wet German shepherd?'

He gestured to indicate that she'd gone around to the front of the house.

Doubling back on herself, Rachel could hear the sound of voices as she headed down the corridor to the lounge. Caroline had obviously come in via the front door. As she walked in, she could see that a wet but clean Jasper had installed himself in front of the fire. Malachi and Caroline were sitting opposite each other, the coffee table between them. Malachi gestured for her to come and join them.

'Sit down, please. I've got some news on the notebook you found on your bed, Caroline, but it involves both of you.'

Rachel plumped down beside Caroline as Imogen appeared holding a tray with three coffees on it. Malachi half rose to help her unload it.

'Thanks. Can you keep an eye on the front door so we aren't disturbed?'

'No problem, just shout if you need anything.' Imogen turned and headed back to reception.

Rachel dropped a lump of sugar into her coffee. 'So spill – what's happened?'

Malachi leaned forward on the sofa. 'There was a faint partial print on the cover of the notebook. We didn't see any glove smudges, so it's possible he wasn't wearing them. Perhaps he was in a hurry and thought he could be careful enough. There are fibres caught in the lid of the lipstick, so it looks like he used the hand towel to hold it when he was in the bathroom. Which makes it all look very opportunistic.' Malachi paused. 'Anyway, the important thing is that we got a hit on the print we found.'

Caroline looked at him, her eyes wide. 'Holy cow. Who was it?'

'Have either of you heard of a guy called Declan Flynn?'

Rachel could see Caroline shaking her head. She looked across at Malachi; he was frowning, his face serious.

What was going on?

'Me neither – who's he?'

'He's a director of Nemo Freight. Remember I said two of them were from Cork? Well, he's one of them. He's been living in London for years, though.'

Rachel sat back in astonishment. 'How … I mean, why would he have been trying to frighten Caroline? She's got nothing to do with Nemo Freight. If Zack's right about seeing a Nemo Freight truck in Alfie's car park, surely I'm the one with the link to them?'

Malachi nodded. 'Which is why you needed to be here for this conversation too. I think it's to do with Caroline being a journalist. There's obviously a story that links Nemo Freight to Hare's Landing that we don't know about, but that this Flynn character felt like you might be on to.' He looked across at Rachel. 'I'd guess he hasn't realised you're connected to the homeless guy, Rachel.'

Caroline leaned forward, her face excited. 'Have you got a picture of him?'

Rachel looked at her; she couldn't see why Caroline looked so animated. Right now, she was feeling sick. She twisted her ring as Malachi opened the Manila file he'd put on the table in front of him and swung a picture around to face them.

Caroline looked at him, surprise written over her face.

'That's the taxi driver. The hotel taxi driver who picked me up from the airport.'

Malachi pulled out his notebook. 'Which was when?'

'Last Thursday. I wasn't expecting anyone to meet me, but he was standing there with a card with my name on it.'

Rachel looked at the photograph. She didn't recognise the man – in his fifties, he was heavily built, his hair an unnatural shade of black. The photo was a press shot: some sort of charity reception with American flags in the background. He was wearing a dinner jacket and bow tie, his shirt straining across an ample midriff. Holding a glass of champagne, he was standing in the middle of a group of unnaturally skinny women with too much hair and slinky evening dresses. He didn't look as if he was struggling for money.

'Are you sure? He's the guy you said had asked all the questions? He doesn't look like a taxi driver here.'

Rachel pulled the picture closer to her, to get a better look.

'Yes, and then he picked me up again to take me to the village to do the workshop with Ava on Saturday, and met me to bring me back—'

Malachi cut in. 'And have you seen him since?'

'No. Rachel's got her Land Rover here so I didn't need him again. Imogen might know more?'

'Will I get her?' Rachel stood up.

'If you don't mind – let's see what she knows about him. Don't tell her who he is.'

A moment later Rachel returned with Imogen. Malachi beckoned to her to come closer and pushed the photograph across the table. She leaned in to look at it.

'Recognise him?'

'That's Mrs Travers's nephew, Declan. He's in London a lot but he helps her out when he's here. He has a taxi ...' Imogen looked around at them in surprise, obviously wondering why they were discussing him. 'What's wrong?'

Malachi frowned. 'Who would have organised for him to pick Caroline up at the airport?'

'Bronagh, I'd guess, Mrs T probably said he was here. Bronagh likes to give him a bit of work when she can. He used to help out here years ago – for the Smyths – before he went to the UK.'

'Has he been back from London long?'

Imogen shrugged. 'I assumed he must have come for Christmas, that he was staying with Mrs Travers. I haven't seen him the past few days, I guess I thought he'd gone back again. Bronagh would know, she would have called him when Mrs T. got sick.'

'That's brilliant. I just need to make a call.' Malachi stood up and stepped out into the hallway, his mouth to his radio.

Imogen turned to Rachel. 'He's not in trouble, is he? He's a bit creepy, but he really looks after Mrs T. when he's here.'

Rachel smiled reassuringly. 'It's nothing to worry about, I'm sure'.

Malachi came back into the lounge.

'Thanks, Imogen. I need to talk to Bronagh. I'd appreciate it if you didn't mention to anyone that I was asking about Flynn.'

'Of course.' Imogen hesitated. 'Do you need me for anything else?'

Malachi shook his head. 'No, you've been great, thank you.'

'Grand. I'll be in reception anyway. I'll come and clear when you're finished.'

Malachi waited for Imogen to leave before he continued.

'You need to be careful, Caroline – Declan Flynn's not someone to mess with, and he clearly has access to the Boathouse. The Nemo Freight situation is escalating and my colleagues in the UK are very interested in his whereabouts. Finding him is a priority, but until we do I'm not sure how safe you are staying down there on your own.'

Rachel turned to him. 'It's okay, Jasper and I have moved in for the time being. But Jasp did hear something outside the other night. Do you think Flynn could still be around here?'

'I've no idea. We'll get someone to call over to Mrs Travers's cottage, and check out any cars registered to here or that address. I'd better go.'

'Bronagh's at the hospital, she should have a signal there.' Rachel hesitated. 'Like Imogen said, I'd imagine she's been in touch with Flynn to tell him about Mrs Travers. She must have called Sheridan Smyth too. He must know Flynn as well, if he worked here.' She frowned. 'Do you think Sheridan Smyth has got anything to do with Nemo Freight?'

Malachi scowled. 'No idea, but that's something else we need to look at. I'll keep in touch.'

He headed out towards reception. A moment later they heard his car door slam and the engine start, the skid of wheels on gravel as he pulled away.

Imogen appeared back at the door. 'Will I clear now?'

'Thanks, here, let me help.' Caroline reached over and picked up Malachi's cup as Imogen bent to put down the tray. 'How do you know Sheridan Smyth is here, Rach?'

Rachel was only half listening; her head was starting to join dots. She frowned.

'He was here, just now, looking for a room.'

The tray full, Imogen straightened up. 'I told him we didn't have anything available – he wasn't impressed.'

Rachel put her finger to her lips, deep in thought. 'You know, when Mrs Travers keeled over she'd been looking through the papers. She must have been reading the articles and realised Flynn was in serious trouble.'

'And then she saw the photo of the house and it finished her off.'

Caroline lifted an eyebrow as Rachel nodded slowly, still thinking hard.

'He used to live with Mrs Travers, Declan did,' Imogen said. 'They were very close. I always got the impression she was pretty upset when he decided to go to the UK.'

Glancing out to reception as if to check that the phone hadn't started ringing, Imogen headed out back to the kitchen with the tray in her hand. Listening to her footsteps going down the tiled corridor, the two of them were silent for a moment, both thinking.

'Hang on. Where's my bag?' Caroline reached for her shopper at the end of the sofa and pulled out her diary. Leafing through it, she found Honoria's letter. 'Look. I knew it. It's addressed to *My darling D*. Could Declan Flynn have been the one having an affair with Honoria? Imogen said he used to work here.'

'From that photo Malachi had, Flynn looks like that sort of chancer, doesn't he?' Rachel screwed up her face. 'He must have been about ten years younger than her. But he obviously likes the ladies. Photos really can tell you so much.' Rachel bit her lip and turned to look into the hall, talking half to herself. 'Sheridan Smyth got really cross when he saw that picture over the mantelpiece. He said he wanted it taken down immediately, that he was going to call Bronagh and tell her. But who would even know it was Sheridan Smyth in the picture? Why would he have got so upset?'

Standing up, Rachel climbed over Jasper's hind legs and went out into the hall. In front of the fireplace, she stood looking at the photograph for a moment, then reached up, catching it by the bottom edge of the frame and jiggling it until the string unhooked. She held on tightly and swung it down from the chimney breast. Holding it out in front of her, angling it towards the light, she looked at it hard.

Caroline followed her into the hallway. 'What are you looking for?'

'I don't know, but the devil is always in the detail. When we compared this with the photo of J. A. Stafford on Facebook, that's all we were looking for. But I think Sheridan Smyth saw something else.' She peered at the photo, turning slowly and bringing it to the reception counter where the light was better. 'When I first started in film, I worked in set design. When we have to reshoot something, we have to make sure every single detail is replicated. We take hundreds of photos. I've spent a lot of my life looking for stuff that's out of place.'

She angled the picture and kept looking at it. She moved it slightly again and then she saw it. She took a sharp breath.

'Oh, Jesus Christ. I think I can see what Sheridan Smyth's problem was. We need to call Malachi back.'

Chapter 48

WHILE THEY WAITED for Malachi to get back to Hare's Landing, Rachel brought the picture into the lounge and put it carefully onto the coffee table. Caroline sat down opposite her.

'Are you sure?'

Rachel opened her eyes wide. 'Look at it yourself again. You can see a reflection in the porch windows behind the boys. I'm sure it's her. The photo in the paper you showed me was really clear – she had frizzy blonde hair, made worse by a nineties-style bleached perm. You can see her hair in the reflection in the glass, blowing in the wind. She must have been here – she took the photograph. She didn't disappear when she was in Dublin – she disappeared from here.'

Caroline pulled the picture over towards herself and, picking up Rachel's phone, flicked on the torch to illuminate the area she was talking about. The image was ghostly, but Rachel was right: you could see a girl reflected in the glass of the porch window – the outline of her hair, the curve of her elbow as she held the camera up to shoot.

'Are you sure that's Meg? Ava's hair is bit like that now. It could be her?'

'Meg was really tall and slim. Even with the perspective, you can see whoever this is, is taller than the two boys in the picture. See in the reflection? Ava's the same size as me.'

Caroline ran her hand into the roots of her hair, thinking. 'We don't know for sure when this was taken, though. It could have been another summer. You heard Ava say Meg did all sorts of odd jobs, perhaps she helped out here too.'

Rachel looked at her impatiently. 'But the T-shirt Stafford – Alfie – is wearing looks new, it's hardly faded, just like the photo on Facebook. It has to be the summer of 1990. It can't be earlier, The Who were on tour in the UK in late 1989 and that picture on Facebook looked like it was taken at Christmas. If it was 1991 or '92, wouldn't it look washed out?' Rachel let out a breath. 'I know that doesn't sound very scientific. But don't you think Ava would have mentioned if Meg had worked at Hare's Landing? Bearing in mind we're both staying here. If Meg had had a summer job here, she'd hardly have forgotten. *And* Ava would have said if Meg was friends with Sheridan too, wouldn't she? Any connection with the house would have come up in that conversation.'

Caroline didn't look convinced. 'It's not evidence, though. There's no date on the photo. It could have been taken that summer, but before she even went up to Dublin for the interview.'

'I know. The police can check to see if there's a date on the back or on the original spool, but *Sheridan knew she took it.* I saw him react physically to seeing it – and that wasn't my imagination. He got a fright, his whole face changed. Why react like that if he had nothing to hide?'

Caroline screwed up her face. 'Okay, so if Meg was here, and she took the picture—'

Rachel interrupted her. 'Why didn't he come forward to say he'd seen her? When she disappeared, I mean? Everyone thought she was in Dublin. Something must have happened

287

that made her leave and never want to come back. Maybe it was something to do with the O'Connor lad, the boy who disappeared at the same time?'

Caroline inclined her head. 'That actually plays right into it *not* being the same weekend at all, don't you think? Sheridan Smyth might not have felt the need to come forward if this was taken months before. Perhaps he was in the UK and didn't even know she was missing.'

Rachel let out a sharp breath. 'But then why did he go bright red and get all agitated when he saw it? It's just a picture of two friends. There has to be more to it … And you're forgetting something else.'

'What?'

'The body in the septic tank. What if it's the boy – O'Connor? We know Meg's safe and well somewhere, but for some reason she seems to be too frightened to come home. Maybe there was a party that weekend, and O'Connor was at it too – and something went wrong. You should have seen how Smyth reacted to this photograph. Something happened when it was taken, I know it.'

As she spoke, a door slammed somewhere upstairs and the fire suddenly spluttered. Jasper lifted his head and growled. They both looked at him, but a moment later he put his head back down. Caroline looked at Rachel, her eyes wide.

'This goddamn house.'

'It's old, it's just a draught.'

'The music I keep hearing isn't.' She straightened her glasses. 'This would be a whole lot less weird if I was one of those people who actually believed in ghosts.' Drawing a breath, Caroline glanced quickly at the portrait over the mantelpiece and then looked back at the photograph. 'If we're right about J. A. Stafford and Alfie being the same person, you've been saying all along that Hunter believed something happened that he couldn't deal with mentally, and as a result of that, he ended up on the streets because he couldn't cope with real life. If something terrible happened that weekend, that would fairly prey on your mind, don't you think?'

Rachel nodded slowly. She got up and came around to Caroline's side of the coffee table.

'Let's have another look at that Facebook picture. Did you save it?'

Caroline reached for her phone. 'Yep. The problem is we don't know for sure that J. A. Stafford was Alfie.'

'But his bank statement was in Alfie's bag, which makes all this a massive coincidence if it's not him. I mean, what are the chances of Alfie having a bank statement that belonged to someone who knew Sheridan Smyth at university?'

As Caroline scrolled through the images on her phone, Rachel pulled her own phone towards her. Some time between now and when she'd looked at it last, it had picked up a glimmer of reception and updated. It showed eight missed calls from Hunter.

'Oh crap, Hunter's been trying to get me. I'd better call him on the landline.'

'Do that while I look for this Facebook photo. Malachi might need to see it when he gets back here.'

As Rachel hurried into reception, Caroline continued scrolling. She was sure Rachel was right: that Stafford and Alfie were the same person. And as they were seeing here, it wasn't what was in the photo that was sometimes significant – what *wasn't* in it could be just as important.

Like the photos of the Christmas party.

She'd emailed Tim as they'd passed the cafe on the way back through the village. Even assuming he'd read it, he wouldn't have had a chance to check where Nancy had been yet. He'd have to think of a clever way of asking the other staff – and the other thing she'd suggested, she knew he'd need some time to get his head around.

Caroline had been thinking about Meg, about locations, about how today you could track someone, but how impossible it had been when Meg disappeared, and *that* had led her to thinking of a way to find out where Nancy had been during the Christmas party. Actually, two ways.

When she'd thought about it, it was really so simple to find out where Nancy had been that night. Google would have recorded her locations and travel – Tim just needed to access Nancy's Google account. Caroline knew Nancy had her location switched on – she always used the app to file her mileage at the end of every month. Tim would just need her password. And *that* would be saved on her terminal in work. A warning message about her account being accessed from an unidentified computer would pop up if he tried from anywhere else, so ideally he needed to go into the office, log in, find out where she'd been, and then print everything out.

Caroline was pretty sure that if Nancy's location could be cross-referenced with Greta's husband Clive's, it would make for some interesting conclusions.

And if that didn't work, she had a plan B. Like hers, Nancy's cell was company issue, which meant technically Greta, as her boss, was the account holder. So Greta – or Tim's firm, as the company lawyers– could request all the text and call data from the service provider, which, if that wasn't damning enough, would include the location information.

Caroline was pretty sure Tim could ask the mobile service provider for it directly himself, but it would be better with

Greta's approval. If Nancy's Gmail location data gave him the information she expected, Caroline could imagine that Greta would be more than happy to dig into Nancy's text history. Tim just had to find a way to handle the whole conversation delicately.

Caroline looked at her phone. There was no reception right now, and a message from Tim hadn't flashed in while she wasn't looking. It didn't matter. If he was going to access Nancy's location history from the office, he'd need to go in fairly late when there was only a skeleton staff working.

The more Caroline thought about it, the more she was convinced she was right.

Nancy's plan was clever – it would get rid of Caroline and land her the top job, while at the same time completely throwing Greta off the scent about Clive.

But Caroline's job was tracking down information, and often criminals, and Nancy had damned sure crossed over when she'd invented that lead. It had landed her and Joni freezing their arses off for hours, watching a perfectly innocent girl trying to work two jobs to achieve her dreams. If they'd taken that information one step further and Caroline had notified her friends in the cops that she was on a stake-out, or even casually mentioned it, who knows what could have happened? In the current political climate, if the wrong people got involved, it was very likely that a young girl would have been arrested and her family deported, whether there were grounds or not.

Nancy didn't think about consequences.

Caroline checked the time again. It was just a case of waiting now. Waiting and keeping an eye on her messages.

Finally finding the image she'd saved, she zoomed in on the section of the image featuring J. A. Stafford and held her phone up next to the framed picture again. They were right, she was sure of it. It wasn't just the T-shirt. The resemblance was uncanny. She was sure the boy in the photograph taken outside Hare's Landing was J. A. Stafford.

Chapter 49

RACHEL HEADED INTO reception, her heart beating hard. What on earth could Hunter want? He'd called so many times it had to be urgent. Did he have news of Nemo Freight? He'd go nuts if he thought she was here on her own with Declan Flynn hanging about, trying to intimidate Caroline. There was no point worrying him; he couldn't get here to help, and getting upset would only slow down his recovery.

Imogen was back behind the desk and looked up as Rachel crossed the tiled hall.

'Do you mind if I use the phone? My partner's been trying to get hold of me.'

Imogen started to lift the desk phone onto the counter, then changed her mind.

'Why don't you go into the office, it's more private?'

Sitting down at Bronagh's desk, Rachel pulled out her phone to find Hunter's number. When she was a child she'd remembered everyone's phone numbers, but now she only knew her own. Lifting the receiver, she punched it in. The call went straight to his voicemail. She dialled again, shaking her head. Had his battery died? She left a message.

Putting the phone down, she bit her lip. She'd told him if he needed her urgently to call the hotel reception, so perhaps he just wanted a chat and was impatient that she hadn't answered. Being stuck in a hospital bed must be driving him insane with boredom.

About to try again, Rachel heard a car pull up outside. *Malachi?* Half standing from the desk, she tried to see out of the office window, but the car had stopped short of it. Her stomach fluttered with anxiety. Would Malachi think she was nuts, dragging him back here to show him a shadow of a reflection in a degraded photograph?

She hoped not; *she was sure she was right.*

The front door banged and Rachel stood up, heading back out of the office through the door in the panelling. She glanced over at Imogen as she passed the desk.

'Couldn't get him, I'll try again later.'

'Sergeant O'Brien just came back, he's …'

She didn't need to say 'in the lounge'. Rachel could see Malachi's dark uniform through the glazed panel door connecting the lounge and the hall.

Inside, he was already poring over the framed photograph. He looked up as Rachel came in.

'We'll need to get it enhanced to be sure, but you've got great eyesight is all I can say.'

'I might not have thought to look if Sheridan Smyth hadn't made such a fuss.'

Rachel sat down beside Caroline. Sitting forward, his face serious, Malachi studied the image, then glanced up to make sure Imogen was busy in reception.

'This is obviously confidential, but we've just got the pathologist's report. He has more tests to run, and for a positive ID he needs DNA, but he thinks the body is a teenage girl. She had a fractured skull.' His face was grim. 'With the level of decomposition, the pathologist thinks it has to have been there for at least thirty years. Which might well tie in with your photograph here, given Sheridan Smyth's age. A bracelet was found in the tank too. It had a charm on it, a letter A. We're checking missing persons reports to see if anyone with the initial *A* went missing around thirty years ago.'

'Could it be Meg Cassidy? You'd need to check to see if Meg ever borrowed any of her sister's jewellery.'

Rachel looked at Caroline, shocked. 'But Ava's got postcards from her – she's in America.'

Caroline clicked her tongue thoughtfully. 'Ava *thinks* she's got postcards from Meg. What if she was murdered and someone sent cards to make it look like she'd left the country.'

'But her handwriting?' Rachel sat forward on the sofa. 'Wouldn't Ava have recognised it?'

Caroline looked pensive. 'It's not hard to copy someone's handwriting if you've got some sort of sample. And Ava wanted to believe they were from Meg.'

'Good point. In the light of what you've found here, I think we need to look for a DNA sample for elimination purposes. If the worst is confirmed, we'll need to look at those postcards.'

'Do you have a sample of Meg's fingerprints?'

'I'll need to check the original file. But we have handwriting experts up at Headquarters in Dublin who will be able to tell us if Meg wrote them or not.'

'If the body turns out to be her, someone sure wanted to make it look like Meg was still alive.' Caroline adjusted her glasses thoughtfully.

'Could it have been Flynn?' Rachel put her hand to her forehead. Everything was flying around inside her head: names and faces; the photographs they'd found; Caroline's notebook. 'The secret was fairly safe once people had stopped looking for Meg. Then you turned up here, Caroline, and everything seems to have kicked off. He wanted to stop you finding something out – perhaps that something was this.'

'It would certainly explain why he was trying to frighten me away.'

Malachi looked at Caroline. 'Sounds like you were lucky that's all he did. But if that's correct, and he was involved in Meg's disappearance and in writing these postcards, perhaps he was as sloppy with them as he was with your notebook. Ava will be able to tell us if he ever had access to them, or handled them after they arrived and she stuck them on her noticeboard.' Malachi's voice was serious as he continued, 'He must have got some shock when you booked in, Caroline. He must have thought you'd been sent here by the paper. But I'd guess he couldn't risk harming you or your bosses would have brought us in. And there'd be a chance we'd find the body.'

Staring into the fire, Rachel let out a breath.

How had they landed in the middle of this? And how did Alfie fit in?

She was starting to get a bad feeling about how he might have been involved in whatever had happened thirty years ago.

'Have you found him? Flynn, I mean?'

'I'd only got to Mrs Travers's cottage when you called. The lads are searching it. It looks like he was living there and has cleared out, but we've alerted all the ports and airports.'

Caroline's voice was quiet. 'Do you think you *will* catch him?'

'We should do. This is an island – it can be tricky to get on and off.'

Rachel ran her hands into the roots of her hair, thinking. So many things were falling into place now. But there was just one more thing bothering her.

'If you're right and this *did* all happen here, perhaps Honoria was away that weekend – in London? In the letter she says something about going to the doctor, and that can't have been here in Glencurragh, surely? She died very soon afterwards, according to that funeral report we found. Perhaps that was when she realised she was pregnant?'

As she spoke, Imogen came in from the bar, bringing more coffee. She slipped the tray down on the table and hesitated for a moment.

'Are you talking about Honoria Smyth?' She blushed, obviously conscious that she was intruding on their conversation. 'She wasn't pregnant.' Caroline and Rachel looked at her in surprise. 'She had ovarian cancer. I probably shouldn't say it, but it was such a long time ago. Her specialist was in London.'

'How on earth do you know that?'

'My grandpa was her doctor. He got the post-mortem reports. I remember him saying to my dad that it was such a tragedy, because it could have been treated. Whenever they talked about anyone getting cancer, he'd mention her name, like a reminder that they needed to keep a really close eye on whoever it was.' With them all looking at her, Imogen's colour rose even more. 'I didn't think anyone else knew. How did you …?'

'I found a letter from her – I've been meaning to show it to you but with everything happening it totally went out of my head. It's hard to read, but we think she wrote it to her lover. The way it was written, it sounded like she was pregnant.'

Imogen shook her head. 'I'd love to see it, but no, she definitely wasn't. My dad probably still has her file with the post-mortem report, you can check.' As she picked up the empty tray, the phone in reception started ringing. 'I'd better get that – it might be Bronagh.'

Rachel looked at Caroline and pulled a face. 'Do you think he left her because she was ill? He couldn't face the thought of her treatment?'

Caroline's face clouded. 'Who knows? But if he *was* here then, and he knew Meg was in the septic tank, he wanted to disappear and this gave him a reason. I bet if you look at the date Nemo Freight was established, it'll be post 1990.'

Malachi stood up. 'I'll check. But it sounds like Sheridan Smyth has got some questions to answer, too.'

As Malachi finished speaking, Imogen appeared back at the lounge door, her face troubled.

'That was Bronagh. Mrs Travers is worse, and the papers are saying the body in the tank was a girl. It's all online. They're saying she wasn't dead when she went into the tank.'

Caroline's hand shot to her mouth. 'My God, that's awful.'

'Jesus Christ, how did that happen? We wanted to keep all of that under wraps.' Malachi shook his head. 'It sounds like the post-mortem report has been leaked. If you're right about the timing of this photograph, Rachel, Sheridan Smyth will know we're looking for him now.'

Caroline looked at him. 'Is it true? That she wasn't dead? That makes this all so much worse.'

Malachi let out an impatient breath as he answered. 'It's absolutely not for the public. Whoever leaked it's going to be for the high jump.' He said it quietly but Rachel could see he was seething. 'Something like this can compromise a trial. There will have to be an investigation, and damned fast.'

While he was speaking, Rachel could see Caroline was frowning, obviously deep in thought. She leaned forward as she spoke.

'If we're right, I think Smyth might come to you now. He knows the law, and, if this photograph was taken that day, that there were potentially three people involved in whatever happened to Meg – himself, Flynn and his friend J. A. Stafford. A jury is going to have to prove beyond reasonable doubt he actually dropped her into that tank. He might think he can bluff it out, pretend that he didn't know what had happened, that it was all Stafford or Flynn, who's already wanted by the police – Sheridan must have read about Nemo Freight's problems. He's a judge, a man of fine character – he'd be arrogant enough to think he could persuade a jury. And he's got time to work it all out.'

Rachel bit her lip. 'He'll want to get hold of this photograph, though. I think he saw the reflection too when he looked at it. And this is potentially the only evidence that connects him directly with Meg.'

Caroline stood up. 'And he believes he's the only one who knows about it. I think he'll come back for it tomorrow. He needs to downplay its significance. Perhaps he'll say he hasn't got any pictures of the house and try and buy it – that's what I'd do. Maybe we should keep it safe in the office tonight, or bring it back to the Boathouse with us.'

'What if he comes back for it tonight?'

Rachel looked at Malachi, her eyes wide. He drew a breath in through his teeth.

'We're releasing the scene – the pathologist is confident he has everything.' He paused. 'Everyone's looking for Flynn so we won't have anyone on duty here tonight.'

Caroline shook her head. 'I really don't think he'd do that, it's too big a risk. He needs to maintain the outward appearance of innocence and credibility, that's crucial to his story – and his career. If he tries to buy it "for old times' sake" –' she did the rabbit ears thing with her fingers – 'the assumption of innocence is in the mix. If he tries to steal it, it sends out a whole different message.'

Malachi was nodding as she spoke. 'Let me talk to the team. I'll make sure someone is back here in the morning, just in case. If Mrs Travers has got worse, I'd guess Smyth will go to the hospital tonight. He needs to show he's not worried by the press report, that he's a compassionate guy. If he does, our lads can pick him up there and invite him in for a chat.'

Chapter 50

Closing the front door of the Boathouse behind her, the framed photograph in her hand, Caroline leaned back onto it and looked at Rachel. She was already spooning dog food into a chrome bowl, much to Jasper's delight. He was sitting expectantly in the middle of the kitchen floor, his ears cocked forward, his eyes bright.

'What I don't understand –' Rachel scooped out the last spoonful – 'is how on earth they can know whoever she was, was still alive when she went into the tank?' She put the bowl down on the floor with a clatter. 'There we go, Jasp, that'll sort you out.'

Caroline sucked in a breath through her teeth and put the photo on the kitchen counter.

'I think it's to do with the diatoms. They are microscopic algae that are present in water – they're one way to tell if someone's drowned. I've worked quite a few cases where bodies have been immersed. I'm pretty sure that once they get into the bloodstream they can be absorbed by bone. The pathologist didn't have a lot to work with, so he'll have done every possible test on what he has.'

'So that means she inhaled the water in the septic tank?' Rachel winced at the thought.

'It meant she was alive long enough for the diatoms to get

into her bloodstream. Which means she drowned – she didn't die from the bump on her head.'

'If she was alive when she went in, it means if someone had called an ambulance when they found her, she could still be alive today.'

Watching Jasper eat, Caroline scowled. 'If Smyth has got hold of the PM report or reads the papers, that piece of information will give him some shock.'

Shaking her head, Rachel headed for the kettle. 'My God, what happened that day?'

'If Flynn was involved in drugs back then, he could have given them all lines or pills. Who knows?'

Caroline slipped off her coat and began heading into the living room, stopping beside the end of the counter before she got there.

'Poor Ava, though – it's like losing Meg twice. And if someone did try and cover up her death by sending those postcards, that's just so awful. It's positively psychopathic.' Caroline shook her head. 'My money's on Declan Flynn. Psychopaths are often charming, and chatty – he certainly is. But they can be impulsive – I don't feel whoever daubed my notebook really thought that through. If it was him, let's hope he forgot to put on gloves when he was handling the postcards too.' Caroline leaned on the counter, rotating her neck.

She looked as tired as Rachel felt.

'Do you think Flynn was following Smyth's career, knew he'd become a judge?'

Caroline shrugged. 'I'd guess so. And if I was Smyth, I'd want to keep tabs on everyone involved. I'd guess he knew exactly what Flynn was doing. If Flynn was involved in the drugs trade everyone keeps talking about being rampant around here, it doesn't take a genius to work out that a freight company is the ideal cover. But the more illegal activity Flynn got involved with, the better for Smyth.'

'Very true.' Rachel reached up to the cupboard for two mugs and a box of camomile tea – they both needed something to help them relax before they went to bed.

'How are we going to find out for sure if Alfie and J. A. Stafford were the same person?'

'Hopefully the police in London will be able to check dental records. Or even familial DNA – Stafford's family will be easy enough to find, presumably, through the university records.'

Rachel nodded slowly. 'Do you think Flynn thought Honoria was pregnant and murdered her too?'

Caroline put her hand behind her neck and shivered. 'Poor woman. Reading between the lines of that letter, he as good as murdered her by leaving when she needed him most. She must have been distraught – you know how at the end of a relationship it always feels like the end of the world? There's nothing worse than getting dumped. And she had a potentially terminal illness, she could have been feeling really sick – you can see how she might have felt she didn't have anything to live for.' She paused again, thinking. 'I don't feel like she had many friends around here, if any. If "D" is Declan Flynn, he could have been her whole world.'

'She had Mrs Travers.' Rachel raised her eyebrows as she made the tea. 'Everyone says she was devoted to Honoria – and she must have had friends in London. But perhaps she'd lost touch with them.'

She handed Caroline a steaming mug. Taking it into the living area, Caroline sat down on the sofa and kicked off her boots, curling up. She stared at the unlit stove as she took a sip, her mind obviously busy.

'I wonder, if we're right, if Smyth knew about Flynn and his mother?' Caroline took another sip. 'Do you know something? I think Mrs Travers knows what happened – maybe not all the detail, but most of it, and that's why she's stayed here all this time. She was protecting Sheridan Smyth and Flynn by making sure nothing happened to the septic tank.'

Rachel brought her tea over to the living room and sat down in the armchair.

'I think you could be right. She was left the gate lodge, wasn't she? That cottage she lives in. She could have sold it and moved into Glencurragh. I mean, there was no real reason to stay here once Honoria was dead, and it would be a lot more practical.'

Caroline sipped her tea. 'And it would explain why she panicked when she saw my email on the booking. And why she told Flynn. I can't imagine Bronagh broadcasting who I was, she's much more discreet than that.'

Jasper padded over and put his chin on Rachel's knee. Holding her mug of tea in one hand, she tickled his ears.

'How could Mrs Travers have known, though?'

'Perhaps Flynn or Smyth got drunk and told her, or maybe she saw what happened. You know how she lurks. Perhaps she's always been like that and saw what happened with Meg. She was the housekeeper, she must have known to expect Smyth and his friend that weekend, made sure she had food in. Perhaps she saw them arrive with Meg. She was very dismissive of the case when I was reading about it in the paper, like it was Meg's own fault what happened.'

Rachel pulled a face, about to reply, when Caroline yawned suddenly. 'Sorry. God, I'm whacked. I'm going to go up, will you be all right down here? I'll take the picture up with me and put it in the wardrobe.'

Rachel yawned too. 'You've started me now. We could both do with a good night's sleep. This is the last place Declan Flynn is going to turn up tonight, thank God – he's probably on the run already if they've searched Mrs Travers's cottage.'

Caroline uncurled her legs and stood up, her mug in her hand, heading for the sink.

'It sounds like she's on her way out. Bronagh's so good to stay with her all this time. Flynn's hardly going to turn up at the hospital either. He must know the guards are after him.'

'I'm absolutely sure Mrs Travers sent Flynn to collect you from the airport when she saw your email address. Between Honoria Smyth's suicide and teenagers disappearing, there was plenty for you to investigate here – no wonder she was frosty when you arrived.' As Rachel spoke, their phones suddenly came to life on the kitchen counter. A variety of pings and whoops rang out as everything updated. 'Ooh, we've got reception. Middle of the night, that's handy.'

Caroline laughed. 'To be fair, it's only nine o'clock.' She passed Rachel her phone and picked up her own. 'Tim's texted, and mailed. Oh God. I'm feeling sick now, I hope to God I was right.' She looked at the screen and back at Rachel, pulling a face.

'About the photographs?'

'It's four in the afternoon in New York. Just keep everything crossed. The text says to check my mail. God, I'll kill him for not just saying it in the text.'

Rachel checked her own phone as Caroline opened her email and scanned the message Tim had sent. Her mouth fell open and her eyes opened wider as she read.

'What? What's up? Don't keep me in suspense.'

'You won't believe it. Tim went to see Greta this morning. He said he made up a story about cryptic messages that could be threats to Nancy.' She glanced over at Rachel, her eyes gleaming. 'You *could* call my messages cryptic and a threat to Nancy – he's very good at being honest, is Tim.'

'Go on, what then?'

'He says he went to see Greta and said he was concerned about the secret project. Nancy wasn't in the office again. He said he really wanted to at least know her location so if anything happened, they could be there to jump in.' Caroline laughed, shaking her head. 'He explained about the Google location thing, so Greta goes to Nancy's terminal and finds out where she's at, right then.'

'And where was she?'

Rachel could see Caroline trying to keep a straight face.

'Wait for it, that's the punchline. So there's Greta looking at Nancy's location live on the screen, and she rings her cell to see where she is.' Caroline couldn't help herself laughing. 'Tim says Greta had Nancy on speaker and she's all breathless. She tells Greta that she's following someone and can't talk, that she's just run down the block into Macy's.' Caroline fought to keep her face straight, 'But she wasn't at Macy's. She was in Greta's apartment. The address came right up.'

'Jeepers, what happened?'

'While Tim's acting all shocked, Greta shoots out of the office and goes home.'

'Surely Nancy had left? She was hardly still there?'

Caroline smirked. 'Nancy isn't that clever. I think she's been promoted because Clive's been putting in a good word.'

'What happened?' Rachel swung around in the armchair to look at her properly.

'She walked in on them. At least that's what Tim thinks must have happened. He got a text from Greta telling him to notify accounts that Nancy was leaving the company. He was still in the office watching her location, and she only left after Greta texted him.'

'Good God. Where does that leave you?'

'Well, it means Greta knows it wasn't me having the affair and that Nancy is a manipulative little bitch. Tim says he told her about the 7–Eleven stake-out, and it being a bum lead and how annoyed I was that I missed the party.'

Caroline looked at her phone for another minute.

'Yikes. There's an email from Greta here. Hold on.' Rachel watched as she scanned it quickly. 'She's giving me an update on the case. She calls it "nonsense" –' Caroline made rabbit ears with her spare hand – 'and she understands from Tim that I have all my data, and she's looking forward to seeing me in the office after my vacation.' Caroline shook her head in disbelief. 'I bet.'

'So that's great, isn't it, that she's backing you?'

'I guess. But do you know what – she shares a lot of characteristics with Mrs Travers. She's just … I don't know.' Caroline shivered, 'She's like a snake. I can't work with an editor who doesn't have my back. If she doesn't know I'm good at my job, she can go take a running jump. I'm going to have a few chats as soon as this case is settled. Even if it doesn't get to court, I'm going to write an article about the whole thing – and my investigation – which, with a bit of luck, might bring in a few job offers. The media are like lemmings, they all jump together. If I'm in the news, I'm hot property.' Caroline looked back at her over the top of her glasses. 'Let me mail Tim back and we can get to bed.'

Rachel laughed. 'Don't you love it when a plan comes together?' She sighed. 'Hunter's been trying me again, he's texted to say call him. In capitals. Why do people do that? He's just like Tim, it must be a man thing. Why not just say in the text what the problem is?' She hauled herself off the sofa. 'Have you got reception? Mine's gone dead again – I'll have to call him from the landline in the hotel in the morning, I can't face going back up there now.' She shook her head. 'I should have remembered before I came down.'

'Try my phone to tell him. I don't know if the signal's strong enough, but you're very welcome to give it a go.'

Chapter 51

A VOLLEY OF BARKS woke Rachel with a start. She hadn't been able to reach Hunter on the phone last night; she'd texted instead, hoping it would get through. She'd slept fitfully, worrying about why he needed her to call.

'Jasper? What's up, Jasp?'

Wide awake, her heart thumping, Rachel rolled over on the sofa bed to see Jasper pawing at the front door, an unmistakable black shape in the darkness. He barked again, whining, and ran back to her, grabbing the duvet covering her and tugging it off.

As she swung her feet over the side of the sofa, the light went on upstairs and Caroline came down the spiral staircase, pulling on her bathrobe, her feet bare. Her hair was ruffled from sleep, dark circles under her eyes.

'What's happening?'

'I've no idea, Jasper's gone mad. There's something outside.'

'Christ.' Caroline was fully awake now and pulled the robe around herself protectively. 'What do we do?'

Rachel's mouth had gone dry, her heart in overdrive. She'd never seen Jasper like this. He jumped up at the front door, barking madly, the sound reverberating around her head. Caroline looked at Rachel, and at Jasper and the door for another second.

'Let's get dressed, then … then … I don't know, but I can't think in pyjamas.'

Jumping out of her makeshift bed, Rachel searched for the clothes she was wearing yesterday; her mud-spattered jeans would have to do. She pulled on a T-shirt and then a sweatshirt on top of it. Her wellies were over by the front door beside Caroline's boots. Both pairs had fallen over on their sides where Jasper had knocked into them in his frenzy.

As Rachel pulled her socks on, Caroline came down the stairs, buckling the belt on her jeans, her socks almost silent on the wooden treads.

'Let's see if we can see anything outside. Don't put the lights on. We don't want anyone seeing in.'

Caroline moved quickly to one of the round windows beside the front door and stood on tiptoes to look out.

'What can you see?'

Following suit, Rachel went to the window on the opposite side of the door. Their view was limited by the surrounding trees, but it was a cold, clear night and as her eyes adjusted Rachel could see the neat paved ornamental circle immediately outside the house.

On the other side of the door Caroline had her hands around her eyes, peering out.

'That lamp on the post is on a movement-sensitive timer, like a security light. It goes off at around eleven and only clicks on again if something comes within range.' She hesitated, as if she was checking to be sure. 'And it's off now.'

Rachel's mind flew down a hundred blind alleyways, all dark and cold and terrifying. What on earth could be upsetting Jasper so much? She could feel Caroline's anxiety, arcing like an electric current, as raw and real as her own. Caroline glanced over to her.

'If the light hasn't come on, whatever Jasper heard, it wasn't people-sized.'

'Or they could have been people-sized but know how it works.' Rachel cupped her hands around her eyes to look out again. 'If you were sharp enough you'd just keep out of the way of the sensor.'

She peered into the darkness of the trees. The rain had moved on, but the wind was strong, stirring the branches in the woods, their movement like the sound of waves on the shore. The moon was in its last quarter, giving some light, but very little.

'Oh Jesus.'

Caroline pulled away from the window and went to open the front door. Rachel put her arm out to stop her.

'What, what can you see?'

'Fire. The house is on fire. You can just see the light over the trees when they move in the wind.'

'It can't be – you must be seeing something else.'

'It is. What else can it be?' Rachel could see the fear and anguish in Caroline's face as she continued. 'Grab your cell. If we walk around a bit, one of us has to pick up enough reception to make a 911 call. We're on different networks.'

Rachel looked at her, stunned. 'Remember what you said about whoever was in the house before, trying to get you outside, and how you didn't want to get attacked in the wood?' Her intonation at of the end of the sentence conveyed her disbelief. 'What if this is some sort of stunt.'

'It's a stunt all right. Someone's set fire to the house. Seriously – let me open the door and you'll see. I promise I'll close it super quick if I'm wrong. And we've got Jasper.'

Rachel reached down to grab his collar. 'Wouldn't the guards call for the fire brigade? We'd have heard engines by now.'

'Malachi said they've cleared the scene. They don't have anyone here tonight.' Caroline was starting to sound desperate. 'We've got to go and check. Bronagh could be home by now – her apartment's at the back of the house. Malachi said she was planning to come back here instead of staying at the pub another night.'

'Okay, let me get the phones.'

Still holding onto his collar, Rachel sidestepped, trying not to trip over Jasper, who was pulling to get away. Reaching the counter, she picked up the phones they'd left charging.

'Ready.'

Caroline pulled open the door and they were immediately hit with the acrid stench of smoke carried on the wind. Above the sound of the trees swaying, they could hear the crackle of flames licking dry timbers.

'Jesus Christ.' Jasper tried to jerk away, his front legs rearing up as Rachel held him back. 'Lead, I need his lead.'

Caroline looked around frantically and, seeing it on the floor where it had snaked off the counter, she left the door and grabbed it.

'Here, quick, we need to find a signal.'

She took her phone from Rachel and checked the reception. Clicking Jasper's lead on, Rachel wrapped it around her wrist, her phone in her hand.

'Put on your coat and let's go.'

As if he thought she was talking to him, Jasper hauled Rachel out of the door, almost knocking Caroline over. One eye on the reception bars on her phone screen, Rachel tried to watch where she was going, at the same time leaning back to try and slow him down.

The moment they were out of the door, the smell of smoke grew stronger, flecks of ash raining down on them. The lamp flicked on as soon as they got within reach of the sensor. Rachel glanced back briefly at Caroline as Jasper hauled her up the path through the trees. She stumbled forward, searching her screen for a hint of reception, her eyes focused on her phone.

With each step they took, the fire grew brighter. Rachel could feel her lips drying, the smoke making her cough as the wind carried it out to sea.

Bursting onto the drive, they could see the whole of the front of the house was burning, flames creeping up the walls, the windows shattered by the heat.

'I've got reception! Shit, it's gone again.' Behind her, Caroline took a step backwards and frantically dialled with her thumbs, putting the phone to her ear as she looked at Rachel, her blue eyes full of fear. 'Hello, hello? Yes, I need the fire service. And police …'

Rachel turned back to look at the house. Smoke was catching in her throat, making her eyes sting. It was a terrifying sight. Half turning to Caroline, she pointed to the stable yard.

'I'm going to look for Bronagh.'

Caroline nodded, her eyes open wide, the phone pressed to her ear as she glanced up anxiously at the burning house.

'Be careful, don't go in whatever you do.'

If Rachel thought her heart had been beating hard before, it was nothing compared to the thundering she could feel now. As she ran across the gravel around the front of the house, Jasper panting beside her, the wind altered direction, bringing the smoke inland. Skirting the turret room, she ran on down towards the lane that connected the stables with the main drive. The fire seemed to still be mainly confined to the front of the house, but the smoke was getting thicker as she tore around the corner into the stable yard, coating the back of her throat, drying her mouth. She felt as if her tongue was swelling; she could smell the unmistakable scent of burning wood interwoven with something sharper, more acrid, something that stung her eyes and made her want to retch. Bending to unclip Jasper's lead, she doubled back, taking him to the edge of the woods. She was going into this voluntarily but she couldn't risk him being overcome by the smoke.

'Stay, boy, I'll be really fast, I promise.'

As she turned back, she realised the fire alarm wasn't going off.

Why wasn't it working?

Questions careered around Rachel's head. She'd managed so many fire scenes over the years in studio and on location, working with fire officers, production managers and the fire brigade to ensure that the end product looked convincing but that no one was hurt. She knew exactly how fast fire could spread in an old building.

How long would it take the fire brigade to get here?

She had no idea where the nearest station was.

Running into the stable yard she faltered for a moment, waiting for the security lights to come on. Nothing happened – the fire must have affected the power. The darkness was complete, oily, acidic – like black coffee on an empty stomach. On the other side of the house she could hear the fire taking control, licking and spitting, glass shattering. Even at the back of the building, the sound was like the roar of a jet engine, like hell itself.

Bronagh's apartment had once been the coach house at the very back of the U-shaped stable block. It could be reached through the main house, but a smart red front door opened directly into the yard.

Running up to the door, Rachel pounded on it, the heel of her hand stinging with the force. She couldn't see any lights on inside – surely the sound would have woken Bronagh up?

Rachel had no idea what time it could be. Realising she'd left her watch in the house, she pulled her phone out to check; it was just past midnight.

Could Bronagh still be at the hospital? How would they know?

Rachel turned back to the door and pounded on it again. Still no response. She took a step backwards. She could find something to break down the door with, but that would take time and Bronagh might not even be here. Rachel whipped around, looking at the stables themselves. There were no horses here now, but one of them was a garage where Bronagh kept her car, Rachel was sure. The only problem was, she had no idea which one, and the smoke was getting thicker, trapped by the horseshoe of buildings. She *really* didn't have time to search for the car.

She needed to get back to Caroline – if Caroline had reception on her phone, they could call Bronagh's mobile or the hospital to see if she'd left.

In the distance Rachel suddenly heard the sound of sirens. *Help at last.*

She turned and ran back to the stable-yard entrance, whistling for Jasper. He was beside her in a second, just as a huge cloud of smoke enveloped her. Bent double, coughing and retching, gasping for air, she was totally disorientated. Then something warm and wet hit her in the face and she felt Jasper's tongue. Closing her eyes tightly, she grabbed hold of his collar.

'Find Caroline.'

Her voice was little more than a rasp but she felt him pull her forwards. Bending down as low as she could, one hand over her mouth, she felt him guide her through the smoke, the sound of the sirens growing louder. She couldn't see where they were going, but she trusted him absolutely.

As he led her away from the house, the air gradually became clearer. Breathing more easily, she opened her eyes, wiping the tears from them. They stung like crazy but she realised Jasper had brought her around to the edge of the drive. Ahead of her a fire tender had pulled up, blue strobes cutting through the swirling darkness. A moment later huge arc lights flooded the drive with harsh white light. Looking at the house, the flames leaping hungrily from what had been the lounge, the downstairs windows framing the glow inside, Rachel shivered. How had this happened?

Chapter 52

STANDING IN THE shelter of the trees on the other side of the fire tender, Caroline waited anxiously for Rachel, pulling her parka around her, glad of the thick cashmere sweater she'd pulled on over her jeans. Despite the heat from the flames, she felt chilled. The wind had changed direction and the smoke was billowing away from her, but it was fanning the flames eating into the main body of the house, sending them deeper into the building. Beside her, the fire crew moved fast, switching on huge bright white lamps, unrolling hoses. In the dazzling artificial light, the shadows were darker, even more ominous.

Caroline wasn't sure if it was the shock or the smoke, but she felt physically sick. The destruction was devastating.

But the water was coming through the hoses now – she could see them jumping where the fire officers had snaked them across the drive. She'd never seen people move so quickly or efficiently. They worked like a machine, the reflective stripes on their jackets lit by the flames, each knowing his role, equipment checks shouted and answered. How many times had they done this before?

The heat was cracking her lips, the intensity and sheer noise of it terrifying. She was staying well back, out of the way, but these guys were running towards the house, focusing on their job and not on the danger. Suddenly water was gushing from several hoses at once, the teams holding them bracing against the force of the pumps. Caroline wiped her face with the back of her hand, realising that tears were streaming down her cheeks.

Never in a million years had she expected this trip to turn out the way it was going so far … and now this? At the start of the year she'd picked up a book called *The Five-Minute Journal* in Barnes & Noble. It was all positive thinking and focusing on what you were grateful for. With the tension in the office, she'd felt she needed something to centre herself, a way to make her think about the good things in her life. It advocated a morning and evening routine, thinking about what you were grateful for in the morning, and listing what amazing things had happened that day, each evening.

The book was still in her suitcase – she *had* brought it with her at least – but when this fire was under control, and she got back to the Boathouse, she was damned sure she was going to find it, and start using it again. When there was so much bad in the world, you had to hold tightly on to the good, or your own sanity would be tested, just like Alfie's had been.

Lost in thought, transfixed by the burning house, she hardly registered the Garda car that had pulled up behind the fire tender, or the uniformed officer who got out of it.

'Caroline, you okay?'

Malachi's voice cut through the jumbled sounds of men shouting, the roar of the flames. Behind him the firefighters were struggling with another of the hoses, with the weight and power of the water pumping from its nozzle. There were two tenders now, hoses snaking across the drive as if they were alive.

'Caroline, are you okay?' He said it again, then paused. 'Where's Rachel?'

She felt his arm go around her shoulders, bringing her out of her thoughts.

'Come and sit in the back of the car, it's safer there.'

He guided her towards it, opening the back door of the patrol car. As she sat down she heard a volley of barks.

Caroline turned as Malachi dipped his head out of the back seat and looked over the car roof in the direction of the sound. They heard it again and Rachel stumbled around the back of one of the tenders, her hand on Jasper's collar. Pulling her, he swerved around the trailing hoses and guided her to the back of the car. She was coughing violently, her face streaked black.

'Christ, where've you been?'

Malachi ran around the car, catching her as she stumbled towards him. Turning, he guided her to the rear door on the opposite side to Caroline. She flopped into the back seat beside her, coughing, trying to catch her breath.

'I can't find Bronagh, I thought she was in her apartment.'

He leaned into the car. 'I've just spoken to her. Mrs Travers has rallied – they think she's going to be okay. Bronagh was just on her way home. She'll be here shortly.'

Caroline winced. 'My God – after all her work restoring the place.'

Malachi's face was grim as he agreed. 'At least she wasn't in the house – and neither were you.'

As Rachel continued to cough, Caroline could see she was struggling to breathe. Malachi had obviously noticed it too. He turned and waved over to one of the firefighters, gesturing that he needed help. A few minutes later Rachel was wrapped in a silver foil blanket. The firefighter briskly fitted an oxygen mask over her face as her body began to shake uncontrollably.

Thank God she was okay.

That was the first thing going into the journal when they got back – top of her list of three amazing things that had happened today. Caroline closed her eyes and lay her head back on the rear seat, immediately feeling something warm and wet on her hand. With the firefighter blocking the other door, Jasper had come around the car and was pushing at her, trying to get inside, his feet on the running ledge.

'It's all right, boy, she's going to be okay. You did good.'

Caroline ruffled his ears and then put her arms around his neck, burying her face in his fur and hugging him hard.

And Jasper was the second thing on her list.

He stank of smoke. He barked as the firefighter leaned in to check Rachel's oxygen mask.

'You're in shock, love, take another slug of the O$_2$ there, that'll sort you out.' He picked up her hand, clipping something onto her finger. 'We just need to check out the oxygen levels in your blood. It won't hurt, it uses a laser strobe to test your blood through your fingernail.'

Jasper yelped again, trying to climb onto Caroline's knee. She leaned back to make way for him and pulled him in. Tangled in the silver foil blanket, he tried to climb across to Rachel's knee and prodded her with his nose, his tail thumping. The firefighter gave him an affectionate rub and unclipped the monitor he'd put on Rachel's finger.

'You'll be grand in a few minutes. Just keep breathing slowly.'

Rachel nodded, and put her arms around Jasper's head.

Before Caroline could speak, they heard the growl of an engine and the inside of the patrol car was lit by the headlights of a car pulling up behind them. It had to be Bronagh. From somewhere closer to the house they heard a voice amplified by some sort of megaphone.

'Sector one clear. All persons accounted for. Fire under control.'

Chapter 53

'**O**H MY GOD!'

They heard Bronagh before they saw her. She passed beside the patrol car as if in a trance, unaware they were sitting in the back. Caroline eased herself from under Jasper and hauled herself out. Bronagh was standing stock-still, staring at the flames, their light picking up the colours in her red hair. She was holding both hands over her mouth. Coming up behind her, Caroline put her arm around her shoulders. There wasn't anything she could say to make it better.

Malachi appeared on Bronagh's other side, his voice low and calm but urgent.

'Caroline and Rachel said Imogen locked up when she left. I've been in touch with her and Conor. They are both safe.'

Almost as if she hadn't heard him, Bronagh frowned. 'How did it happen? I mean ... we're so careful with the candles, Imogen's always telling me to blow them out, and we've only just had the wiring done ...' She tailed off, barely able to speak.

'We don't know yet, but we'll find out.'

Caroline glanced at Malachi as he spoke, his voice hard. Beside him, Rachel appeared, hugging the silver blanket around her, Jasper at her side.

'Why didn't the alarm go off? And the security lights weren't working in the stable yard.' Rachel coughed again, catching her breath.

'That's something else we need to find out.'

Malachi tried to sound light, but Caroline could see Rachel swing around and catch his eye, her eyebrows raised. Bronagh wasn't taking in what they were saying. Suddenly her face contorted with panic.

'What about Ava? Is Ava okay?'

'She was here? Ava Cassidy?' Malachi's voice was sharp.

'Yes, she called me. She was here earlier, she wanted to talk … I can't remember …' Bronagh put her hand to her forehead. 'I'm sorry. I think I need to sit down.'

'Come down to the Boathouse, I can make you some tea. We have power, or at least we did when we left.'

Caroline glanced back up at the main house. It was going to be a long time before anyone would be able to go inside. The fire crews had extinguished much of the fire, but a hose was still trained on the roof where the occasional tongue of flame leaped. The rest was dripping and black, and stinking.

'That's an excellent idea.'

Malachi began to guide Bronagh towards the path through the trees. Still in shock, she walked slowly, continually turning to look back at the house.

'I need to call Leo …' She tailed off.

'We can patch a call through to him, don't worry. Let's get you warm first. I'm afraid I need to ask you a few questions.'

Walking ahead of them, Caroline glanced back to see Bronagh nodding slowly, her face dazed. Opening the front door, she pushed it wide to let them all in.

Once inside, she went straight into the kitchenette and filled the kettle.

As if tea solved everything.

Ahead of her, Malachi led Bronagh into the living room. She hovered, looking at Rachel's unmade bed and duvet helplessly for a moment.

'You just sit here and we'll sort everything out.'

Malachi steered her into the armchair as Rachel bent down to pick up the duvet. Without taking off the sheet, she flipped the mattress back into the base of the sofa, sliding the metal legs of the bed into place and looking around for the huge cushions. Finding them, she dropped her pillows over the end of the arm onto a rug and slotted the back cushions into place.

'Now we can all sit down.'

'I'm sorry, I ...' Bronagh started to speak but Rachel sat down on the sofa and held up her hand.

'Don't be sorry, it takes less than two minutes to make up the bed. Not a bother.'

Malachi sat down beside Rachel, his notebook in his hand as Caroline brought Bronagh a mug of tea. He looked gratefully at the coffee she handed him.

'Now, what were you saying about Ava?'

Bronagh put her hand to her head. 'She called me tonight, she was on her way here, I thought. It was late, around 9.45, I think. She said she needed someone to talk to. She thought I'd be home.' Bronagh frowned, obviously trying to recall the conversation. 'I told her I was still at the hospital.' She took a sip of her tea and shook her head. 'I wasn't really concentrating on what she was saying, to be honest. Mrs T.'s on the mend but she had a bit of a turn.'

Malachi stood up. 'I'll just get someone to call to her house.' He frowned deeply, his hand already on his radio. 'I'll be right back.'

Chapter 54

WHEN RACHEL WOKE up the next morning, she felt like she was trapped in a bubble, the sounds strangely dull, her blood pumping in her ears. She lay on the pillow for a few moments, staring at the honey-coloured wooden ceiling, trying to work out where she was and what had happened. As she gradually became aware that the acrid smell clinging to her was smoke, it began to come back. Beside her she could feel a heavy weight. She reached out, half expecting Hunter, instead finding Jasper's thick coat at her fingertips instead. He flopped his head back and licked her face.

She had no idea what time it was. The gauzy curtains covering the windows at the far end of the room let the light in and it was bright, so it was definitely morning. Rachel reached for her phone. She'd kept it beside her when they'd come in last night, despite the lack of reception – its proximity made her feel safe.

Now she really needed to talk to Hunter.

Bronagh hadn't stayed long in the end, once Malachi had established Ava was home and safe. She'd gone back to the pub, her clothes still in her suitcase in the boot of her car. She'd wanted to call her husband undisturbed. Last night their dreams had literally gone up in smoke.

Rachel closed her eyes and an image of the smouldering

remains of Hare's Landing appeared on the inside of her eyelids. Would she ever be able to forget it?

There was a creak from the room above and Rachel heard the boards whisper as Caroline crossed the floor to the top of the stairs. Rachel heard her hesitate before coming down the spiral staircase, her feet bare. Arriving at the bottom, she looked like Rachel felt. Without her glasses hiding them, Rachel could see her blue eyes were puffy, slightly bloodshot. She tightened the belt on her robe and pulled her hair back out of her face with both hands. Her voice was croaky when she spoke.

'How are you doing? Did you sleep?'

Hearing her voice, Jasper rolled over and made a disgruntled noise somewhere between a growl and a whine. He sounded like an old man annoyed at being disturbed. They looked at each other, shaking their heads.

'He wants a lie-in. Too much excitement.'

Smiling, Caroline headed for the kettle. Jasper sighed loudly and Rachel laughed, feeling her chest tighten as the laughter became a bout of coughing. She fell back on the pillow until it had passed and then, taking a deep breath, swung her legs over the side, and stood up. She felt dizzy for a moment but it passed quickly.

'I do hope you're planning to make a very big pot of coffee.' Her voice was working but raspy.

Caroline picked up the kettle, turning on the tap to fill it. 'That's exactly what I'm doing. I've never drunk as much coffee in my life as I have here, but this morning even my pores need it.'

Rachel came to the end of the L-shaped breakfast bar and put her elbows on it, running her hand into her hair.

'Poor Bronagh.'

'At least she wasn't in the house.'

'True. It's the smoke that's the problem. It gets everywhere and it's almost impossible to get rid of the smell, it clings to everything.' Rachel shook her head. 'She's put so much work – and money – into making it so lovely, it's heartbreaking.'

'When she can see what the actual damage is this morning, she'll have more of an idea where she is. I wonder what Ava wanted last night? It's pretty late to be popping over.'

Rachel frowned. 'If she saw the press report that a girl's body had been found, she probably wanted to talk about Meg to someone who knew her. Do you think Malachi will talk to her today, about getting a DNA sample? They can't do much until they've got a formal identification.'

Caroline sighed. 'I'd guess so. The quicker they can find out who it is, the better.' She paused. 'You know, if it hadn't been for Mrs Travers having a rough night, Bronagh could have been in the house. She did right in the end. Her timing couldn't have been better.'

Rachel shook her head, her eyes wide. 'The irony of it, really.'

'I know, she's a challenging woman. I'm absolutely sure she knew all these years about what happened to Meg. And she must have had an idea about Declan Flynn's activities – he's her nephew, for God's sake. I'm *sure* you're right about him and Honoria.' She scowled. 'Mrs T. and Flynn are made from the same stuff. I guess she'll be interviewed as soon as she's well enough.'

Rachel sighed. 'I'd like to be a fly on the wall then. Will we get dressed and go up to the house? It was so crazy last night, and those huge lights were dazzling. I feel I need to see what the damage is before I can move on in my head. And I really need to talk to Hunter now. I think I'll have to go down to the village to get a proper signal.'

'Good plan. I feel we should drop into Ava too. She doesn't have any family and the guards arriving to take DNA samples is all going to be a huge shock for her. I just need to wash my hair. I'll hop up and use the shower first, then you need to – you stink of smoke, if you don't mind me saying. I'll leave the hairdryer out for you.'

'Ha, that's nice. I'll sort out the coffee while you shower.'

Caroline grinned and headed up the spiral staircase.

*

Jasper almost pulled Rachel off her feet as they walked the short path from the Boathouse to the hotel. He seemed desperate to explore and wasn't at all impressed at not being allowed to.

'You should let him have a run.' Caroline almost laughed at his enthusiasm for the new day.

'He'll get covered in muck and soot and we may never get him clean. Once we get back from the village he can run all he likes, I can take him into the sea if he gets filthy. I think he knows it's almost time to go home – he wants to get down to the beach.'

'He probably wants some proper fresh air after all that smoke. If you think about it, if the smoke's strong to us it must be sickening for him. Aren't dogs supposed to have a sense of smell forty times stronger than ours?'

'Yes. Especially him.' Rachel raised her eyebrows. 'Did I tell you what he did when he was working with the police?'

Caroline shook her head as they started to walk slowly towards the house.

'Just that he was a police dog. They chase criminals, don't they?'

'He was a cadaver dog.'

'A *what*? You mean he looked for dead bodies?'

'Yep. He belonged to a good friend of Hunter's. He was in a specialist unit in the Met but he got shot on duty. Jasper was close to retirement age, so Hunter took him in while Amit's family got sorted out.'

'Poor Jasper. Sorry, I should have said "poor Amit" – what happened?'

Rachel frowned. 'It was some sort of riot situation. He was dead before the paramedics could get to him. Jasper brought down the shooter and won a medal for it. The guy could have killed a load of people. Jasp had always had a soft spot for Hunter – it was only going to be temporary to start with, but then it sort of got extended.'

'I'm very glad you didn't tell me that before, or every time he went after a rabbit I'd be having a nervous breakdown.'

'I probably should have paid a lot more attention when he was in the stable yard. He kept running back in there and barking. You wouldn't think bones would have a smell, would you?'

Caroline did a double take. 'He's a dog, bones are their thing – they can smell them from miles away.'

Rachel screwed up her face. 'You're right, but under all that concrete? It doesn't matter – they were found – but I still feel bad.'

'You couldn't have known. He might be very highly trained but you're not, are you? You don't know what his responses are. It could have been rats he was after. Come on, let's see what this place looks like. It might not be as bad in the daylight as it seemed last night.'

Chapter 55

RACHEL STOPPED ABRUPTLY as they emerged from the trees. The house in front of them was a mess. Only the two majestic statues of hares outside seemed to be unscathed, still standing nobly guarding what was left of the front door. The whole of the porch area, the lounge and the office had been gutted. Taking a step forward, they could see the roof was still intact, and the upper windows on the third floor looked like they had escaped the worst of it, but downstairs the windows were all broken, and charred beams lay haphazardly.

Caroline let out a deep sigh. 'My God. I wonder how far the damage goes in. Maybe they stopped it before it got to the kitchens.'

'It looks like they got here in time to save the main part of the house. At least if it's still structurally sound, Bronagh will have something to rebuild.'

As Rachel spoke, a man in a white overall crossed behind one of the shattered windows like a ghost.

'Morning, ladies, how are we today?'

Malachi's voice behind them made them both jump. Rachel spun around.

'Malachi O'Brien, is creeping up on people part of your job now?'

'Certainly is.'

'How's Bronagh?' Caroline looked at him anxiously.

He raised his hand in a 'so-so' gesture. 'She's spoken to her husband – he's flying home today, so at least she'll have some support. I'm sure she'll be up here shortly. I've just been to see Ava. It's safe to say she's not in great form either. She doesn't believe for one minute the remains are Meg, says it has to be someone else. She kept talking about the postcards. Sometimes this job …' He tailed off, shaking his head.

Jasper tugged at his lead, whining to be let off as Rachel turned to look back at the house.

'How come the alarms didn't go off?'

'Because …' Malachi paused, measuring his words. 'Someone had cut the security system wires out on the main road.'

As Rachel looked at him, she could feel herself paling. 'So it wasn't an accident?'

'Doesn't look like it. There's a technical bureau team coming down from Cork. They should be here shortly. They're fire specialists.'

Caroline shook her head angrily. Rachel could see from the look in her eyes that her temper was flaring.

'But who would do that to such a lovely place? And anyone could have been inside.'

Malachi's mouth was set in a hard line. 'It seems highly likely this is somehow connected to the discovery of the body. Obviously that leak to the press fairly opened up the playing field, but let's just say Declan Flynn is right up there at the top of our list, along with Sheridan Smyth at the moment.' He narrowed his eyes. 'It was definitely Smyth who was driving that navy-blue Merc yesterday?'

'Definitely. Caroline reckoned it was a hire car. He was in the hall when we got back.'

330

Caroline pulled her jacket around her as a gust of wind cut through the woods, chilling them.

'Why do you ask?'

'Because the lads found a new Merc stuck in the mud on the back lane down to the stable yard. Whoever was driving it took that bad bend too fast and wrapped it around a tree. I thought it might be the same car that almost creamed me, but it was going too fast for me to get the number the last time.'

'Do you think Smyth *did* come back for the photograph? Obviously my theories on human behaviour are way off, unless he really wasn't thinking straight.' Caroline paused. 'But how did he get in? Imogen locked up when we went down to the Boathouse. Conor drove them both home.'

'Our guys will be able to tell us when they've finished examining the scene. When I asked her, Ava said she drove almost all the way here but then thought to check Bronagh was home, and when she wasn't, turned around. Smyth could have been on his way here then, too.'

Malachi's radio buzzed.

'Won't be a sec.'

Rachel watched him walk away from them towards the house, and turned to Caroline.

'I still can't believe it, it's such a mess. We were just blessed you managed to get a call through and the fire crews got here so fast.'

Before Caroline could answer, Malachi was back to them.

'You were right about the car – it was rented to Sheridan Smyth at Cork Airport. The question is, where is he now? And we're still looking for Declan Flynn.'

Rachel winced. 'But why burn down the house? Do you think Smyth was trying to destroy evidence? What could there be? It can't have been the photograph, surely – you wouldn't burn down a whole house just to get rid of a photograph.'

'As far as we know, only Smyth knew that photo was here, unless he called Flynn to tell him. Assuming that's what this is about, whoever was here must have realised it had been moved. I can imagine they might have been feeling a bit desperate that someone else had realised who was in the picture. Maybe they were looking for more photos – they'd have known there were more on the roll – and when they couldn't find them, decided to set fire to the place. They'd already cut the alarm wires to get in, so they knew they'd have plenty of time to get away.' Malachi scowled, his face puzzled.

Caroline shifted from one foot to the other as another blast of wind chilled them.

'Do you think they watched for Conor and Imogen to leave? If they'd checked Bronagh was at the hospital, the coast would be pretty clear.'

Malachi wrinkled his nose. 'Apart from you two being on site. I'm wondering what other evidence could have been hidden in the house.' He paused. 'Perhaps Smyth's plan was originally to stay here so he could retrieve something, and when he couldn't get a room, he knew he'd have to come back. Then he saw the photo and it all became a bit more urgent.'

'What other evidence, though? It was all so long ago.' Caroline stuck her hands deeper into her pockets.

'There's always been a question over Meg's missing watch.'

'What watch?' Caroline looked at him quizzically.

'It's been kept out of the press, but Meg had a watch on when she disappeared. It was a man's watch but she'd made a strap for it. She wore it all the time apparently. We didn't find it in the septic tank, so I think it could have been hidden in the house. If someone picked it up and didn't think to wipe it, their fingerprints could have been on it, which would be unequivocal forensic evidence linking them to her.'

Caroline looked back at the house, frowning.

'It could have been in one of the drawers, hidden like Honoria's letter, or that film, just forgotten. Then, when news leaked about the body ...'

Rachel put her hand to her forehead, trying to remember something that was just out of reach. Someone had mentioned a watch ... She ran her fingers into her hair, trying to remember.

Why had a watch come up?

'Ava mentioned the watch when we talked to her. She said Meg had made the strap. Remember, Caroline? She said Meg loved vintage shops. She found it in one in Dublin. But someone else ... Someone's mentioned a watch to me recently.' Rachel snapped her fingers as it suddenly came to her. 'It was Hunter. Hunter said there was a watch in Alfie's bag. It was inside a sandwich bag, in his carrier with the stuff for his violin.'

Malachi's eyebrows shot up. 'You sure?'

'Positive. I need to call him. I'm sure he gave the bag to the police when we realised there might be a link between his accident and Alfie's death. If we're right that Alfie really was J. A. Stafford, and he was here that night, maybe he kept it all this time as some sort of insurance policy. Maybe it *does* have fingerprints on it or something.'

'We'll need to get it examined. I'll put in a call to London.'

Malachi took a step away from them to use his radio.

Chapter 56

ONCE THEY GOT onto the main road, Rachel and Caroline had called ahead to the pottery to say that they were on their way. Ava must have been watching for them. She opened the door as soon as they pulled up, stepping out to hug them both as they got out of the Land Rover.

'Bring your dog in, he'll be fine inside.'

Letting Jasper out of the back, Rachel flipped her seat into place and pushed the door closed. Obediently, he waited to see where she was going, his ears cocked forward, tail wagging.

'Don't worry, we'll go for a walk in a few minutes, Jasp. Come and say hello to Ava first.' She turned back to Ava, who was waiting for them beside the front door, her arms crossed against the cold. 'Will he be okay in your studio? His tail has a bit of a mind of its own.'

'He'll be grand. Come through to the kitchen, we can have a cup of tea.'

Following Ava into the studio, they went straight through to a brightly lit room. It was beautiful, white and bright, a bespoke kitchen with gleaming granite surfaces leading into a huge morning room, a scrubbed pine table dominating the space, one end piled high with ledgers and notebooks crammed with clippings. The entire end wall of the room was glazed and overlooked a concrete patio cum drive and a well-kept walled garden, the old stone weathered. Ava's white four-wheel-drive jeep was backed up to the sliding door, the boot open.

Rachel walked to the far end of the room to look outside, as Ava filled the kettle.

'This house is stunning, Ava, and you've a beautiful garden, it must be lovely in the summer.'

'Thank you – I love it. The end gets the sun all day. When I had the patio built I designed it so I could bring the jeep in to load it. I've a show in Dublin next week, it's a really big one. It always takes me ages to get ready.' She indicated the boxes waiting beside the sliding door, the contents tightly wrapped in sugar paper. 'I've got loads more to do, but at least I've made a start.' She paused. 'Tea or coffee? I've herbal if you prefer. It helps me sleep.'

'Breakfast tea for me, please.' Looking out of the glass, Rachel took in the back of the jeep, the toolbox and the boxes already in there. 'It's a long drive up to Dublin from here.'

'It usually takes me about four and a half hours.'

Rachel turned back to the room and came to sit down at the table, Jasper sticking to her leg like glue.

'This house is in such a fabulous location, Ava. Do you have a boat too? I saw them on the edge of the quay?'

Ava shook her head, 'No, I get seasick looking at boats. I keep thinking I should get over it. In the summer the roads get a bit mad around here. It would be quicker to get into Ross Haven to deliver stock by water than road.'

Ava put the pot of tea on the table. Sitting down, she passed Rachel a jug of milk and put both her hands to her temples.

'How's Bronagh?'

'She's very shocked. Her husband's on his way.'

Rachel leaned forward. 'She said you were looking for her last night?'

Ava put her hand to her mouth and rubbed her face.

'I just needed to talk. With everything going on, she seemed the most sensible person. We've known each other for years.' Ava sighed, taking her time to find the right words. 'She knew what Meg was like ... I was halfway there before I remembered she might not be home, so I turned around. I can't believe the fire – have the guards got any idea who did it?'

Rachel could feel Caroline watching her. 'They're looking at the CCTV in the area, they're confident they'll find whoever it was. There's a forensic fire specialist team coming from Cork.'

Ava picked up the teapot to pour. 'It's so awful the house has gone.'

'Thankfully it's not totally destroyed. Bronagh thinks once they get the insurance sorted out they can start renovating again.' Caroline added milk to her own and Rachel's mugs. 'She was quite positive about it all actually. She said she's going to contact everyone who had just finished to come back and do it all again. With a dry run they should be even faster, and she was never completely keen on the colour of the hallways upstairs.' She sipped her tea. 'She'll get through it, I hope.'

'Have you both moved into the village?' Ava looked from one of them to the other. Rachel shook her head. 'I've moved into the Boathouse with Caroline. I think I'll have to get back to London soon, though.'

Ava nodded slowly. 'The sergeant from Ross Haven was here earlier to take my statement about the fire and to get a DNA sample. He said they were reopening Meg's case, they think it was her body in the septic tank. There was some report the other night, it was all over social media, about how the girl died. I keep telling him it's not Meg.'

'I think there's a lot more to discover. That sergeant is Malachi, Malachi O'Brien – he's a friend of mine from school actually. I know he wants to do his best to get answers for you.'

Ava had paled to almost the same colour as her ivory sweater. She drew in a breath.

'Why will nobody listen? It's not her.'

Rachel reached across the table for Ava's hand.

'They'll have news soon.'

Chapter 57

OUTSIDE THE POTTERY, Rachel looked at her phone. 'I've got reception, I *really* need to call Hunter.'

Caroline took hold of Jasper's lead. 'Let me take him down to the beach for a run, catch us up when you're done.'

Smiling her thanks, Rachel headed for the Land Rover, already dialling Hunter's number as she climbed in. This time he answered after one ring.

'You took your time – I've been trying you since yesterday.'

'Sorry, I tried to call you back, but you know what the reception's like here. Why didn't you ring the hotel?'

'I did, I left a message. Did they not give it to you?'

Rachel pulled the driver's door closed behind her.

'No, but there's been a lot happening here.'

She opened her mouth to tell him about the fire, but before she could, he cut in.

'The police have found the BMW that hit me in a car park in Heathrow. Looks like it went straight there after the accident. They've found out who it was registered to as well.'

Wriggling into the seat, she turned the engine on to get the heater running.

'Who?'

'I'll tell you in a minute. There's more. Alfie sent me a letter.'

Rachel ran her hand into her hair, her mind on the car

park at Heathrow – she could guess exactly where the driver had gone. Heathrow was one of the airports that had direct flights to Cork. But how had Alfie sent a letter? When had he sent it?

Hunter cleared his throat. 'He must have posted it just before he died. The postmark is ages ago, but there's only a second-class stamp on it and then it was stuck at the marina office for days. I got Zack to collect the post today. And before you ask, I found the emails from the insurance company, they'd all gone into spam. I've sorted everything out.'

'Good, that's good. What did Alfie say?'

Rachel kept her voice calm. She knew Hunter was blustering about the delay in the delivery and the insurance because he was upset. She could hear it in his voice. At the other end she heard him clear his throat again.

'It's pages long and it's handwritten, so it's hard to read.'

'What does it say?'

She heard him take a ragged breath, as if he was trying to hold himself together.

'He starts by saying thank you, to me.' His voice cracked.

She waited a moment; she didn't want to interrupt him but she was bursting to tell him what she'd found out. He sniffed at the other end – he needed a few moments to pull himself together, so she took the plunge.

'I think I've found out when he was here.'

She heard him sniff again. 'Seriously? You've found him?'

'I think he really was J. A. Stafford. It was his own bank statement in his bag, not a piece of scrap paper. We've found an old photo of a J. A. Stafford with a friend whose family used to own Hare's Landing. He was here – Stafford, I mean. The police need to check to see if that's who Alfie really was.'

'You've got a photo?' He sounded stunned.

'Two actually. It's just that there's more. Quite a lot more. If we're right, I think he might have witnessed something – something awful – and that was the reason he ended up on the street.'

'It was to do with a girl.'

Rachel felt her mouth go dry. 'Yes. How do you know?'

She heard Hunter sigh. 'It's in his letter. He says he went to Ireland with a friend, someone called Sheridan. Who's called Sheridan anyway?'

'That was Sheridan Smyth. His mother was American.'

'According to Alfie, the summer they graduated from university – he went to Oxford, Rach, can you believe that? – they got the ferry over from Holyhead and drove down. Sheridan had a sports car. He drove like he was in Brands Hatch. They were heading out of Dublin on the Cork road, and there was a girl hitchhiking. Meg, he said her name was. He said she'd lost her wallet or it was stolen or something. This Sheridan knew her a bit, so when they stopped she was happy to go down with them.'

'And what happened?'

Hunter sighed. 'I think we need to give this to the police.'

'They're already involved.' She paused; there was no easy way to say it. 'A body's been found here.'

'Jesus Christ, why didn't you tell me?'

'There's been so much happening … that's only the start. What did Alfie say? Tell me.'

He drew in a shaky breath. 'I can't read it again, babes, but basically he said he and Meg got on really well, she loved music and so did he. When they got to the house, this Sheridan asked her to stay and party with them. It was summertime, really hot, and Sheridan's mother was away so they had the whole place to themselves. There were some other people there, another girl – I can't remember her name, but she was dating this older guy who worked there. The two girls knew each other, though, but they argued. Alfie says the other one was a real bitch – but you can guess what happened next, babes. They all drank too much and the older guy, Declan, I think, gave them some lines.'

Declan? Rachel felt her stomach react. *Could that have been Declan Flynn? Was he right in the thick of this?*

Hunter stopped speaking and she heard hospital noises in the background. His voice caught as he continued.

'It sounds like Alfie had sex with Meg, but then Smyth had a go as well. I think he raped her. Alfie passed out. He's not sure what happened but he reckoned she must have run off. The next thing, he comes to, and hears this guy Declan telling Smyth she's dead. He said she'd tripped and hit her head on some statue.' Hunter kept his voice low. 'This guy and his girlfriend get Smyth to help them take her to some stable yard, and there's this metal trapdoor thing and they drop her in. Alfie didn't know what it was, he said he thought it might be the cellars.'

'It was the septic tank.'

'Holy crap.' Hunter let the words out like steam escaping.

Rachel shifted in the seat. She was so tense her neck was starting to hurt.

'What happened then?'

'That's the thing. That's why he wrote the letter. He saw this dude again a few weeks ago, in his car park, and the dude recognised him.'

'Who do you mean – Sheridan Smyth?'

'No, the Declan guy. He was there, driving a Nemo Freight truck.'

'But how did he recognise him after all those years? Alfie didn't look anything like he used to?'

Hunter sighed again. 'Christ, this is all my fault. Alfie

cleaned up, he had a shave and his hair cut for the filming. He was going to play that Mozart piece and he wanted to look smart. It gave us all sorts of continuity issues but he didn't know that. Maybe he didn't look that different, just older. Maybe he only thought he'd been recognised. I don't know.'

'It's not your fault. You just got caught in the middle.'

As she spoke, a seagull swooped down and perched on the bonnet of the Land Rover.

Who was the other girl?

Unaware of her thoughts, Hunter continued. 'It's the documentary that's made it all worse.' She heard him shift in his bed. 'I don't know. Maybe this guy didn't know him at all, but Alfie just thought he did, because Alfie had recognised him – and whatever had been going on in the car park, they thought Alfie had seen. We know he was paranoid, even Frank said that. He said in the letter he thought he was being followed, that he was in danger, and that was why he was writing. If anything happened to him, it was because of this Irish dude who had links to Hare's Landing but worked for Nemo Freight.'

'Declan Flynn.'

'How did you know his surname? Never mind. The thing is, the car in Heathrow belonged to someone called Declan Flynn and was registered through Nemo Freight.'

'Jesus. He killed Alfie and he tried to kill you.'

'We don't know that, but it doesn't look good. I reckon they thought Alfie was just another homeless bum nobody cared about, and no one would miss.'

Rachel opened her mouth to reply but Hunter cut her off.

'I've got to go, babes, the doc's here. Talk later?'

And with that the call dropped.

Rachel looked at the phone in her hand, stunned. She needed to talk to Malachi.

Chapter 58

RACHEL COLLECTED CAROLINE and Jasper at the beach and headed straight back towards Hare's Landing. On the way, Rachel updated her on Alfie's letter.

'So Alfie *was* there. He was J. A. Stafford. We were right.' Caroline looked across at Rachel, her eyes wide.

'And the photograph *was* taken that weekend.' Rachel kept her eyes on the road, her voice hard. 'I wonder if there's anything else in the rest of the pictures that we didn't see because we weren't looking for it. I've just realised Mr Mahony still has the negatives at the shop. I think we need to pick them up before he mentions them to someone and gets his shop burnt down.'

She glanced across at Caroline as she indicated and pulled up outside Mahony's.

The bell over the door gave a hearty jangle as Rachel pushed it open. She left Caroline waiting in the car with a grumpy Jasper, not in the slightest bit impressed his walk had been cut short.

A voice greeted her from behind the counter. 'Good morning, lass, how are you today? I heard—'

Before he could launch into whatever gossip was circulating around the village, Rachel cut in.

'John Francis, you know those photographs you developed

for Bronagh? Didn't you say you'd keep the negatives in case she needed more done?'

'I did indeed, lass, I did indeed. They're all ready for her here, although it'll be a while before she's needing them, I'd imagine.'

'You could be right there. I'd like to drop them in to her though. With everything going on she might forget to collect them.'

'Very good, lass, but I'll look after them, I won't forget. Doesn't sound like there's much left of that house, is there?'

Rachel silently drew in a breath, but she wasn't about to give anything away.

'It's hard to tell at the moment. Bronagh will know more once the fire inspectors have been through the place. I know she'd love to have those negatives.'

'Oh, okay, lass. Give me a minute and I'll get them.'

Clearly reluctant to give up something that connected him to the drama, the shopkeeper lingered for a moment too long. Rachel continued as if she hadn't noticed his hesitation.

'Thanks so much. I need some supplies, will I collect everything while you get them? I haven't the energy to go into Ross Haven.'

The possibility of a sale played to his practical side, and John Francis grinned.

'Take your time, lass. If there's anything you can't see, just ask.'

Rachel hid her eye roll behind a smile and turned to the shelf beside her, frantically looking for something to buy. Spotting a section full of tins, she grabbed baked beans and sweetcorn and put them on the counter. There was milk and bacon in the fridge beside the counter. She added them to the pile and turned back to find the bread.

Satisfied she was going to make a purchase, Mahony disappeared into the back of the shop and, she presumed, his dark room.

*

'I got them, but it cost me a fortune.' Climbing back into the driver's seat of the Land Rover, Rachel passed Caroline the bag of groceries. 'You'll have to mind those or Jasp will eat the lot. I got things we can leave for Bronagh when she moves in.'

Caroline hid a grin. 'I thought it took you a long time. I guess you got the Spanish Inquisition as well?'

Rachel started the engine and threw the Land Rover into gear.

'You guessed right.'

As she pulled out, Caroline slipped the grocery bag into the footwell.

'I got through to Malachi. He's still up at the house but he has to get back to the station.'

'We'll be there shortly. Hunter's texted me images of the letter so Mal can see it, and he's giving it to the officer who's in charge of Alfie's case.'

The road was clear almost all the way back to Hare's Landing, except for a stray sheep. She'd switched down a gear to take the corner when it hopped off the wild verge into the road. As Rachel braked hard to avoid it, Jasper lurched forward in the back of the Land Rover with a yelp.

'Holy God, where did he come from?'

'Isn't it a she?'

Jasper made a growly sound in the back of his throat. Caroline looked over her shoulder into the back seat at him.

'He says he doesn't care, just don't hit it.'

'God, could you imagine, on top of everything else? Why do sheep have no road sense? You'd think they'd be a little bit spooked by the noise of the engine, it's not exactly quiet.' The sheep ambled to the side of the road, unfazed by their presence. On the other side of the road there was a tractor coming towards them.

'Why do these obstacles appear when you're in a hurry?'

Oblivious to its near miss, the sheep had now been joined by two friends, all intent on eating the grass on the road side of the low stone wall that bordered the narrow two-lane 'main' road. It was wider than the lane leading across the estate, but not by much, and didn't even have cat's eyes down the middle. The tractor passed and Rachel pulled around the little flock.

As they pulled up outside the hotel, they saw Malachi coming around the side from the stables, deep in conversation with a forensic officer in a white suit. Caroline opened her door and jumped out, pushing her seat forward to let Jasper out, trying to catch his collar. Deliberately dipping his head, he pushed past her and ran off at high speed down towards the beach. She staggered backwards.

'Boy, he's strong when he's on a mission.'

'Sorry, I should have put him on the lead before we opened the door. He hates having his walks cut short.'

Rachel climbed out and looked after him, but he was already lost in the trees. As she spoke, Malachi arrived beside them, nodding a greeting.

'This is Gerry Roche from Cork.'

The officer reached out to shake their hands.

'Have you any idea what started it?'

Rachel felt herself colour at Caroline's directness, but the forensics officer didn't seem to be fazed.

'We've got a lot more work to do – we begin with the least damaged areas and work our way in, looking at the heat and smoke patterns. The flame plumes make patterns on the ceilings, so we can tell a lot about the way a fire has travelled. We think there was an accelerant used in the lounge area, it seems to be the heart of the blaze, but we need to do more tests to find out what it was.'

'Really? So it definitely wasn't a forgotten candle falling over.' Rachel frowned. 'I wonder if Ava passed anyone on the road last night. We were just down with her. She's convinced it's not Meg you found. Did you ask her about the bracelet?'

'I did. I was there this morning. Ava said she used to have a bracelet with a charm on it, but she's been here so many times when she could have dropped it, that it doesn't prove anything.' Malachi looked thoughtful. 'She didn't get to the house last night apparently. She turned back – she must have been upset to come out here though, so I'm not optimistic she was paying much attention to who else was on the road.' He raised his eyebrows. 'Now, tell me about this letter – Caroline gave me an outline on the phone. She said it puts Smyth, Flynn and your homeless guy at the scene?'

Rachel nodded. 'I forwarded you Hunter's photo of it. It should arrive when you get a signal.'

She opened her mouth to continue, but as she did so they heard the sound of frantic barking and Jasper appeared, weaving through the trees beside the house. As soon as he saw them he let off another volley of short sharp barks and ran back the way he'd come.

'What's he up to?'

Caroline looked at him, mystified, as he did it again, running towards them and then away again. Seeing they weren't following him, he broke out of the undergrowth and raced back over to Rachel, grabbing the hem of her jacket, pulling her, the jerk jarring her.

She tried to catch his collar. 'Holy God, what's up, Jasper?'

Caroline looked at him, her voice serious.

'Rachel – this time you need to listen to him. He tried to tell you about Meg and he's sure as hell trying to tell you something now.' She glanced at Malachi. 'Turns out he's a cadaver dog. I think we'd better follow him.'

Chapter 59

JASPER SEEMED TO have decided the quickest way through the woods was as the crow flies, but in the absence of wings he was weaving between the trees as if it was some sort of Olympic slalom. Unable to follow him on his direct route, Rachel tried to keep pace along the path, Malachi and Caroline behind her. Heading back down to the Boathouse, she turned left in front of it, taking the tiny path that led to the fields and the beach.

'Can you see him?' Rachel called behind her as she jogged ahead, the path only wide enough here for one person. Her heart was thumping, the rasp of her breathing drowning out the sounds from the wood and the crash of waves. They were only yards from the shore here, following the path that ran parallel with the sea.

Rachel emerged from the protection of the trees and could immediately feel the force of the wind. It was bitterly cold, coming in squalls, blowing freezing rain onto the shore and causing the waves to crash onto the beach below her. It filled her ears, drowning out the laboured sound of her chest.

The same wind that had fanned the flames last night.

Stopping to catch her breath, Rachel looked deep into the trees, catching flashes of gold as Jasper's coat merged and contrasted with the shadows. A deep cough suddenly constricted her chest. Emerging from the trees, Malachi and Caroline caught up with her.

'Where is he?'

Malachi didn't sound like he'd been running at all. Rachel pointed as another cough gripped her.

A moment later Jasper was heading diagonally across the field ahead of them, the wind rippling the long grass where the field sloped down to a drystone wall just above the beach. On the far side, the castle stood lonely and stark against the sky, the earlier blue replaced with heavy steel-grey cloud. A simple squat shape, its stone walls were hewn from blocks of sombre granite, with corner keystones of lighter stone. Ivy and brambles now tumbled out of the tiny windows that must have once been barred.

The field was soft, the grass uneven. They set off to catch up with Jasper, but as Malachi was about to overtake Rachel, jogging easily, his radio bleeped into a burst of static. Slowing, Rachel glanced at him as he stopped to answer it, turning around with his back to the wind.

Ahead of them, Jasper reached the castle and, stopping outside the open wooden panelled door, barked sharply. He stretched out his front paws and wagged his tail, exactly as he had done in the stable yard. Rachel felt her skin chill, more than the wind could possibly chill her, as if some sort of electric ice current was passing through.

What had he found?

'He's trying to show us something!' Caroline's words were almost whipped away by the wind. She pulled her hair back from where it had blown across her face. 'We need to go and check, there could be someone injured.'

Rachel had a horrible feeling that wasn't it at all. She glanced back to Malachi but he seemed to be intent on his conversation – whatever it was, it had to be important.

A second later they'd covered the open ground to the foot of the castle. Jasper whined when they reached him, barked again and darted inside. The door stood partially open, the paint peeling, the wood underneath bleached by the sea and weather.

'We should wait ...'

Rachel glanced back at Malachi. He was turning to head in their direction, but Caroline pushed past her and put her hand on the door.

'There may be no time.'

She pulled the door hard – it creaked as it inched open, stiff and complaining. A bird took off above their heads, circling the parapet, squawking in protest at the disturbance.

Rachel glanced at Caroline and stepped forward.

It took a moment for her eyes to adjust to the darkness; the smell of decay and damp was strong. The dim winter light was filtered through the ivy and brambles tangled around the windows. More brambles had taken over the floor, pushing through the gaps in the flagstones. She looked around. Loose stones were piled where they had fallen from the internal walls as the floors and joists had rotted. Jasper had scampered over to the far right-hand corner. He let out a sharp bark, calling her. Even with her eyes adjusted to the gloom, it was hard to see anything except the overgrown piles of stone strewn across the ground. As Rachel picked her way towards Jasper, he started to scrabble at the dirt, digging frantically.

Pulling her phone out of her pocket, switching on the powerful torch, Rachel glanced at Caroline and turned it to the spot Jasper was digging in.

'What is it ...? Oh!' Caroline gasped, as Jasper barked again and moved over enough for them to see what he'd found.

'What's he got?'

They both jumped as Malachi came up behind them. Protruding from the dark soil, yellowed but unmistakable, was a bone. It had been a long time since Rachel had done biology, but not so long since she'd got the skeleton that had been parked in her office for the last eight months back out to the warehouse. She felt her stomach turn over, fear opening up a dark hole of anxiety. From its size and shape, she was pretty sure the bone was a humerus, the main bone that ran from shoulder to elbow. Jasper scrabbled again, making the hole he'd dug deeper, revealing more.

Rachel reached for his collar, trying to keep her voice level.

'Good boy, come here out of the way.'

'Okay, ladies, I need you both to leave.'

Malachi clicked his radio on and was about to speak into it when, beside them, Caroline shrieked.

'What?'

They said it together and both turned to look at where she was now pointing.

Above them, in the darkness of the farthest corner of the tower, a body was hanging from one of the roof rafters. Shocked into silence, Rachel stared at it. Above the sound of the wind outside they could hear a gentle creak, like a door on an unoiled hinge or wood protesting a weight as it swung gently.

Rachel felt Caroline reach for her arm, gripping it.

'Like Honoria.' It came out as a hiss.

'Do you think …?'

As she spoke, the body turned and swung towards them, a dark shape: a man, heavily built, but from this angle it was impossible to see his face.

'Ladies, please, you don't need to see this …'

The wind picked up and began to whistle around the walls of the building, lifting the thorny branches wrapped around the empty windows.

Rachel was turning to speak to Malachi when she caught a glimpse of something bright white, incongruous in the tumble of stones in the middle of the floor.

'Look, there's something on the ground.'

Without thinking she headed over to it, still holding Jasper's collar. He yelped, wagging his tail frantically.

It was a piece of paper, weighted down with one of Ava's tiles from the hotel, a china blue hare decorating the centre. As she leaned in closer, Rachel could see it was written in a flowing hand in fountain pen. Rain had dripped onto the ink, smudging it, but it was still legible.

'He left a note.'

Nodding sharply, Malachi spoke into his radio again. He indicated with his thumb that they needed to leave the way they had come in.

Outside Rachel breathed in deeply, savouring the freezing salty air. Beside her Jasper yawned and lay down, his tail thumping, ears cocked forward on full alert. Rachel could see he was pleased with himself. She bent down and put her arms around his neck.

Beside her, Caroline crossed her arms tightly and looked at Rachel, her eyes full of questions. Rachel shook her head; she had no idea who Jasper had found in the ground, or hanging from the rafter. From what she could see of the second body, its size and shape, she guessed it was Flynn or Smyth. They'd only know when someone arrived to take him down.

A moment later Malachi reappeared, easing himself around the castle door without touching it. He'd put on a pair of blue latex gloves, held what looked like a sheet of white paper in his hand, now encased in a plastic bag. The wind pulled at it as he walked away from them, his mouth to the radio clipped to his lapel.

Rachel felt sick. As she watched him, he turned and came back towards them slowly, his face grim.

'Ambulance is on the way.'

'Isn't he dead?' Rachel's hand few to her mouth. 'Shouldn't we try and take him down?'

'I think it's too late for that. We need a doctor to certify death. The ambulance team will look after him. It's procedure.'

Caroline looked at him. 'And the other one?'

'Pathologist and the technical bureau also on the way.'

'Who is it? Did it look like Declan Flynn?'

Somehow as she said it, Rachel knew Declan Flynn wasn't the type to take his own life. From what they knew of him, he was as slippery as they came, would double-cross and murder before he'd risk his own skin.

Malachi shook his head. 'This note's been signed by Sheridan Smyth.'

Chapter 60

THE BOATHOUSE WRAPPED them both in a warm embrace as they came in, Jasper at their heels. He'd raced off after some gulls as they'd trudged back across the field, had worn himself out dashing around the beach. He flopped down on the kitchen floor. Caroline took off her coat, suddenly feeling exhausted.

'Damn, I left the shopping in the Landie.' Rachel pulled the brown envelope containing the negatives John Francis had given her out of her pocket, and put them on the counter. '*And* I bought a chocolate cake in the shop, which is exactly what we need now. That and sweet tea. If I go up now, I might miss Malachi.'

Caroline sat down on one of the kitchen stools and leaned on the counter, her face thoughtful.

'Malachi's going to be ages. They'll probably be there all night.'

'Oh God, I hope they get the remains out before dark. This space is spooky enough with the doors slamming all the time and you hearing things.'

Caroline scowled playfully at Rachel and adjusted her glasses. She didn't have the energy to get into a debate about the supernatural now. She'd explained her theories about trapped energy to Rachel, *and* her thoughts on draughts.

'Who do you think the bones could belong to?'

Rachel shook her head. 'I've no idea. That Johnny O'Connor seems to be a likely candidate, unless there have been more disappearances around here that we don't know about.'

Caroline ran her hand into her hair. 'Do you think he started the fire? Sheridan Smyth, I mean. It's weird. He didn't need to destroy evidence of Meg's presence if he was planning to top himself, did he?'

Rachel pulled up a stool and sat down beside her, half on it and half off. Caroline could tell the adrenaline from the shock of their latest find, after everything that had happened in the past few days, was still coursing through Rachel's veins. Caroline had been like that at her first homicide, the images still etched on her brain. Rachel interrupted her thoughts.

'I don't think Sheridan Smyth, despite his grandeur and his posh accent, was a very clear-thinking sort of person. I mean, he seems to have been at the heart of this mess since the beginning, and I haven't seen one occasion where he's exactly shone as a human being.'

Caroline stood up and pulled her phone out of the back pocket of her jeans. She glanced at the screen as she put it on the counter.

'I googled some of his cases while I was checking out Honoria the other day. He came down really heavily on anyone who harmed women. You *could* conceivably conclude from that, he felt guilty about whatever happened here and was trying to absolve his conscience.'

Rachel raised her eyebrows. 'If that's the case, and he saw that news report about Meg not being dead when she went into the septic tank, it can't have sat well with him.'

Caroline shifted on the stool. 'For sure. I was wondering if he was the one who leaked it? With his connections he could have got hold of a copy. Maybe he realised the game was finally up and wanted to spook Flynn into doing something stupid.'

'Like running?' Rachel opened her eyes wide. 'Which automatically makes him look as guilty as hell. But why worry about coming here last night then, and why try to burn the house down?'

Caroline bit her lip, frowning. 'Let's think about what we know. Okay, so some of this has to be hypothetical, but let's assume Smyth's not in a good mental state when he heads over. He's focused on getting the photo, and he knows how the security system is wired from when he lived here, so just in case he has to break in, he cuts the wires. Not hard, it's probably one cable.' She pushed her glasses up her nose. 'He's keyed up and anxious, takes the bend on the stable yard road too fast and collides with a tree. Now he's potentially hurt, as well as being massively stressed. He's *really* not having a good day. He gets "home" –' Caroline did the rabbit ears thing again – 'and he finds the picture is missing. Panics, presumably, and goes off to look for it. He also *maybe* knows Meg's watch could be somewhere on the property. He *does* know for sure that if Bronagh has found one photo from that day, she must have the full film – he's going to be worried there could be other photographs that put Meg at the scene more clearly. There's no way he'd remember exactly what shots were taken.'

Caroline screwed up her nose before continuing.

'The house holds some very bad memories for him, so, when he can't find the picture we had framed, or the remaining photos – we can safely assume he's had a really good look in the office, potentially made a bit of a mess, and may not have had the foresight to wear gloves given the pressure he's under – he decides the best way to destroy all the evidence, as well as the traces of his presence, is to set the place on fire.' She scowled, thinking. 'He probably thought someone had just moved the photo. He wouldn't have expected us to have brought it down here.'

She put her head on one side, her mind ticking over. There were still loose ends in this whole set-up that were bothering her, and a helluva lot of maybes, but the picture was forming.

Rachel suddenly clicked her fingers. 'You know when Jasp started barking last night? I think it was because he'd heard Smyth going past the front door on his way to the castle. That's what started him off, then, when the fire took hold, he really went mad.'

Caroline grimaced. 'Without Jasper leading us to the castle, Smyth could have been hanging there for months. The estate will be closed to the public while Bronagh and Leo concentrate on rebuilding – they'd have no reason to go down there.'

'And by then his note would have been pulp.'

'True.' Caroline wrinkled her nose, thinking. 'It's not a castle, you know. I know it's built like one, but it was the original gaol. Hare's Landing belonged to a customs officer. I wondered if there was any significance to Honoria ending her life there rather than in the house – perhaps she felt like she was in gaol. Perhaps Sheridan felt it was time to pay his penance. He'd be the type to make his passing some sort of grand metaphor.'

Rachel glanced across at her, surprised. 'That's a bit deep. Do you think either of them were thinking that rationally?'

Caroline made an open handed gesture. 'Who knows? It's just interesting, don't you think?'

Rachel stood up decisively. 'You mind Jasp and get that fire lit. I'll go and get the shopping and move the Landie or it'll be in everyone's way. And if Malachi comes while I'm out, keep him talking.'

'That won't be a problem.' Caroline raised her eyebrows innocently.

A few minutes later, watched critically by Jasper, Caroline had the fire in the stove crackling, tongues of flame licking the turf briquettes and sticks.

'There we go, boy, you'll be warm as toast now.'

He whimpered and, as she collapsed onto the sofa and kicked off her boots, came and jumped up beside her. She rubbed his ears. Next time she came to Hare's Landing she'd make sure she was better kitted out; she hadn't realised quite how city orientated her wardrobe had become.

Which was another sign it was time she got a life and did something with her time off that didn't involve more work.

Hanging out with Rachel and Jasper had totally changed this trip. Getting outside, even in the rain, walking on the beach and breathing in crisp, clean air, seeing the mist swirl down the estuary, had cleansed her soul as well as made her muscles ache. In a good way. When she got back, she was going to look at walking holidays, or weekend hikes – she'd see if she could persuade Tim to come with her. He was a skier, after all; he loved being outdoors. And if she couldn't, she'd look for those holidays for adventurous singles. Who knew what doors might open?

Jasper put his head in her lap and Caroline closed her eyes for a moment. Having Rachel here had been a blessing. Someone whom she totally clicked with and who had a very powerful and reassuring dog permanently at her heel. Caroline knew if she'd been staying here alone, having someone creeping around the place pretending to be a ghost would have rapidly sent her into the village. She felt safer in the Boathouse than she would have done rattling around a big, lonely country house, but not by much, and she wasn't totally stupid. Scare tactics made her mad, but there really was zero glory in being a dead hero.

Jasper lifted his head, looking up at the door, and Caroline opened her eyes, craning her head back, waiting to see if there was a knock. Suddenly she could hear male voices outside: the forensics team and pathologist arriving. It was killing her not to go and open the door and stick her head out, but she needed to keep Jasper out of the way and she was sure Malachi would be here in due course. They'd already blundered into a crime scene once today; she wasn't about to do it again.

Chapter 61

RACHEL ARRIVED AT the top of the path from the Boathouse at the same time as a large white Garda Technical Bureau van pulled up alongside its twin, already parked in the driveway. Outside what had been the front door of the hotel, Malachi was deep in conversation with another officer, someone in plain clothes Rachel hadn't seen before. At least he was half in plain clothes – he was wearing a distinctive-looking navy windcheater over a suit. Malachi acknowledged the driver of the van with a wave and, catching the sound of her boots on the gravel, turned to her, nodding a greeting.

She pointed at the Land Rover and mouthed *will I move it?* He shook his head.

Rachel went to the passenger door to retrieve the bag of shopping as he briefed the driver of the van, who went around the back and swung the doors open. Several guards already in white forensic suits climbed out, gripping stainless steel toolboxes. Their hoods up, it was impossible to tell if they were men or women. As Rachel watched, Malachi gave them directions to the castle and they headed down the path towards the Boathouse in single file.

Malachi came over to her as she slammed the passenger door shut.

'Are you sure it's okay to leave it here? I can move it to the stable yard.'

Malachi shook his head. 'It's grand for the moment, the pathologist's already on site, we've not got too many more vehicles coming now.' He paused. 'We think it's Smyth. He seems to have a large contusion on the side of his head – the doc reckons he received a heavy blow some hours prior to his death. He'll know more when he does the PM.'

'Really? Do you think he could have fallen?' Rachel transferred the heavy shopping bag to her other hand as she spoke.

Malachi crossed his arms. 'We can't speculate at this stage. And formal identification will take longer, but Sheridan Smyth apparently signed that note. It said he's lodged papers with his solicitor in London – a sworn statement. Our lads are getting in touch with the solicitor now to find out what it's all about …'

Before he could continue, they heard another car arriving. Rachel turned as Conor pulled into the driveway, Imogen sitting in the passenger seat beside him.

His hair tied up in his distinctive man bun, he opened his door and half got out of the car, leaning between the roof and the open door to survey the damage. Imogen got out of the other side, tears flowing down her face. Rachel and Malachi exchanged glances.

'Hello, you two. Have you spoken to Bronagh?'

Rachel put the shopping bag down on the drive beside the Land Rover and headed over to give Imogen a hug.

Imogen's face was strained as she answered. 'I can't believe the house is gone, and all Honoria's paintings and furniture. And her portrait. I loved that house so much.'

Rachel put her arm around Imogen's shoulder. 'It'll make

your thesis all the more important as a historical record. In fact, with everything that's happened, you could probably write a book about the place.'

Conor looked over the roof of the car at her. 'We're just heading down to the village. Bronagh's at the pub.'

'She is, but we're off home tomorrow, so she'll be able to move into the Boathouse. It'll be easier to mastermind operations on site.' Conor nodded slowly as Rachel continued. 'She'll be delighted to see you and she can tell you the plan. She's still got all that extra furniture in the stables, and she's already started calling the tradesmen who did the first restoration.'

Imogen sniffed loudly. 'How are you and Caroline? And Jasper?'

'All good. Look, here's my card.' Rachel pulled her business card out of the pocket of her jacket. 'Keep in touch, will you? Fire me an email and then I'll have your address.'

Imogen looked at the card and wiped her eyes. 'Bronagh said you worked for a film company.'

'I'm a location scout. But I work right across the business and we're always looking for good stories. I think you might have one here.'

Imogen's eyes filled as her tears returned. Rachel patted her on the shoulder.

'I'll see you soon? I'm going to need to bring Jasper back when the place is up and running again, he loves it. In the meantime, I've got to give this member of the local Gardaí a cup of tea before he keels over.'

'There's a big team here.' Conor frowned, nodding towards the vans.

Did he suspect there was more happening than the fire?

Catching what he'd said, Malachi walked over to join them.

'Fire investigators, down from Cork. Obviously not enough to keep them busy there.' He looked speculatively at Rachel.

'I'd better go, will you two say hi to Bronagh from me? Oh, and tell to her to get the paintings in the Boathouse valued. I don't think she knows what they're worth. Caroline was checking them out – I think Bronagh will get a nice surprise. She could do with some good news.' Rachel rubbed Imogen's shoulder again.

Conor lifted his hand in a wave and got back into the car, Imogen sitting beside him, closing her door. He did a stylish three-point turn, the heel of one hand on the steering wheel.

Malachi watched them go and grabbed her shopping bag.

'Well played. We need to keep this quiet for a bit longer. Is Caroline down below? We've still got a lot of details to check, but I can give you both the gist of what was in Smyth's note. And I need to collect that photograph before anything else happens.'

Rachel wasn't sure why, but she could feel her skin beginning to prickle.

*

The marine-blue door of the Boathouse opened as Rachel raised her hand to knock. Caroline stepped back to let them past, Jasper at her side. She held on to his collar as they both came in.

'He knew it was you.'

Malachi passed Rachel the shopping bag and took off his hat, holding it in his hand as Caroline headed into the living area.

'Come and sit down, the fire's lit.'

Rachel put the shopping down on the counter as he shook his head.

'I can't stop too long, too much happening. I just need to take that photograph.' Malachi paused, looking for the right words. 'And Rach was asking me what Smyth's note said. I wanted to update you. But this can't go any further.'

'Let me get the photo. You sit down for a minute – you're making the place look untidy.'

Caroline skipped up the spiral staircase as Rachel turned and pulled out one of the stools from the breakfast bar.

'It's not very comfortable, don't worry – you won't be tempted to stay.' He chuckled as he sat down. Reaching for the envelope on the counter, she passed it to him. 'I collected the rest of the negatives from Mahony's. Your forensics people may be able to find something on them.'

He unzipped his bomber jacket and slipped it into his inside pocket.

'Thanks for that. We need a more concrete indication of the date that picture was taken – let's see what magic they can work.'

A moment later Caroline came back down the spiral stairs. She put the framed photograph on the end of the breakfast bar and went around it, to sit down herself.

'What's happened? Do you know who the bones belong to?'

Malachi sighed, perching on the edge of the stool.

'The forensics team have found a wallet beside the skeleton. It must have been in his pocket and his clothes have rotted, but it's made of plastic. Obviously we need DNA confirmation – it might not even be his wallet – but it belonged to Johnny O'Connor, that lad who went missing at the same time as Meg. The body cavity also contained pieces of what appeared to be torn condoms with a white residue in them.'

'Oh.' Caroline raised her dark eyebrows. 'Drug mule.'

'Looks like it. I guess one of them burst and whoever he was working for couldn't risk dumping his body at sea in case it came back in.'

Rachel looked confused. 'Don't they normally swallow the drugs to get through airports?'

'Just because his body is here doesn't mean he died here. Perhaps he got back to his handlers and it all went wrong.' Malachi's voice hardened. 'We'll find out.'

'And what did Smyth's note say?' Caroline leaned forward, eager to hear.

'Not a whole lot, as it turns out. I was telling Rach, he's left a statement with his solicitor, we're getting that now. But the note was signed, "Forgive me".'

'Forgive him? For what? The fire – or for Meg's death?'

Malachi rubbed the back of his neck. 'Hard to say at this stage.'

Frowning, Rachel leaned back on the counter, looking at the floor. 'Do the fire people know how it was started?'

'They think petrol, they need to do more tests but—'

Caroline interrupted him. 'But where did he get that? If he had it in his car boot and brought it down to the house, then he must have planned to set the place on fire. If he was also planning to commit suicide, why not take a load of pills and drink and burn with the house? Why go to all the trouble of lugging a ladder from the stable yard all the way to the castle?' She wrinkled her nose, her face puzzled. 'Something's not right there. It doesn't make sense. He wasn't a fit man. It's like he killed himself because the house was burning. Like it really was some sort of final symbolic act.'

Rachel looked at Malachi, her face creased in a frown. 'Ava had a petrol can in the boot of her jeep. I noticed it when I was looking at the stuff she was packing for her show. I thought it might be for an outboard motor, but she said she didn't have a boat.'

Caroline looked at her quizzically. 'Don't people here carry spare gas?'

Rachel pursed her lips. 'Not when their car's a diesel.'

Chapter 62

A SHARP BLAST OF wind sent a volley of rain against the brightly lit window of the studio as Ava checked the temperature in the kiln. Distracted by the sound, she looked over her shoulder, her eye catching the studio phone sitting on the windowsill.

Her hand still on the heating dial, she hesitated. Would she call? A lot had been happening here, and she'd been waiting for contact since news had leaked that the body had been found. It had been in all the papers, all over the internet – there was no way Flynn could have missed it, not with everything else going on. She ran her hands down the front of her apron. They were sweating despite the chill she felt inside.

Sheridan Smyth was an idiot.

It hadn't taken her long to find that out when she'd followed him to London, but silence didn't come cheaply.

She might have guessed he'd lose his nerve in the end, but it didn't matter; she'd looked after everything. She hadn't found the rest of the photographs but they'd be ashes by now.

She still couldn't believe he'd wanted to give it all up. She took a ragged breath.

The anger had swept over her the minute he'd started talking.

She'd left him there on the floor to go up with the house.

He'd been stirring, but she reckoned the fumes would get to him fast enough, and with a blow like that to the head he'd been utterly stunned when he hit the floor.

He wasn't her problem any more.

They'd think he started the fire; she'd make sure they did.

Now she *really* needed to talk to Flynn. But if she called, it could – no, *would* – be traced. Would the line be tapped? Would someone be listening in? She put her finger to her lips, thinking. With everything that had happened, she'd have to assume it probably was, and that her call could be recorded.

She'd need a good reason to get in touch, and to be very careful what she said …

She looked back at the kiln, biting her lip as an idea slowly formed in her head.

She could backdate an order, a piece that 'broke' in the firing that had had to be replaced.

She'd be calling to say it was ready. If she got his voicemail she'd leave a message to that effect – or should she text? She could do that after she'd spoken to him, something about her needing to double-check the Eircode on the shipping address. She thought fast, her mind flicking through the pieces – bowls and tiles mainly – she'd put into the kiln to fire yesterday.

Would any of them be big enough to justify a commission?

She turned around, rubbing her face with her hand as another gust of wind blew in from the sea, rattling the glass as if it was trying to get in.

But the piece didn't actually need to be firing now; nobody would be able to check.

The important thing was that she *was* firing this afternoon. She'd even told a few people – that Caroline and her friend, and John Francis when she'd gone for the paper – so the timing of the call would be entirely logical.

Hurrying back into the kitchen, Ava pulled out her order book from the pile on the end of the table and looked for her notebook in the muddle of samples and paperwork. A moment later she had the number. She opened the order book with the pencil she had marking it, and flicked through it. She could do this later, but she just needed one page that she hadn't fully filled out. One from just before Christmas.

Licking her forefinger, she leafed through the pink and yellow carbonised pages and a moment later found one with no name on it. The jug for Dr Carroll, Imogen and Connor's father. *She'd marked it paid but hadn't bothered to fill in his name.* Perfect.

Ava closed her eyes, trying to steady herself. Her heart was racing now. But she needed to know. She just needed confirmation that he'd sorted out the final loose ends. He'd called her from London from a burner phone a couple of weeks ago, to tell her about the documentary crew, to warn her to watch out for any calls from journalists, or any strangers asking too many questions. He said he'd deal with it. And when nothing had happened, she'd assumed he had.

Then John Francis had told her about Caroline Kelly booking into Hare's Landing.

She knew he was back in Ireland by then, so she'd called the gate lodge. Their conversation had been brief, but he'd told her not to worry. If he already knew there was a journalist sniffing around, why hadn't he alerted her? He'd said he'd look after everything.

Where had she heard that before?

He always thought he was the one in control.

Even with their history, Ava didn't know why she'd trusted him. You couldn't trust anyone in his world except yourself.

She could feel her anger rising, like a hot tide that threatened to overwhelm her.

Look at Meg, her own sister.

As if being beautiful and talented wasn't enough for her, she'd had to take what was Ava's too.

When she'd walked in on them, on Meg and Sheridan, she'd felt physically sick. And the anger had come, faster than she'd ever known it. Meg *knew* Ava had her sights set on him – she knew. And there she was on the lounge floor, half-naked with her legs wide open, clawing at Sheridan's T-shirt. The little bitch had deserved everything she got.

Ava felt the pencil snap in her hand. The sound brought her back from a hot summer's night and a dusty stable yard, the sound of the lid ringing as it landed back into its concrete surround, reverberating through her head.

Her notebook in her hand, she went back out to the studio and straight to the phone resting in its cradle. The light bounced off the walls in here, making it look outside as if night was already encroaching on the estuary and the little harbour. She glanced through the window. The wind was whipping the sea over the edges of the harbour, tearing at it, like fingers grasping for safety. Her hand on the smooth white receiver, Ava paused for a moment – should she call?

She needed to talk to him.

Flipping open the notebook with her free hand, she punched in the number. She could feel her mouth dry as she listened to it ring. And ring again. The tone was Irish, though, so he hadn't left yet. She was quite sure, after everything in the papers, he'd be heading to Spain. He had contacts there, could disappear.

Which was fine by her.

He still wasn't answering. Then, just as she was about to hang up, she heard a click on the other end.

'Oh, hello, it's me.' She corrected herself quickly. 'Ava, Ava Cassidy. I'm calling about the jug you ordered, it's ready now. We need to talk – I need to get a shipping address.' She hesitated for a second; how could she tell him about the fire? She continued quickly before he had a chance to reply. 'I hope Mrs Travers is on the mend, it's terrible news about Hare's Landing. I heard they needed two fire engines to put out the flames. Someone said Sheridan Smyth was there, but I don't know how true that is.'

There was a pause before he spoke.

'Sheridan? Was anyone injured?'

Wherever he was, his voice sounded hollow. In the background she heard some sort of tannoy announcement. Was he at the airport already? Ava smirked to herself. She'd been right. He was so predictable.

'I haven't heard. I do hope he didn't get caught in the fire. That house has so much history, it's a tragedy for sure.' Her emphasis on the last two words, she took a breath. 'How was your boating expedition? Did you get everything you needed?'

It took him a moment to realise what she meant.

'Oh, yes, that's all been sorted out. I had my team make sure we got everything. They took care of it all. Nothing to worry about there.'

'Good, that's good. I think everything's been tied up, then. All the ends. I just forgot to get an address for this jug – or I can drop it into the gate lodge if that's handier and you can collect it next time you're here.'

'Yes, that sounds sensible. There's no point in paying a fortune in shipping when I can collect it. Thanks for calling. That's very helpful.'

He clicked the phone off and she took a sharp intake of breath. From the sounds in the background, she was sure he was at the airport. The sooner he got to Spain the better.

She glanced across at the postcards pinned to her noticeboard. Crossing the studio, she looked at them, firmly secured by all four corners, the shiny pictures turned away from the light and prying fingers. He said he'd been careful when he'd posted them, but she knew what he was like. Attention to detail wasn't his strongest suit. There was every chance there were all sorts of fingerprints on the other side, preserved against the cork since they'd arrived. What did they say about the devil being in the detail? It certainly was. The postcards had been a good idea at the time, but now they could prove invaluable. Her insurance policy.

Ava hurried back into the kitchen to make sure her order book was up to date. She was sure she'd thought of *everything*.

Her mobile was on the table. Would she text just to confirm the conversation, in case there wasn't anyone listening? Perhaps that would be overkill? She couldn't resist a smile at the word that had popped into her head.

As her thumb hovered over the phone, she heard a loud knock on the front door. She looked up sharply. It came again. Urgent, insistent. Part of her stomach went into free-fall. Who could be calling down to her in this weather?

Chapter 63

THE NEXT MORNING dawned bright and clear, a warm shaft of sunlight falling across Rachel's face as she surfaced from sleep, the smell of coffee and toast calling her from the kitchen.

'Sorry, did I wake you up?'

Rachel rubbed her face, turning in Caroline's direction.

'I don't think so. What time is it?'

'Ten, I think, a bit after. Toast's nearly done.'

A few minutes later Rachel had pulled on a sweatshirt and was sitting at the breakfast bar, her hair held back off her face with a scrunchie. She took a bite of her toast, chewing thoughtfully.

'I was thinking last night, it's really evil, isn't it? I mean, whoever sent those postcards – making it look like Meg was alive all this time.'

Caroline pulled a stool around to the opposite side of the bar and sat down herself.

'There's been a lot of crazy stuff going on around here. Literally since the day I arrived – it's like there's something in the air.'

Rachel looked at her knowingly, her face amused. 'Crazy is right. I'm convinced Honoria led you to that roll of film. And thank goodness she did.'

Caroline looked at her witheringly. They'd been over this so many times. Before she could speak there was a knock at the door.

'Oh, crap, who's that? I'm not even dressed.'

Caroline looked at her critically. 'You'll do, you look like you've been to the gym.'

Rachel did a double take. 'The gym? Here in the middle of nowhere?'

Caroline laughed as she pulled open the door to a blast of cold air and Malachi filling the doorway.

'Not disturbing you, am I?'

Caroline held the door wide to let him in. 'Nope, you're just in time for toast – want some?'

He shook his head. 'No thanks. I had breakfast at the station. I'm almost ready for lunch at this stage.'

'Sit, tell us what's happening.'

Rachel patted the stool beside her. Malachi sat down as Caroline, unasked, poured him a mug of coffee and put it down in front of him.

'Quite a lot actually. The boys in London got hold of Sheridan Smyth's statement yesterday afternoon. It was very detailed, basically reinforced exactly what was in the letter Alfie sent, give or take a few details. The only difference is that Alfie thinks Meg hit her head accidentally. Smyth says he witnessed an argument during which Meg was pushed – she hit her head when she fell.'

Rachel knew Malachi well enough to know something big was coming, could feel her heartbeat picking up in anticipation.

He cleared his throat. 'In Smyth's version Alfie was more involved, and Smyth was an onlooker, but ...' He pursed his lips. 'Smyth says Ava was there that night. Flynn had invited her. They had some sort of casual thing going, but she was more into him – into Smyth. She was pretty bitchy when they

– Smyth and this James Stafford character, your Alfie – turned up with Meg in tow—'

Rachel interrupted him, aghast. '*Ava* was there?' She looked across the counter at Caroline, who looked as surprised as she felt.

Malachi nodded, continuing. 'When they arrived, Ava had already been drinking. It was a hot night – it sounds like it got a bit out of hand. She had a row with Meg and slapped her. And then she pushed her hard enough for Meg to fall backwards and hit her head on one of the hares.'

'My God.' Caroline shook her head, slowly absorbing the information.

Rachel felt herself blanch. Alfie said another girl was there and she and Delcan Flynn got Smyth to help them put Meg's body through a trapdoor.

Malachi clicked his tongue on the roof of his mouth. 'This is where things get tricky. Smyth says it was Declan Flynn and Ava. And obviously, as our only two surviving witnesses, they will probably say precisely the opposite and implicate the other two.'

Rachel looked from Caroline to Malachi. 'But the postcards? Someone sent them in a deliberate attempt to conceal Meg's death. If you can find out who sent them, surely that will count for something?'

'Indeed. The detective unit called into Ava's last night. She denied owning a petrol container. They did have a warrant but they couldn't see one in the house or her jeep, which is logical enough. She's hardly going to have left it in the middle of the kitchen table. And she was happy to give them the postcards. Rather surprisingly so, they thought, given the circumstances. But there's more.' Malachi leaned forward to take a sip of his coffee. 'You know how Ava has that huge house overlooking the harbour?'

Picking up on something in his tone, Rachel frowned. 'It's gorgeous. Bronagh said she does really well internationally with her pottery.'

'So people say. But she's got no international outlets listed on her website – just a shop in Cork and one in Dublin, and I checked, they're pretty small craft-type places. You'd need to sell an awful lot of pots to afford a house like that.'

She could see Caroline was nodding, but Rachel raised her eyebrows. 'So how?'

Malachi continued. 'According to Smyth, Ava's been blackmailing him for years. Apparently after Meg "disappeared" –' he slipped his hat under his arm and did Caroline's rabbit ears gesture with his fingers – 'Ava went to live with him in London. She had some crazy crush on him, but she made his skin crawl. After everything that happened that weekend, I'd guess she threatened to derail his legal career if he didn't humour her. Needless to say, whatever she thought they had didn't work, so he persuaded her to come back to Ireland if he continued to support her. I bet he paid for her to go to art college in London too.'

Rachel felt her jaw drop in surprise. 'That's mad – Sheridan Smyth paid for her *house*?'

'That's *seriously* nuts.' Caroline shook her head. 'All this explains why she was so edgy around me. It explains a *lot*.'

Malachi sucked in a breath between his teeth. 'I've only just finished reading the statement, it's very detailed. Now we need to wait for a DNA match to prove it's Meg, although the circumstantial evidence is very strong – the bracelet, her age, the letter from Alfie and the statement from Smyth. There's a file of documentation with it apparently. Smyth made sure justice will be served, even from beyond the grave.'

Chapter 64

SITTING IN THE kitchen of the Boathouse, the sunlight flooding in, Rachel felt it all seemed so unreal. *It was no wonder Alfie had gone off the rails.* He must have spent a lifetime living with the possibility that he might be arrested as an accessory to murder. Had he had any idea how manipulative Ava was? How she had maintained the facade that Meg was still alive all these years? So many questions jostled for attention in Rachel's head, it was starting to hurt.

'She thought she had the whole incident covered up, but Ava didn't count on Alfie and Sheridan Smyth's consciences. And let's see what your forensics people can tell you about the watch in Alfie's bag. I think it was his insurance policy.' Rachel shook her head. 'You know, I still can't get over those postcards.'

Before she could continue, Caroline turned to Malachi.

'Is that your phone ringing? How on earth have you got reception? We only get occasional blasts down here.'

Malachi looked at her, his face confused. She opened her hands in an 'isn't it obvious' gesture.

'The gypsy violins?'

He shook his head. 'My ringtone is Liam Neeson from *Taken* …' Both women looked at him blankly. 'You know that line: "I don't know who you are … I don't know what you want …but I have a very particular set of skills …"' He blushed hard. 'Definitely not violins.'

'I can't hear anything either.' Rachel raised her eyebrows. 'I think it's happening again.'

She looked pointedly at Caroline. She wasn't going to say anything in front of Malachi, but ever since Caroline had arrived she'd been hearing violins, and Rachel had literally just worked out why. Perhaps it was the first time she'd thought about it properly. With ghostly traces of Honoria Smyth constantly appearing, it should have been obvious that it was Alfie, it had to be.

How had it taken her so long to realise?

Rachel felt like slapping herself in the forehead. Whatever wavelength Caroline was on, it was one that seemed to be a lot more in tune with Honoria Smyth and Alfie Bows than she realised. And this was Hare's Landing – hares were supposed to be mythical messengers from the Otherworld, after all.

Perhaps there was more to the name of this estate than just maritime history.

Had Meg been trying to contact her too?

Caroline shivered and glared at Rachel. 'Maybe I'm hearing things. Go on, Malachi, ignore her.'

Malachi cleared his throat. 'We should have information on the watch back this morning. And the postcards. Then we can have a proper chat to Ava.'

'Do you know where Declan Flynn is now?' Rachel twisted her ring, frowning, worry seeping into her tone.

'In police custody at Dublin airport. He tried to leave last night, using a false passport.'

'That's a relief. Can you arrest him for Meg's murder as well? It *was* murder if she was alive when she went into the septic tank?'

Malachi rolled his hat between his hands. 'We've already got proof of Flynn breaking in here and handling your notebook, Caroline. His car was involved in the accident that landed Hunter in hospital. It's only a matter of time before the boys in London find something to link him or Nemo Freight directly to the break-in on your boat, and Alfie Bow's death. If his prints turn out to be on the watch, it'll be the icing on the cake.'

'He deserves everything he gets. He has to be the "D" in Honoria's letter. I can imagine what he was like all those years ago, if he's like this now.' Caroline tapped her nails on the counter again, obviously deep in thought. 'Do you think Smyth arranged to meet Ava at the house, to talk about Meg? Maybe Ava called Bronagh on the way, to make sure she *wasn't* there?'

Malachi gave Jasper's ears a rub. 'We can only work with the evidence we've got, but it's gathering. We'll know more when we get the full post-mortem report on Smyth. It looks like Ava's got a lot of explaining to do either way.'

Upstairs the bathroom door banged shut and they all started. Jasper's head shot up at the same speed as Malachi's.

'Jesus, what was that?'

Jasper whimpered, the high-pitched sound turning into a yelp. But he didn't move from beside Malachi. Malachi patted his neck and bent down to pick up his hat where it had fallen on the floor.

Rachel looked at Caroline pointedly as Malachi continued, oblivious to their exchange.

'We'll check Smyth's mobile traffic to see if he contacted Ava that evening. Bronagh's call log will confirm the time of Ava's call to her. It's certainly strange, Smyth and Ava both turning up here straight after he spotted that photograph.'

Malachi shifted on the stool. 'The pathologist will know from Smyth's lungs if he was present when the fire started.'

Rachel tucked a loose curl of hair back into her scrunchie.

'She must have hated Meg. Do you remember, Caroline, how she told us Meg was really talented? Ava said she had an amazing voice. You could see from the picture in the paper that she was stunning.'

Caroline shivered suddenly. 'Have a look at the heating there, Rach, it's gone freezing in here.'

'Really? You sure about that?' Rachel looked at her. 'Can you smell anything?'

Caroline looked at her sceptically and sniffed hard. 'Only your perfume. Stop winding me up.'

'I'm only out of bed, I'm not wearing any perfume.'

'Then it must be your shower gel or something, it's definitely not Chanel No. 5 anyway.' Caroline cleared her throat. 'With two signed confessions, have you got enough to arrest Ava?'

Upstairs the bathroom door slammed again.

Malachi looked upstairs, startled. 'Holy feck. How does a closed door slam? Does this happen a lot?'

Rachel shook her head. 'Only since you got here and started talking about all of this.' She looked at Caroline. 'It's something to do with her – she's been hearing violins and smelling perfume since she got here.'

'Don't be ridiculous, there's a perfectly rational explanation, we just need to work it out.'

Malachi looked at her, his face as sceptical as it could possibly be. He cleared his throat. 'We've got a lot of circumstantial evidence, enough to bring Ava in for a chat for sure. We'll see what she says when she's questioned.'

As he spoke, his phone pinged with a text, rapidly followed by Caroline and Rachel's, the sounds of them updating muffled by pockets and bags. As he pulled his phone out of his pocket and read the message, a slow smile crossed his face.

'What? Spit it out.' Caroline opened her eyes wide in expectation.

'He's singing – Declan Flynn. They've only had him in the interview room for an hour and he's given them Nemo Freight on a plate, chapter and verse as they say – and he's just implicated Ava. The detective unit have enough to arrest her now, so they're going back to her place to pick her up. I'd better go. I don't want to miss her face when they present her with everything we know.'

Caroline smirked, her eyes sparkling. 'That's the one thing we all forgot about – Declan Flynn's survival instinct. I bet he's after a plea bargain. He's an absolute snake. He's got nothing to lose by turning Ava in. And he's a real live witness a barrister can cross-examine.'

The phone pinged again and Malachi looked back at it, whistling between his teeth.

'And guess what? Flynn's fingerprints are on those postcards. That's going to take some explaining in court.' He looked across at Caroline. 'Obviously there's a strong chance we're going to need both of you as witnesses to attend the trial – I hope you're both able to get back here again.'

Rachel hid a smile as Caroline nodded.

'I think we can manage that. I want to look Declan Flynn in the eye across a courtroom. The clock has been ticking on him for a very long time. We weren't here to help Honoria and Meg – or Alfie – but we can now.'

Malachi grinned cheekily. 'Like Charlie's Angels. But there are only two of you.'

As if he understood, Jasper jumped up and put his paws on Malachi's knee, barking sharply.

'Sorry, my mistake. Perhaps that should be Alfie's Angels – and there are definitely three of you.'

Upstairs the door banged again. They all looked at each other. Malachi raised his eyebrows, his eyes wide. Caroline shook her head in disbelief.

'It's a draught, people. For God's sake, I don't even believe in ghosts.'

Rachel twisted her ring thoughtfully.

'Maybe not, but they seem to believe in you.'

Epilogue

'JUST MIND YOURSELF … that's it.'

Rachel held the passenger door of the Land Rover wide open as Hunter swung around to put his crutch on the loose tarmac. He looked at her, his lips pursed. He'd been in foul humour since they'd woken up this morning, the sound of rain like spit shot on the deck above their bed. The long journey here from London hadn't helped one bit.

'I'm not a total cripple, you know. I'm perfectly capable of getting out of the bloody car.'

Before she could answer, she heard the crunch of boots and a voice behind her.

'Ah, Hunter, I'm so pleased you were able to make it. How are you doing – healing well?'

Rachel turned to see Frank standing behind them, a thick multicoloured scarf wrapped around his neck and buttoned into the front of his padded jacket. They'd been guided by Google Maps along the winding country roads until they were convinced they were lost. Rachel had been relieved to see the sign for the crematorium and Frank's battered red Micra waiting for them. He'd been on the phone as they pulled up.

'Getting there. It's just a lot damn slower than I'd like.'

His hands thrust in his pockets, Frank nodded sagely.

'It's not until something goes wrong that we realise how fragile we humans really are.'

As if agreeing with him, Jasper sat up in the back seat and bumped his nose against the back window, barking sharply. Rachel shook her head; from the moment today had started, she'd felt like she was in charge of a pair of toddlers. She nodded to Jasper.

'He's got the hump because he has to stay in the jeep. He thought we were taking him to the park.'

'Perhaps he can run around later, when we're all finished. Sandra, Alfie's ...' He corrected himself, 'I should say *James*'s sister, has organised some sandwiches afterwards down at the Wicked Lady, they've a huge garden. I can't imagine it will be very busy today.'

He looked up at the sky, still heavy with clouds after the thunderous showers of the morning. Rachel had had the windscreen wipers on full tilt all the way around the M25. She was just relieved it hadn't started snowing.

She put the car keys in her pocket.

'What's she like – Sandra, I mean?'

With so much happening, today was the first time they would get to meet her properly. Hunter had brought his MacBook to show her some of the out-takes he had of Alfie – Rachel couldn't get used to calling him 'James'.

A faint smile flickered across Frank's face and he looked at his feet. Rachel could see he was struggling with his emotions.

'Lovely – a really nice woman. And so much like him. She's an opera singer, goes to Bayreuth every year. Music obviously runs in the family.' He smiled sadly. 'She asked for Mozart's "Concerto No. 5" to be played during the service.' Frank glanced over his shoulder towards the gates of the crematorium. 'I'm sure she'll be here in a minute. It's just her coming, I think, their parents are gone a long time.' He cleared his throat. 'It's hard to believe he never got in touch with her.'

Hunter pivoted on his crutch and fished his hat off the dashboard, cramming it onto his head. Manoeuvring himself around the door, he closed it, leaning back on the side of the Land Rover.

'She said in her email the family thought he'd committed suicide. When he came home from Ireland, they could all see he was very distressed but they never found out why. Then he vanished. She remembers it like it was yesterday—'

Pulling up her collar against the chill breeze rolling across the open lawns of the crematorium from the fields surrounding them, Rachel cut in.

'And she said she tried to contact Sheridan Smyth at the time, but he pretended everything was fine, that they'd had a great weekend and whatever had happened must have been on the way home.'

Hunter shook his head. 'Smyth was in it up to his neck.'

Standing hunched against the cold, Rachel pushed her hands deep into her pockets.

'Even with Flynn's evidence, I wondered, with the conflicting statements in Smyth's affidavit and Alfie's letter, whether the jury would be able to convict Ava beyond reasonable doubt. Flynn isn't exactly reliable – but Mrs Travers? My God, I still can't believe she knew exactly what had happened all this time and never said a thing – she *saw* it.' Rachel shook her head. 'She's a horrible woman.'

Leaning his elbow on his crutch, Hunter reached over to rub her arm.

'She is, and she got everything she deserved. That judge

having her arrested as an accessory as she was leaving court was a master stroke.'

Rachel nodded, tight-lipped. Perhaps because it was an election year, Ava's trial had been scheduled considerably more quickly than they'd expected. Rachel had only got back to Cork for the day she was needed to testify, but Caroline had kept her informed of every detail. Despite his plan to curry favour with the judiciary by testifying against Ava, Declan Flynn had been found guilty alongside her. He was still facing charges in the UK for his activities as head of Nemo Freight – for Hunter's 'accident' and for orchestrating Alfie's murder. Rachel knew Hunter was planning to attend every day when the trials eventually began.

She shivered. 'Will we wait for Sandra inside? It's freezing here and there aren't any photographers yet, but I wouldn't put it past any of them to hide in the hedge.'

Frank rolled his eyes. 'With the level of tabloid interest this has got, at least your documentary will get good viewing figures, Hunter. There are some important stories there.'

Hunter lifted his eyebrows, sighing. 'It's been moved to next spring now, but Sandra's been doorstepped ever since that Flynn character took the stand in Ireland. Hopefully they haven't got wind of today.'

Frank turned towards the main door of the modern single-storey building.

'They love a good headline. You can't get much better than "Homeless Millionaire in Thirty-Year-Old Murder Mystery Leaves Fortune to Shelter" really, can you?' He was about to continue when, behind them, they heard the sound of a car pulling through the gates. A silver Mercedes drew up beside Frank's car, a blonde woman behind the wheel. 'Here's Sandra.'

As the door of the Mercedes swung open, Jasper started

barking frantically in the back of the Land Rover. He'd swivelled around in the back seat and was looking out of the opposite window, pawing at it, his tail thrashing from side to side.

Hunter twisted on his crutch, trying to see what he was barking at.

'What's up with him?'

Rachel took a step backwards and looked over the bonnet, across the grass dividing the crematorium entrance from the low hedge bordering the lane.

'Good God, it's a hare. Across the road – can you see it? It's sitting … No, look, it's running across the field now. Wow, it's so fast.' Jasper barked sharply again as she turned to the two men, both of whom were looking at her, their faces puzzled. 'Didn't you see it? It was right there.'

'Come on, babes. Let's get inside.'

Shaking her head, Rachel glared playfully at Hunter, but before she could say anything someone opened the door to the crematorium building. The sound of violins spilled out, filling the cold air. Halfway across the tarmac on her way to join them, Sandra Stafford stopped and turned. Frank was already on his way over to her.

Rachel glanced back at the field.

Was the hare still there? Had she really seen it?

She felt Hunter's hand on her arm.

'It's time now sweet pea. Come on, let's go.'

Acknowledgements

No story arrives in the writer's head complete. It's the melting pot of ideas, of many micro-stories, snatches of conversations, news, places and people that come together to form a whole – often a whole that is quite different from the original influence.

The idea for *The Dark Room* started in Cornwall, with an image that arrived in my head of a dark-haired woman in green shorts jogging down a beach at low tide, a German shepherd lolloping along beside her. From there, hares kept appearing in my life, in ceramics and in print, and Hare's Landing was born. The customs officer's house and the ancient gaol were inspired by one just across the Helford River from where I was sitting when the woman appeared with her dog in my head.

That same summer, the wonderful Mel Chambers, who is a real ceramicist and runs the incredible Alchemy Tiles, just up the lane from Helford Passage in Mawnan Smith, took me to see her kiln. When she invited me up to her studio, neither of us had any idea how that trip might spark an idea and influence a story, or how it would evolve. You can find her stunning hares and many other beautiful ceramics at www. melchambers.com.

A special thanks to crime writer Arlene Hunt, whose fabulous German shepherds Archer and Lana influenced Jasper – follow her on Twitter @arlenehunt and you'll see them in all their glory. And to Dominic Perrem for his love of Land Rovers – they made it into a book! Many moons ago I quizzed John Reilly, then Station Officer at Dun Laoghaire Fire Station, on how his team dealt with an incident similar to the scene described here. He was incredibly generous with his time and any procedural mistakes are entirely mine. Huge thanks too, to Aisling Kelly, who was on hand to talk me through CPR. Andrew and Jude Jones brought the last piece of *The Dark Room* puzzle to the story – Andrew was at the Who's 25th anniversary gig in Birmingham, part of the 1989 The Kids Are Alright Tour, and, wonderfully, still has the crucial T-shirt!

The shaping and polishing that is vital to bring any book to fruition couldn't be done without my incredible editor at Corvus, Sarah Hodgson, and I was thrilled to be working again on *The Dark Room* with Steve O'Gorman at Full Marks Editorial Services, who is the best copy-editor in the business. I'm blessed to also have the best literary agent in the business – Simon Trewin. He gets to hear the first few mad ideas before a solid book-shaped concept appears, and has endless patience. His advice is always pure gold. Without him, you wouldn't be reading this book.

I put the words in front of each other, but it's a team that puts it into your hand. To *everyone* at Corvus: Will, Hanna, Kirsty, Jamie, Clive, Gemma and Patrick, to the guys at Gill Hess who look after PR in Ireland, to Steve O'Gorman and to Simon Trewin, THANK YOU – you're the dream team.